SERVED COLD

SERVED COLD

A Nathan Parker Detective Novel

James L'Etoile

LEVEL
BEST BOOKS

"Revenge is a dish best served cold."

—Pierre Choderlos de Laclos,
Dangerous Liaisons 1782

Praise for the Detective Nathan Novels

For *Devil Within*

"James L'Etoile is such a talented and terrific storyteller! His real-life experience in the criminal justice system gives his compelling, high-stakes thrillers an authenticity that only a savvy insider can provide. You'll be turning the pages as fast as you can!"—Hank Phillippi Ryan. *USA Today* bestselling Author of *One Wrong Word*

"An incredible story that grabs you by the throat and tosses you across the room. L'Etoile is a gem."—J.T. Ellison, *New York Times* bestselling author of *It's One of Us*

"*Devil Within* is an exceptional follow-up to L'Etoile's Anthony Award nominated novel *Dead Drop*. A propulsive thriller with nonstop action, well-rendered characters, and a truckload of twists and turns. Impossible to put down!"—Bruce Robert Coffin, award-winning author of *The General's Gold* and the Detective Byron mysteries

"Borders are blurred, lines are crossed. Nathan Parker navigates an intensely personal case, uncontrolled emotions threatening his good judgement. Brilliant prose, crisp pacing, and well-developed characters make L'Etoile a must-read for every thriller enthusiast. An unforgettable story."— K.J. Howe, international bestselling author of *Skyjack*

Chapter One

State Trooper Chris Yarrow took his patrol assignment on the graveyard shift on Interstate 10 as a kick to the crotch. The desolate stretch of asphalt from Quartzite to Tonopah was as straight a preacher's spine and as exciting as a Sunday sermon.

Six months. He was given six months on this worthless chunk of highway as punishment. His sergeant warned if he didn't adjust his attitude and become a team player, Yarrow would be on the outside looking in. Halfway through a shift cruising down the empty westbound lanes of I-10, Yarrow hadn't pulled over a single speeding motorist. Not because he didn't want to. There was no one out on this God-forsaken patch of asphalt. Not so much as a headlight in the distance.

He backed off the accelerator at the exit for the Devil's Well rest stop. Yarrow cruised through the freeway rest stop to ensure the truckers who pulled off for the night didn't have paid female company from Buckeye. Last week, Yarrow turned a van full of young women away as they drove up, much to the disappointment of the lonely truck drivers.

Four eighteen-wheelers were parked in diagonal slots. Yarrow's eye went to a cargo container strapped on a flatbed trailer. The tractor and driver were nowhere to be found.

Yarrow stopped behind the trailer and shown his spotlight on the boxy cargo container. No company markings or brand names adorned the side. The trooper pulled his computer console over, preparing to run the trailer's plates. His light found the empty place where the registration should have been.

1

Yarrow stepped from his SUV and approached the trailer-mounted cargo box, casting his flashlight under and around the steel frame.

"If it ain't officer buzzkill," a voice sounded from a truck window to the left.

Yarrow swung his light to the truck cab and recognized the driver as one of the frustrated truckers after the ladies of the night were turned away. His faded and frayed Dodger's ball cap, more grey than blue, was tucked on his head over a ring of red curls.

"You happen to see who left this trailer?"

"It was here when I pulled in," he checked his watch, "about four hours ago."

Yarrow strode to the front of the container, shone his flashlight at the end of the brown steel container. "Something leaking."

The trucker stepped from his cab, hitched his pants up, and joined Yarrow.

"Looks like the A/C unit bit the big one."

Yarrow avoided stepping in the puddle of refrigerant. "I'm gonna have to call the DOT crew out and get this cleaned up before it runs off in the desert."

"God forbid a coyote gets an upset tummy. Tree huggers like them woke DOT weenies is what makes everything we do more expensive."

"Why would a driver take the plates and leave his load," Yarrow asked.

The driver shrugged. "If he saw his A/C was busted, he knew his load got spoiled in this heat. If he's not a company driver, he could drop and run. Especially if he already got paid for the trip."

Yarrow circled around the trailer to the rear. The heavy steel hasp was secured with a heavy gauge padlock and a foil seal on the door.

"A customs inspection sticker," the driver said, pointing at the foil.

"This came over the border? All this way, and the driver just drops it?"

The trucker leaned in, an ear close to the container. "Hear that?"

"What?"

"Listen."

Yarrow leaned closer to the container. "I don't hear anything."

Another voice from behind startled Yarrow. "What ya got going on,

Buck?"

Buck, the driver in his Dodger's hat, glanced at the other trucker, "Might be an abandoned load."

"Saw a guy in a white Kenworth tractor with no trailer burning outta here about five o'clock. Coulda been running into Phoenix to get a mechanic for his A/C."

"Phoenix? We're in the westbound lanes."

"Like I said, the guy was in a hurry; he crossed the center median and headed back east, toward Phoenix."

"I think he's hauling bees," Buck said, straightening his ball cap. "I don't like bees. I keep me an EpiPen in my glove box."

The other driver drew close and put an ear against the metal cargo box. "I hear them. I heard about bee rustlers stealing hives. Think deputy Do-Right here broke the case?"

"Would you guys back away? Quit touching the lock, Buck."

Buck turned the lock loose and put his hands up in surrender.

"It might be evidence."

"How you gonna know unless you look inside," Buck said.

Yarrow pondered his options. If he called it in to his supervisor and it turned out to be dead grandma's patio furniture from Sun City, Yarrow was done. The thin foil customs seal hinted at something more. Smuggled drugs, maybe. If Yarrow could break a major drug trafficking case, he'd earn his way out of this nighttime purgatory of an assignment.

Sensing Yarrow's leaning, Buck said, "I got a pair of cutters in my truck."

Buck trotted over to his rig, opened a tool box, and withdrew a pair of heavy bolt cutters with two-foot-long handles.

Yarrow held them, surprised at the weight and forced the lock off the cargo door. He handed the bolt cutters back to Buck. When Yarrow slid the bolt a metallic clang echoed from within.

"You don't mind, I'ma gonna take a step back. I don't need no bee stings."

The buzzing sound increased, and Yarrow began to second-guess his decision to open the container. He pulled the heavy door aside, and a swarm of insects flew from the crack.

Buck screamed and waved his arms against the winged attackers. "I need my EpiPen!"

Yarrow ducked behind the door as the insects flew from their prison. When they lessened, he leaned around and clicked his flashlight inside. He dropped the light on the blacktop and staggered back. The smell was overpowering.

No stolen beehives and no cache of smuggled heroin or fentanyl were waiting for Yarrow. Inside the darkened cargo container, dozens of dead men lay in a heap on the steel floor.

Chapter Two

Detective Sergeant Nathan Parker pulled into the Devil's Well rest stop and parked his SUV as the sun crested Superstition Mountain to the east. The view was obstructed by the purple remnants of monsoon clouds. He hoped they didn't forecast a dark day ahead.

Four eighteen-wheel long haul trucks were tucked in along the rear of the rest area and in the middle of them was a small, squat cargo box with the rear door ajar. A uniformed Maricopa County Sheriff's deputy held a yellow tape ribbon, unsure where to tie off the end.

Next to the restroom building, a State Trooper stooped over, one hand holding himself upright against the wall. The Statie was grey and sweat lined his forehead, what Parker could see of it.

"Detective, you got here fast. I've asked for a couple more units to help with this one." The young deputy strung out a length of tape and tied it to his patrol unit twenty feet away.

"I live on this side of the valley. Wasn't asleep when the call came in." The bouts of insomnia were a constant companion in recent months. "You the first county unit on scene, I take it?"

The deputy joined Parker outside the tape, twenty feet back from the cargo container. "Yes, sir. Officer Yarrow there," the deputy jutted his chin at the State Trooper, "opened the container and found—you best come see for yourself."

Parker scanned the deputy's name tag. Mason. He couldn't recall meeting the young deputy, and they all looked young to Parker anymore.

"I got it from here, Mason. For now, you're in control of access to the crime scene. We don't need it more contaminated than it already is." Parker glanced over at the four truckers sitting at a picnic table downing their morning Monster energy drinks.

"Was the cargo door open when you arrived?"

Deputy Mason nodded. "Two of the truckers were using their cell phones to take photos of the victims. The trooper, he's a bit under the weather."

"Great. This will be all over social media before we know what we're dealing with."

"I confiscated their cell phones. They hadn't sent any messages ."

"They gave them up?"

"Basically, said how would they feel if it was their family in there."

"The call from the Watch Commander didn't say how many victims we're dealing with. What's the number?"

"Don't know," Mason said.

"What do you mean you don't know?"

"Go look for yourself…"

Parker didn't get the sense the young deputy was playing him. The kid looked rattled but was doing his best to keep it contained.

He approached the trailer on a wide path. At the Trooper's front bumper, the sun was all the illumination he needed. A leg. An Arm. Body after body came into view with each step closer. When Parker stood at the back of the trailer, he finally understood what Deputy Mason meant. Dozens of bodies all intertwined on the steel floor. They all looked similar—brown or black hair, with dark skin. Twenty. Thirty. Parker couldn't tell.

"Mason. You call the evidence techs and Medical Examiner?"

"No. You want me to call it in?"

Parker didn't answer the deputy and pulled his own cell from his pocket. His finger shook as he tried to dial. He needed to start over before he finally connected.

"Morris," the voice responded with a graveled impatience.

"Captain. It's Parker. I'm at the scene of a mass casualty event. Undetermined number of victims at this time—over twenty. Appear to be

6

Hispanic males. They were left in a shipping container and dumped at a rest stop on I-10."

"Another undocumented migrant dump? Their coyote get cold feet?"

"This is west of the city—well past the border. No, there's more going on here." Parker glanced at the long-sleeved dress shirts worn by the two victims closest to the door. Not the clothing of migrant farm workers. None of the bodies he could see wore work boots. Athletic shoes and leather slip-on loafers peeked out from the mass of bodies.

"I called you first because we're gonna need a mass casualty response from the Medical Examiner and more transports for the victims than we have on standby. I've got Johns and Tully on the way, but I'll likely need more. The media will pick up on this, and you remember what happened in Texas last year when they pulled over that semi full of dead and dying migrants?"

"It was the only story on the news for a week. You have any lead on the driver, like they did?"

"Nope. Driver dumped the trailer and took the plates with him."

Parker ran his finger over the foil customs seal. "I'm going to reach out to Homeland Security and see if they know anything."

"I'll start making calls." After a pause, "Any women and children?"

"Doesn't look like it."

"Small mercies. Keep me posted, Detective."

Parker hung up, and the sound of two Maricopa County SUVs arriving drew his attention from the abattoir in front of him.

The deputy behind the wheel of the black and yellow SUV asked Parker where he wanted him. Parker directed him to the highway offramp to the rest stop. "Block it off. We don't need Mom and little Timmy getting an eyeful of this."

The SUV backed up and slid diagonally across the exit ramp. The deputy began setting road flares warning motorists of the closure.

Detectives Barry Johns and Pete Tully strode from the second SUV and joined Parker.

Tully read Parker's expression. "That bad, huh?"

"Worst I've seen. I mean, we've come across migrants left for dead on the trails coming over. This one—"

"All right. Where do we start?" Johns said.

"Barry, how about you begin with our trucker friends over there? Get statements and contact info. I don't want to have them slip out before we nail their stories down."

"On it." Barry strode to the picnic table where the truckers gathered. Two of them stiffened at the sight of a six-and-a-half-foot-tall Black man coming toward them.

Barry was a gifted college athlete and after his sports eligibility ended a pair of Black colleges offered him teaching positions. He turned them down to come back to the desert and joined the Maricopa County Sheriff's Office.

"Pete, our driver, snatched the license plates from the trailer before he split. Can you go over this thing and see if there are any identification markers we can use to find out who this might have belonged to?"

"Sure, there should be a serial number stamped on the cargo box."

Parker hit a number he saved on his speed dial.

"M.E.'s Office. Dr. Lison speaking."

Parker closed his eyes and bit his lip for a moment. Dr. Lison was new to the Medical Examiner's Office and was a bit of an officious prick. Graduated from a prestigious east coast medical school and made sure everyone knew it.

"I'm looking for Doctor Sherman," referring to the Chief Medicolegal Pathologist who ran the office.

"Dr. Sherman is on vacation. I'm acting in her stead. How can I help you?"

"Dr. Lison, we've met. I'm Detective Parker, MCSO."

"Yes." The response didn't come across as a pleasant memory from the doctor.

"I'm on scene of a multi-victim homicide..."

"I'll make that determination, Detective."

"We need your teams out here to..."

8

"I'll decide what my staff need to do, if you don't mind. And why isn't this coming through the regular channels from your dispatch to our controller?"

Parker drew a deep breath before he continued. "This isn't the kind of situation you want on the radio. I need an M.E. on scene, preferably more than one."

"Why would I send more than one to a crime scene? I need to cover the entire county, detective."

Parker disconnected the call. He thumbed through his contact list and found Dr. Sherman's cell phone number.

It rang twice before Dr. Sherman picked up the call. "I didn't leave instructions at the front desk for an early morning wake up call." Her tone was playful and Parker regretted calling her on a hard-earned vacation.

"I'm sorry, Doc, but I need your help."

"Let me guess, Dr. Lison isn't being his helpful self this morning?"

"You could say that."

"All right, run it down for me," she said.

Parker gave her the scant details of the scene at the Devil's Well rest stop.

"Damn. We haven't had a migrant worker caravan dumped in a couple of years."

"You're right, and this one feels different on a number of levels. I don't know how many bodies we're dealing with until we start untangling them— and I don't want to do that without your people on site."

"I understand and good thinking. We don't want to miss anything on a scene this complex. Able to secure it until I get there?"

"I thought you were on vacation?"

"A staycation, and I'm bored as hell already. This sounds like an all-hands call-out. I'll get everyone rolling."

"Thanks, doc. I'm sorry I cut your vacation short."

"I'll let you make it up with coffee when I get there. I live in Buckeye, so I'm like ten minutes away. See you soon."

Parker pocketed his cell as two ambulance units pulled into the lot. Deputy Mason must have called them when he arrived on scene. They weren't running red light and siren, they knew the fate of the people trapped in the box.

Parker glanced up at an approaching helicopter with blue and white markings identifying it as the Channel 6 "News Copter." It swung lazy circles around the rest stop, trying to find the perfect angle for the camera mounted on the belly of the beast.

"Great. So much for keeping this quiet," Tully said as he circled around the box.

Parker grabbed a purple nitrile glove from his pocket and used it to gently close the cargo door. Give the dead a little bit of decency from the prying eye in the sky.

A caravan of six Maricopa County SUVs roared into the lot. Captain Morris stepped from the lead vehicle and paused until he spotted Parker. He joined him near the box.

"Morning Detective. I've got two crime scene investigation units here and wasn't sure what else you needed. I dropped the PIO off at the highway exit, and she'll handle the press on this so you can focus on the scene. Have a couple of uniforms to help out wherever you need."

"Thanks, Cap. Good thinking on staging the Public Information Officer out there." Parker motioned to the exit as a news van pulled to a stop.

"Right now, the public line is the case is under investigation, and we're not saying much else. You can feed her the number of victims or any other case details as you deem appropriate."

A white Maricopa County Medical Examiner's van pulled to a stop behind the tape. Dr. Kelly Sherman stepped from the driver's side and strode in their direction. Her blue coveralls were cinched tight at the waist and tucked into black work boots.

"Gentlemen," she said.

"You weren't kidding about getting here quickly, Doc. I feel bad about ruining your vacation."

"It's part of the job, Detective. She glanced over her shoulder at the hovering news helicopter. "I take it our victims are inside?"

Parker nodded.

"I'd like to get some screens up to keep the lookie-loos away. I have them

10

in the back of the van."

"I can give you a couple of hands to help," Captain Morris said.

The Captain strode off to conscript a few deputies.

"Might as well sneak a peek at what I'm working with," Dr. Sherman said.

Parker cracked the door a few inches. The odor of decomposing flesh was stronger now than it was when he first approached the box.

Dr. Sherman deftly donned a face mask and pressed to the opening, her blue eyes squinting into the darkness. She snapped a small flashlight from her belt and clicked it on, surveying the contents.

She returned the flashlight to her belt and shifted her eyes to Parker. "I'm glad you called. I'm going to set up a tent there," Pointing to an open space in the lot to the right of the cargo box. "I'm calling La Paz County to have them roll in mutual aid on this one."

Dr Sherman strode back to her van with her cell to her ear and motioning with her free hand as she spoke.

"Serial number's been scrubbed from the trailer frame. Might be able to get the lab geeks to do an acid etch," Tully said.

Parker turned. "Wait. You hear that?"

"The helicopter?"

Parker went to the cargo box door and turned his ear to the opening. "There. There it is again."

"What? I didn't hear anything."

Parker opened the door wider and listened. "Maybe nothing."

As he turned away a slight moan carried from within the container.

"I heard it that time," Tully said.

Parker opened the door and despite not wearing protective booties, he stepped inside the cargo box.

The stench was overpowering. Tully handed him a flashlight and joined Parker in the shipping container.

The flashlight beam's bright white contrasted with the dead and bloating faces staring back at him. Arms, legs, heads, all intertwined like a Hieronymus Bosch portrait of the damned. Parker listened for another sound—nothing. Maybe it was his imagination. The dead do give off gas as they bloat and decompose. That must have been—there it was again.

Parker swung his light to the source of the sound and searched about halfway back to the right. He nearly missed it. A hand sticking up from beneath another body. It moved.

Chapter Three

"We've got a live one!" Parker yelled.

The call from within the box was absorbed by the metal sides and the dead.

Parker waded through the bodies to the upraised fingers. When he grabbed hold, he felt it tighten against his gloved hand.

Tully rolled a dead man off of the pile, uncovering a young Hispanic man in his late twenties holding Parker's hand. There was a flicker behind his eyes, but they never opened.

Dr. Sherman appeared behind Parker and pressed her hand to the young man's carotid artery. "Slow and thready. Let's get him out of here."

"I'll grab one of the ambulance crews," Tully said.

Parker and Dr. Sherman lifted the man to a seated position. She nodded and Parker grabbed him under his arms and dragged the young man from the box. The air getting lighter with each step from the bowels of the container.

A pair of EMTs took over when Parker reached the doorway. They swept the man up and gently placed him on a gurney.

In the daylight, Parker noticed the man was dressed in black pants and a white button-down shirt. One black loafer was missing. The man's hair was cut and styled. While he took a deep breath of fresh air outside the container, Parker swung around and aimed his flashlight inside once more. All of the victims wore the same clothing—dark pants and white button-down shirts.

"Good catch, Nathan," Dr. Sherman said.

"I can't believe he survived, for one, and no one bothered to check if there were any survivors until now—including me."

"The decomposition of his travel mates didn't give much hope for finding anyone alive. He's lucky you were looking. No telling how long he would have lasted in there."

"Any idea if he'll make it?"

She shook her head. "I need to get started. Oh good, the calvary has arrived."

Parker glanced over her shoulder and spotted three white Medical Examiner's vans. Dr. Stephen Lison hopped from the lead vehicle, dressed in a starched white lab coat. He stood with his hands on hips and looked crestfallen when he spotted Dr. Sherman on scene.

"I'll get the evidence techs to start documenting the scene," Parker said.

Dr. Sherman didn't respond and looked back to the cargo container and the screens the Captain's men jostled into place.

Dr. Lison began barking orders at the M.E.'s techs to use the colored tarps to prepare a triage area. A pair of them looked at one another and rolled their eyes.

Ignoring Lison, one of the techs asked Dr. Sherman where she wanted them to set up. She pointed to an area next to the last semi-truck in the lot. "Tent?" Dr. Sherman nodded.

Lison strolled over and looked down his thin nose. "I've directed my staff to establish the proper triage area so we can best assess—"

"You've never been on the scene of a migrant dump before, have you, doctor?"

"Policy says in mass casualty events, we must—"

She didn't let him finish and grabbed him by the starched sleeve, pulling him to the open cargo box door.

"Still want to set up a triage area in public? Who are you going to triage, doctor?"

"My God. What—what happened?"

"You're the pathologist. You tell me."

"There's so many." Lison's face grew white.

14

"Next time Detective Parker tells you he needs our office to respond, get it done."

Dr. Sherman donned a pair of protective booties for this trip into the box. "Let's go doctor. These people are waiting for us."

He retreated back to the van and found a set of coveralls and protective equipment.

When he returned, Dr. Sherman and one of the technicians were taking photographs of the dead in situ to document the scene.

Dr. Sherman looked at the tech, a newer hire to the staff, to assess how he was holding up. The man kept focused on the camera lens, shooting off shot after shot, the bright strobe highlighting the accumulated trauma on the floor between them.

"Ever see anything like this before?" The tech asked, working the single-lens reflex camera on one of the victims.

"Every scene is different. And no, I've never seen anything quite like this. You notice something—unusual?"

"The whole thing is unusual if you ask me. But yeah, they're all dressed like some church group on the way to a box social."

She nodded and waded deeper into the mass of tangled flesh. Dr. Sherman stopped at a body pressed against the side of the metal container. She gently rolled the man on his back. His arm was loose in her hand. "Rigor has come and gone. The heat in the box will complicate pinning down the exact time, but eight hours, maybe a little less."

Parker stood at the doorway while the doctor performed her preliminary walk through. When the body rolled away from the wall, Parker noticed a sliver of light in a seam on the cargo box wall.

"Hey doc, to the victim's right, on the wall—was he trying to get a breath through a gap in the metal?"

She bent down, shot her flashlight to the gap, then turned to the man she'd rolled and directed her light to his eyes.

"I'm seeing petechial hemorrhage."

She shifted and checked two other victims. "Same. Looks like they suffocated and died of asphyxiation."

"This thing isn't exactly airtight," Parker said.

"No, but the number of people who were rebreathing the same air with increased carbon dioxide levels—pretty much the same thing."

"The first responders said the A/C unit went out," Barry Johns said as he joined Parker at the rear of the unit.

"You think these men all died from lack of oxygen?" Parker asked.

Dr. Sherman straightened and surveyed the scene around her. "It's likely. I'll know more when I get blood gas results and see if they present with dilated blood vessels as their bodies were trying to pull oxygen from the air around them.

"These two," she gestured to the man she rolled and another nearby, "positioned themselves to try to breathe in air from a small gap. Another over there looks like he took a punch to the face. There may have been a struggle in here when they realized they were running out of air."

"They knew what was happening?" Parker asked.

She nodded. "They did, and unlike the movies, they didn't just fall asleep. Some of them show signs of panic, fingernail scratches on their necks, vomiting, if any of them had asthma, they would have been among the first to show signs of breathing problems."

Pete Tully tapped Parker on the shoulder. Tully had removed his usual sports coat, rolled his sleeves, and was a mass of sweat in the warming desert sun.

"We got the tent up."

Parker glanced at Barry Johns, who still looked fresh and unsoiled. "Looks like your camping merit badge paid off. Next thing, you'll be selling Thin Mints on the corner," Johns said to Tully.

"Thin Mints are a Girl Scouts thing, and if we're talking merit badges, you'd get one for taking photos of yourself in your fancy suits on Instagram."

"One time. I did that one time."

Tully drew a long pull from a water bottle. "I'm not saving any Thin Mints for you either." He set his jaw toward the parking lot. "Two units from La Paz County's M.E. rolling in."

Dr. Sherman stepped to the rear of the cargo box. "Good. We can get to processing this scene. Tommy? You get photos of what we need?"

"I think I've got it covered, Doctor S."

Doctor Sherman met with the new arrivals from the neighboring county's medical examiner, explaining the scene.

Parker, Tully, and Johns backed away, finding a slice of shade near the comfort station at the rest stop. The State Trooper joined them while the medical examiner's teams began extracting body after body from the cargo container and placed them side by side under the tent.

"I've—I've never seen anything like this," Trooper Yarrow said.

"I bet it's not what you expected on your patrol last night?" Parker said.

"Not even—I mean, sure, I've pulled over a van half-full of undocumented workers. But nothing like this. Who would leave them here like they didn't matter?"

"That's the right question to ask."

"I called DOT and got freeway traffic cam footage of a white semi-tractor heading eastbound about the time a trucker spotted one leaving the rest stop."

Parker turned and noticed a bit of color returned to the trooper's face. "Good thinking. Pete, can you see what Trooper Yarrow found?"

Dr. Sherman stepped outside the tent and removed her gloves, tossing them in a hazardous waste bin, signaling she was finishing up.

Parker strode over to join her, and the sight in the tent rattled him. Twenty-eight identically dressed young men were laid out in two rows.

"This is—"

"Disturbing?" she finished.

"What is this, a cult or something?"

"That's more of a *you* thing. What I can tell you is it appears from the preliminary exam they all died from asphyxiation. I'll be able to confirm when we get all the post-mortem exams completed, blood gas analysis, and see if we have any other substances in their system."

"I'll start looking for ID on the victims."

"They don't have any. We checked as we processed. We have twenty-eight John Does."

Parker ducked into the tent and walked down the aisle between the dead. There were all brown-skinned, approximately the same age, and the odd choice of clothing started to itch in his brain.

Halfway down the tent, Parker stopped and took a glove from a nearby box, put it on his right hand, and bent over one of the dead men. Parker grasped the man's wrist and examined his hand. He laid the hand down, removed his glove, donned another to avoid cross-contamination, and checked another victim.

"Doc, you notice their hands?"

"Specifically?"

"The guys we pull from coyote runs or pick up near the border—they have some miles on them. Their hands have a lifetime of labor etched into them. Callouses, scars, blisters, even a missing finger here and there. These guys—nothing. I'd venture to say these victims have never seen a day of hard work in their lives."

"Who are they?"

"Maybe our lone survivor can tell us. I'd like to know why they were disposable?"

Chapter Four

Parker was the last to leave the scene. An hour after a caravan of ambulances, coroner's vans, and a refrigerated truck moved the bodies to the Maricopa County morgue, the cargo trailer was tarped and taken to the Sheriff's Property Management Division, where it would be combed for trace evidence.

It was his practice to stay behind at the scene long after the activity of first responders, evidence techs, and crime analysts finished their work. Parker wasn't a believer in the spirits of the dead remaining behind, or some psychic connection lingering where they died. But, in the quiet that followed, he often pieced together what pulled the victim and suspect together.

The driver panicked when he discovered his "cargo" had become a liability. He fled east, toward the city. The origin, unknown except for the Custom's seal on the cargo container.

His quiet ended when a minivan pulled into the reopened rest stop. Four kids and a Golden Retriever tumbled out of the van. Mom wrangled the kids toward the restroom structure while Dad grabbed the dog by the leash and let it sniff and pee.

Another two cars entered and an ill-tempered man in a black and red tracksuit opened the rear door of his Nissan Sentra where a young girl climbed out with a backpack nearly as large as she was.

Six slots down, a woman stepped from her older model Toyota and opened her arms for the child.

A custody exchange. Parker guessed the girl was no more than ten and waddled under the weight of the heavy backpack toward Mom.

The girl turned to wave goodbye to her father, but he'd already gotten in his car and was backing out of the lot. She looked crestfallen, with her little hand caught in mid-wave and her lip starting to quiver.

Parker never had children of his own and couldn't imagine the push and pull of a tempestuous custody battle. No one wins. He'd seen these exchanges go down before and was called out to supervise a few back in his patrol days. Tense exchanges like these were often in public locations like police stations, shopping malls, and parks where cameras—

Parker wheeled around and spotted it at the peak of the comfort station. A camera directed at the parking lot entrance. It wasn't the DOT traffic camera the state trooper mentioned, and it might provide a view of the trailer drop and if it was supposed to be a handoff, like a custody exchange.

There weren't any markings on the plain brown plastic housing and Parker made a note to find out who operated the rest stop camera.

His cell phone vibrated in his pocket. The caller ID made him smile. It was Miguel, his eighteen-year-old foster son. The state agreed to continue foster home placement with him because of the unusual circumstances of Miguel's case.

Unusual was an understatement. Parker met Miguel as the boy was traveling alone from El Salvador after his family was murdered by Salvadoran gangs. He set out north to find his own path—a path which led to his abduction last year and left for dead in a cargo container, much like the men at the rest stop.

The path to recovery was long and twisted. There were nights Miguel couldn't sleep in his room, and it took him months to return to college. But he was on track to graduate from Glendale Community College and was sorting through applications to a dozen four-year universities.

"Hey, Miguel, you get my message?"

"Yeah, you snuck out early. Finished with my morning classes, and I wanted to let you know I'm heading over to the Immigrant Coalition offices."

"What's going on over there?"

"Billie's getting ready to make a supply run down to the migrant camps outside of Hermosillo. She needs a hand with the inventory and packing."

Billie Carson was a millionaire. On paper, at least. The former Executive Director of the Coalition, Roger Jessup, left her over three million dollars to keep the Coalition up and running after his murder a year ago. Billie was a desert nomad who preferred living on her own, off the grid. Her lifestyle choice was partially driven by staying off the cartel's radar after testifying against them in a human trafficking case and not feeling like she belonged anywhere. Even though she fell into a fortune, she still lived in a broken-down trailer. She did buy a new truck, though, for her regular relief trips to Hermosillo.

Parker told Miguel he'd meet him at the Immigrant Coalition since it was on the way back to the Sheriff's headquarters.

When he arrived at the Coalition office, Miguel's Toyota Camry and Billie's Blue Ford F250 were the only cars in the lot. The rest of the strip mall hadn't recovered from the pandemic lockdowns. The vacant storefronts were a reflection on the rest of the community off Thunderbird Road. The largely Hispanic enclave sheltered a community which included undocumented migrants who attempted to start a new life in a new land. Government services during the lockdowns never reached the invisible people.

The need was so great in the community that Billie found the Coalition assistance programs stretched to the limit. Sure, the program was well-funded after Roger Jessup's death, but without sustained donation, there was a limit.

Parker pushed open the door and found Miguel and Billie huddled in front of a monitor. Miguel's brow was knitted into a scowl. He glanced up at Parker.

"Have you seen this?" Miguel asked.

Parker walked around to face the monitor and saw the news banner displayed on the bottom of the screen in bright red script. It read: Migrants Left to Die.

"I was just there," Parker said.

"Is it true? What they're saying? Some coyote abandoned a truckload of migrants?" Miguel said.

Parker pulled up a rolling chair and sat, rubbing the muscles in his thighs stiff from standing at the crime scene.

"I'm not sure what to make of it. Someone left a—" Parker stopped himself before he mentioned a storage container like the one Miguel nearly died in last year. "Left them at a highway rest stop. Didn't seem like typical coyote dump and run."

"If they thought the heat was on, wouldn't be the first time one a them dropped and split," Billie said.

"I wanted to ask you if you've heard about any large groups moving over the border and maybe heading to California?"

Billie tugged on the brim of a faded and frayed Diamondbacks ball cap. "Theys always coming through here and movin' on to Cali. The fields over the border in the Imperial Valley are harvestin' now," Billie said.

"I don't think these guys were headed to the fields."

"What makes you think they wasn't?" Billie asked.

"None of these men worked in the fields—like ever."

"It doesn't matter. The outcome was the same. They are all dead because their lives didn't matter. People like them—like me. We're all invisible and disposable," Miguel said.

"How many?" Billie asked.

"Twenty-eight. One survivor. He's in bad shape, and I hope he pulls through so we can find out what happened out there."

"How come they was dropped at a rest stop? Most coyotes who dump and run leave the van way off in the desert, so it won't be found."

"The whole thing is off, if you ask me," Parker said. "Where they were left, the age range of all of the men was the same, and talk about same, they were all wearing the same clothes, dark dress pants and white long-sleeve shirts."

Miguel turned away from the news station. "That is weird."

"It looked like they were all working in a retail store or belonged to a cult."

"All of them?" Billie asked.

Parker nodded and rubbed the knot at the back of his neck.

"I ain't heard nothin' 'bout church groups goin' missin' or whatnot. I can ask around and see if anyone knows about what's the deal with these guys."

"Yeah, it might help. Be careful about who you ask. We don't know why these people were killed," Parker said.

"I will."

"Miguel said you were prepping for a trip to Hermosillo."

"I need to make a supply run down there soon. The camps outside the town are growing again. People waitin' to make the crossin' and tryin' to save up enough to pay a coyote."

"Is the cartel pressuring them to move product north again?"

Billie nodded. "There's been more Sinaloa presence. Them bottom feeders are on the lookout for someone who is vulnerable and alone."

"When you gonna make your run?"

"I dunno. I got a notice from the county saying I got thirty days to move my camp, or they's gonna tow my trailer away. Got no call to bother us."

"Us?" Parker asked.

"We got a group of six or eight living out by Rocky Wash."

The mention of Rocky Wash sent a chill down Parker's spine. The isolated stretch of remote dirt road was the source of his greatest failure. Five years since he watched his partner bleed out on the road after stopping a suspected coyote. The killing, partially caught on a blurry dashcam video, was the work of Esteban Castaneda, the ruthless leader of Los Muertos. Castaneda had evaded capture, and Parker carried the guilt of letting his partner die. The guilt took a toll on Parker's life, relationships, and he swore he would avenge his partner's murder.

"Rocky Wash isn't the most hospitable place in the county, Billie," Parker said.

"It sure ain't since they tryin' to push us out."

"I mean, there's nothing out there for miles."

"Which is exactly why we went there. We ain't botherin' nobody. Then the county comes along and says we're harming the environment or some such. It's just made up to git rid of us."

"Environment? Billie, are some of your 'neighbors' dumping their sewage out there?"

"It mighta happened a time or two. Mostly, everyone runs out to the Carefree Highway and dumps at one of the gas stations."

Miguel tapped on the computer monitor. "Hey, check this out."

He pointed at an image of a Spanish-language newspaper.

"What's that?" Parker asked.

"It's from a small paper published in Mexico City. Two mothers are saying their sons disappeared after they went to work in the city."

"Okay?"

"Look—they put photos of the two missing guys. They're both wearing white shirts and dark pants like you saw. You think it's important?"

Parker leaned over the monitor and took in the grainy photos of the two missing men. They were the right age, but Parker couldn't tell if these two were among the victims he spotted this morning. "Hard to make a connection. They went missing down south, and our victims were found up here. Not likely someone kidnapped them and drove them up here. Does it say where they worked?"

Miguel scanned the article. "No, not by name. Some reference to a tech company."

"Tech isn't exactly high risk, is it?" Billie said.

"What isn't high risk these days? Miguel, can you dig in, maybe call the newspaper, and find out more about those two? Like where they worked and when they went missing?"

Miguel squared his shoulders and turned back to the monitor. "I can do that."

"Thanks."

Miguel began tapping away on the keyboard.

"Now, Billie, what are we gonna do about your living arrangements?"

Chapter Five

Parker left Billie to take her inventory of the supplies needed for the migrants stuck in the temporary camps in Hermosillo. Having experienced the conditions in these camps, Parker knew the cardboard and tarpaper shacks did little to keep out the wind and rain. Exposure to the elements, along with poor sanitary conditions, bred sickness and disease. If the migrants were ill, they couldn't make the trek north. The longer they stayed, the more likely they became prey to the cartels and criminal groups.

Billie tried to do it alone, and there was no way a single person, even one as driven as she was, could turn the tide. Yet she never gave up. It was one of the qualities Parker admired in her.

While he drove, he tried to make sense of the bodies abandoned at the Devil's Well rest stop. If they were migrant farmworkers, it made more sense and, unfortunately, fit with a common coyote practice where van loads of undocumented people were left for dead in the desert when Immigration authorities turned up the heat.

This one, though, didn't have the same urgent dump-and-run feel in Parker's gut. Sure, the cargo container was abandoned, and the occupants were most certainly dead, but it was too clean. Too organized. Were they meant to be found?

More questions and few answers.

The Maricopa County Sheriff's Office headquarters on West Jefferson was a thirty-minute drive from the Coalition headquarters, but it seemed hundreds of miles culturally. From the dense immigrant population in the area around El Mirage to the slick urban setting on West Jefferson, the downtown corridor seemed a different world. And in many respects, it was—few cared about a cargo container full of nameless people left to die. If it didn't affect their non-fat-low foam latte, then it didn't exist.

Parker arrived in the Major Crimes Unit office to find Tully and Johns on their individual phones. He motioned them to his office when they were finished. Johns jutted a chin in the direction of Parker's office door. The name plate on the office said Detective Sergeant Nathan Parker and he was the one person who the Sheriff's Office brass went to for answers.

One of them sat in his office waiting. Undersheriff Taylor Myers perched on a sofa in Parker's office. Parker stiffened, stopping in his doorway.

"Parker."

"Sheriff. To what do I owe this visit?"

"I want to get the straight shit on what went down at the rest stop. This is already bubbling up in the Melendres Order monitoring team, and community advocates are issuing press releases saying this is another example of violence against the migrant community while we sit on our hands."

"That was fast. I mean, I know this was bound to get community attention, but I've hardly had time to sit on my hands. Where is the messaging coming from?"

"You know what the Melendres Order is all about—the federal court is still monitoring our interactions with the Hispanic community, profiling, complaints of indifference, and excessive force."

"Sure."

"Certain people want to make sure it stays on the front burner. We've made progress on everything the court wanted us to address, and if certain attorneys get involved, then it means the court order stays in place, and they keep getting paid."

"Attorneys like Larry Sutton."

"Bullseye."

Parker had a run in with Sutton when a false allegation of assaulting one of Sutton's clients resulted in a temporary suspension. The matter was cleared, and the attorney admitted he'd been deceived by his cartel-influenced client. The man played both sides and his moral compass spun like a top.

"Sutton can't have any idea what's going on—he's blowing smoke."

"And the media see smoke and aren't thinking we've elected a new pope."

The Undersheriff rose from the sofa. "You're going to have eyes looking at you on this one, and we've got to make sure all of our bases are covered."

"Understood, and we always do."

"I know. And to make sure we stay within the lines of the court order, I'm assigning a liaison from Court Implementation to your unit for the duration."

"That's not necessary. We've got it covered."

"I'm not asking, Sergeant."

Parker drew a deep breath.

"She'll be along shortly."

"Who?"

"Me." Deputy Linda Hunt stood in the open doorway in her full uniform.

"You've met Deputy Hunt?" The Undersheriff's brow creased.

"We've run into one another from time to time," she said.

Parker felt a flush run up his neck.

"Oh, good then. Parker I've tasked the deputy with keeping Court Implementation and my office updated on the investigation. We can't afford to be blindsided on this one."

"Yes, sir," she said.

"Got it," Parker said.

The Undersheriff paused and glanced from Parker to Hunt. "Get her up to speed," he said as he strode from the office.

When the number two man cleared the office, Linda smirked and hugged Parker, giving him a peck on the cheek.

"Your face was precious," she smirked.

"How did—does he know we?"

"He has no idea. Why, are you ashamed of dating a mere deputy?"

"No, no, that's not it. But it does kinda complicate things if we're working together.

Pete Tully was the first to the office. "Hey, Linda. Good to see you again. You taking him out for lunch?"

"Something like that," Parker said. "Get Barry off the phone. We need to go over this together."

Tully squinted. "Ah, yeah, all right. I'll go get him. He's probably on the phone to his image consultant anyway."

"How did you wrangle this assignment? I mean, you've been in Court Implementation for less than two months."

"It was Captain Morris's idea. He knows you are going to need all the help you can get on this one. He said I wasn't corrupted by the Court Monitors and attorneys yet."

"And he knows about us."

"He does and told me to make sure you keep it professional."

"I bet he did."

"Not in those exact words anyway."

"You wanted to see us, boss?" Barry said, knocking on the doorframe. "Hey, Linda."

She nodded in response.

"Yeah, come on in, guys."

Tully and Johns took chairs opposite Parker's desk. "What's up?" Tully asked. "The Undersheriff pull us off the case and turn it over to the feds?"

"Not yet. You remember the fine line we needed to walk last year when we were looking at the Immigrant Coalition?"

"And a good thing we did—nobody there was who they pretended to be," Tully said.

Parker pressed on. "The corner office is concerned about the public perception of our case this morning. Like we did with the Coalition, we need to be mindful of how our investigation is characterized in the press. We can't be perceived as writing this off as another border crime. We've already had some pushback from community advocate groups. We can't afford to be seen as profiling, or not giving this case all our attention."

"The bodies barely hit the morgue, and we're profiling? Want me to check in with Court Implementation, like last time?" Johns said.

"Good thinking, and that's why Deputy Hunt is here. She's going to be pitching in on the investigation and will be our liaison with Court Implementation. The Undersheriff wants to make certain we don't cross any lines which would extend the federal court order on the Melendres injunction."

Tully high-fived Linda. "Welcome to the dark side."

"Where do we start?" Linda said, holding a notebook in hand.

"Pete, run it down for us."

"Sure. We have twenty-eight male victims between the ages of twenty and forty, who were locked in a cargo container at the Devil's Well rest stop on I-10. Twenty-seven were deceased on scene, and one victim was transported to Banner Memorial in critical condition. We have no ID on any of the victims. Dr. Sherman will let us know if they get any hits when they Livescan their fingerprints at the morgue."

"Twenty-eight? My God," Linda said.

"Barry, any update on the traffic cam footage?"

"Not as much as we hoped. Witnesses at the rest stop reported a white tractor trailer, they believed it was a Kenworth, pulled out of the lot in a hurry, shot across the westbound lanes, through the median and headed east. The traffic camera at the 10 and 101 caught it moving fast. No plate on the back end. The next camera at the 17 interchange didn't catch it."

"He took the 202?" Parker asked.

Johns nodded. "But which way, north to Scottsdale, or south to Chandler?"

Parker strode to a county map on his office wall. Tracing his finger along the pathway Johns described, he stopped and tapped a spot on the map. "My bet is here," tapping the spot once more. "South. He could drop back on the southbound 10, or, more likely, the driver is hiding here in the Guad."

Guadalupe, or "The Guad" was a desolate enclave south of the city. If there was an equivalent to South Central Los Angeles, or the Southside of Chicago in terms of gang violence, weapons offenses, and drug busts in the one-square mile community, The Guad was it.

"If I were a coyote, this is where I'd hide," Parker said.

"Wouldn't be the first time. Remember Cardinale, the dude connected with the Cartel? He ran his operation from there."

"If the cartel's back in play here again, we'd have heard, wouldn't we?" Tully said.

"We need to check in with ICE and Homeland." Parker turned back to the map again. "If a guy let two dozen migrants die in a metal box, how welcome is he going to be in this neighborhood?"

"Not if they know about it," Tully said.

"Or if he's connected to the cartel, everyone is too afraid to talk," Johns said.

"Always a possibility." Parker's mind scrolled back to Cardinale and the bodies he left buried in the desert north of the city.

"We need to start poking around in the neighborhood. We know they won't be open to talking with us," Tully said.

"There are lots of undocumented who live there with their families. The only interaction they've had with law enforcement hasn't been positive."

"Want us to do a drive-through and see if we happen to spot our truck? I mean, it's too big to hide in someone's garage," Tully said.

"Yeah, go hit that and, Barry, let me know if we get anything from the Livescan prints from our victims. Linda and I will go have a chat with the feds and see if they've picked up a cartel connection on similar cargo box moves. Miguel is pitching in, informally, he's got a notion this might have a connection to a pair of missing kids in Mexico City. It's a long shot, but I wouldn't write it off."

"Can I ask a question?" Linda said. "I know I'm probably out of line, but can we get photos of the victims out there to see if anyone might know who they are? That many people coming over at one time—seems like someone should know?"

Parker couldn't hold back a grin. "Good thinking, Detective."

Linda blushed and stared down at her shoes.

"All right, that gets us a start. You guys take a chamber of commerce tour of the Guad, and Linda and I will see if the feds have intel we can use to make sense of this. Let's connect back here this afternoon. Linda's going to need to report to the boss on what you've been up to, so make it look good."

Linda's head snapped up, her eyes wide. "It's not like that."

Tully laughed. "We know, we know. We'd much rather have you here working with us than the court monitors looking over our shoulder. Or the Public Information Officer trying to run the investigation for the headlines."

"Don't worry, Linda. We know you have a job to do. Besides, it'll be nice to have a real cop working with the court watchers."

The two detectives gathered their radios and ballistic vests and headed out.

Linda glanced at Parker. "Detective, huh?"

"You are if you work here. Now go get changed into plainclothes. We have a stop to make before we drop in on the feds."

Chapter Six

The Law Offices of Sutton, Wimmer, and Hoster were in an upscale smoked glass office building in Scottsdale. The waiting room was appointed in dark leather and mahogany, which made the space come off as more of a smoking lounge than a waiting room for mobbed-up cartel hitmen.

"Do you have an appointment, Mr.—?" The receptionist asked.

"It's detective, Detectives Parker, and Hunt. Let Mr. Sutton know it might concern a client of his—a client from down south."

"Have a seat, and I'll ask if he can see you. Coffee?"

"Thank you, and no."

Linda leaned close to Parker, shot her eyes to the photos on the wall, and whispered, "The guy runs in some pretty high-powered circles."

"The ones who aren't on the wall are the ones to worry about," Parker said.

"I've heard Sutton likes to file excessive force complaints on cops in California, Nevada, and Arizona."

"Excessive force, racial bias, policy violations, over-policing, and his latest tactic is conspiracy. When an arrest goes bad, and there's more than one cop on scene, he claims it was a conspiracy."

"Every time we call for backup, it's a conspiracy?"

"It's how he plays it."

"Is any court buying his line?"

"Not yet. But, he's tying up resources, clogging up the system, and departments are settling these bogus complaints to avoid the hassle."

"Nuisance money."

"Exactly."

The receptionist rose from her desk, smoothed her grey pencil skirt, and gestured to a door to the left of her desk. "Mr. Sutton will see you. If you'll follow me."

She opened the tall, dark wood doors into a hallway and directed them to a conference room decorated with more legal trophies from the firm's clients.

While they surveyed the who's-who of litigation on display, a voice called out from behind.

"Come to confess your transgressions, Detective Parker?"

Larry Sutton stood at the head of the table, dressed in an expensive-looking dark blue suit, cut to his exact proportions—tall, thin, and a little wiry. Parker thought it was perfect for a weasel.

"Thanks for meeting with us. This is Detective Hunt."

"A pleasure, Detective. I do hope you don't let your partner's bad habits rub off on you. Now, Parker, what is it you need? You know I cannot divulge anything about my clients, *past* or present," he said with emphasis on past associations.

"I wouldn't ask you to. I know you hear a lot of information in your day-to-day interactions with the fringes of society you represent."

Sutton took the dig with a grin. "Everyone deserves representation, Detective."

"We're working on an investigation—and it's taking on some unusual aspects. Dozens of migrants left for dead—"

"Yes, yes, we all know this story too well. What does this have to do with—my clients' interests?"

"That's where we're hoping you can help us. Can you tell me if you've heard anyone mention bringing large groups over and the people were talking about weren't migrant farmworkers."

Sutton pursed his lips, exhaled a deep breath, and closed the conference room door. He opened a drawer on a credenza and removed a metallic bag. He opened it and placed his cell phone in the bag. "Yours as well."

Parker and Linda followed suit and dropped their cells in the Faraday bag, shielding them from any electronic eavesdropping.

"One can't be too careful," Sutton said.

He took a chair at the head of the table and gestured for the detectives to do the same.

"I'm not going to breach client confidentiality. When you mentioned the people you're concerned about aren't farmworkers, what were you implying?"

"No implications at all. I have twenty-seven dead, left in a cargo container on a major interstate highway. None of them looked more than thirty, and not a single one had as much as a callous on their hand. Sound familiar at all?"

"None of my clients are involved. Past or present. What you're describing—it doesn't sound like straight-up human trafficking. Any sign of drug smuggling?"

"None. Of course, whoever dropped the cargo container could have taken the shipment with them."

Sutton nodded. "I have overheard talk about a flow of workers coming over the border. Customs was somehow involved. I don't know the extent, other than palms had to be greased to make the connections work."

"That tracks with what we found. But they weren't day laborers," Parker said.

"I didn't say they were, Detective. Don't be so xenophobic. I said workers. Since the great pandemic, businesses can't get enough employees to fill their openings. Inflation and the economy mean they can't increase wages enough to recruit qualified, motivated domestic employees."

"What businesses are smuggling people over the border to fill their vacancies?

"I can't say, my clients aren't using these recruitment methods. Someone is, though."

"How long has this been going on?" Parker asked.

Sutton didn't pause before his response. "Six months, maybe a little longer. Two employee crews a month."

Parker worked a quick calculation in his head. "Means there have been around three hundred of these workers illegally crossing the border."

Sutton nodded. "Seems about right. I have heard this isn't the first 'shipment' to have 'problems' getting to their destination."

"It's the first we're aware of. What can you tell me about the other incomplete runs?"

"Two I know of—or rather heard about. One never made it to the border and was stopped on the Mexican side. The second—a competing entity stepped in and intercepted it."

"Who would that be?"

"It was an issue of drawing attention to established routes of international commerce, from what I understand. My clients had no part in it but were not altogether displeased with the message."

"Did you hear where this 'message' was delivered?"

Sutton paused, put both hands flat on the table. "Detective, I can't afford to be your confidential informant. In my business, I've learned not to ask questions I don't want to know the answer to."

Sutton stood. "Now, if that will be all…"

He handed the metallic Faraday bag to the detectives after removing his phone.

"One last thing, Mr. Sutton. Why bag the sheriff's office in the press about this investigation only hours into the case?"

He smiled. "It got you here, didn't it?"

The attorney smiled and left the detectives in the conference room. The receptionist was on deck to escort them from the inner sanctum.

Once outside in the parking lot, Parker leaned against his SUV. "Detective, tell me what you thought."

"Kind of a waste of time. He wasn't going to tell us anything about the men in the cargo container, or who's responsible for smuggling them over the border. He seemed to have more of an interest in working you through the ringer, making you come to him and beg for information."

Parker smiled. "Sutton told us a lot. The negative press release was his smoke signal to us—to me. He knew it would get my attention, and I'd come to him. He can't be seen going to the authorities. When he had us put our phones in the Faraday bag, it meant he knew he was being watched, and his offices were probably bugged."

"Who? Who'd bug his office?"

"The cartel, most likely. And we know the cartel didn't want these worker shipments to interfere with their established drug smuggling routes."

"The routes of commerce he mentioned."

"Exactly. Cartel controls the crossings, and they didn't want this new venture drawing attention to their smuggling routes."

"Sutton said a lot without saying a lot." She shook her head. Will I ever get to understand these guys?"

"You can't take anything at face value from people like Sutton. I am worried about the fact he thinks he's being watched. And the second smuggling run, intercepted by another, non-cartel group. It means either the cartel is using third-party muscle, or someone might be trying to move in on a smuggling route."

"How will we find out?"

"That's our next stop with the feds," Parker said.

The pair went silent, with Parker leaning on his SUV.

"What are we waiting for?" Linda asked.

"I want to see what our friends over there do."

Linda looked over her shoulder and spotted a dark sedan. Two silhouettes shown through the smoked glass. The car was on the opposite side of the street in front of the law office building.

"Who are they?"

"Only one way to find out." Parker pushed off the SUV and strode toward the sedan. When he took a step into the street, the sedan pulled from the curb. He snapped a photo of the car as it pulled away.

Using his SUV's onboard computer, Parker tapped in the license plate number from his cell phone photo.

In seconds the automated system spit back a response. The car was a federal government car from their motor pool. It wasn't an undercover car because the plate didn't come back restricted.

"Government? Were they watching Sutton?"

"No, I think they were watching us. Let's go find out why."

Chapter Seven

The FBI offices on Deer Valley Parkway were housed in a sandstone-colored brick complex north of the city. It sat back from the roadway and a thin iron fencing separated the structure from the world.

Parker flashed his badge at the security gate, and the guard let him through. After checking in at the main desk, Parker and Linda received visitors badges and Parker said he knew where he needed to go.

Assistant Special Agent in Charge Lynette Finch's office was on the third floor. Once in the door, Parker spotted Lynne's protective assistant perched at her desk.

"Hello, Delores," Parker said.

"Detective." She had a special way of making the word detective sound trivial and demeaning. "You don't have an appointment."

"Oh, I'm sure I did. You might want to check with Lynne."

"Special Agent Finch is out of the office. Call for an appointment next time."

The outer door swung open, and Lynne strode through. Blonde hair pulled back into a ponytail, dark business suit with a blue silk blouse that matched the color of her eyes.

"Nathan. Linda, how good to see you." Lynne hugged Linda and glanced at Parker with a glint in her eye. "I hope you're not picking up bad habits from this one."

"Detective Parker doesn't have an appointment, Ms. Finch," Delores said.

Lynne grinned. "What's next on my schedule?"

"You have a meeting with the AUSA on the Peterson case in twenty minutes."

"Linda, Nathan, come in. I assume you had reason to drive by."

The detectives followed Lynne into her office, and Nathan glanced back at Delores and smiled. The woman's face could melt granite.

"What's up? Is this a permanent assignment, Linda?"

"I'm a liaison to Detective Parker from Court Implementation."

"Well, he does need monitoring from time to time. Sit, sit."

Linda and Parker sat at one of two sofas facing Lynne's desk.

"Nathan, how's Miguel?"

"The kid is resilient, I'll give him that. He's back to school, looking at a four-year, and working part-time for the Coalition."

Lynne's face softened. "I'm glad to hear it. I don't know too many people who could have gone through the things he did and come out the other side without being bitter and broken. And speaking of bitter and broken, how are you doing, Nathan?"

Nathan laughed. "Actually, pretty good. He glanced over at Linda. Really good." Linda blushed.

"We're working on a case that might have some interest to the feds. This morning we had a cargo container with twenty-eight migrants—"

"I heard. I asked our HIDTA task force for a briefing. That's just what I got back from."

"We have some intel indicating workers are being smuggled over the border and have been for the past six months. It doesn't look like Cartel, but whoever is doing this might have gotten close to a cartel route, and another shipment was intercepted," Parker said.

Lynne nodded. "Our resources in Mexico seem to confirm that also. Large groups of men, mostly college-age, are going missing. The families have no idea where they went. They simply disappeared. They weren't planning on making a border crossing. Their families were stable, employed, and not being pressured by organized crime elements south of the border."

"You have contact with the families?"

"Our liaison at the American Embassy in Mexico City does. Why?"

"If we get you the photos of the twenty-seven victims we found this morning, you think the families could identify them?"

Lynne looked down at her desk. "We can ask the embassy liaison officer to make the contact. You think there's a connection here?"

"It's too similar to ignore. If we get an ID on one of our victims, it might give us a link to how they disappeared there and turned up here."

"Get me the photos, and I'll pass them on. As miserable as it will be for the families, at least they'll know," she said.

"You haven't seen any evidence of what happened to the one intercepted 'shipment,' have you? If it's like the one we found, we're talking over two dozen men," Parker said.

"We've not found movement of that magnitude. Homeland and ICE might know more."

"Excuse me," Linda said. "If these workers aren't being smuggled across for migrant work in the fields, what are they coming for? What kinds of jobs are they finding?"

Lynne rubbed her chin and paused for a moment. "That's a good question. Usually, it's farm work, construction, general labor, sometimes they have relatives who put them to work as mechanics, fabricators, electricians, and teachers."

"Teachers?"

"Some of the migrant communities are mobile and move from crop to crop as the planting and harvesting cycles rotate. The families move with them, including the kids. Some of the larger groups set up their own schools, knowing without documentation, vaccination records, and transcripts they couldn't get into public schools. They also don't trust the school authorities here not to turn them in to immigration."

"It could be any job, any skill level, or trade bringing our victims here?" Linda said.

"Unfortunately, yes. Sorry it doesn't narrow it down for you."

Linda bit her lower lip. "Actually, it might. Instead of looking at the narrow stereotypical view of employment, our victims were coming for, we need to go wider and look for businesses with a labor shortage in the last six months. A shortage severe enough they resorted to undocumented labor."

"Not bad, Detective," Parker said.

Lynne nodded in agreement. "You might have a future in this detective game."

Linda's neck flushed pink. "I'm only saying we have a place to start. It might not go anywhere…"

"Is Espi still plugged in at DEA?" Parker asked. Espi was Special Agent Philip Espinosa who worked several undercover operations for the Drug Enforcement Agency. If there was rumble of cartel activity, or moving significant quantities of drugs over the border, he was in the best place to hear about it."

"He is. He might have a handle on other reasons your victims came here—like the solar panel manufacturing plant."

"Solar panels?" Linda asked.

"The Sinaloa Cartel was manufacturing and distributing fentanyl from a solar panel facility near Cave Creek. They used forced migrant labor to run the facilities, and the exposure to the chemicals turned out to be deadly for many of them."

"Here? I thought the Cartels were only working south of the border. I mean, I know they run product up here, but a cartel-operated place in Cave Creek?" Linda said.

"It's like a game of whack-a-mole. Hit the cartel in one place and they pop back up somewhere else. Taking down the operation hurt them and disrupted their flow for a while. Espi could give us a heads up on what the cartel's doing now and who's running it."

Delores knocked and entered. "You're expected in conference room two."

"Thank you. Please let the Assistant US Attorney know I'm on my way."

"Yes, ma'am." Delores gave Parker what he thought was a world-class stink eye on the way out.

Parker pressed up from the sofa. "Thanks for your time, Lynne. Before we go, could you have your people check for any intel on Esteban Castaneda?

It's coming up on the anniversary of the murder..."

"I will. I haven't heard mention of him or Los Muertos for a year. He seems to have gone to ground again. He came close to getting trapped up here."

"I'd like to believe that. You remember he threatened to target anyone in my life."

"I'll let you know if we pick up any whisper about Castaneda."

"Thanks, Lynne. We'll be on our way. If you hear anything..."

"I'll be sure and pass it on."

Lynne gave Parker a hug. A sure sign of the thaw in their relationship. It was a slow process mending a breakup. Five years ago.

Once outside, Linda donned her sunglasses and started to their SUV. "It's fun spending time with your ex. And Delores has your number, doesn't she?"

Parker stopped in his tracks. "Who's side are you on?"

"I wasn't aware there were sides. Until today. What the hell did you do to her?"

"What makes you think it was me?"

Linda looked over her sunglasses and narrowed her green eyes.

"Never mind," He said. "It was probably me."

"Probably?"

They climbed into the SUV, and Parker started the engine to get the air conditioning going. The late afternoon heat was beating down on the black SUV.

Parker didn't put the car in gear.

"Five years ago, my partner was murdered."

"I know."

"I didn't handle it well. Lynne and I were living together at the time, and I blamed myself for what happened to Mac. I still do, if I'm honest. I withdrew, didn't want to deal with what occurred out there at Rocky Wash. Instead of taking time to recognize the trauma of having your partner bleed out in your arms, I withdrew, went dark and threw myself into the job, pretending I was okay. I wasn't.

"Things fell apart. Lynne and I stopped trying to make it work. I kind of ignored her and tried to pretend everything was fine."

"And it wasn't," Linda said.

"No, not even close. I let everything fall apart. I didn't feel anything. I was walking around numb most of the time. I escaped into the job as a place to go hide from everything. I pushed all my feelings down and bottled them up."

"Because you're a guy."

"Maybe. But whatever it was destroyed the relationship I had with Lynne, our friends, and honestly, even my work suffered."

"What pulled you out of it?"

"Honestly, I'm not sure I ever did. I went to a few counseling sessions off the books so the deputies I worked with wouldn't think I was weak, and I don't know, maybe they worked, but mostly, it's been time. Time and finding Miguel when I did. The kid's made me more aware of what's going on outside my own little mind, you know?"

She sat back in the seat and placed her hand on his arm. "I've never heard you talk about this before. I met you after you became Miguel's foster parent. Leon came into my life around the same time. You seemed to—I don't know—you seemed to really care about the boy, for someone who had only recently come into your life. I thought it said a lot about you as a person."

"There was a time when I didn't think I could care about anyone else again. Miguel broke those walls down for me. As sappy as it sounds, if it wasn't for Miguel, I wouldn't have met you."

"You mean because he got arrested at an immigration protest?" She smiled after her response.

"Well, that too. But we met at those foster parent meetings with you and Leon."

"But, you didn't ask me out until Miguel shamed you into it," she said.

"I don't think shamed is the right word. Convinced, maybe."

"We can agree to disagree on that point."

"Whatever—what I'm trying to say is I wouldn't have risked a relationship with someone like you without letting myself open up a bit. And Miguel helped me regain a little piece of myself again."

She patted his arm. "A relationship, huh? Are we like going steady, like in high school?"

"You're impossible, you know that?"

She leaned over and kissed him on the cheek. "So are you."

Parker glanced at his watch. "You want to grab some dinner and meet up at my place with the boys?"

"Sure, Leon should be off work and he's always hungry.

Parker pulled out of the FBI lot and headed back to the sheriff's office. A little relaxed after his talk with Linda and thinking about what to grab for dinner, he didn't notice the dark sedan following him once more.

Chapter Eight

Parker dropped Linda off at the Sheriff's station so she could give her report to the Court Implementation unit and the Undersheriff. They agreed to meet up at Parker's place in two hours.

The Major Crimes Unit evening shift was setting up for the night's prostitution stings. Detective Karen Rollins was typing up an action plan for the evening's round-up. Dressed in leather hot pants, boots, and a matching leather vest, the detective was the bait for the evening.

"Where to tonight, Karen?"

"Scottsdale, near the hotel strip."

"How did you draw the short straw?" Parker asked, gesturing to her clothing.

She tugged down the hot pants legs. "It was either me or Jimmy Corwin."

Detective Corwin was three-hundred and fifty pounds and six-foot-three.

"I dunno. I think Jimmy would do those hot pants justice. Anyway, be careful out there, and don't break any hearts."

"Yeah, yeah," she said, focusing back on the report.

Detectives Johns and Tully returned from their tour of the Guad, and Johns gestured with a shrug and palms up to Parker. They'd come up dry on their search for the white truck.

Tully followed Parker into his office.

"Nothing, huh?" Parker said.

"We hit more than half of the Guad and no sign of the truck. There are a couple of storage yards on the east side and a few more blocks we're gonna hit in the morning. We started losing daylight."

"The FBI didn't know much more than we did. They knew about runs bringing workers here, but don't know where they were supposed to go. I'm going to reach out to Espinoza at the DEA tomorrow."

Johns entered the office. "Got a message from the morgue. They're gonna start on the post-mortem exams on our John Does in the a.m. They ran Livescan on the first ten, and nothing hit in the system. Want me to run down there and cover?"

"Why don't you guys finish the Guad, looking for any sign of the truck? Think they could have started stripping it out already?"

"It's possible. We'll hit some of the salvage yards in the area," Tully said.

"I'll see Dr. Sherman tomorrow and learn about our victims. Oh, Linda had a good idea about showing the photos of the victims to families in Mexico who reported college-aged family members disappearing. The FBI Liaison in Mexico City is going to help out."

"Worth a shot. We've got nothing else to ID these guys yet," Johns said.

"Oh hey, I forgot to mention, could one of you track down who's running a camera set up at the Devil's Well rest stop? It's mounted over the comfort station and might give us a view of the truck driver, or anyone else who had an interest in our cargo container. I think it was being used to monitor child custody exchanges."

"I'll track it down," Johns said.

"All right, let's hit this fresh tomorrow. We've been running on this straight for about sixteen hours. Keep me posted on what you find in the Guad."

"You got it, boss," Tully said.

Parker snapped off a quick text to Linda asking about what to grab on the way home.

Seconds later, his screen brightened with her text in response. His mood fell at the message. "I need to ask for a rain check. Trouble at home with Leon."

"Is he all right?"

"Yes. Maybe. I don't know."

"Want me to come over?"

"No. I have it managed. I'll catch you up tomorrow."

"Pick you up at 7:30?"

A thumbs up emoji was the response. Linda was distracted and didn't want to tell him what her foster son's problem was about.

He clamped his eyes shut and knew he had blown it with his oversharing after the FBI meeting. She must think he was a total head case and was having second thoughts about their relationship. He didn't blame her. He was more trouble than he was worth.

He shot a second text to Miguel, letting him know he was on his way home, and what did he want him to pick up for dinner on the way home. The second he hit send, Parker mumbled out loud, "Please don't be pizza, please don't be pizza."

"Pizza from Ernestos. Extra cheese, extra pepperoni," Miguel replied.

Parker smiled and shook his head. The kid was assimilating into American culture.

"You sure?" Parker messaged.

"Yes! Please…"

He told Miguel he'd be home in thirty minutes, he logged off his computer, and turned out his office lights.

"Happy hunting tonight, Karen," Parker called out to the detective as she tugged on the tight leather vest.

Parker balanced the pizza box in one hand as he punched in the entry code on his front door. One of the security upgrades he'd done at the house in the last year. It was probably obsessive, but he wasn't going to take a chance.

Inside, Parker heard voices from the kitchen. Miguel and someone else in conversation. He closed the door, carried the pizza box through the living room, and spotted Miguel with a young woman.

They were making a salad. Miguel was chopping tomatoes, and she was tossing lettuce, green peppers, and mushrooms in a large wooden bowl.

Miguel looked up from the cutting board. "Hi, we thought a salad might be nice with the pizza. Oh, this is Sarah."

Sarah wiped her hands on a towel and extended hers to Parker. "Nice to meet you, Mr. Parker."

Parker shook her small hand and said, "I imagine the healthy salad was your idea. Because I've known Miguel to eat absolutely zero salads."

"I might have suggested it."

Sarah bounced back to the salad bowl. She was maybe five-three, Parker guessed, a wisp of a thing with chestnut-colored hair and dark brown eyes, with dimples when she smiled. Miguel was smiling, too.

Parker dropped the pizza box on the dining table. He noticed it was set with three places with dishes from the cupboard instead of the paper plates he and Miguel tended to use in their bachelor lifestyle.

"Be right back, Parker said. He retreated to his bedroom and locked his duty weapon into a fingerprint-activated gun safe. He changed into jeans and a t-shirt and joined Miguel and his friend.

Parker stood under the air conditioning vent and let the chilled breeze waft over him. A shiver crept over his body at the thought of the men trapped in the cargo box when their A/C broke down. He shook his head to clear the thought.

"What's everyone want to drink?"

"Water for Sarah and me."

"Salad and water? What have you done to him?"

Miguel grinned and carried the salad bowl to the table. "Someone has to set an example in this house."

Parker poured cold water from a pitcher in the refrigerator and filled everyone's glasses.

"How did you two meet?" Parker asked.

"It's kind of embarrassing. We met at school."

"Sarah's in one of your classes?"

"You could say that."

Parker caught Sarah elbowing Miguel.

"She's teaching the class." Miguel blushed.

Parker held his slice of pizza suspended between his plate and his mouth.

"Teacher? You're a college professor?"

It was Sarah's turn to flush.

"I'm a graduate student assisting an instructor at the college. I'm working on my master's in ecological studies."

It meant Sarah was older than Miguel by at least a couple of years, Parker figured. You couldn't tell by looking at her.

"You know the Earth Sciences class I was having trouble with?"

"You mean the one you said was a waste of time?"

Sarah turned to Miguel with a questioning expression.

"I never said that."

"I seem to remember the exact words were, 'Who cares about rocks and dirt?' and 'When will I ever need to know about the jet stream's impact on the Mexican Jumping Spider'?"

Sarah caught a wink from Parker.

"Really? Is that why you came begging me to tutor you?" she said.

"I didn't say that. Dad, tell her you're kidding."

"Why would I make up such things?"

Miguel took a bite of his pizza so he wouldn't have to respond. After he swallowed, he said, "My grades went up, didn't they?"

Parker's cell rang, and he excused himself to answer. The caller ID showed Linda's number.

He grimaced because he knew she was going to react to his oversharing and exposing his vulnerability a bit more than he should have. He didn't blame her.

"Hi, Linda. Hey, I'm sorry about the whole—"

"Nathan, I wanted to say I'm sorry for cutting you off earlier. Leon sprang some crap about wanting to drop out of school."

"Why is he talking about leaving school? He was doing well at Glendale, wasn't he?"

"He was. I guess his grades came in, he didn't show them to me, but he's all butt hurt about them and says it's not worth it."

"Did he say what he wants to do if he drops out?"

"No, he's frustrated and doesn't know where he wants to go in life."

"I get it, I do. Miguel goes to Glendale. Want me to see if he knows about what's got Leon thinking about leaving? I know they were close, but I don't know if they spend much school time together."

"Might be a good idea. Miguel had a way of getting through to him."

"Oh, and Miguel has a girlfriend here from school—and get this, she's a teaching assistant in one of his classes."

"Miguel's hot for teacher?"

"Something like that, she does seem nice though. Even has him eating salad."

"You could do with the occasional salad, too," she said.

Parker instinctively sucked in his gut.

"Yeah, yeah, yeah. Listen, I'm sorry about earlier, if I got all morose like a weepy teenager."

"You did no such thing. In fact, it was nice to hear a man strong enough to talk about his feelings."

"Oh, God, you used the F word. I may never live this down."

"I thought it was—charming."

"I'm charming?"

"I didn't say that. And yeah, could you ask Miguel if he's seen any change in Leon? Maybe I'm overreacting, and he's blowing off steam."

He promised he would and confirmed he'd pick her up in the morning at her place.

Back in the kitchen, Miguel and Sarah were finished cleaning up.

"Hey, that was Linda. She's kinda worried about Leon. Claims he's thinking about dropping out."

Sarah and Miguel exchanged a look.

"What?" Parker said.

"Leon's been kinda off the rails lately."

"What's that mean?"

"He stopped coming to my class, for one," Sarah said.

A dark cloud passed through Miguel's eyes. "You know, last year, when the Coalition had a presence on campus, organizing rallies and protests?"

"Sure, didn't those stop when the Coalition folded up—before Billie and you reinvented the organization?"

"Nature abhors a vacuum. I learned that from Sarah. There are other groups springing up to fill the void. Not all of them are about doing what's right."

"Leon got hooked into one of those groups?"

"He did. It's one of the more extreme elements. They believe in some of the things most of the undocumented would agree with—a path to citizenship, amnesty, and extending DACA. But this group will do anything to get people talking about their cause. I think they were behind the firebombing of the federal building last month."

"I remember. No real damage, as I recall, but it disrupted a meeting with the Mexican Counsel General. What's the name of this group?"

"It's Soldiers for something or another—"

"Soldiers for Justice," Sarah said. "They're more anarchists and antifa than anything thing else. Disrupt, obstruct, and intimidate."

"What's Leon doing with them?" Parker asked.

"I have no idea what he sees in them. He's been kinda distant. If he's talking about dropping out, it could be the only way he knows to get away from them. You remember how non-confrontational he is."

"Which is why I don't see the attraction. Can you talk to him? Find out what's going on?"

"I can try. Hey, Sarah and I are going to head out and catch a movie. Can I leave you unattended for a few hours?"

It was Miguel's way of asking if it was all right.

"I'll manage. Have a good time. Nice to meet you, Sarah."

"You too, Mr. Parker."

The two hadn't left the driveway when Parker's cell phone rang.

"Parker, here."

"Hi, Nathan, it's Dr. Lison at the Medical Examiner's Office. I think you need to come over. Dr. Sherman's been exposed. We think it's from the cargo container."

Chapter Nine

Parker made the trip to the Medical Examiner's Office on West Jefferson after leaving a note for Miguel. The offices were open and readied for the families of the recently deceased to receive confirmation of their loved one's death. The scant waiting room was a place where good news never dropped. Families didn't leave here with their souls intact.

The receptionist waved at Parker through a glass panel and buzzed him through the locked door. Inside this corridor, the mood shifted to a clinical and professional place, with less warmth than a dollar store. When families came here to claim or identify their loved ones, no one cared about the paint color on the wall. With over forty thousand deaths a year in the county, the time for niceties was limited.

He found Dr. Sherman at her desk. She wore a pair of light blue scrubs and looked fresh out of the shower with damp hair.

"Hi, Doc. I heard you were exposed. Dr. Lison got me worried. You all right?"

"I'm—okay. Dr. Lison meant well, but he got a little excited."

"He said you were exposed in the container. Drug residue?"

"Not quite. It's more of a precaution than anything. We have to decontaminate the bodies, and the process might strip away any trace evidence we need. I'm pissed."

"What happened? Fentanyl? I know you guys use respirators..."

"Respirators wouldn't do anything for this." She turned her monitor so Parker could see. Two staff members in HazMat suits with "Medical

Examiner" stamped on the back were hovering over a corpse on a stainless-steel table. The clothing was held by forceps and placed into a biowaste bag marked "Do Not Incinerate." The body was doused with a shower hose mounted above the table. When the shower stopped, one of the protective suit wearing people held a box-shaped object over the body and ran it from head to toe.

"All clear," a voice sounded over the computer speaker.

"All clear of what?" Parker said.

"Radiation."

"What?"

"The cargo container was exposed to radiation. We found it on the victims' clothes. What we don't see is any sign of radiation poisoning. No evidence of widespread nausea and vomiting, other than what we first associated with asphyxia. We didn't see any burns, or radiation dermatitis from high-level exposure. As you saw in the feed, the body itself isn't a source of further contamination."

"You were exposed?"

"I handled the bodies and the clothing and was considered to be exposed."

"Jesus, Doc."

"So were you. We were both inside the container this morning." She shuffled open a drawer and tossed him a small orange pill bottle. "Potassium Iodine. Bottoms up."

"I'm exposed? Am I radioactive or something?"

"You're not going to glow in the dark. You got exposed in the range of 20 millisieverts. Like the amount you get from three chest X-rays."

"Twenty sounds like a lot."

"You get about three millisieverts walking out in the sun. The people who got sick at Chernobyl got hit with about 700."

"The pills are a precaution?"

"They are. If you have any nausea, vomiting, dizziness, headache, you get your ass to the hospital. I swear to God, if I lose my hair, I'm gonna find out who's responsible and get medieval on someone. Oh yeah, hair loss is another symptom."

"I was home before I came here. Is my place contaminated? Is Miguel in danger?"

"There shouldn't be a problem. I would gather up the clothes you wore and run them by us for testing."

Dr. Sherman handed Parker a water bottle. "Now bottom's up."

Parker unscrewed the bottle, poured one of the pills into his palm, and tossed it back. "So, I'm cured?"

"The potassium iodide stops your thyroid gland from absorbing any radiation."

Parker took another nervous pull from the water bottle. "Where did it come from?"

"An exposure like this, it's not a massive meltdown, or what you'd see from a dirty bomb. But it's concerning. We're going to have to report this event to the feds."

"Oh, this's going to be a cluster."

"We need their help with decontamination of the cargo container and determining where it came from."

"And you're okay? You were in there handling these bodies for a long time."

"I'm fine. Pissed because this is delaying everything, but I'm fine. I have to carry one of these around." She clipped a small rectangular card to her scrubs. "A dosemeter to register exposure. If this dot changes color, it means radiation is present." She shuffled her drawer open again and tossed him four of them. "Might as well have your team wear them."

"Thanks, I think. It's kinda scary to think about."

"We're talking lower doses here, like I said, but it's still troubling—how it got onto our victims' bodies in the first place."

Parker gathered up the radiation badges. "If I start glowing in the dark, I'll let you know." He stood and took a step to the door when Dr. Lison pushed through.

"Dr. Sherman, you need to see this." Lison was out of breath and handed a folder to Dr. Sherman.

She opened the file and a series of photographs were clipped to the file.

She flipped from one to another, until the last in the set of six.

"We had to delay this part of the examination until the bodies were fully decontaminated. Only six of them showed signs of exposure. The rest were clear. None of them registered near to a fatal dose."

"Only six of them?" Sherman said.

"Yes. There rest were clear of contamination."

"Dumping contaminated bodies, even six of them—it wasn't an accident," Parker said. "Someone went through a lot of trouble to get rid of these victims. Why?" Parker asked.

"The answer is on your side of the fence, Detective."

"The fence keeps getting taller. I'm glad you're okay, doc," Parker said to Dr. Sherman." Parker hefted the file folder. "Mind if I keep these?"

Lison tucked in his chin and accepted the affirmation. "Of course."

"Without any hit on Livescan, we're looking at identification through photo, distinguishing characteristics, and dental. Unfortunately, none of those are automated at this point. What we do have is an FBI Liaison Officer in Mexico City who's willing to take photo lineups to families who've reported college-aged sons and brothers missing."

"We can work up a digital photo package for you. Dr. Lison and his team will take care of it."

"Absolutely," Lison said.

"Thank you. I guess I should head back home and bag up my clothes."

"Drop them off here, and we'll check them over and get an idea of how much exposure you might have received. You weren't in the box very long, but I'd feel better knowing you've taken every precaution. I'm sure I don't have to tell you, but take a shower after you bag up those clothes, as a precaution."

"One Silkwood shower coming up," Parker said.

"I don't think you'll need someone with a stiff brush scrubbing you down."

"Oh, our lone survivor. I remembered. Does the hospital know about the contamination risk?"

"We took care of it, Detective," Dr. Lison said. He's in isolation, and they've disposed of his clothing. He didn't read positive for radiation when scanned."

"Any update on his condition?"

"Not that I'm aware of," Lison said.

"Thanks again, and let me know when you have the photo package ready. I'm sure the families would appreciate it if they're able to find out what happened." Parker didn't use the word "closure." There was never any when it came to the death of a loved one or family member. It stayed with you, and depending how you dealt with the memory, it was a comfort, or a dark shadow in the corners of your nightmares.

Parker's memories of McMillan were of the later variety. Survivor's guilt. The first few months, every night, included an inventory of all the decisions and actions he could have taken to change the outcome that night. One of the most painful memories was the replay of delivering the news to Mac's pregnant wife that he wasn't coming home.

Closure was bullshit.

Chapter Ten

Parker made it home, bagged up his clothes from the scene, right down to his favorite Merrill shoes, and tossed them in a triple layer of plastic bags. If double was good, triple was better. After a long hot shower with a cheap caustic soap he kept on hand for those times he worked on his Jeep, he felt like a layer of skin went down the drain.

By the time he got out of the shower, it was time to get the morning routine underway, rousing Miguel, getting coffee going and heading out to pick up Linda.

The smell of fresh, dark brew drew Miguel from his room.

"Morning."

"Mmm," Miguel said, smelling the coffee. He poured a cup and sat at the counter.

"How was the movie?"

"It was another superhero thing. I've lost track of which one, they all have powers and everyone dies."

"Did Sarah like it?"

"She's way into that scene and can tell you the difference between DC and Marvel, and all I know is Spider-Man got bit by a bug, and Batman lives in a cave."

"At least I know how your grade in her class improved."

He grinned.

"Let me know what you hear about Linda's kid, Leon, would you? She sounded worried about him."

"I will. I'm heading out to the campus in about an hour. I'll see what I can find out."

"I don't need to tell you to be careful when it comes to fringe groups, right? I'd hate for something to happen."

"I know, I know. You're like a worried old woman. Just Chill."

"Chill? You used the word chill with me?" Parker put down his coffee.

Miguel glanced up, a crease in his brow. "What, didn't I use the word right?"

"Yeah, you did. It sounded funny coming from you, the most unchill kid I know."

"What? I'm chill," Miguel said.

"Sure, sure you are. Work after school today?"

"Yeah, for a couple hours."

"I'll grab some chicken or something and grill it up for us tonight."

"Maybe. Sarah and I were talking about going somewhere."

"Oh, okay then. She's welcome here if you want. Let me know so I can make sure we have enough."

He nodded and took another sip of coffee.

"All right then, I'm off," Parker said.

He got in his SUV and pulled out of the drive, thinking his time with Miguel was becoming less and less. Miguel never talked about what happened to his family in El Salvador. From the bits and pieces Parker was able to cobble together, his parents were murdered in front of him after Miguel refused to join a local offshoot of the MS-13 gang. Parker knew the kid blamed himself for their deaths. Miguel fled the Central American country to escape the violence and start a new life. It wasn't an easy adjustment, but in some ways, Miguel and Parker filled the voids in each other's lives. Parker hoped he'd given him enough of a foundation in the short time they had together to let him succeed. Is this what an empty nest felt like?

He pulled up to Linda's place at seven-thirty on the dot and she was waiting for him at the curb.

Parker picked up on the worry lines and handed her a travel mug of coffee when she got in.

"I need this."

"Not much sleep last night?" Parker asked.

"I stayed up talking with Leon for most of the night, trying to get a handle on what bug bit him on the butt."

"The dropping out of school thing?"

Parker pulled off the curb and headed south toward the Guad.

"There's more to it. His attitude about everything has changed. He doesn't want to go to school, he won't talk to me about it, he hangs out with these sketchy people in La Mirage, and is starting to spout off all these notions about defunding the police and abolishing ICE."

"You remind him the 'police' is paying for a roof over his head?"

"I did, and it went over like a fart in church. He said I was part of the establishment and part of the problem."

"You know, it sounds like he's getting his head filled by some radical fringe groups. Miguel was telling me a few of them popped up on campus lately."

"I don't want him to toss everything away. He's gone through so much, and if he does something stupid and endangers his visa status here, I don't know what I'll do."

Parker put a hand on her knee. "We'll make sure it doesn't happen."

"I hope not." She wiped a stray tear away with a knuckle. "Thanks for letting me vent."

"It was your turn…after yesterday."

"Listen, I'm sorry if I came on strong yesterday. It's just seeing you with your ex—"

"Nothing to be jealous about there. Like you witnessed, I burnt that bridge and swept away the charred remains. There's nothing going on there."

"That's not what I mean. But I guess I am jealous of the relationship you two still have. She still cares about you, and I think in your way, you do too. I don't have that with my ex-husband. When Tim and I split, it was over."

"You never mention him."

"There's a good reason."

Parker waited her out. He sensed Linda wanted to open a door into her past.

"It happened slowly. I didn't see the signs until it was too late."

"Alcohol?"

"That was part of it. When he drank, he became abusive."

"I'm sorry. I didn't know."

"I didn't want anyone to know. It was like it was my shame."

"You weren't at fault, Linda."

"It wasn't. I know that now. But at the time…"

"I get it," Parker said.

"I'm not out for sympathy here. Leaving him proved I was the strong one in that relationship. I have no idea where he is, and I don't care. But there's a small part of me that would like to have the kind of relationship with Tim that you have with Lynne."

"Cold, distant, and spiteful?"

Linda smacked him on the knee.

"What's the game plan for today?" she asked.

"I've gotta drop by the Medical Examiner's Office, then I thought we'd head out to the Guad and give Pete and Barry a hand looking for our truck."

"The Medical Examiner? I've never—do I have to watch an autopsy?"

"Not today—there was a complication last night?"

"Last night?"

"I got called out to go see Dr. Sherman. Long story short, they thought she was exposed to radiation. She's fine. But, some of our cargo container bodies were contaminated with low-level radiation."

"Radioactive? You? You were in the box with them. Are you all right?"

"Looks like it. Dr. Sherman had me take some Potassium Iodide as a preventative and wanted us to carry radiation badges while we're on this investigation." He pulled one of the badges from his jacket pocket and handed it to Linda.

"I need to wear this?"

"We don't know the source of the radiation. It's not a bad idea. If the dot turns color, we need to back out."

"If we aren't doing the autopsy this morning, why are we heading to the M.E.'s office?"

"Laundry."

Before he could respond to Linda's curious expression, his phone rang.

"Parker, here."

"Nathan, it's Lynne."

"Good morning, Lynne. What's up?"

"I hope you still think it's a good morning. Where are you? Sounds like you're driving?"

"I am, Linda and I are heading out to—"

"Put me on the speaker. This concerns both of you."

Parker hit the speaker button, "All right, you're on. What's up, Lynne?"

"We got a hit on Los Muertos."

Parker's knuckles tensed on the wheel.

"Where?" he asked.

"Two Los Muertos hitters were intercepted at the Border near the Sasabee crossing."

"That's a good thing, right?"

"It is. What worries me is what they were found with."

"What's that?"

"They had photos of you, Miguel, and Linda with them."

Parker involuntarily pulled his foot off the gas. "What are they saying?"

"Nothing. You know these types. They're holding their mud. I've got Agent Collins in with them now."

"When you're done with them, I'd like to see what you've got, maybe take a crack at them. If they wanted me so bad, they might break if they get close."

"I don't think these guys are going to tell us a thing. The only thing they've asked for is to contact the Mexican Consulate."

"What's that about? The Mexican government and Los Muertos aren't exactly seeing eye to eye."

"Yeah, it was a bit peculiar."

"Speaking of peculiar..." Parker gave Lynne a short update on the last night's radioactive discovery.

"You're okay, though?" she asked. Parker felt a genuine concern in her voice. There was a time, not long ago, when Lynne couldn't have cared less what happened to him. At least that's how it felt.

"Dr. Sherman doesn't think there's anything to worry about. She said she was going to reach out to whatever federal agency deals with this kind of thing. Thought it might be important for you guys to know about."

"Thanks. I'll get the word out. Any thoughts on where the contamination occurred?"

"Not yet. The containers were sealed with a customs sticker and opened at the rest stop."

"The customs seal could have been applied anywhere."

"We have the techs looking at it, might be phony. Still, we don't know where the contamination occurred."

They ended the conversation with an admonition from Lynne to be extra vigilant. When Los Muertos found out their two men were captured, more would follow.

Linda took in the first part of the conversation calmly as if getting placed on a gang hit list happened every day. When Parker disconnected the call, Linda twisted sideways in her seat, facing him.

"You, and me, I understand. We can deal with whatever they throw at us. But Miguel? Why go after a kid? He's never interfered with their business. That's all these clowns care about, isn't it?"

"Los Muertos isn't the typical street gang. They came up as a tool for the Sinaloa Cartel to use when they didn't want to get their hands dirty. Using them as muscle to kidnap, assassinate, or intimidate gave the cartel some deniability. Los Muertos are mercenaries."

"Mercenaries go where the money is," she said.

"Exactly. Been their M.O. all along."

"Who's paying them now?"

"I'm not sure. They fell out of love when Los Muertos tried to take over the fentanyl operation from the Sinaloa Cartel. Someone's got to be bankrolling them. Castaneda is a wildcard. He wants me, and it's personal.

He made sure I knew he was coming when he left me a message after the sniper killings last year."

"I remember."

"I'll reach out to Billie and have her keep an eye on Miguel and Leon. I don't trust Los Muertos to not go beyond the names Lynne found."

Parker pulled into the Medical Examiner's parking lot to find more security than when he left last night. Phoenix police blocked off the entrance to the facility and a uniformed Phoenix PD officer waved him off when Parker turned into the entrance.

"No access to the facility," the officer said. An older guy with a handlebar mustache Parker knew was an inch or two beyond regulation.

"Detective Parker, MCSO. Dropping something off for Dr. Sherman."

"Not today, you aren't."

"She knows this is coming in—it's important."

"So you say. Beat it."

Linda leaned over and took her sunglasses down to engage the officer. "You know why they're locking this place down, right?"

"Yeah, of course."

"We're carrying some of the 'material,' and Dr. Sherman told us to deliver it to her."

"You can't come into the facility."

"How about we give it to you, and you can bring it inside to her? Although, if she's right, you'll never be able to have children again, officer," Linda said.

The officer took a step back. Another Phoenix PD officer came to Linda's side of the SUV. She was a younger officer, and the look on her face said she was exasperated with her partner.

"Let me call inside and see if we can figure this out," the officer said. Her brass name tag read Brennan.

"Thanks," Linda said.

Officer Brennan took a step back and dialed a number on her cell. A few seconds later she walked around the SUV to her partner, handed him the phone while she unlatched the gate, pushing it aside for Parker.

The officer approached Parker's window. "Sorry for the delay. Dr.

Sherman's office said they would have someone meet you at the loading dock."

"Thanks," Parker said.

"Sorry if we caused a problem with your partner," Linda said.

"Training Officer."

"It gets better, I promise," Linda said.

"I hope so."

The training officer came over, handed Brennan her cell, and waved his hand. "Come on, get moving," like it was his idea to approve their entrance."

Parker pulled through and watched the younger officer secure the gate while the training officer stood and did nothing to help.

"He's one piece of work. The kid's got it hard. Glad my first T.O. didn't treat me like that."

"Of course, he didn't. You're a man."

"That's got nothing to do with it—the job's the job."

"It's got everything to do with it. Every woman who's ever worn a badge deals with people like him. They don't want you in their all-male club. Tell you, you don't belong."

"It's not every T.O."

"Enough to make it feel like they don't want you here and will go out of their way to let you fail. There's no training. It's wait until the rookie does something wrong."

"Is that what you got?"

Linda nodded. "Sure did. Almost told him to stuff it where the sun don't shine and walked off. Lucky for me, I had a couple of role models to sit me down talk, and sense to me. They told me it was never going to be easy. I had guys like Officer asshat watching me. I'd have to be better than him to get the same amount of respect from other deputies."

Parker reached the loading dock, and two HazMat-wearing techs were at the ramp. Parker rolled his window down and told them a bag of clothing was in the rear of the SUV. He hit the remote latch, and the rear gate opened. One of the techs used long stainless-steel forceps to lift the plastic bag from the rear of the vehicle. A second ran a scanning device in the rear of the cargo compartment. Parker waited to hear the clicking of a Geiger counter, but these were more sensitive, sophisticated devices.

"All clear." And the tech shut the cargo door. He stepped around the driver's window. And Parker recognized him as one of Dr. Sherman's techs he'd met out at crime scenes.

"Dr. Sherman wanted me to ask if you have your dosimeters?"

Parker showed him his, and the tech waited for Linda to lift hers into view. The tech nodded.

"How's the doc this morning?"

"Cranky. She doesn't like being behind schedule. She did say she was able to Livescan all the bodies. We'll see if we get a hit in the system."

"Let's hope."

"Oh, she said you'd have the photo package of our victims later this morning."

"Great. Tell her thanks; we appreciate it."

Parker rolled the window up and left through the rear entrance.

Linda's phone lit up with a message.

"Johns and Tully want us to see them at the corner of Los Aztecs and Guadalupe. There's a Mexican market on the corner. They've spotted something."

Chapter Eleven

The community of Guadalupe, known as the Guad to locals, was a Phoenix suburb east of the 10 and south of the 60 where the motto was officially, "Where three cultures meet." Others knew it as the most crime-ridden scrap of land in Phoenix. More gang crime, shootings, and assaults took place in the Guad than in the rest of the metropolitan area combined.

People who wanted to hide came here. People who wanted to be left alone lived here. When those two populations come together, one of them is bound to lose.

Parker spotted Tully standing next to his SUV in the market parking lot.

Parker pulled in alongside as Johns was exiting the market, holding three paper cups of coffee.

The tall detective came to Linda's window. "Morning team."

Linda took one of the hot paper cups and handed it to Parker, then took one for herself. "Thanks Barry, I'm gonna have to get used to drinking more coffee around you guys," she pointed at the travel cup in the console.

"Oh, you won't want to drink this. I think it's left over from last night. Smells like burnt rubber. I needed to talk with the store owner and buying a couple of cups of coffee broke the ice."

Linda smelled the coffee she'd been handed. "Oh, my, that's strong."

"Yeah, I wouldn't recommend it."

"Pete's drinking it," she said.

"He doesn't know any better. He may come off as a professor, but he's a Philistine," Johns said loud enough for Tully to hear.

Tully waved it off.

"What you guys get?" Parker asked.

"Store owner saw what sounds like our truck last night. Across from the house she lives in. Truck came in, and the man pulled it around back."

"Where was this?" Parker said.

"Corner of Calle Carmen and Calle Maravilla. East side."

"Carmen's one of the dead-end strips, right?"

"It is. One way in and one way out."

"Wanna do a drive-by to see what we can see?" Parker asked.

"Already done. Can't see it from the street. No sign of a truck at all."

"How confident are we the shopkeeper saw a truck?

"I'm believing she saw a truck, whether it's our truck or not, I don't know."

Pete Tully joined the discussion. "How you want to handle this. As of now we got no probable cause to go search if the guy opens the door and tells us to pound sand."

"The storekeeper tell you about the driver?"

"A little," Pete said. "She claims he is a truck operator, mostly long haul, and he'll be gone for like a week at a time. Lives by himself. Doesn't put him in with the gang elements in the area. Seems to think he's legit."

"Legit until now," Johns said.

"What's the next street over from Maravilla? The one behind it?"

"That'd be Calle Sahuaro," Johns said.

"Let's take a drive."

Parker led the way through the narrow streets to Calle Sahuaro. The homes were older and suffering from a lack of upkeep. The paint was faded on most of them, and the stucco cracks were the most stable feature on a few. The front yards were barren, and the desert had reclaimed the land. Cars, trucks, and motorbikes were parked in the dirt yards.

As they cruised down, shadows lurked in the windows behind thin curtains.

One home halfway down the block was a burnt-out husk.

Unlike other trips into the Guad, Parker didn't find groups of men hanging out, proclaiming the street as their gang territory. Maybe it was too early for a gangbanger display.

Parker pulled to the curb at the last home on the right. The one opposite the home where the shopkeeper had reported seeing the white truck.

The house was older, but a broom leaning next to the front door meant someone was still trying to fight off the dirt, dust, and desert grime from overtaking the yard.

Parker got out of the SUV and told the others to wait back at the curb. He was certain the neighborhood already knew the government was crawling up the street but there was no need to cause a panic.

Parker rapped a knuckle on the door. An older, weathered face appeared in the window next to the doorframe. "Yes?" she called out through the window.

"Hi, ma'am. I'm Detective Parker with Maricopa County. Can I talk to you for a moment? You're not in any trouble, I promise."

"I've heard promises before. What is it you want, Detective?"

"Your neighbor, the one who lives behind you—what do you know about him?"

Her expression marked her distrust with the narrowed eyes, stiffened posture, and a slight tip of her bony chin.

"I do not get involved in the business of others. I keep to myself."

Parker figured it was probably a good tactic for survival in this neighborhood.

"That's not what I mean, Mrs.—"

"Ortiz. Celia Ortiz."

"Mrs. Ortiz. Thank you. How long have you lived in this area?"

"Twenty-five years. My husband and I came here after he retired from the Navy."

"I bet you've seen some changes."

"It was a nice community. A lot of us had families in central Mexico. We had similar backgrounds, la cultura, and wanted our families to have every advantage. Then the drugs and the gangs came. They don't have any respect for life."

Parker nodded. "I see it everywhere. It's not only here."

"These people turned their backs on the church and their community. We see it all the time."

"Have you heard about young men coming here to work—not in the fields, but coming here in large groups?"

"The fields, landscaping, janitors, construction, there is nothing new about this. Jobs your people don't want to do, my people will take to feed their families."

She didn't seem to know about the particulars of the cargo container victims.

"Your backyard neighbor, he's a truck driver. Did you hear him early yesterday morning?"

"He's always coming and going. Insists on parking his truck in the backyard so the young vatos leave it alone."

"Mrs. Ortiz, will you give me permission to look over your back fence? I'm trying to see if your neighbor's truck was the one we saw abandoning a group of undocumented men yesterday."

"The one from the television yesterday? On the freeway?"

"Yes, ma'am."

"How could someone do that to another human being? He is not a coyote," she gestured a gnarled finger at her backyard. "Go look and see what you need to see."

"Anyone live with him? Family? Kids?"

"No. He lives alone, works all day, sometimes for a week, then comes home. He doesn't bother anyone. His name is Ernesto. Ernesto Lopez."

"Thank you. I won't trouble you again."

"Yes, you will." And she disappeared from the window.

Parker motioned to Linda and the detectives to wait a moment while he looked out back.

He was taken with the patio and succulent garden in Mrs. Ortiz's backyard. A pergola with linen curtains, a small copper fire pit, and saltillo tiles made for an oasis in the middle of a war zone.

The yards were separated by a cinderblock wall taller than Parker and topped with shards of broken glass to discourage unwanted visitors, both animal and human. Parker stacked two wooden boxes and used them as a step to peek over the top of the wall.

A white Kenmore tractor sat in the middle of what was once a back garden. A rusty children's swing set sat to one end of the yard. It bore no evidence of use in decades, as did the home. Broken windows were covered with plywood, gang graffiti tagged the back wall, and the rear door was warped and broken. The door hung open awkwardly and a large black boot print on the door wasn't comforting.

Parker climbed down and jogged to the team waiting at the curb.

"Truck's in the backyard. Signs of a break-in at the back door. Don't have a good feeling about it."

"We need tactical backup?" Johns asked.

"I think we can take the direct approach on this one. It looks like this guy is a legit truck driver and might have gotten in over his head. The neighbor confirms he lives alone—no family."

Parker motioned with a finger twirling in the air for everyone to mount up. Parker led the SUVs around the block and parked in front of the truck driver's home.

Parker and Linda went to the front while Tully and Johns covered the rear exit in case the man tried to run.

Parker slid to one side of the door and tried to peek through a grime-coated window. The curtains were pulled and hid the interior. He knocked on the doorframe. "Mr. Lopez, Sheriff's Office."

No response from inside. He rapped the door harder a second time and still nothing from the trucker.

"Maybe he's not home," Linda said, off to the other side of the door.

Johns returned to the front of the home. "Boss back here."

"Barry, stay here with Linda. I'll go back with Pete."

Parker followed the dirt path around to the rear of the home. Up close, the Kenworth truck was bigger than he thought it would be. It was one of the large units with a sleeper compartment behind the driver's seat.

"Pete, we check there?" Parker motioned to the truck?"

"Yeah, no one hiding in there."

"What'd you see?"

Tully tipped his chin at the warped and broken back door. "That's recent. The dirt on the boot print flakes off if you touch the door. Someone broke in."

"You're thinking exigent circumstances?"

Tully nodded.

Parker knew entering a private home without a warrant could exclude any potential evidence. But if there was reason to believe someone might be in danger, officers could enter the premises.

Parker snapped a series of quick photos with his cell and tapped out a quick text to Barry, that he and Tully were going in.

Parker pushed the broken door inward, and it hung limply on one hinge. He and Tully pulled their weapons and stepped through.

"Sheriff's Office. Mr. Lopez, are you home?"

Parker pointed at a trail of dirty boot tracks, like the one on the back door, leading into the home.

They stood in the kitchen, and it was well-ordered, neat but sparse, fitting for a man who was on the road a good deal of the time.

Following the trail of footprints, Parker turned into the darkened living room and directed Tully to the left hallway.

The shades were pulled over the front windows, and Parker flicked on a light. There he was. Mr. Ortiz was face down on the living room carpet, hands bound behind him. A single gunshot wound to the back of his head.

"Pete, over here!"

"Oh, man," Tully said.

Pete reached to check the man's vitals despite the gunshot wound. Victims have survived worse.

Parker grabbed his arm.

"We have to treat him as if he were contaminated like the other victims. I'll call it in."

While Parker called, Tully let Linda and Johns in the front door. Parker noted the victim's pockets were turned inside out. There was slight bruising on what he could see of Mr. Ortiz's face. A robbery and beating, or search

71

and interrogation?

"Dr. Sherman said she's on the way. She's gonna have some gear to detect radiation, so we need to be careful not to touch anything." Parker glanced at Linda's dosemeter, and the color hadn't changed on the telltale dot.

"Let's watch our radiation badges, people."

"Doesn't look like anything was torn apart like you'd expect from a home invasion."

Parker glanced around the living room. "Laptop computer, other electronics, stuff that's easy to pawn was left behind."

"We'll divide and conquer here. Pete, you and Barry stay with the deceased, document the scene as best you can without touching anything. Linda and I will take a look at the truck and see what we can see."

Parker led Linda out the back door.

"You doin' okay?" he asked.

She nodded. "Not my first DB, but my first homicide scene. It seems a little surreal."

"It feels a little that way. When you don't feel anything when you walk onto the scene, you need to call it quits."

"How do you keep doing this and not let it get to you, you know, change who you are inside?"

"Part of it will always affect you. You can't be human and not walk away with some of this on you. Some go to counseling after all this accumulated trauma from the job; others compartmentalize their lives as a survival mechanism."

"Which do you do?"

"I'm not a good example. For reasons we talked about yesterday. But, if I focus on keeping the work at work, and not bring it home, it makes it easier to deal with. Unfortunately, I've had a few instances when it followed me home, literally."

"Okay. What do you need me to do out here?"

"Without touching the truck—we need to get all the info we can—to document everything about the scene. The truck, the backyard, the house— because once we have the response here, everything will get trampled, and when we leave, this place will get picked over by vultures."

Linda grabbed her cell phone and opened the camera app. She began taking shots, cycling around the truck.

Parker focused his attention on the gang graffiti near the back door. It looked familiar with its angular slanted script. He snapped a few photos of the tag and messaged them to Sammy Bachman in the gang unit.

Sammy was the leading gang expert in the valley and was on the gang enforcement task force until he was hit with a lead pipe during a raid. After a year of surgery and physical therapy, he could walk with the assistance of a cane, but his time as a peace officer was over. The sheriff's office didn't want to lose his years of experience, so they created a job for him in the unit where he took in and analyzed gang intel from deputies on patrol.

Parker's cell rang a few seconds after sending the message.

"Sammy. What you make of this?"

"Hi to you too, Parker. Expect me to drop everything and cater to your every whim?"

"Sounds fine to me."

"It would. Where'd you find this exquisite example of street art?"

"Down in the Guad."

"Huh, unusual."

"How's that?"

"It's a tag from a gang. One with origins near the border, as violent as MS-13. These guys are a little crazy like their MS-13 brothers, but they don't get all the face tattoos and advertise themselves. They can hide under the radar."

"Where have you seen them before?"

"The tags have been showing up down south in Tucson and as far north as Casa Grande. Nothing up in the valley before. Give me some context. What's you got going on?"

"The tag is on a home where the victim inside was bound and shot, execution style. No evidence of robbery. This was targeted."

"What we've been hearing is these dudes are guns for hire."

A chill ran up Parker's spine.

"You got a name for these guys?"

"Los Muertos."

Chapter Twelve

The medical examiner's crew arrived and donned white protective HazMat suits in the front yard. The neighbors took little interest in the display because they had seen it before when meth labs were taken down.

Parker and his crew waited out front while the technicians went in with their monitoring equipment.

Dr. Sherman exited the home and pulled her mask up. "All clear in here. No readings whatsoever."

Parker joined the doctor on the porch. "Nothing on his clothing, or in his home?"

"Nothing, and the truck is clear too."

"Did you have a look at our victim yet?"

She nodded. "I took a preliminary look. I'll show you what we've got." She said.

Parker motioned for Linda to follow. They gathered near the downed man.

"Dr. Sherman, this is Detective Hunt's first scene. Can we walk it through with you?"

"Sure. We have a Hispanic male, estimated fifty years of age, suffering what appears to be a single GSW to the occipital portion of the skull. No exit wound, and the size of the entry marks this as a small caliber weapon. Powder burns and contact bruising noted."

Dr. Sherman lifted the man's body with the help of a tech and rolled him on his side. "We find lividity here on the chest and upper torso, so he died face down in the position you found him. Still in rigor, and combined with the liver probe temp, I'd estimate time of death at three to four hours."

Linda leaned in. "You can tell from a quick look? I thought you'd need a full autopsy."

"The bodies can tell us a lot if we stop and take the time to observe."

"His pockets were turned out when we got here. Anything found on his person?"

"Nothing. I do see a wallet on the floor by the sofa. But, I'm not a detective, so…"

Parker followed the doctor's eyes and next to a small wooden side table, he spotted a nylon wallet, nearly the same color as the threadbare carpet.

"Nice catch, Doc. If you get tired of this coroner gig, we might have a place for you."

Parker pulled on a fresh set of nitrile gloves and knelt for the wallet. He grasped the edge of the wallet to avoid smudging any prints the evidence techs could pull from the pebbly nylon surface.

Parker pulled on the Velcro strap and found an Arizona Driver's License issued to Ernesto Lopez. The wallet was jammed full of coupons, receipts, and a single photograph of Ernesto and a woman. The light inscription on the back read, "mi amor – 1981."

He slid the wallet into an evidence bag and handed it to Linda. "When we get a chance, we'll need to go through all the paper in there and see if we can retrace his last few days. Maybe a receipt could tell us where his route with our cargo box started."

"I can take care of it," she said.

Parker motioned to Linda to follow him into the bedroom. "Let's look for anything he might have kept showing who he hauled for, or anyone he might have associated with. Some friend, another truck driver, or drinking buddy might have overheard him say where he was going."

The two of them searched the bedroom, each taking half of the space. Lopez was neat and ordered with his possessions. A Timex watch laid out on his bureau, next to a cheap rollerball pen. "Look for a notepad, or notebook."

"He's a trucker. They keep mileage logs, assuming the last trip was on the books."

"Good thinking. You're not just a pretty face."

Linda gave him a stink eye. "I could say the same thing, bucko."

Parker pulled open the top bureau shelf. "You think I'm pretty."

"Shut it and get back to work," Linda said.

Parker pulled the drawer all the way out and placed it on the bed. He'd found hidden drugs, weapons, and stolen property tucked away in or under furniture more than a few times. Not that he believed Ernesto Lopez was hiding guns and contraband. It was part of Parker's process. He pulled the remaining two drawers out and laid them on the bed next to the first one. The bureau frame was empty, no illicit material secreted inside.

The truck driver kept a half dozen t-shirts and pairs of socks in the dresser and little else. Parker stood back and surveyed the collection. A single dark suit, a dozen long sleeved shirts, and four pair of jeans hung in the closet. A single pair of black dress shoes were arranged on the floor, next to worn and scuffed work boots.

"Where's the rest of it?"

Linda had been looking under the bed with a flashlight. She leaned upright on her knees. "The rest of what?"

"Our guy is a long-haul trucker. According to the woman at the market and the next-door neighbor, he would be gone for days at a time. Where are the clothes he wore on those trips?"

"Laundry? He might have clothes stashed out in his truck. We can see what Pete and Barry come up with? There's—under here. Help me turn the mattress over."

Parker checked the bottom of the drawers before he put them back, and then, with Linda, they hefted the old heavy mattress off the frame until it stood on its side.

"There." Linda pointed at a slice in the fabric. "This was cut. A mouse didn't chew this opening."

"Not unless the mouse is wielding a switchblade."

Linda used her cell phone to take a photo of the mattress and the sliced fabric.

"Shall we?" she asked.

"Your find. Go ahead."

She gripped the edge of the tear and pulled down. The age of the material let it rip like onion paper and a small dust cloud of musty fabric kicked up. But what got Linda's attention were the bundles of cash spilling from the mattress.

"Looks like Mr. Lopez didn't believe in the modern banking system," she said.

"How long has he been stashing his cash in there? Parker asked.

"Some if these bills look—they are old. Here, this one has a 1990 date." She handed Parker a bundle of twenty-dollar bills.

The older twenties had the smaller portrait of Jackson and lacked the more modern security devices designed into later versions of the bill. The package wasn't wrapped with a bank issued band, but a length of brown twine.

Linda held another bundle. "These are new. They look fresh from an ATM."

Parker handed the bundle back to Linda. "Okay, you know what to do. We'll do a full count back at the unit. Let's make sure we get everything out from Mr. Lopez's piggy bank."

Linda retrieved the cash bundles from the mattress and sorted them on the floor. Fifty individual bundles of twenty-dollar bills. If the count on the first bundle held true for the rest, each hand tied package contained one hundred bills—two-thousand dollars each. On the floor at Linda's feet was one hundred thousand dollars.

"Hell of a retirement nest egg," Linda said.

"Too bad he didn't live to see it put to good use."

"You think whoever came for him was looking for this?" she said.

"We need to consider it, for sure."

Linda photographed the currency before sealing it in two brown paper evidence bags.

They finished searching the rest of the small home as Dr. Sherman was making notes on her tablet. Two of her techs lifted a bag with Mr. Lopez's body onto a gurney. All that remained behind was a small blood stain where the man died.

"I'm about done here, detectives. I'll get you the results as soon as we get to him. The cargo box bodies will begin today. We're done with all the decontamination protocols. I've got another pathologist coming over from La Paz County to pitch in. We had one of those portable morgue trailers we used when COVID first hit. Seems ironic to put them in a cargo container when they were found in one."

"Thanks, Doc."

Parker and Linda went out the back door. Tully was in the driver's seat of the truck.

"Find anything up there?" Parker said.

"I've got a bag full of cups, gas receipts, a logbook, and some handwritten notes. Can't make much from them right now. It looks like he wrote in his own code, probably to hide what and who he was hauling for."

Barry Johns came from the side of the home. "Just came back from a little sit down with the family next door. Nice people. Been living here for ten years. They say Mr. Lopez generally kept to himself since his wife died about five years ago."

Parker flashed on the photo of a younger Lopez and the attractive woman.

"They did say, the last few months, there's been more traffic coming and going here. The Mrs. said they didn't look like people from here. 'Slick' was the term she used. I think she meant to say gang bangers. Thought they might have been putting pressure on the old man."

"What kind of pressure?"

"I asked and she didn't want to say, other than Mr. Lopez had a truck."

"Smuggling. They wanted him to run drugs or people. We know how that turned out."

"The artwork by the back door confirms her account," Johns said.

"Yeah, it's troubling. Sammy Bachman in the gang unit says it's a Los Muertos tag."

"Oh, not them again. Since your last run-in with them, they've been pretty quiet."

"I hope this is an anomaly and they stay off book," Parker said, although he didn't feel it.

"Now you know they are still pissed at you," Johns said, turning to the truck and Tully.

"Why do you say that?"

"Bottom right of the tag."

Parker faced the graffiti and looked at what he thought was an autograph of the artist. The Letters P, R, K, R, were scrawled in the same slanted script, with a line drawn through them.

"What is it?" Linda asked.

"You know how these guys run their tags, eliminating vowels from them."

"Because spelling isn't their thing."

"More like to hide the message in plain sight. This one is PRKR for PaRKeR. The line through it means marked. It's a personal message for me. I've been marked for a hit."

Chapter Thirteen

The team gathered in Parker's office after the scene was processed. Parker sat heavily behind his desk. "All right, where are we? Let's get a status. Tully, grab a marker and start us out."

Tully took a marker from the tray on the whiteboard mounted in Parker's office. He drew a horizontal slash with tic marks, indicating a timeline. At a point two-thirds to the right, he drew a bubble and wrote "trailer dropped."

"We know when the trailer was abandoned based on statements from the truckers at the Devil's Well rest area. We have traffic cam footage of a white tractor-trailer heading eastbound a few minutes later." Tully marked another bubble "traffic cam."

Johns pointed at the horizontal line. "Dr. Sherman's preliminary take was the victims died eight hours before we found them—plus or minus."

Tully marked a tic line to the left on the timeline and marked "Est. TOD."

"There's a lot of time between time of death and when we found them. Were they dead before they crossed the border?" Johns said.

"Our delivery driver, Lopez, dropped the container here, but where did he pick it up?" Parker asked. "He might not have been the driver to cross the border with it."

"We have a lot of holes in this one. Without ID on any of the victims, we don't know when they went missing, or where they were going to," Tully said.

"All true," Parker said.

A ding sounded on Parker's desk computer. He strode around to the monitor and clicked. "Email from Dr. Sherman's office." He clicked on the email and opened an attachment. A cascading display of twenty-seven faces filled his screen. Three of the victims had tattoos, and a few had surgical scars."

"We have a thread to pull on here. Lynne Finch offered the Mexico City FBI Liaison officer up to circulate these photos. If anyone down there matches one of these people to their missing relatives, we have a place to work back from."

"I'll start sorting out all the paper we found at the scene. If there are gas receipts, fast food containers, or coupons to recreate Mr. Lopez's last few days, it might tell us where he came into contact with the cargo container," Tully said.

"I'll reach out to ICE and Border Patrol contacts to see if the local border crossings at Nogales and Sasabee caught a white Kenmore truck making the crossing. I'll pass on the photos of the truck and the cargo box, but I don't think the container got anyone's attention. While I'm in contact with them, I'll ask about the Customs seal, see what they can tell me about it and if phony ones are common," Johns said.

"I'll reach out to those truckers. If Lopez was a long-haul driver, it means he needed to have connections with shippers—shippers other than this last one. I see him as a wildcat operator and not one aligned with a union. I'll try to find out where a driver would go to pick up runs to make a living," Tully said.

"And it looks like he did make a living," Parker said, gesturing to the two paper bags of cash. "He was paid under the table, so folks might not like to answer the questions you'll have."

"I'll be subtle," Tully said.

"That'd be a first," Johns said.

"You're the one to talk. Remember last year when you went to court on the Miller case? You wore a red suit. Looked like a damn skinny Black Santa."

"It wasn't red. It was maroon. And we got a conviction, didn't we?"

"I'm sure the defense attorney filed an appeal on you distracting the jury."

"Whatever."

"I'm gonna help Linda photograph all these bills and get them entered into the system, see if one of them pops from a bank heist or ATM theft."

"Boss, we gotta talk about the elephant in the room," Johns said.

"And which elephant is that? We got us a zoo here?"

"Los Muertos and the threat against you," Johns said.

"It's more of their bluster," Parker said.

"I'm not sure. On the way back to the unit, I reached out to Bachman. He's not taking it lightly. He missed the message on the tag directed at you. He's also concerned since this is new activity in the Valley, and Los Muertos hasn't claimed territory here before. They've been hit and run. He's thinking this might be a shift and mark the start of turf battles."

"Lynne over at the FBI told me they snagged a pair of low-level Muertos thugs at the border. You guys know the head of that snake, Esteban Castaneda, killed McMillan. He's also made it clear he holds a grudge against me. I'm not surprised by the tagged threat, or the increase in activity. Los Muertos is motivated by money. If they're up here, it's because there's a payoff. We'll be vigilant, but we don't go cower in the corner."

"We can get you a protective detail assigned until this blows over," Tully said.

"I'm not pulling a deputy off patrol to be my shadow. Okay then, we all have our assignments. Let's get to it." Parker signaled to the group he was done talking about Los Muertos.

Parker helped Linda carry the paper evidence bags to a table in the squad room.

"How do we do this? I've never processed this much cash at one time." Linda said.

"We need two people to count and verify. I'll set up a video camera to document the count. After the count, we'll take each bill and photograph the note, then upload it into a system feeding into the Organized Crime Drug Enforcement taskforce. They'll verify if any of these bills are flagged in money laundering, drug transactions, or were part of cash stolen in bank robberies."

"Why don't we use one of those automatic cash counters like you see at the casinos?"

"I want to be able to take the witness stand and tell a jury I personally counted each bill and can verify what I saw and did. I don't know what goes on in the electronic brain of a machine. Sure, it's old school, but it's reliable. And a jury can't second guess the process."

Parker placed one bag on the work surface. He snagged a tripod mounted video camera from a storage locker and set it up at one end of the table.

"Smile," he said as he turned it on.

Linda stiffened. "What am I supposed to say? Is this like an interrogation tape, where I identify myself?"

"Nope, no sound. The camera is another set of eyes on the table to make sure bills don't go missing, we don't add any to the count, and we both verify the totals. Pretend it's not even there."

Parker laid two notepads on the table and took the first evidence bag, noting the number on the bag, writing it on his notepad. Linda followed suit. Parker turned the bag so the label was facing the camera and unsealed it.

He pulled on a pair of gloves and began removing bundles of cash, one at a time, until all twenty-five bundles in the bag were placed on the table surface.

"I'll start us off."

Parker took the first bundle slipped the twine off and counted off one hundred bills. He attached a sticker to the bundle, with number 1 on it and slid it to Linda. She jotted a note on his pad documenting bundle number and the number of bills. "You do the exact thing for each bundle I slide over to you."

She nodded, unbundled, and started counting.

Parker dug back in, and they completed the process in thirty minutes. The tally agreed that one hundred thousand dollars in cold, hard cash came from the truck driver's mattress.

"Now what? Do we have to take individual photos of each bill?" Linda asked.

"For that, we have a little help."

Parker pushed back from the table and returned to the storage locker. He carried a boxy object obscured by a black plastic dust cover. There was a white Treasury Department emblem on the cover.

He set it on the table and plucked off the cover. He unwound the cord and found a power strip.

"Oh, yeah, I need my laptop."

Parker took a laptop from his office and placed it next to the device. He plugged in a USB cord from the laptop into the Treasury device.

"What is this?" Linda said.

"An optical sorter, courtesy of our friends in the Treasury."

Parker took the first stack of bills and laid them on the wire rack on the top of the machine. He pressed power and the bills fed through, faster than a copy machine but not nearly as fast as a cash counter at a casino.

The laptop screen blossomed with row after row of color images of twenty-dollar bills.

"Once we get these downloaded, we send them off to the feds in the cloud, and someone lets us know if these bills have been flagged."

"I bet you Miguel could tell you how it works exactly."

He chuckled. "I'm sure he could. It's like a damn video game anyway."

"I love it when you get all technical."

Parker fed in the remaining bills into the optical sorter and the bills spit out into the collection bin on the bottom tray.

Parker hit enter on the laptop with a flourish. Tap.

"Now what?" Linda asked, looking at the screen.

"We wait."

"Well, that's anticlimactic."

"Let's get this cash booked into evidence and call it a day. Let's stop by the store and grab some stuff for dinner. I'll cook tonight," Parker said.

"What did I do?" She smiled. "I did everything you told me to do today, and you want to make me eat your college dorm cooking."

"What? I'm a good cook."

"How many times have you and Miguel had takeout this month?"

"We're on a busy schedule. Him with classes, his job and working at the

Coalition, me with this stuff. We grab what we can together."

"Not good enough. And definitely not healthy enough."

"You just called me fat," Parker said.

Parker went to shut off his computer and store the optical reader and video camera when his eye caught the screen.

"Huh, check this out." He tapped the monitor and the display of the last bundle of bank notes.

Linda spotted the difference right away. "A phone number written on the bill. Not unusual, but I'm curious where it goes."

"Let's find out." Parker trotted back to his office and returned a few minutes later with a cell phone. "It's a pre-paid cell. We don't want whoever's on the other end to get a caller ID screaming Sheriff's Office."

Parker tapped in the number into the burner phone. "A local number." And waited.

After the fifth ring, a voice called out over the heavy metal music in the background. "Crystal's Gentlemen's Club."

Parker disconnected the call.

"When's the last time you went to a strip club?"

Chapter Fourteen

Parker and Linda agreed a decent meal outweighed a trip to the Gentleman's Club chasing a stale phone number scrawled in blue felt tip, from lord only knows how long ago.

After a stop at an organic market, they arrived at Parker's place, toting grocery bags of vegetables, risotto, and an organic, free-range chicken, which Parker joked meant the chicken died happy.

Placing the bags on the counter, Linda said, "I called Leon, and he'll be here. If there's food, he'll find it."

"Same with Miguel. While we were grazing the Kale and Kelp aisle of the grocery store, I called and told him you'd be cooking. I was a little hurt at how excited he sounded."

"Told ya," Linda said while unpacking the bag."

"I figure tomorrow we'll drop by the strip club and see what's up."

"Nothing like starting off the day with g-strings and glitter,"

A rustle at the front door marked Miguel's return. He strode into the kitchen, tossed his backpack in the corner, and greeted Linda with a hug.

"Thanks for doing this."

"What, you make it sound like you exist on bread and water around here," Parker said.

Miguel swept his hand across a pile of local take-out restaurant menus. "I could make a sculpture out of the empty pizza boxes in our recycle bin right now."

"You like pizza. You're the one who chooses it when we're deciding."

"It's safe."

Parker shook his head. "You want me to help?" He asked Linda as she was prepping the counter.

Miguel sat at the counter. "Hey, I did some checking on those two missing college students I told you about."

"Yeah? What'd you learn?"

"Both of the guys attended a private tech school in Mexico City. I have the name written down in my backpack. They were both studying computer science and technology."

"They come from wealthy families? You know how the cartels and other criminal groups love to target families with money. Kidnap for ransom isn't an unusual thing down south."

"Not as much as it used to be. We—the Coalition have been monitoring the kidnap reports from around the major cities, and there's been a drop-off. The people say it might be the new government's pushback on cartel activity in the cities, or it could be they've found other ways to make money."

"The cartels, Los Muertos, all of them, look for a quick score. They don't care if anyone gets hurt in the process."

"Like these missing students," Miguel said.

"Exactly. I wonder if they were targets of opportunity for whoever took them? I mean, who goes out looking for computer nerds?"

Linda started chopping celery and onion. "I've heard the tech scene in Central and South America is booming right now. Leon told me. Speaking of Leon, before he gets here—Miguel, what's going on with him?"

Miguel rolled his eyes. "I'm not totally sure, but I think he started hanging around with one of the groups on campus who are a little more aggressive when it comes to what they think needs to happen on immigration reform."

"Is he okay?" She asked, putting the knife down on the cutting board.

"I think—I think he doesn't know what to do. I know how he feels, like he has to do something for people like him and me. The organization he hangs with most is kinda radical. They are the in-your-face counter-protesters who force confrontation, block freeways to inconvenience commuters, and plaster signs or graffiti on buildings and businesses they judge as not supporting the immigrant cause."

"You know the name of the group?" she asked.

"Soldiers for Justice."

"Sounds ominous," she said.

"I think Leon is caught in between. He knows what's right. I don't think he wants to do the things this group does. It might have to do with his talk about dropping out of school. Maybe he's getting some pressure from the Soldiers, and he's avoiding them."

Linda thought for a moment and bit her lower lip. "Now that sounds like Leon. He's never been confrontational. But why would he not tell me about this? He had to know I'd support him?"

"Because he feels like he's a grown man and has to face his own problems." Miguel snuck a glance at Parker. Miguel felt the same pull toward independence, but Parker had made it clear he was welcome in the home for as long as he wanted.

"But he doesn't have to go it alone. I'm here for him."

"Does he know that?" Miguel asked.

"Of course he does. I tell him I'll help and support him all the time. He doesn't listen."

"He does. Leon hasn't had any support network in his life before he came to you. You know his story, like mine. His parents died in the violence in El Salvador. It's hard to put too much faith in someone who might be out of your life at any moment."

"It's not like that. He's family."

"He needs to know it."

She blinked away a tear and turned back to the cutting board. "Damn onions."

Parker clasped Miguel's shoulder. He was proud of how far the kid had come.

"You have the names and addresses for those missing students in Mexico City? We've got an FBI contact who can show them photos of our victims."

"You sure they are the best people to do that?" Miguel asked.

"They're already in place down there in the U.S. Embassy."

"That's not what I mean. Think of it. Picture yourself as a parent of one of these guys. Some suit-wearing white guy shows up at your house with photos of a bunch of dead boys. You have to search through them to find your son while this American, this fed, who didn't care about you before your family member disappeared, sits in your house and judges you."

"These families need to know."

"They do. I'm not sure if an FBI agent knocking on their door is the right way to do it."

"That's our only option right now," Parker said.

"No, it's not. The Immigrant Coalition can contact the families."

"I don't know…"

"Think about it. The Coalition runs supplies down to Hermosillo and to the outskirts of Mexico City. People know us down there. There's a trust factor. They know talking to us won't endanger their family members who are in El Norte already. If an FBI agent comes to their home, that will be the first thing on their minds, other than the photos of dead people you're bringing."

"Interesting ideas. I don't know…"

Another rustle at the door, and Leon strode in.

"Hi, Leon. Pull up a chair. We're watching Linda work," Parker said.

"Sounds like fun," he said, pulling out a stool at the counter. "Oh, roast chicken? What's the occasion?"

"Nothing special. Thought it was time to get us all together and have a decent meal."

"Good. I'm hungry, and I'm tired of pizza," Leon said.

"What's this? You don't get gourmet meals like this every night?"

"Are you kidding? Who has time for fancy?"

Linda didn't look over at Parker, but she was smiling.

"How was your day?"

"I hung out at the library, then put in a few hours at the shop. They called and needed some coverage."

"Where you working?" Parker asked.

"A machine shop off of La Mirage. West Valley Machine. I drive delivery trucks for them, moving parts around the valley."

"I know the place." Parker rescued twenty undocumented migrants being held in the place by Los Muertos thugs last year.

"How'd you find that job?" Parker asked.

"Guys at school said they were looking to hire."

"Guys from Soldiers for Justice?"

Leon's eyes narrowed, and he stiffened.

"What of it?"

"I know about the machine shop, and they have a shady past, is all. Be a shame if you got caught up in anything going on there."

"All I do is drive a van around, dropping things off and picking things up."

"You're a smart guy, watch yourself all right?"

Leon grew silent and nodded.

Linda put a roasting pan into the oven and set the timer. "Should be ready in about an hour."

"I'm hungry for food that doesn't come out of a pizza box," Miguel said.

"Same here," Leon said happy for the change in the conversation.

"You two aren't helping," Linda said.

"While I have you two here, you ever see this around the valley?" Parker pulled up the photo of the graffiti on the trucker's house and laid his cell phone on the counter.

Miguel leaned into the screen and shook his head. "No. I haven't seen this one." He slid the phone to Leon.

Leon glanced at the image, then picked up the phone, staring intently at the spray-painted tag.

"Where was this?" Leon asked. His throat sounded dry.

"Linda and I found it on a house in the Guad. You've seen one like it?"

"A couple of times. Some of the places I deliver, I've seen it."

"The same tag?"

"Yes. There's one on the back-alley wall of West Valley machine."

"You know what it means?" Parker felt his pulse rate ramp up.

"I—I don't."

"Our gang experts hadn't seen it until now," Parker said.

"What gang?" Leon asked. He was tentative in his question."

He glanced at Linda, who was now leaning next to Leon, rubbing his back.

While maintaining eye contact with Miguel, Parker said, "Los Muertos."

Miguel's expression was shock and a replay of fear for the hell the gang had rained down on him. "They're back? Here in the valley?"

"We don't know for sure. They did catch a couple of them at the border. But other than this tag, they've been ghosts."

"You've told me about Los Muertos, Miguel. I haven't heard mention about them. I swear. I'd tell you if I did."

"I believe you…"

"Leon, if these are Los Muertos tags like our gang intel people believe, why would they target businesses here in the valley?" Parker asked.

Leon shook his head. "I don't know how they're connected. But if they're half what Miguel has told me, I want nothing to do with it."

"No idea why they had you delivering to tagged businesses?"

Again, he shook his head. "No, and I don't even know what I'd been delivering. It was sealed. I'm sorry."

"You have nothing to feel sorry about," Linda said. "How could you have known?"

"There has to be a link between these tags. I wish we knew what they meant," Parker said.

"I don't know what they mean. But I know who tagged them," Leon said.

Chapter Fifteen

"Salvador Camacho, everyone calls him Sal. He's the head guy in the Soldiers for Justice. He's the tagger."

"How can you be sure?" Parker asked.

"I saw him do one at an auto parts place in Tempe."

Parker slid the phone in front of Leon once more. "Like this, you're sure?"

He nodded. "I was on a delivery run and pulled up to the store and saw him working on it. He tried to play it off when he spotted me in the truck, but I know he did it. He had spray paint on his hand."

"No idea why Sal would tag these places?"

"No."

"No mention of Los Muertos?"

"No. I'd remember if there was, because of what Miguel's told me."

Linda put an arm around Leon. "I'm not comfortable with you going back to work there."

"I can't quit. What else am I going to do?" Leon looked away from Linda, trying to hide his watering eyes.

"You can come and work with me. At the Coalition," Miguel said.

"I don't need charity."

"You're a computer science major. You shouldn't be driving a delivery truck for these thugs anyway. We need someone to work on the Coalition's computers and servers. I don't know enough about that kind of thing, and Billie still uses a flip phone."

"You could do that? A real job?"

"I need to talk with Billie, but I know she won't have a problem with it."

"I'd feel better with you working with Miguel and Billie instead of with people who are into—God knows what they're into. I want you to be safe," Linda said with a hug.

"And speaking of safe, when's that chicken going to be done?" Miguel asked.

Linda glanced at the oven timer, "Twenty minutes."

"Perfect. Enough time for me to crush Leon in a game of Grand Theft Auto."

"In your dreams," Leon said.

The two hustled out to the living room and started playing the video game.

"We need to find out what this Sal kid is all about," Parker said.

"It kind of worries me Sal had Leon delivering packages all over the valley, and Los Muertos had some connection to it. Who knows what they had him delivering—drugs, guns, cash. I'm getting angrier thinking about it. Using a vulnerable kid to do their dirty work."

"I want to press Sal tomorrow on the tags and what he knows about the Los Muertos connection."

"What do you think Sal and the Soldiers for Justice will do when they realize Leon quit."

"They might try to pressure him back into the fold. But I think we might be able to give Sal something else to think about."

"What do you have in mind?"

Before he could answer, a knock sounded at the door.

Miguel paused the video game and checked the peephole in the door. Miguel glanced back at Parker and opened the door.

"Agent Finch," Miguel said.

"Please, call me Lynne."

"Come in."

Parker stepped into the living room. "Hey, Lynne. What brings you by?"

"I needed to talk to you for a minute. Can we—" she tipped her head toward Miguel and Leon.

"Sure, sure, come on in the kitchen."

She followed Parker and smiled when she spotted Linda.

"Thank God someone's here to rescue you from microwave dinners and takeout," Lynne said.

"Is this gang up on Nathan night?"

"The truth can be painful."

"Hi, Lynne, care to stick around for dinner? We have plenty to go around," Linda said.

"No, that's very kind. I came over to talk with Nathan, but I'm glad you're here too."

"What's up?" Parker gestured to a stool at the counter.

Lynne remained standing. "One of the two Los Muertos hitters we caught at the border is talking."

"What's he giving up?"

"We're trying to piece it together, but it looks like Los Muertos is involved in our cargo box deaths."

"Wouldn't be the first time they've dabbled in human trafficking. It never ends up well for the people they trap. What's he saying?"

"He's angling for a deal. But all he'd say without an immunity agreement is there are three more crews in play."

"Three more cargo containers filled with men who might see the same fate as ours?"

"Apparently, yes."

"When are they coming over?" Parker asked.

"He wouldn't say. Either he doesn't know, or he's holding something back as leverage to make his deal."

"Any hint about where these men are going? Our victims were heading to the California border?"

"I've reached out to Los Angeles and San Diego—they've heard nothing about Los Muertos moving people over the border."

"Speaking of Los Muertos, we're spotting these tags in the valley. We'll be rolling up on the businesses they hit. I'm concerned the places are either Los Muertos fronts or being pressured to pay rent to the gang. This is the first real presence Los Muertos has claimed. They've been a shadow organization, moving to where the next paying job takes them. This is a change, and it's troubling, if it pans out."

"There's one more thing."

"Yeah?"

"The guy says he knows where Esteban Castaneda is?"

"Where?"

"Again, he's holding it back until he gets a deal."

"Think he really knows, or is he bluffing? "

"We're going to work on him more tomorrow."

"Any chance you'll let me talk to him?"

"DOJ wants to lock this down as tight as possible. If Castaneda is out there, he could be using this guy as bait to lure you out."

"Let me know if you change your mind. I'd like to press the guy for what he knows."

"We have people who can do that."

"I know, this—this is—"

"Personal? Another reason we need to keep you out of it."

The oven timer sounded, and Miguel and Leon rounded the corner like hungry wolves.

Linda pointed at them. "You two set the table."

"Sure, you don't want to stay?"

"No, I need to get going. Wanted you to know we're homing in on Castaneda, and Los Muertos seems to be bubbling up around here. Please be careful, both of you."

Parker walked Lynne to the door. "Any update from the science nerds on where the radiation originated?"

She shook her head. "Nothing yet. All they've said is it's not fallout from a detonated dirty bomb. Which we would have already known by now."

"True. Keep us in the loop where you can."

"Same goes for you."

"We're going to follow up on a money laundering angle tomorrow, and it might get us close to finding out who funded the cargo box move. Our driver was murdered."

"Where is the money connection?"

"I'm taking Linda to a strip club in the morning."

She grinned.

"You were always the classy one."

Chapter Sixteen

Crystal's Gentleman's Club sat on a lonely corner on Grand, and it looked even sadder in the daylight. Dark purple paint slapped on the siding with what was supposed to be pink candy cane stripes was garish in the morning sun.

"You take me to the nicest places," Linda said as they pulled into the parking lot.

"What's troubling is the lot is half full this early in the morning."

They parked and noticed a young woman exit the club, a long sweater wrapped around her legs. She sat on a cement parking bumper and lit a cigarette. Heavy eyeliner, glitter, and fishnet stockings painted a desperate image of a woman who made choices out of necessity.

"Let's go get an eyeful," Parker said.

"I can't wait."

The woman from the club stubbed out her cigarette on the asphalt as they approached. She didn't attempt to get up, merely pulled the sweater close around her, a protective cocoon against the hand life dealt.

"Cindy?" Parker asked when he and Linda drew close.

She glanced over quickly and tried to look away. "Hey, Detective Parker." She looked less embarrassed over her situation than resigned to it.

"What are you doing here?"

"What's it look like? And you call yourself a detective."

"I guess I mean, why are you here? Last I saw you, you had an electronics trade school thing going on. What happened?"

"What happened is the lockdowns and grant money drying up. I gotta work, so here I am."

"How long you been here?" Parker asked.

"Going on six months. I wait tables and let the gross dudes in there cop a feel now and again for tips. Livin' the life."

"How busy is it this early in the day?"

"It ain't prime time, but then again, Paulie tells me, neither am I."

"Paulie, the manager? I need to talk with him."

She nodded as she lit up another cigarette. She blew out a lungful of smoke. "He's in there. You can't miss him. The fat man with the Hawaiian shirt."

"Thanks, you take care of yourself, Cindy."

"I'm trying, Detective, I'm trying."

As they pushed through the door, Linda asked, "Who's your friend?"

"I feel for that kid, I do. Dropped out of the foster care system and had nothing going for her. I found her turning tricks in Goodyear. Tried to keep her out of the system, and I thought she was going to make it." He glanced back at the girl huddled under the thin sweater. "She needs to catch a break."

The second set of doors held back the earsplitting rock music spilling over the club's speakers. Two stages, but only one was occupied at the moment. Two bikini-clad women in clear platform heels gyrated to the music as they stood on the stage in front of tables with men handing bills to them.

Linda tapped Parker on the shoulder and pointed to a man standing next to the bar. He was six-and-a-half feet tall, with a huge belly covered by a lime green Hawaiian shirt that puckered in the front because Hawaii wasn't that big.

"You Paulie?" Parker asked.

"What of it?"

"I'll take that as a yes."

"Whatdayawant? I'm kinda busy?"

Parker flashed his badge. "So am I."

Linda leaned over and whispered, "I'm gonna check something out."

She strolled to the back of the club, where a pair of women were bussing a table from an earlier party.

"What is it, officer?"

"We found some evidence connecting this place to a murder down in the Guad."

"How so?"

Parker glanced around the club. At least fifty men, some looked like they got off a graveyard shift at one of the manufacturing plants in the area and hadn't made it home yet. Others dressed in suits, late for their corporate gig. "Lots of cash getting passed around here, isn't there?"

"It's largely a cash-based business. Ain't nothing illegal 'bout it."

"Not unless it's laundering drug money."

"Whoa, whoa, just wait a minute there. We ain't into any of that. I insist my girls are clean and don't deal in none of it."

"I'm not saying your girls are doing it?"

"It ain't me."

"Tell me why a bundle of drug money we found had your phone number on it?"

"I can't help who writes a number down."

"If we check the cash you have here, I bet we'll find the serial numbers match up, and it will be hard to explain to the liquor license board."

"Listen, I can't help where people got their money from, but when they come here, they're free to spend it any way they like. That ain't laundering."

"Let's have your barman open the cash register, shall we?"

Paulie put up his hands. "We don't gotta go through all that. I think I may know what you're talking about. Come with me—my office."

Parker caught Linda's attention, letting her know where he was going. She was chatting up two women dressed in the same skimpy costume Cindy wore.

In Paulie's office, the noise level was much lower. The cluttered office was tiny, the owner's encouragement to the manager on duty to spend time on the floor, no doubt.

Paulie opened a floor safe, and he pulled out a bank bag. He unzipped the bag and laid three bundles of currency on his desk. He sorted through each stack until he found three twenty-dollar bills inscribed with phone numbers. Two of the three numbers were the strip club's digits. The third was different. Parker took a photo with his cell phone.

"I remember these came in last week. I was getting ready to make the deposit and saw the numbers. See, these prove it ain't only us."

"I don't know what it proves, But I need to take these three bills."

"Of course you do. Gimmie a receipt."

When Parker and Paulie left his office the tempo of the music had increased and the amount of clothing on the two dancers decreased. Linda was walking back from the table. Parker pulled up a photo of Ernesto Lopez on his phone. It was a crime scene photo so it wasn't user friendly, but Parker wanted to gauge Paulie's reaction.

"You ever see this guy in here?"

Paulie leaned in and jerked his head away. "What the hell happened to him?"

"He had a twenty-dollar bill with your number on it."

Parker pocketed the phone. He looked to Linda, "We done here?"

"One last thing before we go, Linda said. She got close to Paulie's ear and whispered over the music. Whatever she said made the big man go pale. She backed off and patted the man on the chest. "Remember what I said."

"I'm ready," she said to Parker.

They headed for the door, and Linda broke off and found Cindy taking a drink order at a table. She handed Cindy one of her cards. "If that asshole doesn't treat you right, you call me." She made sure Paulie saw her pointing directly at him.

Cindy broke into a slight smile, took the card, and thanked Linda.

Once they were outside, Parker asked, "What was that about?"

"Seems Paulie there's been taking part of the hostess tips and feels like he can grab a handful anytime he wants."

"I can see that coming from him."

"What did you say to him, because the expression on his face was priceless?"

"I told him to respect the girls and leave their tips alone. They earned them."

Linda got in the passenger side and when Parker got behind the wheel, he said, "I don't think those are the exact words you used."

"Close enough. I needed to make sure he understood. If I got word that he touched another woman, I was going to come back and nail his scrotum to the bar."

"Damn, glad you're not angry with me."

"Not yet."

He started the SUV, pulled from the lot, and headed north on Grand.

"Learn anything from the women?"

"I figure if someone was passing flagged cash, they'd probably be the first to see it. They did. They remembered seeing bills with the club's number on them. One of them even mentioned it to the guy who gave it to them. He wasn't very nice about it."

"She able to describe him?"

"Only in general terms. He was Hispanic, which she thought was odd, because this place usually draws white and Asian clientele. No more than thirty to thirty-five years old and dressed nice—button-down shirt and good shoes. His hair was cut short, and she remembered a small star tattoo on his forearm."

Parker let off the gas. A star tattoo on his forearm? Which arm?"

"Left, I think she said. Why?"

"That was Esteban Castaneda. He's here."

Chapter Seventeen

"How can you be sure? I mean, the description could fit hundreds of guys who troll for a little action in places like this," Linda said. They pushed outside into the daylight. Parker paused and scanned the parking lot around the gentleman's club. Nothing seemed out of place among the work trucks and sedans scattered in the spaces. He checked around back where some of the patrons preferred to park, their vehicles hidden from the street, safe from the wife's prying eyes.

Parker pointed to the back corner of the building. Another spray-painted tag, this one without the personal message to him.

"It's him. His description along with another Los Muertos stamp on the building. It's him. I can feel it in my gut."

"You think he's tied into the money?"

"It's a connection. It means Los Muertos is responsible for the deaths in the cargo container. It's not the first time they've left undocumented people to die. We need to go find the tagger, Leon mentioned."

"Sal Camacho. I can run him on the computer in the unit. Leon seemed to think the guy was a leader of the Soldiers for Justice, so he might be hanging at the college."

They returned to the SUV, and Linda typed in Salvador Camacho's name on the dash-mounted keyboard, and there were several matches listed. "I'm betting it's this one." She tapped a Samuel Camacho with an address a block from the Glendale Community College campus. "Samuel. What a poser." His driver's license photo was dated, as were most of the Arizona MVD records. Camacho was five-seven, dark eyes, and light brown hair with

103

frosted tips. Not exactly the hard-core gangbanger.

The short drive to the residence paid off when they spotted a Soldiers for Justice banner on the house along with Defund the Police, Abolish ICE, and black Antifa flags.

"Subtle," Parker said.

The windows were all obscured, with reflective film blocking any view of the interior of the home.

Parker knocked on the doorframe. A few seconds later, the lock unlatched, and a thin young woman opened the door a few inches. Long, straight red hair, parted in the middle, framed her face. Her light blue eyes squinted at Parker. She didn't say a word.

"Hi, I'm looking for Sal," Parker said.

"Why?"

"I need to speak with him."

"You're a cop."

"I am, Detective Parker, Maricopa County—"

"How many innocent kids have you shot today?"

"I need to talk to Sal, he can help us on a human trafficking case."

"Sal's not here."

A rustling from somewhere deeper in the house and the bang of a back door sounded.

"Runner," Linda called from the curb, pointing to the backyard.

Parker spotted a man running down the side yard toward the street and Linda.

He jumped from the porch and started toward Linda when the man tripped over a loose paver and fell face-first on the pavement, sending his messenger bag flying. The old leather satchel skidded on the ground, and three spray cans of paint rolled from the bag.

"Hi, Sal," Linda said. Looking down on the sprawled man. No longer sporting the frosted tips, Camacho wore shoulder-length hair and a patchy beard.

Camacho reached for his back pocket and slipped out a switchblade knife. Parker stepped on the man's wrist, pinning the knife and the man's hand to the pavement.

"Get off me, pig."

"All we were going to do was talk to you, then you go and pull a knife on us," Parker reached and grabbed the knife while Linda handcuffed Camacho.

The red-haired girl stood on the sidewalk with her cell phone up, filming the encounter. "Let him go! He's innocent! Police brutality…" Three men gathered behind her, puffing up their chests.

Another small group of college-aged people started to gather, some shooting video for their social media feeds, others curious about what was going on. Sal's red-haired friend was the only one yelling at the deputies.

"One of the bystanders commented, "Ah, it's only Sal. What a tool."

Parker helped Camacho to his feet, and he felt the man tense under his grip, preparing to fight back. Parker squeezed his shoulder. "Don't do it."

Linda gathered up the messenger bag and spray paint cans and placed them in the back of the SUV. Parker led Camacho to the rear seat and secured him inside.

"Where are you taking him?" Red asked.

"He's got some questions to answer, and pulling a knife on a cop isn't the brightest thing."

"It was self-defense. I have it all on video. You're only after him because of who he is."

Parker closed the rear door, securing Camacho.

"Do you know who he is? Samuel Camacho? Where's the Soldiers for Justice, now? One goes down, and they scurry away."

She looked over her shoulder, and she was all alone.

Parker and Linda got back in the SUV and pulled away. Camacho was running his mouth in the back seat before they cleared the block. "You have no idea who I am. I'll have your badges for this. In fact, you never showed me your badges. This is entrapment. I'll sue you. You didn't have a warrant. You didn't read me my rights. This is an illegal and unlawful action."

Linda turned in her seat. "Sit down and shut the hell up. Don't make me stop this car."

Camacho slid back in his seat and mumbled a smart remark about some lady cop telling him what to do.

"What did you say?" Linda said, glaring over the seat at him.

He slunk back into the seat and looked out the window to avoid eye contact with her.

"I'm seeing a whole new side of you today," Parker said.

"Best make sure you don't get on the wrong side then."

With Camacho secured in an interrogation room, Parker and Linda huddled in his office.

"That's the little prick who's been terrorizing Leon?"

"I'm sure he uses his rat pack to intimidate people around the campus."

"How did he get so influential and for the life of me, I don't see the draw."

"I'm gonna go find out," Parker said. "Wanna join me?"

Linda paused. "You go ahead. I need to make a few calls. Find out what this little turd had going on. Mind if I use your phone?"

"Help yourself."

Parker left her in his office and found Camacho pacing in the interrogation room.

"Sit down," Parker said.

"I demand an attorney."

"I demand you sit, so sit."

Camacho dropped in the chair with a huff and crossed his arms.

"So, Samuel, we have us a little dilemma here. I wanted to talk to you, then you pull your rabbit act and threaten my partner with a knife."

"Lawyer."

"We can play it your way. We have two cops and your little girlfriend's video to corroborate the charge of Assault on a Peace Officer. At a minimum it's going to be a Class 5 felony with a mandatory two years in prison. I have to wonder how you'll survive in prison."

"That's bullshit, and you know it."

"Is it?" Parker opened the interrogation room door. "Hey Potter, got a second?"

"A female deputy appeared in the door. "What's up, Detective?"

"You had a dirtbag pull a knife on you last year, right?"

"Oh, yeah. I don't know what he was thinking."

"What happened to him? He tried to fight the charges, didn't he?"

She nodded. "He tried, but the jury didn't buy into his 'I was in fear for my life' line, and they convicted him in less than an hour."

Camacho swallowed.

"Whatever happened to him?"

"Went away for five years. He's free now, though."

Camacho's chin tilted in defiance.

"Yeah, the Mexican Mafia killed him six months into his sentence."

"Thanks, Potter."

"Anytime." She glanced down at Camacho and shook her head with a dismissive gesture.

Parker closed the door and sat opposite Camacho. He leaned in and spoke softly.

"What if I made sure you got probation?"

"What do you mean?"

"I really did want to talk to you this morning." Parker hefted the messenger bag onto the table. The metallic clank of the paint cans echoed in the small room.

"Tell me about your tagging."

"Tagging? You took me down for vandalism? This is wrong. Artistic expression is protected under the First Amendment."

"I want to know about a specific tag you've been doing." Parker pulled up the image from the truck driver's home. And held it for Camacho. "This is your work. I know it is; don't bother to deny it."

Camacho smiled when he spotted the photo. "Yeah, it's mine. So what? You got nothing."

"Tagging private property with graffiti is vandalism."

"I was commissioned to do them. A series of them."

"Commissioned?"

"Yeah, it means I was paid for my art."

"Let me get this right: people actually paid you to deface their place of business?"

"They didn't think of it that way."

"Help me understand. People paid you for art, and this is the best you could do?" Parker tapped the phone screen.

"It's the image he wanted. I gave it my style, of course, But the patron wanted the exact image. And the locations. He told me I'd be the next Banksy."

"How many places did you tag with this image?"

"Eight."

"Here in the valley?"

"Yep. He called it a collection."

"Who was this patron of the arts?" Parker felt his heart rate increase.

"Don't know his name, and I only met him once. He paid me in advance and gave me the locations he wanted me to paint."

"Like a house in the Guad, West Valley Machine, and Crystal's Gentlemen's Club?"

Camacho tilted his head and furrowed his brow. "Yeah, they were mine. Why?"

"The one at the house in the Guad—anyone home at the time?"

"No. Place looked empty. Did make me wonder why he wanted the place tagged. But, I was getting paid so..."

"Did you add PRKR to the tag in the corner?"

"Uh uh, all of them were the same. Did someone come along and try to claim this as their own?"

"The guy—this patron—he have a name?" What's he look like?"

"Said his name was Esteban. Not too tall, average, I guess."

Parker scrolled through his phone until he found the one he wanted. A photo clipped from the FBI's Most Wanted List. He flipped the phone around, facing Camacho. "This the guy?"

"Yeah." Without hesitation.

"Why did he reach out to you? Of all the misfit taggers in the valley, why you?"

"Probably because he'd seen my work around."

"Doubt it. I understand you help get jobs for students through the Toy

Soldiers for Whatever."

"SFJ is a legitimate social justice organization. People know us, and businesses in the community are willing to help marginalized students by giving them jobs, or temporary housing."

"Some of the same businesses you tagged?"

Camacho thought, and Parker could see the light come on. The kid never made the connection before.

"Some of them, yeah."

"Like maybe West Valley Machine?"

"They've offered a few jobs to our people?"

"Who is the person you work with there to coordinate the job placement?"

"I don't want to get him in trouble. He's trying to help our students who need a hand up."

"If that's all it is, then there's not a problem."

"If I tell you, what do I get?"

"You don't get an intimate relationship with a cell partner for the next five years."

Camacho bit his lower lip. "Screw it. Hector Reynaldo. He's the guy who runs the West Valley Machine business. He wanted me to bring him three students who wouldn't ask no questions and do what they were told."

Parker jotted the name down. "He ever mention Esteban?"

"Yeah, now that you mention it. I thought maybe it was because he hit up Esteban for one of my tags."

Linda entered and sat across from Camacho, next to Parker. Camacho leaned back a bit in his chair.

"So, Samuel. Mommy and Daddy are a trifle miffed at your behavior this morning."

"You called my parents? I'm not in high school anymore."

"Funny you say that, because they tell me they've been paying your tuition, and you still bring your dirty laundry home for Mama."

"Yeah, what of it."

"What of it is, you won't have to bring your stained tighty-whities home to mom anymore."

Camacho looked confused. "What are you talking about."

"I had a chat with the College Provost. The charter for the Soldiers of Justice has been revoked. It seems pulling a switchblade on a peace officer is frowned upon."

Camacho started to reply, but Linda cut him off with a stop gesture.

"The house you and your castaways are leasing belongs to the college. You've broken the terms of your lease with acts of violence, and they want you gone. You can go back and live with mommy and daddy again."

Linda rose from the table and looked down at Camacho. "Time for you to grow up, kid."

When Linda left, Camacho's face swiveled to Parker. "She can't do that. Can she?"

"She can, and she did. Time for you to make a new start and figure out what you're gonna do in life. Because this," Parker grabbed one of the spray paint cans, "ain't getting you anywhere."

"That's my art," Camacho said.

"I'm pretty sure your 'art' will be off limits as a condition of probation. Up, we got to get you booked."

"Jail? I'm going to jail? I gave you what you wanted. You said—"

"I said you could avoid going to prison. And I'll let the prosecutor know you cooperated with us. But, bottom line, you pulled a knife on a cop—you're going to jail."

Camacho's knees buckled when Parker pulled him from his chair.

A uniformed deputy waited in the hallway to take the prisoner to the holding cells where he'd be printed, photographed, and processed.

Linda met Parker in the hallway as the crestfallen street artist was led away.

"He'll probably make bail."

"Mom's in no mood to bail him out," Linda said.

"Really?"

"We had a parent-to-parent moment."

"I don't think he'll be bothering Leon or anyone else at the college."

"He manage to give you anything we can use?"

"He did. Let's go see a man about a water pump."

Chapter Eighteen

Billie met Linda and Parker two blocks away from the West Valley Machine location on Grand.

"Yeah, I know the guy you're talkin' about. Hector. He's a sketchy dude. Used to run with some street gang, and then he magically pops up running a machine shop. He knows nothin' 'bout the business, so he didn't earn his way to the top, if you know what I mean."

"He's running it, but who owns it?" Parker asked.

"I dunno. But you and I both know Los Muertos been in and outta the place."

Parker turned to Linda, "I pulled twenty undocumented people from a room in the back last year. They were being held by Los Muertos thugs until their families paid off the cost of getting them over the border."

"Why is the place still open?" Linda asked.

"My guess is whoever owns the place claimed Los Muertos pressured them to use it."

Parker looked over Billie's shoulder and had to smile at her battered red Toyota pickup truck. Even though she purchased a new Ford, she couldn't let go of the relic.

"Glad to see you could get here."

"Hey, she's got a few miles left on her. But her water pump is leaking and anything longer than twenty minutes and she starts to overheat."

"You know what you need to do?"

"Like you said, drive up and go ask about a replacement water pump."

"See if you can spot anything out of the ordinary, especially if you get an eye on Hector Reynaldo. Don't try and engage, just see what you can see. If they were to see me, or Linda, they'd clam up."

"I get it. I can do that." Billie started to her truck, and Parker followed.

"Billie, be careful in there. If these guys are connected to Los Muertos, they'll be watching. I can't have anything happen to you. If it looks a little off, get out of there."

She nodded. Thanks for sayin' that. Not too many people care these days. Don't worry. I been dealin' with guys like these for years. I can handle myself."

"I know you can, Billie. Be careful."

Billie got in her old truck, and the door creaked as she slammed it shut. The engine struggled to start and finally kicked over and rumbled to life. Parker took a step back from the earsplitting motor noise.

"You never got your catalytic converter replaced?" Parker called out.

"Nah, they'd only steal it again."

Billie pulled away and rumbled out of the parking lot.

Parker joined Linda, and they huddled in the SUV over Parker's cell phone.

"You think she'll remember?" Linda asked.

"Billie's reliable when it comes to this kind of stuff. She'll call when she parks and then pocket the phone."

"She acted like she's done this before."

"Too many times. Especially for the Marshal's Service. You know about her and the cartel, right?"

"Her former life as a coyote, sure."

"Before that, she was in Witness Protection and gave it up when the cartel threatened a couple of families in Hermosillo if she rolled on them."

"Witness Protection? That's new."

"It explains why she lives off the grid like she does. Billie's the kind of person who sees the best in people and would do anything to help someone in trouble. She takes it hard when someone takes advantage of her, or worse, treats her like she's worthless. She stays on her own so people can't hurt her. She comes off all tough and self-reliant, but the truth is she's got a heart bigger than most of us."

"I should be a little jealous," Linda said.

Parker's cell rang, and he punched the speaker button. "Okay, now. Be careful. If it doesn't look right, walk away."

"Yes, mother," Billie said.

Parker and Linda heard the rustle of Billie putting the phone in her pocket, followed by the squelch of the truck door.

They heard the tinkle of a bell when Billie entered the shop. There was a lack of machine noises, the type usually heard from grinding wheels, welding equipment, and cutting torches.

"Hello? Anyone here?"

She heard faint voices in the background. They abruptly fell silent.

"Shit, Billie, what did you do?" Parker said.

"Who are you? You shouldn't be back here?" A rough, angry sounding voice sounded from Parker's phone.

"Weren't nobody out front."

"Get out."

"I need a part for my truck."

The man with the voice followed with, "Go wait out front. You can't be back here. Insurance."

"Sure, sure."

A moment later another male voice, this one higher pitched, perhaps younger came over the speaker. "What do you need?"

"I'm looking for a water pump for my truck. The one out there."

Parker envisioned Billie stabbing a thumb over her shoulder.

"What year?"

"A ninety-seven"

A tapping noise. The man was looking up the part.

"We don't got it. You need to go somewhere else."

"How 'bout a catalytic converter?"

The counterman was silent for a moment. "We don't got any in stock."

"Oh. Sorry I wasted your time."

"But, I can get you one. Come tomorrow with cash. Seven hundred bucks."

"Five hundred."

"Okay, five. You come tomorrow, and I'll have it. You need to install."

"Deal."

The doorbell sounded once more.

"Wait. Your phone."

"Oh shit," Parker said and started the SUV.

"What about my phone?"

"The light's on in your back pocket."

"Dammit. I'm always butt-dialing someone." There was a rustle of fabric. "It's like my social worker not to answer their damn phone anyhow." Then, the line disconnected.

Parker put the SUV in drive and drove across the entrance to the Western Machine parking lot and felt his breath release when he spotted Billie pulling toward the street.

He caught her eye, and she followed the SUV for a few blocks before Parker pulled into a grocery store off Bell.

They pulled in next to one another, and Parker rolled his window down.

"Social Worker? Really?"

"It's alls I could think of."

"You had me worried for a minute there at the end."

"Yeah, damn hole in my back pocket gave it away."

"What was going on in the back room? They didn't like you there."

"Weren't no machine shop operations, for sure."

"I walked in on something they didn't want seen. They was packing up boxes, and it weren't auto parts. Didn't get close enough to look for sure."

"See Hector Reynaldo?"

"Sure did. He was the dude who came up and told me to get lost when he spotted me in the back room."

"He act like he'd seen you before?"

"No."

"Anything stick out in what you saw?"

"Every one of them was packin', and a couple of rifles were behind the backroom door. Oh, them boxes—they all had this symbol on them. I don't know what it looked like—and some foreign language."

"Would you know it if you saw it? We could show you some examples."

"Yeah, maybe. I know it ain't Chinese or any of that. It had some backwards letters in it."

"Sounds European," Linda said.

Parker paused for a moment and rubbed his chin. You got a look at the words on the box?"

"Like I said. I don't know what they mean."

Parker reached in his console and grabbed a notepad, and handed it through the window to Billie.

"Can you draw what you saw?"

"Can I draw it? I don't know what the words mean."

"You've recalled numbers and signs you've only seen once before. This isn't different. Draw what you remember seeing in there."

"I'll try. Still don't see the point."

Billie took the notepad, and her forehead was creased in concentration. She bit her cheek as she scribed out lines and letters. In addition, she scratched out a circle with three triangles pointing inward.

She passed the notebook back to Parker.

"You saw this?"

"Sorry, that's the best I could do."

"You got more than I could have hoped. The circle is a radiation symbol."

Parker placed the notepad on the console and used a scanning app on his phone.

"I've wanted to try this for a while."

He loaded the image into his cell phone's browser and hit enter.

"Billie, you see anyone in there with one of these on their shirt?" Parker showed her the radiation dosimeter he'd received from Dr. Sherman.

"Not that I saw, why?"

"The letters you saw. обережно медичні відходи They were Ukrainian for

Caution, Medical Waste. With the international symbol for radiation."

Chapter Nineteen

"Are you certain?"

Parker's first call was to Lynn.

"Billie saw the markings on the boxes. Los Muertos might be moving radioactive material around the valley. Could be how our victims were exposed."

"What are they doing with radioactive material?"

"I don't know. Whatever it is, it ain't good."

Parker gave her the address and told him to stand by.

"What are we supposed to do?" Linda asked.

"She didn't say, but I think we should go keep an eye on the place until Lynne gets whoever to come scoop up what was getting packed into those boxes."

"What do you need me to do?" Billie asked.

"Head for the Immigrant Coalition. Miguel's been working on a way to connect with the families of some missing college students down there. He might need some help figuring out the best way to make it happen. He didn't think sending an FBI agent knocking on doors would get a good response."

"He's right," Billie said. I'll go see what he's got, and maybe some of my connections in Hermosillo could pitch in."

"Don't get anyone started until we find out what you discovered in the Western Machine shop."

Billie nodded and pulled out of the parking lot.

"You really think Los Muertos is shipping radioactive material? Leon, he

117

drove their shipments all over the valley. He could be exposed..."

"The way Billie ran it down—what she saw, it doesn't seem like Hector Reynaldo and his crew were too concerned about handling hot material. They could be ignorant to what it is they're doing, but it seems more like a smokescreen for something else."

"But the bodies in the cargo container were exposed."

"Yeah, I know. We can't take a risk; that's why I called Lynne. It would be like Los Muertos to get everyone distracted with a radiation scare to keep us from finding out what it is they are really up to."

Parker's cell pinged with a text message.

"It's Lynne. A NEST team is on the way over."

"NEST?"

"Nuclear Emergency Support Team. These are the specialists who know how to search and deal with hot material."

Parker pulled the SUV out of the grocery store lot and turned in the direction of the machine shop. A block away from the shop a white panel van swooped past them and pulled into the Western Machine Parts lot. Parker pulled to the curb.

A man in a pair of plain blue coveralls carrying a brown cardboard box stepped from the side door of the cargo van. Someone inside the van door closed the door.

The deliveryman trotted to the door and pulled in back, resting the box on his hip, and he pushed inside.

Parker's cell chimed again with Lynne's number.

"She's watching us. Wants to know what we're doing here."

Linda looked over her shoulder and tilted her chin at a black SUV down the block.

Parker tapped in a text in response. "I asked if we should follow the delivery van when he leaves."

An immediate reply on his screen. "No. Van = Team Blue."

"Team Blue. The delivery guy's a fed."

A minute later the delivery driver exited the machine shop carrying the same box he went in with. He slid open the side door, stepped inside. And moments later the panel van pulled away from the shop onto Grand.

"What do we do now?" Linda said.

Another chime on his cell. "Lynne wants to meet. My office."

"She's summoning you to your own office?"

A black SUV blurred past, heading south, in the direction of the Sheriff's Office.

"Apparently so."

When Linda and Parker arrived in the Major Crimes Unit offices, Lynne and the deliveryman, dressed in the blue coveralls were deep in conversation with Pete Tully.

"Nathan, this is Dr. Wilson Thomas," Linda said, leaning toward the delivery driver.

"Dr. Thomas. NEST, I take it?"

"Right. I lead one of the response teams. As soon as we got the call from the county medical examiner, we headed here. Then when you called Agent Finch, we positioned resources and made our approach. I have some questions."

"Shoot. Let's go sit in my office. Pete, you too."

They gathered in Parker's office, and Dr. Thomas cleared his throat.

"Let me begin with the cargo container. Radioactive material has a unique signature. The isotopes are like fingerprints. We can tell where any source of radioactive matter came from."

"The cargo box? You know where it came from?"

"Not precisely. Since we didn't find any measurable material, all we have is the reading from the metal cargo container itself. Our first thought, and concern, frankly, was the source of the radiation was the Palo Verde Nuclear Power Plant. As the largest nuke plant in the nation, we have concerns about a safety compromise. We take great care controlling the waste from these generating plants."

"Where does the nuclear waste go? Could someone hijack a transport and make off with a shipment," Parker asked.

"For that very reason, all the nuclear waste generated from Palo Verde for the last thirty years is sealed within concrete and steel cylinders and stored on-site."

"If it wasn't from the Palo Verde Plant, then where did it come from?"

"That's the puzzling part. Even though we can identify individual isotopes, the cargo container was a bizarre puzzle of Cobalt, Iodine, Technetium, and Phosphorus. All medical grade elements."

"Medical grade? Where would our victims come into contact with radiation from medical sources?"

"I can't begin to explain it. The only helpful point is Technetium has a half-life of six hours. It degrades quickly and since it was around in trace levels, there was Technetium in your container less than six hours prior."

"Can those materials be used in a dirty bomb?" Tully asked.

"Any radioactive material would do."

"The timing is troubling. We know the container sat at the Devil's Well Rest Stop for almost six hours. Did you find the same medical-grade isotopes in the machine shop? Those boxes were labeled as medical products."

"No."

"What did they have then?"

"Nothing. We got an absolute zero reading above normal atmospheric levels. There was no radioactive material in the building."

"The boxes were labeled with a yellow and black radiation warning in Ukrainian."

"I can't dispute it. But I'm completely certain there was no source material there."

"Were you in the back room? Where the boxes were?"

"I don't need to be in the same room. The well counter and Geiger Muller counter would pick up isotopes in that and any adjoining building. There was nothing there. This is the same monitor that picked up a cancer patient in the New York subway system because he was being treated with radioactive Iodine for Grave's Disease. It's that sensitive." Dr. Thomas said.

Parker paced the room and rubbed the tension knots in the back of his neck. "What's the connection between the machine shop boxes and the cargo container?"

"Maybe we're trying to make one where there is no connection," Lynne said.

"What are the chances two events, involving Los Muertos aren't linked with one another? I mean, think about it. We get a truck with dead men who turned up irradiated. Then a machine shop is packing boxes marked with radiation and medical waste warnings."

"The boxes are marked as a warning to keep people away from them, right? What if the cargo container was the same thing? Someone didn't want us to look too closely at what's inside," Linda said.

"Interesting take," Parker said. "We don't know what might be in the machine shop boxes, but Dr. Thomas is certain it's not radioactive. Fits with your line of thought. What have we missed in the cargo container?"

"What if the last cargo before your victims consisted of medical waste? Could there have been enough material to give off the levels of radiation our victims were showing?"

Dr. Thomas paused and glanced to a corner of the room, as if he were calculating an invisible equation. "It's possible, but more likely, the two were in the container at the same time."

"Where could someone take medical-grade material to get rid of it?'

"It shouldn't be incinerated, like other medical waste. The ash would be radioactive and if it spread in the wind—it's fallout."

"I can't imagine you can take it to any public dump," Lynne said.

"No, you can't. There are a few facilities, and they are generally very controlled and monitored."

"It comes back to our victims. Finding out why they came here and how some of them were contaminated is key."

Chapter Twenty

After Lynne and the NEST team leader left, Parker plopped behind his desk, picked up his desk phone, and left a message for Dr. Sherman asking if she knew more about the victims. If the answers to this case were tied with them, they weren't giving much up.

"What are you thinking?" Linda asked.

"Forget about the radiation. We don't know who these victims were, so set that aside for now. We know where they were found, how they likely died, and the truck driver was connected to Los Muertos. They either paid him or forced him to drive these men to their deaths. Then he's killed. And we have the Los Muertos tag on his place and other businesses in town, including the machine shop where something was getting packed up for shipping."

"Okay, so we know bits and pieces of the story."

"And the Soldiers for Justice were connected to Los Muertos and setting up people like Leon with jobs in some of those same businesses."

"You think they might have had a connection to the work our victims were doing here?"

"It's a connection we haven't explored yet. Think your new friend, Samuel, will talk with you?"

"I'd love some quality time with that man-child."

"Think they've transported him to county yet?"

Linda got on the phone and tapped in a number and after a quick conversation, she hung up. "He's downstairs. We've got about twenty minutes before he's scheduled to go."

They found Sal in a baggy orange jumpsuit and the only one in an empty iron-barred holding tank. He had a black eye, a new adornment since they last met.

"Making friends, I see," Parker said.

"My parents are going to sue you."

"I doubt that," Linda said. "Mommy sounded like she was about done with you."

Sal shrunk a bit in his jumpsuit.

"We need to talk," Linda said.

"I got nothing to say to you," he said.

"You remember the part about five years?" Parker said.

"I already told you what you wanted. We had a deal."

"The deal's changed."

"Then I don't go to jail."

"You're not in a position to dictate terms here, boy," Linda said. "You answer our questions and play nice, or we'll send you back in the other holding tank with your new friends."

Sal glanced over at the tank with fifteen orange-clad prisoners who were intent on the discussion going on across from them.

"All right, let's get it over with."

Parker cuffed Sal up through the cell bars and had the deputy monitoring the holding area unlock the tank.

"Come with us," Parker said.

"Snitch! I knew it. That weak pendejo is a rat." The cat calls from across the hallway followed Sal into an interview room.

"Looks like you'll have quite the welcoming committee when you hit the cellblock, Sal," Parker said.

He looked sullen and distracted by what awaited him at the jail. "What do you want? You have to promise me I'll be safe."

"No promises, but we'll make sure the jail knows you've been cooperative and houses you in a special unit."

"You arranged jobs for students at places like the West Valley Machine Parts business," Linda said.

"Yeah, I already told you."

"Where else?"

"A couple places. Warehouse work, delivery drivers, dishwashers, places like that."

"Any large groups you found work for?"

"Large groups? I don't think so. Oh, there was one gig, about six months ago. I didn't end up arranging it, but I heard the dude from the strip club, that Esteban guy, he was looking for high-end computer jobs."

"Computer jobs? Like what?"

"I'm not a tech guy, so I couldn't help him, but I knew of a guy."

"He ever say what these jobs were?"

"He said some geek-speak—I didn't know what he meant. Coding, scripts, that kind of thing. I don't know the details."

"And your contact? The one you turned Esteban onto? What's his name?"

Sal looked like he was holding his last poker chip and couldn't cover the bet. "You gotta promise me this don't come back on me. If I tell you, I walk."

"I told you there's no walking out of pulling a knife on a cop. We will ask the District Attorney to let you off on probation," Parker said.

Sal looked to Linda for confirmation, and she nodded along.

"Randy Coyle. Randy runs a software engineering company. If anyone knew about high-tech jobs, he'd be the one."

"All right, we'll check it out. I'll make a call to the jail to make sure they keep you away from your new friends out there.

Linda tapped the table. "One last thing. West Valley Machine Parts. What's going on there? It's not about machine parts. What is being delivered by your drivers?

"Esteban made it clear. It was none of my business. I know it's not good, whatever it is. I used to make the deliveries until I found this kid. Kid started asking questions and got bitch slapped by Hector for poking his nose into Hector's business."

Linda stiffened. She knew he meant Leon.

"No one ever opened the shipping boxes to see what was really being delivered?"

"Hector made it clear. Open the boxes, and you'd be gone. I don't think he meant fired, either. Besides, all the boxes were sealed with this fancy silver seal to make it look all official and shit."

"A seal?" Parker asked while he scrolled through his phone, settling on the foil customs seal on the cargo container. "Like this one?"

"Yeah, that's the one. I remember."

"All right, Sal, I'll keep our end of the deal and let the jail and D.A. know you've been helpful."

Parker helped Sal up from the chair and led him back to the holding cell. Jeers from the other inmates followed Sal back to his tank.

The deputy locked the cell door, and Parker told him Sal should be listed as protective custody at the jail.

"Figured as much," the deputy said.

Parker and Linda left a dejected Sal in his holding cell where he had to listen to the threats and intimidation from the other prisoners. Parker thought it was a little karmic justice for the way he treated Leon and other vulnerable students.

On the way back to the offices, Parker asked Linda how good she was with computers and techie stuff.

"I hold my own. I can update my phone and PC. Why? We going to reach out to Randy Coyle? I'm not in that league."

Parker sent a text message to Barry Johns. Barry responded seconds later saying he was almost back to the office and said Dr. Sherman also had an update for Parker.

Parker pulled up a web browser on his phone as they walked back to his office. Randy Coyle was the CEO and founder of Coyle Technology. The largest tech firm on the west coast. He'd relocated from California's Silicon Valley a year ago because of the soaring costs and business-unfriendly regulations in the Golden State. Since the relocation, three thousand-five hundred jobs were added to the Phoenix-based company and their profit margin blossomed. Coyle was credited for the upturn in the company's bottom line.

"Says the Coyle Tech offices are off of South Verrado in Buckeye."

Barry Johns arrived at the Major Crimes unit the same time as Parker.

"What you need me to do, boss?" Johns asked.

"Fill me in on the Medical Examiner's findings."

Johns put his messenger bag on his desk, unbuckled the flap and pulled single file folder from within. He handed it to Parker.

"Dr. Sherman told me she's confirmed the COD as asphyxia. All of the deceased had high levels of Carbon Monoxide."

"Monoxide? I would have sworn they would have shown high Carbon Dioxide levels from breathing the same air in the enclosed space," Parker said.

"Dr. Sherman thought so. Our evidence techs are taking another look at the cargo container. It could be they died from an exhaust leak."

"What a freaky occurrence. The A/C unit had broken down. I guess it's possible."

"Right now, she hasn't declared the manner of death, but she's leaning toward accidental unless something else pops up."

Johns handed him a USB flash drive. "Here is the photo package on the victims."

Parker palmed the USB drive and said, "How's about you and I going out to Coyle Technology and see if we can get Randy—"

"Randy Coyle? He's like the LeBron James of tech. The man single-handedly changed the face of the industry with his new chip design and is supposed to announce a new operating system to rival Windows and Mac."

"You think you can hold back the fan-boy a bit when we meet with him?"

"I can try," Johns said with a grin.

Parker tossed the USB drive to Linda. "Copy this and try to send it to the Pima County Missing Migrant Project. They are an NGO, so they might balk at an informal dump from us."

"If they are interested in missing and unidentified persons, this should be all they need," she said.

"Make a copy and get it to Billie and Miguel. They have some thoughts on how to reach out to the families in Mexico who reported their sons and husbands missing."

She nodded. "I'm due for my update to the Court Implementation unit this afternoon, too. See you later?"

"Count on it."

"Let go, Barry, off to see the wizard."

Chapter Twenty-One

T he Coyle Technology offices were located in a small campus of squat adobe-colored buildings. After Barry's buildup of the tech giant, the offices were a bit of a letdown. Parker had no trouble finding a parking space because the place was empty, except for a dozen cars spread throughout the lot.

"Is the place even open?" Parker said.

"Hard to tell. Hey, someone just came outside."

They both stepped from the SUV and headed toward the Coyle Technology staffer. The young man flicked a match and lit a cigarette, but what Parker noted was the man's clothing. The same color pants and white button-down as the cargo box victims.

"You seeing what I'm seeing?"

"Uh-huh," Johns said.

"Hi there. You work at Coyle Technology?"

"For now," the man said. Parker judged him to be in his mid-twenties, patchy beard and rail thin."

"That good? I thought Coyle Technology was the place for software innovation."

"It might be, but not when you treat your employees the way they do. I'm out once I get another place to land."

"What's that about?" Johns asked.

The smoker glanced between the two detectives. "You from the SEC or FCC?"

Parker pulled his jacket back to expose his badge. "County Sheriff. Care to tell me why you don't like working here?"

"What the hell, why not? We're not supposed to talk about the company—it's in these stupid non-disclosure agreements we all had to sign. Coyle Tech is a slave ship. They pay us next to nothing, demand we work overtime and refuse to even think about a profit-sharing arrangement with their employees."

"Speaking of employees—where is everyone?" Parker asked.

"Cuts. The corporate overlords cut positions when the rest of the world was forced to go remote. They wouldn't even consider letting us work from home where it was safe. They made us come in and work—the rest of us, the ones they didn't cut. They said—they had the balls to say—our safety and the safety of the projects were on the same level."

"What do you mean?"

"It means Coyle Tech is afraid someone will find out what we're working on and figure out a way to do it cheaper. If that were even possible."

A timer sounded on the smoker's watch. "I gotta go log back in, or it's my ass." He stood and started for the door.

"Is Randy Coyle in?

"Who knows? I've never seen the man."

Parker and Johns followed the trail of smoke into the building. The reception area was vacant. Hallways sprouted off in both directions. The smoker saw them pause and he pointed down the hallway to the left. "Follow the yellow brick road." The carpet to the left was a yellow cactus pattern.

"I'm game, but I'm telling you, I ain't Toto," Johns said.

Parker saw signs of life in three offices, but more than half of the workspaces were vacant. At the end of the hallway, a bronze plaque marked the office of Randy Coyle, Chief Executive Officer and Founder. He half expected the door locked, but it pushed open smoothly on heavy metal hinges.

A young, raven-haired woman sat at a desk in the outer office. She turned away from her computer monitor as if visitors to Coyle's office were an unusual event.

"Detectives Parker and Johns, to see Mr. Coyle.

"Detectives? What's wrong?"

"Nothing's wrong. We need to speak with Mr. Coyle. Is he around."

"He's always around. Let me see if he can break away and see you."

She lifted a sleek black phone from her desktop and pushed a single red button. "Sir—I know, sir—yes, I remember, but there are two detectives here who want to speak with you."

The raven-haired assistant swiveled her chair around and spoke softly into the phone. "I don't know why, sir. They won't tell me."

She jerked her head up as if she was slapped. "Mr. Coyle will be right with you."

The double door flung open, and a thin gnome of a man stepped through. His hair was unkempt, a stained button down and wrinkled pants. This is what the assistant meant by he's always around. He looked like he never left.

Parker recognized the man in spite of his disheveled appearance. "Mr. Coyle, Detectives Parker and Johns. We'd like a moment of your time."

Coyle didn't respond, but instead turned and retreated into his office. Parker took the open door as an invitation. He and Johns followed Coyle inside.

Three six-foot-wide white boards along one wall of the workspace were packed with annotations, notes, reminders, and lines of computer code. Instead of the massive exotic wood, or gleaming metal desk, Parker anticipated, Coyle used a fabric sided workstation, identical to those in the cube-shaped office modules they passed in the vacant hallway workspaces. The six-foot-by-six-foot fabric and laminate structure seemed lost and out of place, as did Coyle himself.

There were a handful of beanbag chairs and two couches, but Coyle didn't offer the detectives a seat. Instead, he turned his back to them and scratched out a note on a blank space on the whiteboard. The scrawl was tiny but very precise. "Server Farm 3 Drop."

Parker used it as a way to begin their conversation. "What's a server farm?"

Coyle snapped the cap on the dry-erase marker and faced the detectives.

"They are the backbone of Coyle Technology. Electronic consumers think of the cloud as some ethereal space where their precious personal data are safely maintained until they call for it. The end user doesn't give it any thought until they need a document, spreadsheet, or great-grandma's recipe for cheesecake. It's all stored somewhere. The cloud should really be called the fog, because all it does is hide where the data are being maintained. Every cloud really means servers, thousands of them. Coyle Technology manages over ten thousand of these servers, and we group them together in server farms. Ten of them."

Parker noticed Johns was nodding along with Coyle's explanation.

"Coyle Technology has a reputation for high-end encryption and data security in its cloud-based applications," Johns said.

Coyle shoved his hands in his pockets. "Everything we have depends on it."

Parker pointed at the note Coyle wrote. "What does it mean when you say, 'server farm 3 down'?"

"Long before the pandemic, cloud storage pushed aside the need for personal hard drives, and the everyday end-user was pushing content to the cloud from their phones, laptops, and home computers. It was convenient and relatively inexpensive. Inexpensive for them. Cloud servers are costly to purchase, maintain, and service. There's constant network routing and coding issues to keep the consumer's data available at a moment's notice. Cloud operators like Coyle Technology struggle to keep the cost low for the consumer.

"The last few years have seen more offshore server farms. Indonesia, India, China. Labor costs are a significant cost driver. Coupled with the fact most of the servers are manufactured in Asia, it's becoming more of a challenge to stay competitive."

"A server farm down means it's offline?" Parker asked, circling back to the question.

"No, no. It means—it could mean offline." Coyle abruptly turned back to the board and used the blade of his hand to wipe off the note. "In this case, I'm noticing a downturn in the production at unit 3. I pay software engineers, coders, and system technicians to keep the software up to date. They've been falling behind."

"What's the significance of falling behind? Grandma's recipes are still in the cloud, right?"

"And we want to keep it that way. There have been over…" Coyle strode to the far right side of the board and circled a number with another marker. "Three-thousand-five hundred attempted network intrusions this year. The software updates and maintenance ensure Coyle Technology keeps the data secure."

"I understand you've reduced your staffing."

"We have to compete with the offshore corporations. All non-essential personnel have been let go. Only the productive staff remain. If you don't give me five thousand lines of code in six months, you're dead weight. I need production."

"And you need it cheap."

"I need it competitive."

"We understand you recruit from the student population at Glendale Community College."

"We draw from many of the colleges and universities in the region."

"Sal Camacho said you were helpful, getting jobs for some of the GCC students."

A knitted brow in response. "I don't know the name. I'm sure we do what we can. I rely on my team to take care of the hiring."

Coyle turned to the whiteboard once more and started drawing lines and arrows from one clump of text to another. Parker couldn't make any sense of it.

Johns cleared his throat. "Excuse me, Mr. Coyle. Have you bought up some of the offshore server farms to stay competitive?"

Coyle threw the marker in the tray and spun around. "Coyle Technology does not operate foreign servers. We were founded on the principle that we operate and manage the world's most secure cloud servers. We cannot rely on substandard foreign regulations, interference by distant governments, or questionable labor pools in other countries. We've managed and operated our own servers."

"Can you tell us who might have worked with The Glendale Community College and Mr. Camacho to recruit students?"

"Entry-level hiring decisions, interns, and the like are managed by Lee Patterson. My assistant can connect you. Now, if you don't mind, I need to get back to this." Coyle returned to the board, wiping a section clean before scribbling lines of new text.

"Oh, one last thing," Parker said. "What's with the dress code? Your staff all wearing white button-down shirts and dark pants."

Without turning from his whiteboard, Coyle responded. "It's neat and orderly. I want people to recognize what we bring to our work."

The raven-haired assistant greeted Parker and Johns as they exited the office. "Here is Lee Patterson's phone number. He's off-site today."

"Were you listening in?"

"Always. Mr. Coyle demands it."

"Let me ask you then, "There seem to be a lot of vacant staff positions here. I get the sense people aren't happy. How does Coyle Technology expect to keep things running?"

"As Mr. Coyle explained, we must remain competitive. To achieve that, we must be lean, and everyone must pull their weight. Mr. Patterson is out recruiting to find us the labor pool we need to maintain operations."

"From local junior colleges?"

"From wherever he can find people who know how to code, maintain cloud servers, and update our software."

"Thanks, and please let Mr. Patterson know we'd like to speak with him."

"He's expecting your call, Detective."

Parker noticed the chart on her desk. "Lot of red lines there."

She flipped the paper over. "Have a nice day, Detective."

Parker and Johns backtracked out of the nearly vacant offices and into the Phoenix heat.

"I guess it's true," Johns said.

"What's that?"

"Never meet your heroes. He's hanging on by a thread."

"Kinda gave me a 'Beautiful Mind' vibe. He's focused on the big picture. The day-to-day operations are falling apart. You catch the chart his assistant was quick to hide? It was quarterly earnings—all in the red. Stockholders can't be pleased about the result."

Parker noticed the Coyle Tech doors open when three identically clad workers came out. Two whipped-out vape pens the moment they set foot on the concrete outside. The third man looked familiar. Medium height, short brown hair, with short, spiked tips on top. Where had he seen him before? Spike climbed into a dark blue, nearly black sedan and pulled from the parking lot.

A tense feeling swept over Parker, and he couldn't place it other than it had to do with that man.

Chapter Twenty-Two

"That guy look familiar to you?"

"Which one?" Johns asked.

"The guy who got into the dark sedan and pulled out."

"Didn't catch him."

"Humor me for a bit. I know I've seen him before. Let's see where he goes."

"Who am I to question your gut?"

Parker and Johns hurried to the car and pulled from the lot. The dark sedan had disappeared.

"Dammit."

"No recollection where you remember seeing that dude before?" Johns asked.

"Can't put my finger on it. Maybe it's nothing."

Parker's cell buzzed from the console. He tapped the speaker button. "Parker."

"Nathan, I'm at the Immigrant Coalition offices to drop off the victim photo pack to Miguel and Billie. There's no one here," Linda said.

"They were supposed to be there. Miguel was going to track down some families in Mexico City who might have connections to our victims."

"There's a sign on the door, says back in five days."

"Billie does that when she heads down south delivering supplies to migrants caught in the squatter camps. Wait, Miguel wasn't there? He didn't answer the door?" Parker felt his anxiety boil. If Miguel decided to go with Billie on the relief trip, it could jeopardize his Visa. He might be

135

trapped on the other side of the border. He'd been angling for a chance to go with Billie on one of her supply runs, but Parker had remained firm. The risks were too great.

"Sit tight, I'll be right there. I'm gonna call Miguel." He disconnected the phone pressed on the accelerator a bit harder and hit the speed dial number 1 for Miguel.

The phone rang unanswered. Parker disconnected. "Shit, shit, shit. Miguel, what have you done?"

"I've heard him mention Billie Carson's adventures down south. You don't think Miguel decided to go along with her, do you? Billie loves the kid, but she wouldn't allow it, right?" Johns asked.

"I don't know what to think right now. Miguel wants to help other people and Billie has really coaxed him out of his shell with the work at the Coalition. Miguel sees people like himself, who're undocumented, and he'd do what he could to give them a hand. I hope this isn't one of those situations."

Parker pulled into the chipped asphalt parking lot in front of the Coalition offices. Linda's Maricopa County Sheriff's SUV was the only vehicle in the lot.

"No sign of either of them?" Parker asked as he got out of the SUV?"

"No. Miguel have school?" Linda asked.

"Off day. Dammit. Where's his car?"

Parker pressed his face against the glass, and the inside was obscured by blinds. He pounded on the doorframe with his open palm. Even if Miguel was inside with headphones on, he would have heard the thunder of the slap against the metal door.

"I'm gonna call Leon, see if Miguel mentioned anything," Linda said.

"Checking out back," Johns said, and he trotted around and peeked down the side of the building.

Parker heard Linda connect with Leon and she leaned in hitting the speaker button. He returned and fidgeted while she connected.

"Hey, honey, do you have any idea where Miguel might be? He mention Billie, or going on a trip with her?"

"Want me to ask? He's right here," Leon said.

"Miguel's there?" she said.

"Yeah, what's the big deal? Hold on."

There was a rustling over the phone before Miguel's voice sounded. "Hey, Linda, what's up?"

"Hey buddy, I've been trying to reach you," Parker said, trying not to let the anxiety slip.

"Oh, yeah. I need to charge my phone."

Parker recognized the casual tone in Miguel's response and felt his blood pressure drop. It left him cool and off balance.

"We stopped by the Coalition offices but it's all locked up. Thought you and Billie were gonna be working on getting a line on those families down south."

"I was too. Then she got all weird and decided to make her supply trip early. Left about an hour ago."

"I was worried you went with her."

"One of these times. I know you keep telling me it's dangerous and how if I get in trouble on the trip, it might cause Visa problems. These people need help, and my problems don't outweigh what they're facing."

"I get it. Thanks for not going off with her this time."

"I wanted to. I asked her. She told me in plain terms she didn't want me with her. Kinda pissed me off."

"She said that to you?"

"Yeah, like I said, she got all weirded out and left early."

"How come?"

"I don't know. We were talking about the men who died in the container. She was reading about it in the paper and got all quiet, then started packing."

"What was in the paper?"

"That's what I asked, and she never said. I read the article after she left. Nothing new. Talked about how they were found abandoned, and there was one survivor. The paper said his name was Armando DeSilva."

"Where'd they get the name?"

"Said hospital sources."

"Where are you and Leon now?"

"We're at the college."

"You don't have classes today."

"I know. But the girls at the library don't care. Besides there's a job fair here today, and since you guys ruined Leon's job, we're looking at what's up." Miguel was playful in his response. He was hurt by Billie's refusal to let him tag along, but he and Leon were doing what boys their age do.

"Wish Leon good luck on his job search. Let him know to stay away from West Valley Machine for good. The more we find out about the place, the more it looks like they were running shady shit out of there."

"I figured as much after what you and Linda said. I think he's over it. Don't worry, I'll keep an eye out, dad."

"I know you will." Parker disconnected the call.

Detective Johns rounded the building. "Billie Carson's old heap is parked out back. No sign of anyone else."

"Got it. She must have taken her new Ford truck on the relief run down south. Barry, can you go back to the office and run down what we have on Armando DeSilva, our cargo container survivor?"

"He's talking?"

"Not yet. Someone leaked the name to the press. While you're at it, see what you can find out about Coyle and his recruiter, Lee Patterson. Coyle Technology—those uniforms. It's too much of a coincidence."

"On it."

"Parker tossed his keys to Johns. "Take mine. I'll ride with Linda.

Linda got behind the wheel and started the engine.

"Miguel's a good one, Nathan. And so are you," She patted his knee. "He called you dad. I've been waiting for Leon to think of me that way. Maybe it's too much to hope for, and he thinks of this as a temporary shelter arrangement until he moves on."

"I think he knows it's more than that."

"I hope so. Still, it would be nice to hear."

"Want me to call you dad?" Parker said.

Linda backhanded his shoulder. "Ass."

"Speaking of asses, someone at the hospital leaked the name of our lone survivor. We've not received any report the guy regained consciousness, so where did the information come from? We're not far from Banner Memorial Hospital, what say we do a drive by and find out?"

While they headed to the hospital, Parker dialed Billie's number once more. No response. "This isn't like Billie. Last time she went dark like this, the Sinaloa Cartel forced her to coyote undocumented over for them."

"She doesn't seem the run-and-hide type to me," Linda said.

"She's not. Totally not her."

Linda pulled into the Banner Memorial Hospital behind a short bus from one of the local senior living facilities, dropping off a handful of silver-haired passengers for appointments. The waiting room was similarly occupied by people who didn't plan on spending a great part of their golden years in medical waiting rooms and pharmacy lines.

The registration desk didn't have a patient listed under Armando DeSilva; the name leaked in the newspaper. Parker asked for directions to the Intensive Care Unit, the place most likely to treat the critical trauma their survivor suffered.

The hospital was a Level 1 Trauma Center and offered over a hundred beds of specialized care for the most critically injured patients. Parker didn't have any trouble spotting their victim's room because of the uniformed deputy in the hall. The younger deputy was chatting with a nurse who handed the deputy his cell phone before she tucked her hair behind her ear and coyly returned to her desk at the nurses' station.

"Get her number, deputy?" Linda said.

"What? I just—it wasn't—Hunt? When did you move over to plain-clothes?"

"Aren't you supposed to be sitting on our shipping container victim?"

"I do—I am—it's not like he's going anywhere. A waste of department resources, if you ask me."

"I didn't ask you," Parker said. Where's your post?"

"Over there," the deputy tipped his head to the far end of the unit. "Number seventeen."

Parker scanned the patient board on the wall behind the nurses' station and found number seventeen—listed as Doe, J.

"Show me," Parker said.

The deputy acted as if he was put out and would rather spend time flirting with his nurse friend. "Can't you find it? You're the detective, after all."

"Let me put this as plain as I can for you. Your job is to stand watch outside that door until relieved by the next shift. You document every living soul going in and out of that room. Nothing else. You understand? Nothing else." Parker glanced over at the young nurse.

"He's not a flight risk, I think you're being—"

"You don't get to make any decisions about my investigation. The man is the only survivor of a mass murder. He is the last link to whoever may have killed these men. Someone might not want him to live to tell what he knows. While you're out here playing patty cake with your little friend, our victim is exposed."

"I didn't think about it that way."

"Show me the way," Parker said.

Parker and Linda followed the deputy to the door of room seventeen. The room had windows, but the curtains were drawn. Parker pushed the door open.

The bed was empty.

Chapter Twenty-Three

The survivor was gone. The space where the hospital bed was parked, now empty. I.V. Lines hung limply from their pumps, and monitors were unplugged.

"Where did he go?" the deputy said. He looked dumbfounded at the empty ICU room.

Linda trotted out into the hallway and to the nurse's station. "Number seventeen. Where is he?"

An older nurse looked at the board. "Nothing listed, should be in his room." She tapped a few keys on her console. "He doesn't have any scheduled appointments today."

"Where is he?" Linda said.

The nurse picked up her phone and tapped in a number.

Linda caught movement from the far side of the nurse's station. The flirty young nurse was moving fast. She broke into a run for the unit door.

"Nathan, we got a runner," Linda took off in pursuit.

"You park your ass right here," Parker told the deputy before he ran after Linda and the fleeing nurse.

Parker bounded through the swinging ICU doors into the main hall at the moment Linda tackled the runaway nurse. The nurse squirmed and tried to pull her arm away from Linda's grip. A wrist lock stopped her resistance, and Linda snapped handcuffs on the woman.

Linda sat the nurse against the wall and snatched the ID from the lanyard around the woman's neck.

Stickers were printed and placed over the hospital identification. Faked.

"What's your name, sweetheart?" Linda said.

"I don't have to talk to you."

"Where's the patient in room seventeen?" Parker asked.

"I don't know."

"If anything happens to him, it's on you."

"I never even saw the man. I want an attorney."

The ICU charge nurse, a tall, thin black woman with silver streaks in her natural hair, came out into the hallway. "Detectives, we found the patient."

"Where?"

"Our patient's on his way back to the ICU. We caught someone loading him into a stolen ambulance."

"You know who this is?" Parker pointed at the handcuffed nurse.

"She said she was from the registry. We're shorthanded and called in for a replacement."

"The ambulance driver? Security has him?" Parker asked.

"Yes, on the first floor."

"Thanks. Oh, the newspaper this morning released the patient's name. When did you release his name?

"My staff wouldn't release patient information."

"When we're done with your Nurse Ratched here, I'd like to talk with you some."

"I'll be around."

Parker and Linda lifted the phony nurse to her feet.

"Steve got caught?"

"The ambulance driver?"

She nodded. "I swear I didn't have anything to do with that part."

"What was your part?"

The nurse clammed up.

"I know you want an attorney. Fine. Let me tell you what happened. You were paid to flirt with our impressionable young deputy while your partner wheeled the patient away."

The nurse's eyes grew wide, telling Parker he'd nailed it.

"Makes you a co-conspirator and an accessory to kidnapping at the very least."

"It was worth the risk," she said in a low voice.

"I hope you still think so in ten years or so.

A pair of uniformed deputies exited the elevator. "Hey, Parker. The hospital called, said you needed a hand."

"Good timing, Clint. You can take this one and get her processed. I'd like one more crack at her. Can you put her in holding?"

"You got it. Come on, miss." Clint took her by the arm and led her away without a struggle.

The deputy who was supposed to have guarded the victim stepped into the hallway with cell phone in hand. "Detective, it's Lieutenant Washington, the Watch Commander."

Parker took the phone. "Hey, Wash."

After listening to the Watch Commander, Parker responded, "You got it. Two in custody. It seems our deputy was purposefully lured away by a pretty young nurse."

"Yeah, I'll tell him." Parker disconnected the call and handed the phone back to the deputy."

"You're to report to the Watch Commander forthwith."

"Means I'm in trouble, doesn't it?"

"What do you think? You had one job—to keep an eye on a patient. You were too busy getting a nurse's phone number—wait—give me your phone again. Show me the number she gave you."

The deputy pulled the phone from his pocket, unlocked it and handed it to Parker, with the number the nurse added to his contacts.

Parker dialed the number and got a recording saying the number was no longer in service.

"No longer in service, which is probably what awaits you in the Watch Commander's office."

The deputy took his phone and slunk away.

"What do you think will come of him?" Linda asked.

"Depends on what else he has against him. This should earn a suspension—a long one—at the least."

A replacement deputy arrived to take over watching the patient and he held the elevator door for an orderly and a nurse rolling a gurney.

"Hi, Detective. I'm taking over for Mullinson, who I gather dropped the ball on this one."

"You know what to do with our guy here, Abrams."

"Won't be out of my sight. Lieutenant Washington's exact words were a bit more to the point, and I won't repeat them in polite company."

"You got this. Detective Hunt and I are going to go to the security office and have a chat with the ambulance driver. If you get wind of who might have leaked our patient's name, give me a shout. Any change in his condition, let me know immediately.

Linda and Parker found the Security offices in the back rear corner of the hospital, in corridors out of public view. There were no motivational posters here urging family members to have hope, positive energy, and happy thoughts. In the bowels of the medical building, it was reminders to use hand sanitizers and avoid sexual harassment in the workplace.

The small security offices were more suited to what you'd expect in a small shopping mall. Two video monitors and a holding room. A red-headed security man with a blue uniform stood behind another older, pot-bellied guard pointing at the monitor. They both glanced up when the detectives entered.

"Hi guys, you have someone we need to talk to?" Parker said.

"Let me see if we can find him. Sorry, bad joke. Yeah, he's in the holding room. We were watching the video playback."

"Show me what you got," Parker said.

"There's sumthin' off about the whole deal. I mean, we know the ambulance was stolen, came from the V.A. Hospital. But check this out. The guy we have isn't the one who backed it up in our loading bay."

The second security man hit play and showed the ambulance backing up into the slot near the loading dock.

"That's what got our attention. This ain't for patient loading. I went down while Wally watched from here."

"Check this out," Wally said.

Another man came into the frame and waited at the rear of the ambulance. The driver stepped from the cab, strode around to the ambulance doors, and threw them open. He tossed an EMT jacket to the waiting man, who disappeared in the direction of the hospital.

The driver took out a cell phone and placed a call.

"Linda, make a note of the time the call was made—timestamp on the video."

"Got it."

The driver hung up, pocketed his phone, and walked away. As he did, he faced the camera for a few short seconds. Parker felt his blood run cold. Esteban Castaneda. He was here.

Chapter Twenty-Four

"What's Castaneda doing here?" Linda said.

"Can you go back and freeze on his face?" Parker asked.

The security man jockeyed the video feed in reverse until the moment the man at the rear dock pocketed his phone and exposed his face to the camera's eye.

"Why are you here?" Parker said to the image on the screen.

Any doubt was eliminated when the captured photo revealed Castaneda's star-shaped tattoo on his left forearm—the same tattoo burned into Parker's memory the night his partner McMillan was murdered.

The camera in McMillan's patrol unit caught the attack, and while the assailant wasn't readily identified at the time, the tattoo belonged to Esteban Castaneda, the head of Los Muertos.

Parker leaned against a wall in the suddenly claustrophobic security office. The connection between Castaneda and the comatose trafficking victim didn't make any sense. Why would Los Muertos care about a twenty-something kid? They wouldn't, Parker knew, unless they needed to eliminate a loose end. A thread that might lead back to them.

Lynne Finch's intel about other worker crews expected to come across the border echoed in his mind. He could imagine Los Muertos smuggling drugs, money, conscripted farm laborers, sex workers, or gang hitmen over the border. Those were commodities to Castaneda. How did a trailer filled with college-aged men fit into the picture?

"Let's talk to our friend in the holding room."

Parker waited while the red-haired security man fumbled with his keys,

146

trying to find the right one for the lock. It testified to the rare use of the hospital holding room. Red unlocked the door and pushed it open, revealing an empty room.

Parker brushed past the security man and the ambulance driver was gone.

It wasn't difficult to figure out what happened. Plaster, dust, and pieces of broken ceiling panels were scattered on the table in the center of the room. A chair stacked on top of the table gave the fugitive a boost up into the plumbing chase hidden above the thin acoustic panel ceiling.

Parker jumped up onto the table and found a three-foot square utility channel, easily large enough for a man to crawl through.

As Parker reached up to the bottom lip of the channel, one of the security men called out. "Got him."

Parker clambered down from the table and bolted from the holding room. The older, pot-bellied security man pointed at the monitor in front of him. "There."

Parker watched the screen. The image displayed was the front entrance of the hospital from inside the lobby and waiting room.

"Is this real-time?" Parker asked.

"It is."

Parker pushed out of the security office and ran down the back corridor hallway toward the main lobby. Linda was steps behind him.

They crashed through the double doors spilling into the lobby, and the doors banged off the stops, causing everyone on the lobby to freeze and look for the source of the loud disruption in the usually quiet place.

Parker scanned the lobby and none of the faces he saw looked like the man in the video.

Linda pointed. "There. Outside."

Parker and Linda rushed to the hospital doors and pushed them open in time to spot the fleeing man hop into a car pulling to the curb. A familiar dark blue sedan.

"Stop," Parker called out.

The man turned and closed the car door.

The deep blue Ford Crown Vic shot away from the curb as the detectives closed.

Parker watched the same vehicle he spotted at Sutton's law offices spirit the ambulance driver away.

"There goes our chance to find Castaneda," Linda said.

"He was never going to lead us back to Castaneda."

"What are the chances we'll ever see him again?" Linda asked.

"Los Muertos and Castaneda don't leave loose ends dangling."

"We're back to square one again?"

"I've seen the car before—the one our ambulance driver escaped in. It's the same one waiting for us when we left Larry Sutton's office. What I can't wrap my head around is why the FBI is behind this?"

"The FBI? That's the car?"

He nodded. "Shit just got weird, didn't it?"

"Can Lynne tell us what's going on?"

"I don't know. If she knew about a fed connection to the case, enough to rescue the ambulance driver, I think she'd tell us."

"Would she? I mean, you two have a challenging history. And by challenging, I'm trying to be diplomatic here. She hasn't come around to trust you again after everything."

"After I saved her ass from a bomb planted under her car?"

"Which she blames on you for having it put there, to begin with. No, I mean you as a person. You let your relationship with her wither and die. She hasn't forgotten, and it explains how standoffish she is when you meet with her."

"She's over it. We're in a better place now."

"You might be—her, I'm not convinced."

"You're saying she's withholding information from us because we broke up? I don't buy it."

"One way to find out…"

"You want me to go confront my ex and claim she's purposely tanking our case because she's butt-hurt?"

"Something like that."

"Lynne wouldn't do that. She's the Assistant Agent in Charge of the whole Phoenix office. She wouldn't put her job on the line to get back at me. That'd be some high school-level stuff there."

"I'm just saying. I know how it looks from my perspective and she's not telling you the whole story."

Parker rocked on the balls of his feet for a moment. Linda had a point. Why would the FBI help a suspect escape? She owed him an explanation, at least. Lynne played her cards close to the vest when it came to her professional life, but she'd never outright lied to him before.

"Fine."

"Fine, what?" Linda said.

"Time to clear the air with Lynne and find out what she's been holding back."

Chapter Twenty-Five

After stopping in the security office, Parker dropped Linda off at the Major Crimes Unit. He thought it would be better to approach Lynne without a wing-woman. Linda agreed and said they needed to clear the air without her as an excuse to leave things unsaid.

Parker headed to the FBI offices and called ahead this time. Lynne's protective assistant wouldn't commit to carving out a few minutes in her boss's busy schedule.

"Tell her to make time," Parker said before he hung up. He was starting to get an acid feeling in his gut—the warning telling him he was headed into the lion's den.

Parker arrived in Lynne's outer office. The haughty demeanor of Lynne's assistant was gone. She looked slightly shell-shocked and didn't flinch with Parker's appearance. "She's waiting for you."

Parker entered, and Lynne wasn't alone. Two suits and a tall, thin man with a bandaged hand stood near Lynne's desk.

"You want to tell me what the hell is going on?" Parker said.

"Nathan, this is Assistant Director Hansen from Homeland Security, she gestured to a man in a dark blue suit with a military-style brush cut. He had the bearing of a former military commander.

"Parker," the Homeland boss said with no effort to shake his hand.

"You want to explain this guy?" Parker jutting his thumb at the tall, thin man wearing an EMT jacket."

"Nathan, I—"

"We don't have to explain a thing to you, boy," the homeland executive

150

said.

"Oh, I think you do."

The man pulled his jacket open and rested his hands on his slim hips. "Here's all the explanation you need. You are interfering with a federal investigation. Back off."

"Or what?" Parker shot back.

"Or you find yourself in federal custody."

"I'd like to see you try."

Lynne pounded a fist on her desk. "Gentlemen! Zip up your flies and sit down, all of you."

Parker waited for a moment before he lowered himself onto one of the sofas in the office.

"All right, Lynne. What's going on?"

"You've stumbled into a complex investigation here, Nathan. Homeland's been running an op for nearly a year."

"What does this op have to do with stealing a comatose patient from Banner Memorial?" Parker glanced at the phony EMT.

"That's on a need-to-know basis," The head fed said.

"Since the man is a victim from my crime scene, I'd say I have a right to know."

"Not your crime scene, or your case. We've taken over on the basis of national security. And the patient is a person of interest."

"A person of—what? You can't act like a seagull, swoop in, and crap on my case before you steal it. And how is a comatose college kid a person of interest in my murder investigation?"

Lynne interrupted, "Because he's a material witness."

"You had an informant in the container? I find it hard to believe. If you did, it means you're as bad as the truck driver who left him for dead."

Hansen glared at Lynne for revealing his secret.

"Where did they come from?" Parker asked.

"I can't tell you," Hansen pointed at Lynne, "and neither will you. This is way more important than a truckload of illegals getting caught in the wheels of a bigger machine—a criminal machine we're finally getting some traction against."

The phony EMT finally spoke up. "Listen, man, I know you don't like having someone else snake your case, but this is way too important to let local cops get caught in the middle."

"Give us a little credit, would you? How did the media get wind of your top-secret program and leak your man's name, Armando DeSilva?"

"That's not his name, but we're trying to run it down now. The leak is what made us jump in and risk moving him in his present condition," the Homeland man said.

Parker pressed up from the couch. "Well, this is nice and all, but I have a killer to catch. Someone's responsible for the deaths of twenty-seven men, and you're acting like it's collateral damage."

"I'm sorry, but we won't allow it."

"Allow it? You pompous piece of—"

"Enough," Lynne yelled.

"Nathan. The DOJ has already confirmed with your Sheriff. The investigative reigns have been passed. For reasons you may not understand."

"Try me."

Parker's cell phone rang, and the number was Captain Morris's direct line.

The homeland man grinned, "You probably want to take that call."

Parker stabbed the accept button. "Parker."

"Detective Parker, I'm in the Sheriff's office right now and there are new developments on the cargo container investigation."

"So I'm learning."

"Homeland Security will be taking point. There is an organized crime investigation they have in play, and this cargo box figures into their game plan."

"We're supposed to ignore the twenty-seven dead men and pretend like it never happened?"

"Detective, the cargo box deaths are theirs, the survivor, who I've come to learn is a material witness, is theirs. The box, the container, and the trailer—theirs. Understand?"

CHAPTER TWENTY-FIVE

"I understand."

"All right, when you're done over there messing with those assholes, get back here. We need to talk."

The call disconnected and Parker shoved it in his pocket and didn't remove his balled fist.

"Nathan, this case—this case could be a big one. The levels of violence on both sides of the border have increased, and we know the primary source." Her eyes glinted. He'd seen this look before, and it never came with good news.

"Primary source? You make it sound like there's only one criminal faction in play."

"Only one has transnational reach. Only one has a web of connections into all of the Cartels."

"Sounds like you're talking about Los Muertos," Parker said. A tight feeling gathered in his chest.

Lynne didn't respond right away, and Parker knew he was right.

"Los Muertos doesn't tolerate dissension in the ranks. They're compartmentalized, and their soldiers don't know what the rest of the organization is doing. If you turned one of those hitters you intercepted at the border. He's not going to give you enough to take down Los Muertos."

"It has to do with the two gang members found crossing the border. We have a source. He gave them up, proving his reliability. Remember, these two had photos of you and Miguel. This informant may have saved your lives."

"You know how these people work. Those two hitters were disposable. If they want to come after me, taking them off the board isn't going to change a thing."

"I think it might. We have certain assurances."

"I don't see how…"

Lynne tapped the intercom button on her desk phone. "Please show him in."

"Nathan, their CI, has a structured immunity deal for his testimony. Don't let your emotions cloud your judgment.

Parker thought it was an odd admonition coming from Lynne. Until the door opened.

Esteban Castaneda strode into the office.

Parker jumped from the sofa and lunged for the killer. The phony EMT and the second Homeland Security man blocked him and pushed him back.

"What the hell is he doing here?" Parker said.

"Mr. Castaneda is a cooperating witness in our federal investigation," the head fed said.

"He's a murderer."

"Am I? Detective Parker, I thought you needed evidence to make such allegations," Castaneda said from behind his federal protectors.

"You killed my partner. What you did to Miguel in the desert. You're a rabid dog."

"Nathan—Nathan," Lynne said, getting Parker's attention.

"You can't be serious, Lynne."

"This came from above my level, Nathan. He's been given immunity on all past offenses, as long as he continues to cooperate."

"McMillan's murder? That's not possible."

"Mr. Castaneda has provided valuable information to us and enabled our team to disrupt Cartel shipments, confiscate a large weapons cache, and he gave us the two Los Muertos gunmen coming for you," Hansen said.

"The gunmen he sent. Can't you see what he's doing?"

"He's enabled us to take down networks we didn't even know existed. The Cartels are weakened as a result."

"Is that supposed to make McMillan's widow feel better? Her husband's killer walks free because he gives up a few of his disposable soldiers."

"He's done more than give up low-hanging fruit."

"He's using you to bring down his competition. Can't you see?"

"Please, Detective, where's your sense of fair play and justice?" Castaneda said with a used car salesman's smile.

"Were fair play and justice involved when you left my partner to bleed out on the side of some godforsaken road?"

"It's unfortunate what happened to your partner. But are you certain it was me? From what I've seen of the dash cam footage, there is nothing to show I had anything to do with it."

"I saw you on the video. You were there."

"I never said I wasn't. But wasn't alone out there."

"Don't try to lay this off on one of your flunkies. His blood is on your hands."

"Why don't you ask your friend, Billie Carson?" Castaneda said.

"What does Billie have to do with any of this?"

"I find it odd she disappeared the second a name was attached to our witness," Hansen said.

"You're saying Billie was with you the night McMillan died?" Parker asked, ignoring the Homeland Security man's probe.

Castaneda shrugged. "You could ask her—oh right, she's disappeared. She has a habit of running off when what she's done closes in around her."

Parker's head spun. Billie was there? No, she wouldn't have been there when Mac was murdered. She said he didn't go on the coyote run with Castaneda and wished it had turned out differently. Doubt crept in. Was Billie there? If Castaneda didn't murder McMillan, then it meant only one other option.

Lynne recognized Parker's dilemma. "Nathan, the grand jury laid down an indictment for Billie Carson this morning. For the murder of deputy McMillan."

Chapter Twenty-Six

Parker stormed out of Lynne's office. She called after him, and he heard Castaneda chuckle as he hit the door. Air. He needed air. The walls pressed down on him, suffocating and crushing the air out of his lungs.

He shoved the doors open and stepped into the heat. Parker bent over a planter and threw up. He was shaking and braced himself on the concrete barrier. His mind swirled, replaying every conversation he'd ever had with Billie over the years. Was it all one big lie? A lie to cover up what she'd done?

The dry desert air wasn't thick enough, and he found himself hyperventilating to get a full breath. He hadn't felt these anxiety attacks since the days immediately after McMillan's murder. Seeing Castaneda walk away from the murder brought it all back like his partner's blood was fresh on his hands.

Billie? She swore she wasn't there. Now, she was indicted for the murder and slipped away over the border. Was it a relief supply trip, or was she on the run again?

Parker closed his eyes and the last moments from the fateful evening came flowing back.

"Got one coming my direction. Dark blue panel van riding low. He's not turning around like the others," McMillan said over the radio.

"Nah. A coyote wouldn't be this stupid. Probably a construction worker heading out to Anthem. I'll chase him back out," Parker replied.

Parker heard a click and static over the radio two minutes later.

"Mac? 10-9," Parker said, asking for McMillan to repeat the message.

Another click in response. The hills and washes in this section of the desert caused garbled radio traffic.

"Come again, Mac?"

Parker never heard another word from Mac.

In the months since, Parker blamed himself for his partner's death, ruminating over every possible decision made that night. Everything he thought he knew was a lie.

Parker grabbed his cell and jabbed the buttons for Billie's number once again. There had to be an explanation. The call rang three times before a voice answered.

"Dad?" Miguel said.

"Where are you? What are you doing with Billie's phone? You're not with her, are you? You promised..."

"Whoa, slow down. I'm at the Coalition office. Billie left her phone in the bottom drawer of her desk. She must have forgotten to take it with her."

He couldn't tell Miguel what Billie had done. Miguel had relied on her and she was responsible for his recovery in large part. She was there when Parker wasn't.

"I need you to think, Miguel. Did Billie say anything before she left?"

"It was strange, you know? She read the thing in the paper about one guy who survived the cargo container, and she said she needed to get on the road."

"Say where she was headed?"

"Not specifically. It's probably Hermosillo. She always stops there because of the people she knew in town."

"Think carefully. Did she say anything you thought was out of character?"

"She was rattled after the newspaper article. Kept saying the man's name over and over Armando, Armando. It was like she knew the name. Then when I was asking her if I could come along, she said something I didn't understand. She said she couldn't make it right. Whatever right was supposed to be. Do you know what she meant?"

Parker was starting to believe he did, and it all tied back to the night out

157

on an isolated stretch of Rocky Wash. "I don't know, Miguel." He hated to lie to the kid but telling him outright that Billie ran away might crush him.

"I think Billie's in trouble," is all Parker would say over the phone.

"What kind of trouble?"

"Los Muertos kind of trouble. Miguel, I need you to look around the office and see if you can figure out where she went. Leaving her phone behind worries me."

"She ran out of here so fast she forgot a lot of things. The phone and everything wasn't loaded up for the trip south. Most of the supplies are still piled up here in the office."

She was on the run. If it was a relief trip, she would have taken the medical supplies with her. Billie, what have you done?

"Listen, I need you to be extra careful. Keep an eye out for what's going on around you. Anything odd, you call me, understand?"

"Yeah, I understand. What's going on?"

"I don't know for sure, but if Los Muertos is involved, we all need to be extra careful."

"Billie's not involved in Los Muertos," Miguel said. Parker was silent on his end of the call.

"She's not. She can't be. Billie hates those guys."

"I know. Is Leon still there with you?"

"Yeah, he's here."

"Good. The both of you keep an eye out for one another. I'll meet you at home later, okay?"

"Yeah, okay. Billie's not involved with those guys. I know it."

"Yeah, buddy. I hope not, either. Some fed types seem to think otherwise."

Parker told Miguel he was going to drop by Billie's trailer and see if she left behind a clue that could tell where she'd run.

The FBI office was not far from the north end of the valley, a twenty-minute ride to Billie's camp near Rocky Wash.

A half mile of yellow road dust clung to Parker's windshield, and every jolt from the washboard road surface turned the dial up on his anxiety. Why here? Why did Billie's most recent campsite end up on Rocky Wash near where McMillan died? The connection was too much to think about. Parker slammed his hand on the steering wheel until his palm stung.

He rounded a familiar corner and spotted the makeshift memorial. Two white wooden strips fastened together in a rustic cross. The very spot where McMillan died. Parker never knew who erected the memorial, but he'd tacked a photo of his partner to the vertical stake. He'd visited once in a while to ask for forgiveness. He didn't think Mac's widow even knew the memorial existed.

He stopped at the site and waited for the dust to blow past before opening the door. Parker spotted a slip of paper flicking in the slight warm breeze blowing up the canyon. He circled around his truck and stood in front of the cross. A folded paper was impaled on a rusty nail.

Pulling the paper off, Parker unfolded it. A Note.

"Don't come looking for me. I'm sorry, but I gotta do this." It was signed simply, Billie.

Parker held the note at his side. Billie was on the run.

He folded the note and stuffed it in his shirt pocket before getting back behind the wheel. A glance at McMillan's memorial in his rear-view mirror was a punch in the gut. Billie knew he'd come out here, and she couldn't leave Parker the message in person.

Another five miles and Parker found Billie's campsite. Her trailer was gone. She'd left behind a pair of ratty folding chairs, where she and Parker had a few beers together. The fire pit ring was there, along with three bags of aluminum cans for the next trip to the recycler. There was a strong sewage odor from where Billie dumped the trailer's tank before hitting the road. Billie did mention the complaints about sewage dumping and he supposed this was her parting thoughts on the subject.

There were three other trailers and camps within visual range. A well-trod dirt path between the campsites said there was a community here as opposed to a collection of off the grid loners.

Parker followed the trail to the closest RV, a thirty-year-old travel trailer listing to one side from a broken suspension. As he knocked on the thin metal door he spotted a shadow drift away from the dust-covered window.

"Sheriff's Office."

"What do you want?" A thin, reedy voice called out from behind the door.

"Can I talk to you about Billie Carson?"

"Billie's good people. Don't be bothering her."

"I'm Detective Parker."

"Harold Miller," the man said. "What you want with Billie?"

"She's gone. Wondered if you might know why she picked up and left."

There was a metal scrape from the lock as the thin man opened the door. He wore an yellow-white tank top and pajama bottoms, both four sizes too large for the balding older man.

"I seen her leave. She knows when the heat is about to come down. Those cactus-loving environmental nuts are all about mother nature until they learn a developer will pay them big bucks to go away quietly."

"What time did Billie pick up and go?"

"Not long. Maybe a couple hours. That new truck of hers is hard to miss. Backed in, hooked up, and gone. Took her less than ten minutes. Guess she knew the code enforcement people like you was coming."

"I'm not from Code Enforcement. I'm only trying to figure out why Billie ran off. Know where she might go? Her trailer isn't the most road-worthy," Parker said.

"She got new tires and had some work done. Like she knew she was going to need to move. I guess I gotta think about moving my rig out somewhere."

Parker glanced over the man's shoulder. A pair of green oxygen tanks with thin rubber tubing was parked next to the dining table, where an assortment of prescription bottles were strewn. One of the bottles had different colors of pills and capsules mixed together.

"Can I get you some help? You know, someone to pick up your prescriptions, get your oxygen tanks topped off, that kind of thing?"

"I can manage. Been doing it for going on seventy years. I'm not as fast as I once was, and I forget a thing or two, but I'm still able to take care of myself."

Parker had seen the early stages of dementia and Alzheimer's when working in a patrol district dominated by retirement communities. When people began isolating, skipping medication doses, or mixing them like Miller, the outcomes were never good.

"I can have someone come out and give you a hand."

"Not necessary," Miller said.

Parker nodded to the prescription bottles. "You have a lot of meds back there. Everything okay?"

"If by okay you mean COPD, kidney failure, and hepatitis, then yeah, everything's peachy."

"Sorry to hear that. Sure sounds like you could use some help. Maybe a doctor's visit to make sure you're doing everything you're supposed to..."

Miller rubbed the salt and pepper stubble on his chin. "Suppose it wouldn't hurt none to get my tanks refilled. Been going on a week without any oxygen. Makes it hard at night, especially."

"I'll make a call and get someone to take care of it for you."

Parker spotted a bulky black object on the table behind the pill bottles. "You have a satellite phone?"

Miller glanced over his shoulder. "Yeah. Don't have no one to call, though. Billie left it before she split."

"She say why?"

"Said she wasn't gonna need it no more."

Parker's skin prickled despite the heat. Billie was cutting off all ties. She pulled up and left with any tether to her life severed. Someone who knew the land, the migrant trails over the border, and how to survive in the harsh Sonoran desert meant if she went underground, no one would find her. It looked like that was exactly what Billie wanted.

Chapter Twenty-Seven

Parker's mood grew dark as he made the drive back to Major Crimes. He'd called Linda and told her to gather Tully and Johns for a meeting as soon as he could get there. When she asked what it was about, he responded sharply, saying, "Just get it done," and hung up.

He immediately regretted the outburst. Linda didn't deserve to get caught on the receiving end. He'd find a way to make it up to her—eventually.

When Parker arrived, the three detectives were waiting. From the tense expressions, Linda must have passed on the pissy communication.

They followed him in the office and he gestured for Johns to close the door behind him. For a supervisor with an open-door policy, Tully and Johns looked at one another and knew all was not happy in the kingdom.

"All right. Where do I start?" Parker rubbed his face. The three detectives were standing and tense.

"Have a seat. We're gonna be here a while."

Tully cut through the tension. "This ass chewing for something we did, or something we didn't do?"

Parker had to smile.

"Nobody's getting an ass chewing. At least not you guys. Okay, the feds are big footing our cargo container case. I got back from a meeting at FBI where Lynnette Finch and a suit from Homeland laid it all out. They don't want us meddling in these murders because it looks like they are linked to an organized crime investigation of theirs."

"RICO?" Johns asked, meaning the Racketeer Influenced and Corrupt Organizations statutes used to prosecute mafia and prison gang members.

"They didn't use the word, but it sounds like where they're going."

"Well, ain't that the nun's balls," Tully said.

"I had a quick conversation with Captain Morris, and he's confirmed it. We are off the cargo container investigation."

"Let me guess, their focus isn't on these murders, but on getting an indictment on some midlevel gang members?" Johns said.

Parker nodded. "They are convinced they have an informant working for them who will give them enough to take down Los Muertos."

"I like the last part, but what are they giving up to get their intel?" Tully asked.

Parker exhaled.

"Too much. Way too much."

"Nathan, what is it?" Linda said.

"They have given their informant qualified immunity in exchange for giving up what he knows about Los Muertos and other organized crime activity."

"If Los Muertos gets wind of the deal, the informant won't last long," Johns said.

"I'd agree if the informant wasn't Esteban Castaneda."

"Are you shitting me?" Tully said.

"No flipping way," Johns countered.

"They had him there at the meeting when they ordered me to stand down. Threatening obstruction and the usual get-in-line rhetoric."

"Wait, they had Castaneda in custody?" Johns said.

"He was there. And not in custody. The immunity order includes all past crimes he's alleged to have committed."

"But not—"

"McMillan's murder included."

"They can't be serious. Are they willing to forgive a cop killer in exchange for some mid-level drug dealers? That's all Castaneda would hand over."

Parker nodded. He felt heavy and exhausted. He plopped behind his desk. "The feds are tunnel-vision focused on making a dent in the organized crime spawned from Los Muertos and the cartels. The head Homeland

Security guy didn't care about anything else and had another theory about McMillan's murder."

"Another theory?"

"Castaneda admitted being there the night McMillan was killed.

"No shit. We all saw him on the dash cam." Tully said.

"He's claiming he wasn't alone."

"Big surprise, he's going to give up some low-level slug to save his own ass."

"The feds have already run with his account of the events and gotten an indictment from a federal grand jury for the alleged killer."

"Well, there's that." He caught Parker's expression. Wait, what aren't you saying?" Tully said.

"It's Billie Carson," Parker said.

"No way," Tully said.

"That's way out of Billie's character. She couldn't do that," Linda said.

"I know. I know. What I can't make sense of is Billie's disappearance. She saw the name of the survivor leaked in the news and split. The minute Billie saw the name, she dropped everything and ran. It doesn't look good."

"Why would she run? She must have been threatened somehow?" Linda said.

"I tried calling her, but she's left her phone behind. She didn't even take the relief supplies to Hermosillo. Once she saw the name in the newspaper, Miguel said she started acting strange, jumped in her truck, and split."

"She can't have gone far," Tully said.

"Maybe. I'd usually agree, but I dropped by her place and the trailer is gone. She pulled up stakes and left. The neighbor said she was in a hurry."

"What do we do?" Johns said. "About the twenty-seven dead, the murdered truck driver, Low Muertos money laundering through the strip club, and now Billie Carson? What's our next step?"

"I'm ordered to go see the Captain as soon as I got here, but I needed you all to hear this first. The feds made it clear we're hands off on all of this. When I spoke with the Captain, he gave me a crack. He was very specific we were no longer investigating the cargo box murders. He said the container, the victims, the survivor, and the trailer were all theirs."

"What about—"

"That's what I'm going to see Captain Morris about. The truck driver's murder wasn't mentioned, and neither was the trail of money laundering coming out of the strip club. I'm also concerned with what's happening at the West Valley Machine business—although our intel on that one came from Billie, so we need some corroboration on what they're actually shipping out."

"You think they'll let us continue on these threads? They're awfully close to what the feds are pulling on?" Johns said.

That's what I'm gonna go find out. Until then, keep pushing on the Coyle Tech connection—there's an odd vibe about the place. The trucker and the money laundering are still on the table. For now…"

Parker entered the Captain's outer office, and his receptionist, Kerri, glanced up and lowered her pencil. "Detective. You've been a topic of discussion here today."

"Not my idea, I assure you. The boss in?" he asked, pointing to the office door.

"He is, and he's been expecting you."

"Bad mood?"

"I wouldn't want to spoil the surprise," she said.

Parker rapped on the door once and entered.

"Captain."

"Detective, what have you gotten us in the middle of?"

"It wasn't my intention, sir."

Captain Morris stood from behind his desk and strode around, leaning on the front edge.

"I know it wasn't. I hate it when the feebs push their way in and cherry-pick the cases they think they can get good press from. Why this one? Part of me wishes them good riddance, and I can't wait to tell the media to go talk to them when they ask what we're doing about twenty-seven murders."

"It doesn't look like those deaths figure into their game plan. They want the organized crime connection to the men in the container. That's all."

"They're going to have to answer to the press about those deaths. They can't brush them aside. You think the community activists thought we were profiling? Wait until they hear the feds aren't even looking at the murders."

"Lynne sprung it on me. This Homeland Security honcho comes off as another hardass bean counter who wants to report how many pounds of cocaine, or the number of low-level drug dealers they've taken off the streets. How safe we are now because they're on the job."

"They have an informant who I don't like one bit. I don't trust Castaneda to not sell them what they want to hear to save his own ass," Morris said.

"Exactly. If Castaneda is giving up cartel and organized crime connections, it's only because it benefits him. If he had to sacrifice a few of his guys in the process, he'd do it in a heartbeat."

"And the A.G.'S office was willing to let him slide on the murder of our deputy. Unfucking believable," Morris said.

"Homeland let it slip this is qualified immunity."

"Which means their rat has to deliver on his promise."

"Exactly right."

"What are you thinking, Detective?"

"If I understood you on the phone call earlier, my instructions are to stay away from the deaths in the cargo container, the container itself, the lone survivor, and the trailer."

"Yes," the Captain nodded and stared back at him."

"Understood, sir. We have other cases which need our attention. The criminal ecosystem being what it is, there may be some overlap, and some of our persons of interest might be related."

The captain nodded. "There's more crime in this valley than some fed taskforce can handle. We're going to continue to do our job, and they can deal with it. If you happen to solve their cases for them, that's the way it goes sometimes."

"Very well, sir. I'll keep you informed if we run into any entanglements."

"Try to be diplomatic, Parker."

"When have I ever not?"

CHAPTER TWENTY-SEVEN

The Captain lowered his chin and looked over his glasses at Parker.

"Thanks for your time, sir."

Parker left the Captain's office and waved to the receptionist as he passed. His cell buzzed in his pocket.

"Parker, here," he said as he walked. He didn't recognize the caller ID.

"Nathan, I think we should talk."

Parker recognized the voice. Special Agent Espinoza of the Drug Enforcement Administration.

"Espi. What's happening?"

"I came across something that doesn't make sense. It involves you."

"I'm not surprised. I just came from a meeting with some of your friends at the FBI and Homeland. I'm not on their Christmas lists anymore."

"That's what I hear. In fact, it was Lynne who called me."

"Lynne named me as persona non grata so I'm sure she wanted to share the good news with you."

"I don't think she had a choice. What I hear is Homeland is running this op, and she was told to get in line."

"Whatever. She can be a good little soldier, and Homeland lets a murderer walk. Any event, I'm out."

"Remember where we faced off with your Cartel buddy running undocumented migrants over the border?"

"The train tracks running alongside Grand? How could I forget? Damn near started a Sinaloa and Juarez Cartel war."

"Come meet me at the market on the corner. You need to hear this before you walk into a trap."

Chapter Twenty-Eight

Parker pulled up to the Mercado Centro, a small mom-and-pop market catering to the Latino population in La Mirage. The tiny market brought a little flavor from home, whether it be Mexico, Colombia, or the Central American nations in between. The place served as an anchor to the world these people left behind. It was also, as Parker discovered, a hub for moving undocumented migrants once they crossed the border.

A small brass bell sounded as Parker entered. An older grey-headed shopkeeper wearing a stiff green apron tilted his head to the back room. Parker thanked him and parted the thick canvas curtain separating the space.

Espinosa sat at a table in the back room, which served as a combination market pantry and migrant bunkhouse.

"Brings back old memories, eh?" Espi said.

"You could say that. Last time we were here, it was a bit more—occupied," Parker said, glancing at the empty bunks.

Espi sipped from a small white China cup. "Want one? The old man has an amazing espresso machine."

Parker pulled a mismatched chair to the table and joined the DEA man.

"What's so important you couldn't tell me over the phone. I know Lynne and her new Homeland playmate want me out of the loop. What gives?"

Espi's hand curled around the tiny cup. "Lynne called me about your face to face with Castaneda."

"Let me guess. She wants you to make sure I don't kill the guy before he gives up what he knows about every petty crime south of the border."

"It did come up. But it's not why she called. She doesn't like Homeland swooping in any more than you do. It wasn't her idea to grant immunity to Castaneda. She thought parading him out like they did was—well—an asshole move."

"Okay, it wasn't Lynne's idea. Doesn't change a thing. Are we done?"

"The immunity deal was a shitty thing to do when it came to McMillan. He and his family don't deserve it."

Parker didn't need to respond to Espi's commentary. He was leading up to something.

"Castaneda decided to come in from the cold because he didn't have any other choice. He's being pushed out by others in Los Muertos. He figures if he rats on them, he'll give the feds what they want and strengthen his standing in Los Muertos."

"Sounds like him. Playing both ends. Who's in line to take over Los Muertos if Castaneda goes down?"

"The guy makes Pablo Escobar look like a boy scout. His name's Ramon Echevarría. Came up through the Los Zetas Cartel then went freelance with Castaneda. We hear he's unhappy with Castaneda's hands-off approach on expansion north and doesn't like the way Los Muertos acts as hired muscle for the Sinaloa Cartel. Goes back to the Sinaloa and Los Zetas history and the massacre at Loredo. Anyway, this guy wants to make a name for himself."

"Sounds like a prince. Castaneda is desperate, and the feds know it. They're milking him for all he's worth. Doesn't change a thing."

"His immunity deal. It's not as ironclad as he thinks. He has to give up Echevarría and his network to pull it off. It's a desperate move and if the Los Muertos structure falls apart on its own, then Castaneda loses his leverage."

"What's the chance of that happening?"

"Funny you should ask. There are people aligned with the Sinaloa Cartel who don't want to see Los Muertos turn into a hostile rival, competing for control over trafficking routes. In fact, you know one of them."

"No one would win in the battle. Lots of innocent people would get caught in the crossfire. Who's trying to broker the peace?"

"Not peace as much as to not lose what they have. And Castaneda has nothin' to give up."

"If he's cut out of Los Muertos, he can't give it up to the feds."

"And his deal goes out the window."

"Who's this we're talking about? You're being kinda precious about it. Spill it," Parker said.

"Turns out Castaneda's girlfriend didn't know about his deal with the feds and he dropped her like a hot rock. You've actually met her. Carmen Delgado, the former PIO for your department."

"Carmen? The same Carmen who set me up on a murder beef and nearly got me killed by the Sinaloa cartel? That Carmen?"

"She surfaced in the Sinaloa compound near Hermosillo. The intelligence we have is she's trying to push the Cartel to eliminate Echevarría as a threat to the Cartel. She's promised an allegiance to them, if she's put in charge. She's not happy with her now ex-boyfriend and is asking the Cartel to take him out too."

"She is a sweetheart, that one. You know you can't trust her."

"Which is why we're not dealing with her. We're watching, but it looks like she's likely to come out on top, if she can pull this off before Castaneda gives it all away."

"I'd say let them destroy one another," Parker said.

"Here's the rub, though. If Echevarría gets pulled under, Castaneda will be next. When it happens, the Sinaloa Cartel will solidify its stranglehold over the territory and the people caught up in the system. Carmen seems to have promised forced labor to move more product over the border."

"Using the undocumented as the smugglers so the cartel's people are out of harm's way. Those people are going to die in the process. We've seen it before. They'll be forced to pay for passage or carry backpacks full of the Cartel's drugs. Families of the smugglers will be held hostage as insurance."

"That's what the intel is saying. Unless Castaneda stays in play."

Parker's head spun with the possibilities. Part of him wanted to let the criminal gangs fight it out and kill one another. But the innocents—the people living in the squatters camps on the outskirts of Hermosillo—they would pay the price. He'd seen them with his own eyes with Billie. Billie. She wasn't going to help them because she was running from her own ghosts.

"What's this all mean?"

Espy pushed his empty cup aside. "Echevarría is going down. Sinaloa will be appeased, and Carmen will step in. Castaneda has the information the feds need to take her down and what's left of Los Muertos."

"Okay. What has this got to do with me? I'm on the outs here, remember?

"You. My friend, need to make sure Esteban Castaneda stays alive."

Chapter Twenty-Nine

"You want me to keep Castaneda alive?" Parker asked. "Are you out of your mind? That man—that animal killed my partner in cold blood. You knew McMillan. You expect me to go out of my way and keep him alive so he can leak questionable intel to the feds?"

"It's the only way we get to bring Castaneda and his entire operation down."

"What about his immunity deal, remember?"

"They didn't give him the total immunity he thought he bargained for. It's use immunity only. His testimony can't be used to incriminate him. If he's out of the loop in the Los Muertos structure because Carmen has pushed him out, his intel becomes stale and useless because the first thing Carmen will do is root out anyone aligned with him and hide the rest. He won't be able to give up what he doesn't know, and his deal will fall apart. Then he's ours for McMillan's murder."

Parker sat back in the wooden chair. "You don't know what you're asking, Espi."

"I do, and Lynne does, too."

"I don't know if I can do that. Keep him alive. I'd feel like I was betraying McMillan's memory."

"Think of it as the only way we'll get Castaneda in handcuffs and in front of a jury to answer for McMillan's murder. And we take down what's left of Los Muertos before Carmen can solidify her standing with the Cartel. We have to do this, Nathan."

Parker stood. "I don't have to do a damn thing. The feds ordered me off the case. Lynne made her play siding with Homeland. I understand what she needed to do for her career. But I don't have to bend over and take it. No, Castaneda is on his own. He deserves everything coming his way. I'm out."

Espy got up from his chair. "I'll give you time to think about it. I know it's a lot. When it happens, it will happen fast. Echevarría goes down soon. Castaneda will be next."

"Don't bother. You want to save that worthless prick? Have at it. I won't." Parker said and strode from the back room.

The old man nodded as Parker passed. A signal he knew what the argument was about? Or about what was at risk?

Parker climbed into his Explorer and drove off, kicking up loose asphalt in the parking lot. He needed to clear his head. The first person who popped in his mind was McMillan. Letting his killer walk was unforgivable. If he did nothing and let Castaneda spill his secrets, he'd literally get away with murder. And to make it worse, Espi expected him to make sure Castaneda stayed alive to do it.

He flashed back to that night. McMillan bleeding out in his arms was one of the worst moments of his life. The hardest was telling McMillan's pregnant wife he wasn't coming home.

That night, Ellie answered the door and smiled when she saw Parker, a smile that fell when she caught the expression on his face, She knew right away. Her hands went to her belly, shielding their unborn child from what was unfolding.

"Ellie, can I come in?" Parker asked.

Silently, she held the door for Parker and a departmental chaplain.

Parker took one of her hands. "I'm so sorry, Ellie."

She collapsed on the sofa and wept. Parker sat next to her and held her hand. He wept for his friend and partner along with her.

After a quiet fifteen minutes, she squeezed his hand. "Tell me what happened."

Parker's throat was constricted. He wasn't sure what to say. He'd delivered death notifications to next of kin dozens of times. This was different This was personal. "He was attacked."

Her face tightened, and her eyes clamped shut. Knowing it wasn't a random car accident made it even more real to her.

"Was he alone?"

"No," Parker said quickly. "I was with him."

She nodded and swiped a tear away. "He never knew…"

Parker waited out her silence.

"He never knew we were having a baby girl."

Parker snapped back from the memory. It felt like it happened minutes ago, and he was reliving the night again. Over five years had passed since McMillan's murder, and that fateful night was one never-ending replay in his mind.

He pulled the Explorer to the curb. He didn't have any recall of driving the five miles from the market to Litchfield Park, close to home. It was also where his partner and his wife, Ellie, used to live.

Parker drove by the house and remembered Mac planting the rose bush near the front door because Ellie wanted one despite the searing heat and the water it would require. The rosebush withered, and Parker saw a dry, brittle remnant in the brick planter bed. Two years ago, Parker asked Ellie if she wanted him to do some yard work take the dead rosebush out, and maybe plant something more desert-friendly. She told him no. She wanted to leave the rose where it was. She never said why, but Parker knew. Mac had planted it for her.

Parker pulled to the curb in front of the house. He didn't want to knock on the door. Ellie hadn't said it, but Parker knew every time she saw him, it only reminded her of what she'd lost. He was about to pull away from the curb when Ellie pulled into the driveway in Mac's black Dodge Charger.

Ellie stepped around to the passenger side and unstrapped a tall, gangly red-haired girl from a booster seat. The child was nearly a mirror image of Ellie with shoulder length hair, light complexion and blue eyes. Ellie waved at Parker and spoke to the girl who skipped off to the front door.

A wave from Ellie looked a bit tentative before she walked to Parker's window.

"Hey there. Lexi is waiting inside. She wants a tea party with Uncle Nathan."

"She's getting tall," Parker said.

"Everyday." Ellie patted Parker's arm. "Come on, let's get inside."

Although Parker had been in the house dozens of times since he broke the news to Ellie that night, he couldn't help but remember every single time.

"Uncle Nathan!" Lexi called as she ran and wrapped her arms around him.

"When did you grow up?"

Lexi grabbed his hand and led him to the kitchen, where she had laid out her tea set.

Ellie smiled. "I'll join you two in a minute. I need to get some things from the car."

"Need help?" Parker asked.

"No, I've got it. I'm used to it." She flushed. "I didn't mean that how it sounded. I usually get Lexi after school, get her inside to start on her schoolwork, then get my stuff from the car."

"School work? At her age? What first grade?"

"Kindergarten. And, yes, they start them young at her school."

Lexi was pouring pretend tea for Nathan. "Careful, it's hot."

"Thank you." He took an exaggerated slurp, and Lexi giggled. "Very good."

Ellie came back in with a pink backpack, a messenger bag, and a grocery tote, setting the collection on the counter.

"Lexi, please take your backpack and start coloring the pages Mrs. Lilly gave you."

"After Uncle Nathan finishes his tea."

Parker made a show of downing the imaginary tea and placed the cup back in the little plastic saucer. "Ahhh."

Lexi hopped from the chair, grabbed her backpack from Ellie, and skipped down the hall to her room."

"I wish I had her energy," Parker said.

"Tell me about it."

"How's work at the cube farm?" Ellie was a manager in a corporate sales center and like him, she used the job as a place to keep occupied and away from the hole that had suddenly appeared in her life.

"Fine, but that's not why you're here, is it, Nathan? I can tell by the expression on your face."

Parker looked away from her blue eyes.

"No. I need to ask you something. I don't know what to do. I need you to hear me out and help me figure this out."

"It has to do with Mac, doesn't it?"

He nodded.

"We found the man who—"

"Killed my husband?" She said in a calm, measured voice.

"Yes, and that's where it gets—complicated. Everything we know from that night shows him at the scene. The grand jury finally indicted him two years ago, and now the feds are making a deal with him."

"They aren't going to prosecute Esteban Castaneda for taking my daughter's father away from her, are they?"

"You make it sound like you expected it."

"I never thought they'd find the man."

"They want to give him immunity and let him roll over on other criminals in the network. I don't know what to do, Ellie. I owe it to Mac to keep the pressure on."

"Whatever happens to Castaneda—nothing will bring my husband back. He's gone. My husband, my best friend, the father Lexi never knew—gone. If he dies in prison, or lives out his life running in Mexico, nothing changes."

"He can't get away with what he's done, El."

"What are you asking me, Nathan?"

"They want me to let this animal go free in exchange for giving up some petty criminals. After what he's done—to you and Lexi. I don't know if I can let it happen."

"Are you asking if I forgive him? Because I don't. I never will. I don't care what happens to him. I spent years hating. Hating the man who did

176

this to us, hating the job that caused Mac to lose his life over nothing. I hated everything, and it started to take a toll on everyone around me. Until one day, Lexi asked me why I didn't smile like the other moms. What was I going to say? Because your daddy was taken away from us? I couldn't be a victim anymore. And I couldn't let Lexi suffer for something she had no control over."

"I'm sorry, El."

"Don't be. That little girl saved me. I could have gone down a bitter spiral and she put me in check. Sure, I'd like to think someday I'll be able to forgive what happened, but that ain't happening. It came down to a decision. I'm not giving Castaneda any more power in my life. He's nothing. And I don't care what happens to him."

Parker sat back and assessed the matter of fact, calm demeanor Ellie presented during what he thought would be an emotional outburst.

"I'm not as put together as you are, El. I could have put this guy down once, and I blinked. What the feds are doing is wrong. That man is responsible for hundreds of lives, not just Mac—hundreds. He has to be stopped."

"You didn't murder him, because it's not who you are. You and Mac shared a lot of the same qualities. Compassion, empathy, and a sense of justice. You're not like Castaneda; you're not a killer. Castaneda would like nothing more than to see you fall. You can't give him the satisfaction."

"Still, I can't turn my back on what he's done."

"Fine. But it doesn't have to be you who makes a stand. You're not the only cop in Arizona, you know?"

"I'm not?" Parker said, lightening the mood."

"You might be the best one, but not the only one. See, the thing is, people like Castaneda, they only know power and control, you know? Take that away, and what are they? Nothing. I won't give him my power or my control, and he's nothing to me."

"You think I should let him go?"

"I can't tell you what to think, Nathan. But I know I don't want to see this man turn you into someone you're not. These people always get what's coming to them—they've hurt and damaged so many lives the universe must balance things, you know?"

"I don't know about the whole hippy-dippy universe balancing thing, but I get what you're saying."

Ellie reached over and patted his arm. "Good. Miguel needs you—who you are, not some revenge-seeking shell. You've been a good example for the boy. But maybe you could learn a thing or two from him. You know how much he struggled to get here, losing his family to gang violence in El Salvador, the grueling trek north. Does he obsess every day about getting revenge on everyone who's wronged him?"

"No, you're exactly right. The kid is resilient. He's finishing up junior college if you can believe it. He's passionate about helping others, especially people who share his migrant experience. Thinks he has something to offer there."

"And he couldn't if he was stuck in the past and bent on revenge. Besides, don't they say revenge is a dish best served cold? Let it go, Nathan. Mac wouldn't want you to kill the guy, or make sure bad things happened to him. That wasn't him, and it sure isn't you."

"Mom! Are you coming?" Lexi called from down the hall."

"Duty calls." Ellie got up and looked Nathan in the eye. "Do the right thing—not the easy thing. Isn't that what you told Mac?" She leaned in for a hug.

"Take care, El. Give Lexi a hug from me and tell her it was the best tea ever."

"Will do."

Parker's cell phone rang, and he let himself out the front door while Ellie tended to her daughter's art needs.

The caller ID spelled out 'unknown caller.' Parker hit the connect button. "Parker, here."

Billie Carson's voice carried over a poor connection. "Nathan, I'm in trouble."

Chapter Thirty

"**B**illie, where the hell are you?"

A rustle over the connection, an accented male voice came on the line. "Is this Detective Nathan Parker of the Maricopa County Sheriff's Office?"

"Yes, Detective Parker, here. Who's this?"

"I'm Inspector Lopez of the Policía Federal. Miss Carson has been arrested. She says you know her. In what capacity might that be, Detective?"

"Federales? What did Billie do?"

"One thing at a time, if you don't mind. You know her then, Billie Carson?"

"Yes, yes, I do," Parker said before his mind began shuffling memories and snippets of conversations. Was Billie responsible for McMillan's death like Castaneda said? And why had she run off abruptly?

"Miss Carson's being held at Cereso during her legal proceedings."

"Cereso? Proceeding for what?" The feds couldn't have acted fast enough to pick her up on the federal indictment for McMillan's murder charge.

"Cereso is the main jail here in Hermosillo."

Billie had gone to Hermosillo after all.

"Is she being charged?" Parker asked.

"Arms trafficking. She was found in possession of over fifty handguns and disassembled assault rifles."

"Weapons? She's never been involved in that."

"So you say, but my men stopped her vehicle, and the illegal arms were in her possession."

"Bail?"

"For these serious offenses, and she is considered a flight risk, there is no bail. She will appear before a judge within seventy-two hours."

Parker knew why she called him and not the American consulate. The state department staff would most likely know about the federal grand jury indictment and begin extradition proceedings.

"What can I do to help you, Inspector?" Parker asked.

"Our government does not take kindly to American citizens bringing weapons to our country. Remember your Justice Department's Fast and Furious operation? We remember here in Hermosillo as most of those weapons ended up in the hands of Sinaloa Cartel members. Many were used against our citizens."

"Why are you telling me this? Sounds as if you already have your mind made up."

"You could give the court and me some confirmation the arms were not part of a government-sponsored undercover operation."

"Call the State Department. They weren't part of any operation I'm aware of.

"The court needs assurance on the matter. Testimony from you could help."

The hair on the back of Parker's neck began to tingle.

"I can send the court a letter. I don't see the need to travel to Hermosillo."

"I see. Let me pass on a word from Miss Carson. She said, 'Tell Detective Parker to pick up his truck parts at West Valley Machine.' I don't know what she means by this, but she seems more concerned about your vehicle repairs than her own predicament."

"Tell her thanks. Would you please let me know when a hearing is set?

The Mexican police inspector agreed and hung up. Parker stood in Ellie's driveway, trying to put the pieces together. Billie had fled south only to be arrested by Mexican authorities for gun running. She'd been a coyote before, shuttling people over the border, but guns weren't her usual go-to. He couldn't think of but one time he'd seen her with a firearm—and she saved his life with it. What's with the Western Machine Parts message? She reported seeing boxes with the warning labels printed on the cardboard.

It struck him. Was Billie telling him the machine shop was packing guns and weapons parts in the boxes camouflaged as medical supplies? It made sense on some level, but why would Billie get caught with them in her possession?

Parker climbed into his SUV and started the engine. The AC spit out the first blast of hot, stale air. It was almost suffocating. Parker wondered if that's what those men in the back of the cargo container felt.

Parker glanced at his watch and figured Miguel would be done with the job fair at the college. Hopefully, Leon got a few leads, or an interview after he and Linda made him walk away from his delivery job.

Parker tapped the brakes in a reflex. The delivery job. Leon was driving for the Western Machine Parts business. Billie claimed there were odd markings on boxes coming from the shop, and Leon would deliver them all over the valley. But Billie had been caught running guns down south. How did those two connect?

Parker hit a speed dial button on his phone.

"Wondered when I was going to hear from you," Linda said.

"Sorry about that. I needed to clear up a few things."

"And did you?"

"Not really. Let's say the outlook remains cloudy."

"Well, aren't you the living, breathing Magic 8-Ball."

"I am a little shook up, I suppose."

"Captain Morris pulled us off the case?"

"Yes and no. All you guys still there?"

"Yeah. Barry ran out to pick up a lab report. Said he wanted to grab it in person."

"When he gets back, we all need to have a sit down and assess what we have."

"We're still in the game?"

"Sort of, and it got a little more complicated. Let's meet off-site. My place? I think Miguel and Leon should be there, too."

"The boys? They've been exposed too much already, don't you think?"

"They have. I don't disagree at all. They might have seen something we haven't keyed on yet. Like the Western Machine connection…I'll tell you more when we meet. Can you get Pete and Barry? I'll get Miguel. He and Leon were hanging at the college earlier."

Linda agreed, but Parker heard the reluctance in her voice.

Twenty minutes later, Parker arrived home armed with three pizza boxes. Linda, Barry, and Pete were seated around the kitchen table. Miguel and Leon were playing a video game in the living room. The screeching special effects game sounds were contained in their headphones.

Linda spied the boxes and narrowed her eyes. "Again?"

"Hey, I'm stress eating. Give me a break. Besides, I don't know what everyone likes."

"I could go for vegan Italian," Johns said.

"There's that greasy taco place a mile down the road," Pete said.

"Or, hey, what about the new Pakistani joint, the one with the homemade Gyal," Johns said.

"It's pizza," Parker said, dropping the boxes on the middle of the table between them. "When did you guys become such foodies? Barry, there's a cauliflower crust one in there."

"Thanks. What's the news from the corner office?" Johns asked while taking a paper plate from Parker."

"It's a mixed bag," Parker said, taking an empty chair.

Parker dropped a slice on his paper plate, and the aroma drew Miguel and Leon to the table.

"It's as we thought. The feds have stepped in and are cutting us out of the investigation into the deaths of the twenty-seven. We can't touch them, or the lone survivor, who they claim is a material witness now, and we can't pursue crimes related to the box, or the trailer."

"And they claim a national security privilege and made a deal with Castaneda?" Tully said.

"They did. Here's where it gets a bit more complicated. I met with Espinoza from DEA, you guys remember him, and he explained there is a power struggle within Los Muertos and Castaneda might be making this deal with the feds because he knows he's about to be pushed out."

"Making a deal while he can," Johns said.

"Right, giving up competitors and the factions within Los Muertos who oppose him. He's still trying to remain in control. But the forces against him are winning the battle. They've joined up with the Sinaloa Cartel."

"Things don't look good for Castaneda. I can't say I'm sorry for him." Tully snagged a slice of the cauliflower crust and dropped in on his plate.

"Here's what Espi laid out." Parker explained the move against Echevarría for control of Los Muertos, the planned hit on Castaneda, and Espi's theory that Castaneda couldn't live up to his end of the deal if he was out of power."

"He also can't snitch if he's dead," Tully said.

"If he's killed off, he can't give the feds what they need to dismantle Los Muertos. If Los Muertos and the cartel join up, there will be innocent people caught in the middle."

Miguel chimed in. "We've seen what that partnership has brought in the past. Anyone trying to cross the border will be at their mercy. The camps. They'll grow again with desperate people looking for a way out."

"Some feds I know won't see it as a bad thing. Them and the whole build the wall crowd." Tully said.

"You think some of that sentiment is behind the Castaneda deal?' Linda asked.

Parker glanced at his untouched slice. "Wouldn't be out of the realm of possibility. The Homeland guy was only focused on what he could bring down from Castaneda's testimony."

"Who's behind the merger with Sinaloa?" Barry asked.

"Another tidbit Espi dropped. Remember Carmen Delgado?"

"The department's PIO who ran off after she was implicated in the drug scandal? You can't be serious?" Tully said.

"Turns out she was Castaneda's girl, and his running off to make a deal with the feds kinda rubbed her the wrong way—enough to make her convince the Sinaloa Cartel to put a hit on her ex."

"A woman scorned," Johns said.

"Let that serve as a warning to all of you," Linda said.

"Where does that leave us?" Johns asked.

"My meeting with the Captain left the window open for us to continue the investigation into the trucker's murder. And the money laundering out of the strip club with the Los Muertos connection. It means we can take a look at what's happening in the West Valley Machine Parts back room."

"And Coyle Technology?" Johns asked. "Because I found some weirdness going on after our visit."

"What can we use?" Parker said.

"I don't know yet. I pulled the financials, and since it's a publicly traded company, it's holdings and share values are out there for the world to see. In the last year, Coyle Technology's stock price doubled. Until six months ago. It's lost all of that gain and more."

"It tracks with what we saw out there. Staff layoffs, empty offices. Coyle looked like he was barely hanging on."

"That's the thing. The stock price is down. You'd expect revenue and production to be down. They aren't. Revenue is down, but production, in terms of server online time, is up."

"You're saying they're running at capacity, but getting paid less for it? Not a good business model," Parker said.

"Coyle Technology was one of the employers at the college today," Leon said.

"You get a chance to talk with them?"

"We did. The company wants anyone with an IT major. They weren't looking for coding, or mainframe experience, not even what programming language people had some proficiency with. They seemed—sort of desperate."

"Barry, remember Coyle telling us one of his server farms was down? He could be looking for a quick labor pool to get back online," Parker said.

"The guy we tried to follow from the offices out there in Buckeye, Lee Patterson, he's got a domestic violence protection order on him and a prior arrest for fraud."

"Sounds like the kind of guy I'd want repping my company," Parker said.

"Patterson? He was the recruiter at the college today. Kinda weird if you ask me. I mean, I'm not a techie like Leon, but this guy knew squat about operations," Miguel said.

"Yeah. He was signing people up if they knew anything about tech. He said they would train new hires to learn their proprietary software. The pay wasn't great; no benefit package to speak of. Other tech firms were outbidding them. Did you see that Patterson dude sign anyone?"

"Two, maybe," Miguel said.

"Yeah, sounds about right."

"The photos he had with all the smiling happy people wearing the same uniform made it look like a cult."

"The dark pants and white shirts?"

"Yeah."

"The same dress code as the dead men we found in the container," Tully said.

"But we're hands off when it comes to the cargo container case," Johns said. But, I may have found a way to connect Coyle Technology to our truck driver." He reached down and pulled a file from his briefcase.

"These are the logs our truck driver kept. Pick-ups, drop-offs, and miles driven. The DOT requires drivers to track hours driven to make sure exhausted drivers aren't out there on the road. Anyway, in the last four or five months, our trucker was all over the place. Albuquerque, Nogales, El Paso, San Diego, but for a guy everyone thought was a long-haul driver, look at all these local runs. Tucson, Phoenix, Buckeye…"

"Buckeye? Wouldn't happen to be the Coyle Technology office address?" Parker asked.

"Not the address we went to. I've got to run these down. It'll tell us where our driver went. The last entry listed was a pickup in Buckeye. Not a border run like we've been thinking. He was coming from Buckeye when he dropped his trailer at Devil's Well."

"That puts a different angle on things. Good work, Barry."

"Western Machine's come up in our investigation. Leon, did you ever get a look at what was in these boxes they were having you deliver? Any idea at all? We know it wasn't the radioactive material Billie claimed she saw."

"Once I got the boxes on the truck, they were sealed, and the first thing they checked when they were unloaded was if the seals were broken. I couldn't leave until they checked every single delivery. It was kinda strange at the time. Now I know why, I guess."

"What about before you loaded the truck. Any opportunity to sneak a peek?"

"A couple of times, I got there before my shift and found the guys all working in the back. I don't know what it was they were doing, but they didn't like me being there. You want me to go back and make another run? I can take a look in one of the boxes and reseal it. They'd never know."

"No." Parker and Linda chimed in together.

Parker was silent for a moment. "I need to leave town for a day, maybe two."

"What can we do?" Barry asked.

"Nothing. It's unrelated to this, I think." He cast his eyes toward Miguel. Linda caught the look and knew there was more.

Miguel caught it, too. "Does it have to do with Billie?"

Parker thought about withholding it from him. He didn't want to start lying to him. Not now. "Billie's gotten wrapped up in something and got arrested in Mexico. I don't know all the details yet."

"I'm coming with you," Miguel said.

"No, you're not."

"I can—"

"Here's the deal. I don't know what kind of trouble she found, and I don't know who's involved in her legal issues. It's—messy. I have the name of the cop down there who's handling her case. I need to go sort it out and find out what she's doing and what made her run after she found out the name of the lone survivor."

"I can help," Miguel said.

"I need you here. Can you work your Immigrant Coalition contacts in Hermosillo and Mexico City to see if the photos are any of the missing college students, and if they've seen or heard anything about Billie? If they have, I need to know right away."

Miguel nodded, unhappy he was being cut out.

CHAPTER THIRTY

"I'll be back in a couple of days."

Chapter Thirty-One

Parker was able to book an AeroMexico flight from Phoenix to Hermosillo International with little notice. The single terminal airport in central Mexico was named after General Ignacio Pesqueira García, former six-term Governor of the State of Sonora. Parker breezed through customs although he paused slightly when asked by the young man in a military uniform, "What brings you to Hermosillo?"

Business or pleasure. It wasn't a vacation, for sure, but he wasn't here in any official capacity either. The last time he was in the city was even less pleasant, stuffed in the back of a tanker truck.

After getting his passport scanned and stamped for his sightseeing trip to the city. The sun was beginning to set, and Parker used a pay phone in the terminal to call the Cereso prison. He was fortunate not to end up with a recorded message in Spanish. He would be able to make out a few words, but not enough to comprehend. A woman prison staffer spoke fluent English and let Parker know visiting hours were over for the day, and they would resume tomorrow morning at seven.

He thought about calling Inspector Lopez as a courtesy. It was standard practice to reach out to another department if you'd be poking around. Cleveland, Nashville, or Hermosillo, the protocol was the same. If you're in another agency's turf, you let them know. Parker wasn't here in any official capacity, and he doubted the Inspector would see the difference.

Hefting his carry-on bag, Parker followed the signs to the taxi stand. He expected to wait at this hour, but four taxis were lined up waiting for fares.

Parker went to the first in line, and the driver hopped out and helped him drop his bag in the trunk.

The driver didn't even bother with Spanish and pegged Parker for the American he was. "Welcome to Hermosillo. Where can I take you?"

"The Colony Hotel on De Los Gandaderos."

"Sí," the driver said with a flick of his eyes in the rearview mirror.

After navigating the traffic out of the airport, the driver said it would be a twenty-minute drive unless there were government checkpoints.

"Checkpoints? What's that about?" Parker asked.

"The National Guard started random checkpoints in the city last month. It's not a big deal. We won't have any problem getting through."

Parker recalled the Inspector's phone call and Billie getting caught up in a checkpoint.

"What are they looking for?" Parker asked.

"Oh, the usual: drugs, money, and guns. The gang violence in the city has increased in recent months. The government had to crack down, or we'd risk giving it all back to the cartels again."

"I was here when the cartel ran everything in the city, including the electricity. I remember an old man telling me wherever there is a light burning, the cartel runs it."

"Es verdad. True. He wasn't, how do you American's say it, pulling your leg. It was very bad here when El Halcón was in power. I have lived here all my life, and I see it coming back again."

Checkpoints wouldn't make a dent in organized crime. Parker knew the real cartel players would have bought off the officer working at the checkpoint to make sure their shipments went through without delay.

A few minutes of silence passed as Parker glanced out the window at the cityscape. Hermosillo was a city of almost one million people. Half of them, it seemed, were out on the roads. To the north, he spotted the Cerro de la Campana, the mountain sprouting out of the desert floor in the center of the city. Lights at the lookout on top flooded down the spiral road to the top.

"Once you get to your hotel, Señor, I suggest you stay in for the night. The area around the prison is not pleasant after dark. But you probably know that, Detective."

Parker noticed the look in the mirror and a glint in the driver's eyes.

"Inspector Lopez sent me to collect you. I'm Sergeant Ramon Medina."

"Why is the Inspector interested?"

"He thought it unusual."

"Unusual enough to have customs flag me when I arrived?"

"He knew the moment you booked your flight."

"I'm not here in any official capacity."

"I know. We checked."

Parker grimaced at the thought of the Mexican consulate contacting Captain Morris and asking about one of his detectives flying off to another country.

After the revelation about the Inspector, Parker was surprised his "driver," Sergeant Medina, pulled into the Colony Hotel entrance instead of some dank police station in the city center.

Medina turned in the front seat. "Inspector Lopez will meet you at the prison at eight tomorrow morning." He popped the remote truck latch for Parker's bag. Parker slid out of the rear seat and thanked Medina for the ride.

"At least this ride was free," Medina said. "One word of caution. If we know you're here. Others will, too."

Medina said,

"Registration is to your left. The hotel dining room is closed for the evening, but room service may be able to get you something light."

"Thank you."

Medina pulled away as Parker dropped his bag at the registration counter, hit a small bell on the polished wood surface, and disappeared.

Parker glanced around and the lobby was deserted. Odd since many Mexican restaurants run late into the evening.

An uneasy feeling swept over Parker. The warning from Medina. Others knew he was here, and the deserted hotel lobby blended into a prickly paranoia cocktail.

He jumped when a door slammed behind the counter. He turned at the shadow appearing in the hallway. Parker reached, grabbing his bag and glanced to the front door.

When the shadow materialized and stood behind the counter, Parker let the bag drop. The five-foot, grey-haired ancient woman wasn't the gangland assassin he anticipated.

She pulled the glasses up from the gold chain around her neck. "Do you have a reservation?"

From the lack of a bustling lobby, Parker didn't think getting a room would be a problem. "Yes, Parker."

The old woman ran a gnarled finger down a printout. "Yes, I see it here." She held a clipboard to Parker. "Please fill this out."

Parker completed the basic form and handed it back to the aging hotelier.

She handed him a key with a brass tag attached with the room number etched into the metal surface. "Two One Two, she said. Stairs are to your right, and it will be the first room to the left."

"Thanks."

On the landing in front of his door, a newspaper lay folded, resting against the threshold. Parker noticed none of the other rooms had a paper waiting for their occupants. Parker grabbed the paper, and the front-page photo was one with Billie in handcuffs, being forced into a police cruiser.

Medina's warning again. "Others will know you're here too."

Chapter Thirty-Two

Parker slept lightly, startling at every creak and groan from the old hotel. He propped a chair under the doorknob. At sunrise, the golden light spilled in through thin curtains. The morning rays glinted off the water glass he balanced on the chair as an early warning device.

The room was dated but very tidy. Not a surface with a hint of dust or disrepair. Parker chided himself at the precautions he'd taken to prevent intrusion.

Parker never changed out of his travel clothes in case he needed to make a quick exit. His bag sat right where he dropped it on the wood floor next to his bed. Sunrise wake up left him an hour and a half before he was supposed to meet the Inspector at the prison.

He considered skipping a shower, because he'd be vulnerable then, but the musty travel smell wafted up and convinced him otherwise.

A surprisingly hot shower reinvigorated him, and a change of clothes didn't hurt either. Despite the lack of decent sleep, he felt rested. He repacked his bag, undid his makeshift burglar alarm, and stashed his carry-on bag in the closet.

The old woman toiled behind the counter when he arrived in the lobby. The dining room was lit, and three tables were occupied. One single man, who dressed like a businessman, based on the oversized briefcase at his feet, Parker pegged him as a sales representative. The other two tables were taken by couples, both in their mid-twenties. The way they doted over one another and held hands across the table, Parker wondered if they were newlyweds.

Parker passed the old woman at the registration desk.

"Was your stay pleasant?"

"It was, thank you. Say, how long of a walk is it to the prison?"

She tensed her jaw before she spoke. "Fifteen minutes at my pace. You have someone inside, yes?"

"I'm meeting someone there."

"I'm very sorry. The place is evil. I pray the person has protection." The woman blessed herself, making the sign of the cross with her hand.

"That bad?"

"If they cannot afford to pay the mordida for food, blankets, or to keep them away from the bandits they have in there—then it's very bad."

Parker wondered how Billie had managed in the foreign jail. She was a survivor, but from what the old woman described, an American woman without outside resources wouldn't last long.

"Please, have some breakfast before you go."

Parker realized he was hungry and thanked her for her hospitality. He sat at one of the empty tables, and a young woman appeared from a backroom carrying a coffee shop and a menu.

"Si, Señor?"

"Coffee please."

"Oh, American." She poured coffee into a white porcelain cup, careful not to spill a drop on the starched white linen. "Would you like something from the kitchen?"

He glanced at the menu, and most of the items were on the heavy side. "How about some fruit and yogurt?"

"Certainly, Señor."

Parker watched the other diners and relaxed a bit since they didn't seem like a cartel hit squad sent after him. The waitress returned and placed his bowl of yogurt and a plate of sliced guava, melon, and berries in front of him.

A glance at his watch told him he needed to get moving to get to the prison on time to meet the Inspector.

He quickly ate and left a tip for the waitress with enough cash to cover the bill.

Parker set out the front doors and took to the sidewalk in the direction of the prison, some five streets away. The surrounding area became more depressing the closer he got to the prison. Bars on windows, signs in Spanish for what he thought looked like check cashing, bail bonds, or stores taking advantage of the families of those trapped in the system.

He heard the crunch of footsteps in gravel behind him. He glanced over his shoulder, and the salesman trailed him, walking at an angry pace. Parker's paranoia ratcheted up because it seemed unlikely a salesman would have business in this desolate part of town.

Parker rounded the corner to the left and ducked behind a dumpster reeking of spoiled meat.

The salesman took the same corner, and Parker sprung out at him, pinning him to the steel wall of the garbage container.

The man's eyes grew large.

"Why are you following me?" Parker said with his forearm tight against the salesman's chest.

"Please, don't hurt me," the man said in accented English. He dropped the briefcase.

Parker kicked the briefcase, and its contents spilled on the asphalt. Packages of instant noodle soup, cookies, cigarettes, tissues, and beef jerky fell from the case.

"Take them, please."

"You're following me," Parker said.

"I'm not. I'm going to the prison. My wife."

Parker let up on the man's chest. "Your wife?"

"Si. They have her, and she needs these things."

Parker looked at the assortment of goods on the ground. He stepped away from the man, releasing him.

"I'm sorry. I thought—"

"I know. You aren't used to how things work down here. We have to do this, or she won't be able to buy her safety."

"I've heard…"

"You have someone in there?"

Parker nodded. "I do. She's—" Parker didn't know what to call her. Billie was a close friend. A friend before he found out she was with Castaneda that night. If she was involved in Mac's death… She lied about it all. He cleared his throat. "She's a woman I know from up north."

"She might be in with my wife. They don't have very many women in there. Only the ones they consider high risk, or someone they can sell."

"What is it they say your wife did?"

The salesman straightened his suit jacket and grimaced. "She didn't do anything. The federales claim she was providing refuge to cartel members. She did no such thing. She works at a farmacia. She has no control over who comes inside. What is it your friend is accused of?"

"Arms dealing. I don't know what she got herself involved in."

"That's serious, too. The government has been making a big effort to rid us of arms dealers and smugglers. I hope, for your friend's sake, she did not do what they are accusing her of. It won't be good for her."

As much as Parker was confused over Billie's involvement in McMillan's death, fleeing Phoenix, and being caught with illegal firearms in her possession, he didn't wish her harm in prison.

"I hope not either. I only know what the Inspector told me."

"Which Inspector, if I can ask?"

"Lopez."

The man's eyes widened again. "Lopez is one of them."

"One of what?"

"Los Muertos."

Chapter Thirty-Three

Lopez was Los Muertos? Was it possible? And Parker was walking straight in to meet him.

Parker waited across the street from the prison's entrance. Yellowed pock-marked concrete walls marked the prison with round turrets on the corners, watching both the street and inside the walls. There was no mistaking the purpose of this fetid place.

With visiting hours set to begin, a line of family members snaked half a block, ready to enter the prison. In American prisons and jails, Parker knew, visitors could not bring anything inside with them. Here, though, bags of food, clothing, and comfort items were collected for the incarcerated. Some would make it to the family member. There was a certain amount lost to bribes, and the visitors expected staff to paw through the bags, taking a few "confiscated" items.

Parker checked his watch. He was ten minutes overdue for his meeting with the Inspector. The line started to shuffle forward, admitting the visitors one at a time. A light blue Saab sedan slowed and pulled to the curb in front of the prison. A man of medium height, with thin black hair swept back and held in place with a shiny product of some sort, stepped from the passenger side. He tossed on a pair of aviator sunglasses and adjusted the sleeves of a light cream linen suit as the car pulled away.

The man exuded authority, and the people waiting in line recognized it. They parted when he passed through the prison gates. Parker knew. Inspector Lopez had arrived.

As Parker thought, after another ten minutes, the visitation line had disappeared inside. The Inspector stepped through the prison gates to the street and glanced in both directions. Hurried. A man not used to being stood up. He snatched a cell from his jacket breast pocket and placed a ten-second call. Within a minute, the light blue Saab returned and picked up the Inspector.

Parker's cell phone buzzed, and from his vantage point, he could see Inspector Lopez holding a phone to his ear. The caller ID on Parker's phone displayed an unknown number message. Parker tapped the decline button. Lopez threw his phone on the dash and ordered his driver to leave with a quick hand gesture.

After the blue Saab disappeared, Parker stepped into the street and crossed to the prison. Entering the institution was like what he'd found north of the border. IDs were checked, name of the prisoner he wanted to visit was called in, and after passing through a metal detector, he was escorted to a large open space, a patio where inmates and visitors mingled. It was hard to tell the difference because most of the inmates were wearing the clothes they came in with, not prison uniforms.

His prison escort pointed at an empty table and ordered Parker to wait, at least what he thought the man said. It was such a rapid clip of Spanish Parker could only make out the word for table—mesa.

He was one of the few white faces in the mixed visiting space and exercise yard for the female prisoners. Inmates and their visitors were eyeing him with suspicion or sizing him up for a potential mark. Parker noted gang tattoos were prevalent and recognized a few of the skin tags designating street gangs north of the border and MS-13 from El Salvador. He'd never encountered a woman MS-13 member before. They were traditionally hardcore male and violent.

A door unlocked and Billie walked through after the escort pointed to the table where Parker waited.

She was dressed in her jeans, a thin tank top, and a pair of cheap shower shoes. Her sun-bleached hair hung limp around her face, framing a fresh black eye and a split lip. The blood had crusted over into a black vertical slash on her bottom lip.

"Jesus, Billie."

"Yeah, these gals don't play."

Parker noticed a few of the prisoners glared at Billie's back and whispered.

"You made a few friends, I see." Parker jutted his jaw at one of the tough, inked-up women.

Billie glanced over her shoulder. "That one there is a real charmer. Her husband, or boyfriend, or whatever, was a low-level coyote working for the cartel."

"She using his cartel muscle."

"Not so much. She's in here for murderin' him. Turns out he'd been sleepin' with the women he smuggled over the border."

After a pause, "Billie, what are you doing here?"

"I was hopin' you wouldn't come down here, Nathan. I don't know where to start," she looked away.

"You ran off, Billie. As soon as you found out the name of the container survivor. What gives?"

"I don't know who was in the container. But the name, Armando DeSilva, was a code name."

"Code name? What the hell are you saying?"

"There are families in Hermosillo who help me and the Coalition deliver supplies where they're needed. You 'member the family Los Muertos threatened if I testified against the Cartel? We arranged a signal. If they were bein' threatened again, they was to use the name."

"How did the name get in the paper and tagged on our survivor?"

"The local paper was the place where the Armando DeSilva name was supposed to appear. Always on the front page, always above the fold so it would show up. We have a friend at the paper who agreed to put it in some article when the people here tell them they are in trouble."

"Why not call you?"

"It's too dangerous. These people risk everythin' to get medical supplies, tents, warm clothes to those who need them the most. They're bein' watched all the time. And 'sides I don't always have a phone handy."

"Armando DeSilva has nothing to do with the man in the hospital?"

"No."

"Then it doesn't make any sense why the feds went through all the trouble to try and bust him out of the place. "

"Don't know what they did. But, Once I saw the name, it meant the people down here was in trouble."

"Why take off with your trailer and everything? You see how it looks, right?"

Billie huffed. "I was able to call down here once I got the signal. Los Muertos was closing in on them—and they was scared. If Los Muertos was after them, then they'd come for me too, so I grabbed everything and left. I didn't want none of this to spill over on Miguel, or you. If I was gone, then them idiots would follow me and not bother you."

"Pulled your trailer all the way down here to help your friends? Still doesn't explain why you're sitting in here."

"That's where things got sideways. It was a lure."

"A lure? Who lured you?"

"Let me lay it out. I got the signal—the name. Then I called and the people I know down here said they's goin' to get killed if I don't do what Los Muertos wants."

"Which was?"

"I hadn't even left Phoenix, and I get a call. They's tellin' me I have a relief shipment to bring down to Hermosillo. 'Cept it weren't no regular supply run on account of my medical supplies don't come from Western Machine Parts. I think it had somethin' to do with me pokin' around in there the other day. Anyways, I go to the machine shop, and they has them boxes all lined up ready for me to load up, and they's all labeled medical supplies, perishable, or vaccines and whatnot. I put them in the back of my truck with some other medical supplies I had already loaded, stashed my trailer, and headed south."

"No one bothered to inspect the boxes at the border?"

"You know how it is. The inspectors are lookin' at what's coming into the country, not goin' out. The Mexican border people see me on the regular, so it didn't look like nothin' to them."

"Then what?"

"A federales checkpoint is what happened. They're up all the time, it ain't unusual. What was different this time was they singled me out and opened the boxes. Ain't never done it before. Like they was told what to look for. That's when they found them guns."

"You had to know what was in those boxes. They came out of a Los Muertos front."

"I didn't know exactly, but I figured it weren't no good."

"But you did it anyway? Billie, I don't know what they're gonna do to you because of it."

"They wanted them guns and me."

"Why you?"

"I sit on the Coalition's money, and they want it."

Sergeant Medina clamped his hand on Parker's shoulder.

"Inspector Lopez is waiting for you."

Chapter Thirty-Four

"You too, Miss Carson. Come with me."

Parker followed the Sergeant. The Inspector must have gotten a phone call from the prison when Parker checked in.

"Billie, you wanna tell me what's going on?"

"I wish I knew. This Inspector guy ain't right. I hoped you wouldn't fall for his B.S. and get pulled down here."

"Heard Lopez is Los Muertos," Parker said softly, keeping it from their escort.

"That fits. He questioned me. Not about where I was goin' with them guns, but who told me to take them here. They—they don't know."

"There's a split within Los Muertos."

They reached a door at the end of a dank hallway where the driver paused and looked up to a camera mounted up behind a thick spiderweb. The door popped open with the buzz of an electric lock.

Inside, Inspector Lopez sat behind a table in his linen suit.

"Detective, Miss Carson, come in."

The driver gave Parker a shove in the back when he didn't comply.

"Your name isn't Lopez, is it?" Parker said.

The man smiled, "It's one of the names I use when it suits me."

"Echevarría?" Parker said.

"Very good, Detective. Now we know one another let's get down to it. Who were you delivering the weapons to, Miss Carson?"

She looked at Parker. "Someone was supposeta contact me once I got to Hermosillo."

"Who?"

"Don't know."

"Don't play games with me. You do not take an illegal arms shipment across international borders if you don't know where it's going."

"You do if people you care about are being threatened."

"Armando DeSilva. Yes, we know. It's why we set up the checkpoints. The people who sent the message are safe."

"Why should I believe you?"

"Because my disagreement is not with them, unless you make it one."

"I can't tell you what I don't know."

Parker cleared his throat. "The way I have it figured, there is only one real possibility."

Echevarría grinned. "Really, Detective? Please enlighten us."

"Casteneda."

The man's eyes went cold. Parker noticed the man's hand ball up into tight fists.

"Why would Esteban send weapons here, Detective?"

"Carmen. She's positioning herself to push you out. She's made a deal with the Sinaloa Cartel to assume leadership of Los Muertos and pledges allegiance to them. Maybe she needs them to take you out."

"Preposterous. Carmen is loyal to me." There was doubt behind the words.

"Carmen doesn't agree with where you want to take the organization; surely you've heard her talk. We both know she doesn't hold back on her opinions."

"Why? Why would she think about such a move when Castaneda is still controlling most of Los Muertos? It would be suicide."

"Unless she's made a deal with the Cartel to take Castaneda off the table, too."

"Impossible. She doesn't have the muscle to make a move like this."

"With your law enforcement connections, you know how your interests in Los Muertos have been—compromised."

"Of course. Castaneda is working with your FBI. He's giving up factions of Los Muertos who he considers disloyal."

"Like you?"

"He can try."

The deafening roar of a gunshot in the small room made Parker's ears ring. Echevarría slumped in his chair, a dark hole in his forehead. Blood trickled onto the crisp linen suit.

Parker spun around only to face the barrel of the gun now facing him.

The visiting salesman tossed the gun on the floor and backed out of the room, leaving Billie and Parker alone with the dead Los Muertos shot caller. He left the door open behind him.

Parker went for the door and looked out into the empty hallway.

"Billie, come on. We don't want to be here when they figure out where the gunshot came from."

They both crept into the hall, and alarm noises sounded. An urgent announcement spit from the intercom speaker, garbled and choppy.

"Says there's a disturbance in the visiting area. All inmates are to report to their units."

"A diversion. Let's go."

They jogged up the hallway and found a door propped open with a chair. "Must be for us."

Parker led Billie through, then kicked the chair out of the way, letting the door slam shut behind them.

"Who was he?"

"A guy posing as a visitor. He followed me from the hotel. I figure Casteneda got him to pull the trigger—his wife's in here."

They pushed on an exit door and it dumped them into a staff area where all the visitors were being rushed out of the visiting patios. Parker and Billie slipped out and joined the stream.

"Keep your head down, Billie."

The staff were more interested in keeping the crowd moving than looking for anyone hiding within the mob. Billie's dirty blonde hair made her look like an outsider, so staff waved her on with the others.

Ahead, Parker saw the entrance where he'd first come in. Two armed officers stood post and stopped every visitor trying to exit. They were trapped. The press of fleeing visitors behind them pushed them to the gun-wielding pair ahead.

The gunman on the right locked eyes with Parker and shifted his glance to Billie. Recognition washed across the man's face. A quick word to his partner and both armed guards homed in on them.

"We got trouble, Billie."

"I see. I know the one on the right. He's been hasslin' me the whole time."

The crowd pushed them closer.

Six feet.

"Any ideas?" Parker said, glancing for any possible exit.

They were trapped in the sallyport. Above them, another armed officer watched the flow.

Three feet now. The gunman on the right shifted his weapon.

Parker knew how it would play out in the international media. "Lawman and gun runner from the United States killed during an attempted prison break." It was a setup from the beginning. Grabbing Billie as bait to lure him here. He fell for it, and now they'd both pay.

The gun barrel jerked in their direction.

"Stop."

Parker closed his eyes and thought about Miguel as the gunman closed in.

Chapter Thirty-Five

The gunshot didn't happen. Instead, the armed officer shoved a hard plastic object in Parker's hand and pushed him out. Billie followed behind him, and ten seconds later, they were both on the street outside the prison.

"What was all that?" Billie asked.

"I'm not sure what to make of it, but I'm not waiting around to ask questions."

Parker grabbed Billie by the shoulder and tugged her down the street away from the crowds and police vehicles starting to arrive to quell the latest disturbance at the correctional facility. He glanced down at the object in his hand—a cheap burner phone.

"I'm beginnin' ta think it'd be easier to kill us out here and blame us for shooting the police Inspector."

"Leaving us alive—while I greatly appreciate it—was done for a reason. Someone wanted us out here." Parker clicked the phone's power button and it flashed to life. Although the screen was in Spanish, the call history displayed a single number. Parker hit the redial button and raised the phone to his ear while they walked. They needed more distance between them and the prison.

The phone rang twice and connected. "I'm happy to see you enjoying your time in Mexico, Detective," Castaneda's voice echoed over the connection.

"Castaneda. What's your play here? Killing the leader of the opposition?"

"It had to be done. Los Muertos is mine. It will always be mine. Echevarría thought he could take it away. His approach upset a delicate balance, and

205

you witnessed what happens when you defy me. Carmen will soon realize it, too."

"You think your new friends in Homeland Security will let you kill your way back in control?

Parker and Billie made it back to the corner across the street from the Colony Hotel. Three police cars with flashing lights occupied the entrance. They held back as uniformed officers ran inside.

"They are grateful for the service I provide. They get to claim they are taking down criminals who threaten the great nation of Los Estados Unidos. It's all they truly care about."

"Why didn't your man take us out in the prison-like he did Echevarría?"

"He wanted his wife released, and he did as I ordered. As for you two, I have other things in mind. You both need to finish what Billie started and complete her delivery."

"The police have the guns you were smuggling down here."

Billie squinted and pointed across the street. The police were leaving the hotel, satisfied the killers they sought were not hiding in Parker's room.

"You need to make certain they don't. Billie knows her friends down here will pay the price if you fail. Tell her Armando DeSilva is waiting." The call disconnected and Parker shoved the burner phone in his pocket. It was then he remembered he'd left his cell phone at the prison entrance when he checked in to visit. Another connection to the police inspector's assassination.

Parker pulled Billie back to the corner as a police car cruised past.

"Billie, it's time you come clean with me."

"About what?"

"The fact you need me to narrow it down for you should be enough of an explanation. Castaneda. I need to know. I deserve to know."

She swallowed hard. "Castaneda's people took the DeSilva family, and they're holdin' them until them guns get delivered. The same family he and the cartel threatened when I was set to testify in federal court."

"When you dropped out of witness protection?"

"Uh huh, the same. They's good people and don't deserve what been done to them. It's my fault for bringin' it down on them. I was supposed to drive them guns to a spot east of Hermosillo and deliver them to Castaneda's people. They gonna need them to fight off Echevarría's takeover."

"Echevarría is out of the picture now."

"Cut the head off the snake, and the serpent sill wriggles around a bit. And if you're not careful, that head can still bite."

"Or there's a whole other snake out there in Carmen Delgado. Homeland Security is convinced she's making a play for control. With Echevarría gone, there's nothing in her way."

"Whoever gets them guns, the DeSilvas and a whole lot of other people who don't got no dog in this fight are gonna get hurt."

"Billie—where were you the night McMillan was killed?"

Billie fell silent and avoided eye contact with Parker.

"I done told you about that."

"Tell me again, Billie. This time, tell me about you being there with Castaneda."

She twitched.

"Billie?"

She fell back against the wall.

"Castaneda has the feds believing you killed Mac. A federal grand jury has indicted you for his murder."

Her eyes grew wide. "No. I din't kill no one. That's a lie."

"I don't know what to believe anymore, Billie. Tell me again what happened. You told me all along you weren't with Castaneda. "

"Nathan, I swear I wasn't there when Deputy McMillan was killed. I shoulda been. I started out on the run with him. We stopped at a bar down near Tucson."

"I know the place, Quiet Eddie's—the roadhouse down south."

"We was changing vans, putting the people in a blue panel van for the rest of the trip to Flagstaff. I heard Castaneda say to the men who brought them up—I heard him say he was gonna bury me out in the desert on account of bein' of no more use to him. He knew the route and didn't need me no more. I snuck off before he left in the blue van. Nathan, I swear."

Parker saw the hurt in her eyes. She was never able to hide her emotions and he could tell she was anxious over what happened that night and for earning his distrust.

"Why the lie before? You said you never went on the run with him?"

"I—I din't want you to think I had anything to do with it. I coulda stayed and maybe stopped Castaneda from killing the deputy. I din't want you to think even less of me." She broke off eye contact and wiped her eye with the back of her hand.

Parker exhaled. "Billie, I believe you. If you'd have stayed with that animal, there would have been another murder on his hands. You know what happened to the migrants in the van, remember?"

"Yeah, he left them to die in the desert."

"We still have a problem. The feds believe Castaneda. They're blinded by the stories he's telling them and the low-level thugs he's turning over. Too bad there's nothing to disprove his version of that night."

"There is."

"What do you mean?"

"There's someone who can swear on a stack of bibles or whatnot that I wasn't there, that I bailed at Quiet Eddie's bar."

"That would be a start, if they can testify you weren't there. The feds would have to listen. It won't be easy, though. Who is the witness?"

"Armando DeSilva."

"Thought you said that was a code name."

"It is. Had to change his name after. Armando was with me that night. We managed to run off before Castaneda left with the van. Armando wasn't a migrant making a run for the border. He was supposta come and learn the route. He told me Castaneda was bragging about how he din't need me no more. Armando said they was gonna make an example outta me. I got scared and ran—Armando and me. He saved my life."

"Now you feel like you owe him."

"I do. Him and his family."

"What are you thinking, Billie? You can't bring a load of weapons to Los Muertos. You know what that will bring down on anyone who gets in their way."

"I know, Nathan. I got an idea. It might be enough to spring Armando and his kin and get Los Muertos off our trail for a bit. I need to get my truck."

"You know where they stashed it?"

"I got me a good idea. Echevarría was keeping them for his-self. We was delivering it to Castaneda's men. It won't be far from where they took me down north of the city."

"You think it's still there?"

"I have to steal it back."

"Steal it back from an armed gang?"

"I know how it sounds. But I got a plan."

"I'd like to hear it."

"Well, it's mostly an idea about a plan."

"I'm gonna regret this, aren't I?"

"You ain't going. This is my problem to fix."

Parker pointed to the hotel. "I need my passport from the safe in my room. Then we'll see about getting your truck. Besides, I need Armando's statement to help nail down Castaneda once and for all."

Chapter Thirty-Six

The Colony Hotel lobby was as vacant as it was when Parker checked in. He bypassed the registration desk this time and headed straight to his room. If there was someone watching the hotel, he didn't want to waste time.

He used the stairs, taking two at a time to avoid the bell chime in the elevator. Turning from the landing, he spotted a housekeeping cart in the hallway a few doors down from his room. Beyond the cart, a uniformed officer stood outside his door.

Parker backed into a recessed door across from the stair landing. Pressing his back to the door he was out of sight from where the officer stood. He peeked around the corner and when he officer glanced the opposite direction, Parker leapfrogged to the next door where the housekeeping cart was parked.

He slid inside the room startling the housekeeper as she was stripping the bed.

"Aye Dios mío," she said.

Parker put his finger to his lips and pointed down the hall. The housekeeper nodded, understanding the police officer was nearby.

Parker crossed the room, drew open the patio door and stepped outside. The rooms had narrow patios, wide enough for a chair and a small table. More important to Parker, they were a few feet apart and were lined with wrought iron railings.

Stepping on the patio chair, he stepped up on the railing, steadying himself against the wall. One smooth stride let him reach the next patio railing with his right foot. Balancing between the two patios, he pushed off with his back foot and landed on the patio next door, bumping the chair and knocking him off balance.

On the street, he spotted Billie watching from the intersection. She waved and repeatedly pointed at the balcony next door. The patio door to his room slid open, and the uniformed officer stepped outside.

The rumble of the heavy chair when he landed on it must have roused the officer. Trying the door to the room where he was trapped—it wouldn't budge—locked.

As the officer turned, Parker sat in the patio chair with his back to the officer.

The scratch of a match and the pungent sulfur stench meant the officer was taking a smoke break outside rather than checking on the noise from his balcony hopping.

"Buenos Días," the officer said.

Parker waved, not looking behind him. "Buenos Días."

Parker cringed, waiting for a question in Spanish he couldn't understand or answer. The next thing he heard was the officer's footsteps and the balcony door closing.

He waited until the faint thump of the hallway door sounded, indicating the officer had resumed his post in the hallway.

Parker climbed the railing once more and pushed off. His right foot landed on his room's railing, and it gave way folding in toward the patio. The collapsing railing sent him off balance and he sprawled on the concrete patio surface, landing on his stomach.

He got to his knees and glanced in the window, expecting the officer's return.

The door was unlocked. Parker drew a sign of relief the officer hadn't locked it after his last smoke break. Parker slid inside and the room was much as he left it. The open drawers and closet marked the sloppy remnants of a quick search. His carry-on bag was gone.

He crept to the hotel safe in the closet. It was next to the front door. Parker slowly turned the room's deadbolt and the small metal flipper serving as a secondary lock. Returning to the safe, he pressed the buttons quickly, each one sounding like a siren to wake the dead. The safe door popped open, and he snagged his passport.

Parker ran to the patio, jumped the downed railing, and climbed over the next, ducking into the housekeeping room as the door in his room crashed open.

He visualized the officer, gun drawn, forcing his way into the room and out to the balcony. The broken patio rail would be telling.

Startling the housekeeping staff once more, Parker jetted from the room and made for the stairs.

The hotel lobby was still silent when he crashed down the stairs. He took a deep breath and strode though the lobby trying to act like be belonged.

"Señor Parker," a voice echoed in the lobby.

The old woman beckoned him from the registration desk.

"I'm in a bit of a hurry," he said.

She hefted his carry-on bag from behind the counter and dropped it on the surface.

"Then you will want this."

Parker turned course for the registration desk. "How did you?"

"When the police come, we knew what happened. We managed to take this before they stormed in. I told them you checked out."

"Thank you, you didn't need to do that. It was a risk for you to get involved."

"It's what we do."

"We?"

"Casa Segura."

"Thank you…"

"Here, take this," she handed him a brown paper bag. "Some food for you and Billie."

"You know Billie Carson? You knew who I was going to visit at the prison?"

"Of course, Casa Segura only exists because of Billie. You'd better get on your way."

Parker laid his hand on the old woman's arm. "I hope I can come back and visit under better circumstances."

Parker shouldered his carry-on and grabbed the paper bag. Walking out the Colony Hotel's front entrance, he embraced the sounds of the city. He and Billie would need to hide in that anonymity while they worked their way to the location north of the city where Billie claimed her truck was kept.

Getting out of the city was going to be a challenge. They couldn't walk the distance, and by now, the police would have figured out Billie had escaped, Echavarría murdered, and he was involved. There would be roadblocks and checkpoints.

Parker met up with Billie, and she asked for the burner phone.

"Who are you gonna call? It's not like Castaneda is going to give you a ride."

"You sure? He wants them guns, don't he?"

"You can't trust what he says."

"I know." Billie tapped in a number from memory and waited for a connection.

She spoke in Spanish, and one of the few words Parker recognized was Casa Segura, the group the old woman at the hotel mentioned. She hung up and gave Parker the cell phone.

"Should be about five minutes," she said.

"What's Casa Segura?"

Billie bit her bottom lip. He could see in her eyes she wasn't going to give him a straight answer right away.

"The woman at the hotel mentioned you and this Casa thing. What have you been doing on your trips down here? It hasn't all been relief supply runs, has it?"

"It's still about gettin' the medicine, clothing, and supplies to where they need to get. After over half of what we brung down was stolen by the cartel, or bandits, we needed to find a better way. We created our own network—underground—to make sure the people who need the stuff git it."

"How'd you manage to do that?"

"Weren't only me. Miguel's a big part of connectin' these people together. The boy is a wiz when it comes to the internet."

I've heard you two talk about a network of people, like when Miguel was going to show those photos to the families down here. Is that what we're talking about?"

"It's part of it. There's also people who are more active."

"Active?"

"Sometimes, we gotta take back what got took from us."

"Like a militia?"

"Nothing so organized. Just a group to move when somethin' needs moved. Like us. Here's our ride," Billie pointed to a truck rumbling in their direction.

Their ride was a rusty-looking box truck with a faded logo for a carnecería based on a happy cow's image on the side.

The truck pulled up and the young man rolled his window down and beamed. "Billie. Good to see you. Where to?"

Parker and Billie climbed into the cab, and the air conditioning spit moisture-laden air at them. Billie gave the driver a long hug. The young man put the truck in gear and pulled into traffic.

"Nathan this here is Armando DeSilva."

Chapter Thirty-Seven

"**A**rmando? I thought Castaneda had you?"

"He has my family. I was delivering supplies to the camps when they came for them."

Armando shoved the stick shift into third and merged onto Highway 15, heading north.

"Is your family okay?" Billie asked.

He nodded. "So far. I get a feeling the men holding them aren't all aligned with Castaneda. It could go very bad, and I'm afraid they will be hurt when it happens."

"When what happens?" Parker said.

"Is it true? Echevarría is dead?"

"It is," Parker said. Armando looked to Billie for confirmation, and she nodded.

"Then we must hurry. If they find out Echevarría is gone, I don't know what will happen."

Armando kept the truck going north.

"Are there any roadblocks or checkpoints?" Parker asked.

"Not on this highway. The authorities were told you were spotted heading to the airport, so all the police went that way."

"Good thinking," Billie said.

"Armando, Billie told me about a night five years ago in Arizona. You were there?"

"I was. I was twelve, and they told me I had to start leading groups over the border and making sure the drugs they carried were delivered. I didn't want to do it, but they threatened to kill me and my family."

"What happened?"

"What happened was Esteban Castaneda. He was bragging to his men it was going to be Billie's last trip. He was going to slit her throat and dump her on the trail as a sign for others. We came up over the border in a small truck, and we stopped to change vehicles. A blue van was waiting for us. That's when I heard Castaneda again. He was getting ready to kill Billie right there. I told her, and we ran."

"You weren't there when his van got stopped by a deputy in Arizona?"

"No, I heard about what happened. What Castaneda did."

"If you weren't there, how can you be sure?"

"He was driving the van. Everyone else was locked in a cage in the back. It was him."

"I believe you. It might not be enough for the grand jury to drop their charges against Billie, though."

"Billie was with me, down near Tucson."

"I wish we had something to prove all of this."

"There is."

"What's that?"

"The deputy had a body camera, and Castaneda took it. I've seen it."

When Parker rushed to his dying partner's side, his badge and body cam were missing. The camera hadn't uploaded to the cloud, because the techs said McMillan turned it off. There was no image to hold anyone directly accountable for the murder. There was only the slice of video from the dash cam where Castaneda appeared.

"Where's the body cam you saw?"

"Castaneda kept it. He shows it off to people he wants to impress."

"Where's the last place you saw it?"

"His girlfriend has it."

"Carmen Delgado?"

"Yes, you know her?"

"We're acquainted—and not in a good way."

Parker mulled over how to find Carmen and get his partner's body cam.

216

She wasn't about to let him knock on her door and ask for it like he was selling solar panels.

Billie pointed ahead at a sign reading Casa Magnolia Jardin Eventos. "It's near the event center.

Armando nodded and took the exit from the highway into El Encanto. The small town looked dry and forgotten in the shadows of Hermosillo. Still there was a vibrancy on the streets and brown walls enclosing homes and small businesses.

"There. That's where they took my truck."

Armando searched for a parking lot on the next block and they were able to scan the building as they drove past. A squat tan adobe style building with a single roll up door in the front. No windows.

"Looks like a fricken fortress in the daylight," Billie said.

"You sure this is the place?" Parker asked.

"This is it. Armando pullover right there," Billie pointed to the rear of the lot next to an adobe wall a hundred yards away from the building.

Parker and Billie climbed down from the cab of the truck.

"What's the plan, Billie?"

"The truck, what else?"

"They're not going to let us walk in and drive off."

"That's exactly what they'll let me do. Castaneda wants his delivery. Castaneda's men are in there, but they can't risk gettin' caught with the stuff, like I did. They'll turn it over to me."

"Remember, Billie, there are men from Castaneda and Echevarría's camps in there," Armando said. "My parents…"

"We'll make sure they are safe," Billie said.

Armando stepped from the cab and hopped down to the dust-covered pavement. Five foot two and a hundred twenty pounds, Parker picked up on his anxious energy.

"Best you stay here. If things go bad, we don't need you being used as another hostage," Parker said.

"They are my family."

"Mine too," Billie said.

"You need to be ready to get them away from here and keep them safe. Let Billie and me know where you are."

Armando nodded.

"Wait here, okay?" Billie said.

The young man huffed but agreed.

"Come on, let's get this done."

Billie and Parker approached the block-shaped building. No movement sounded from within.

"There anyone here?" Parker asked.

"Sure should be."

Billie pounded a hand on the steel roll-up door, and the sound reverberated off the sheet metal.

A rustling from within. A scraping sound as latches were thrown back and the jangle of a chain pull as the door inched up.

When the rollup door was open chest high, another metallic sound repeated, the charging handles on a pair of AK-47s. Two men, one on either side of the garage opening, covered Parker and Billie.

"We're here for the truck," Billie said.

The gunmen didn't move, but they didn't shoot them either. Parker remembered Billie and Armando saying there were four Los Muertos soldiers watching the arms shipment. Where were the other two?

Parker glanced to his left and saw a boot sticking out from behind a wooden crate. One faction had taken the other.

Billie took another step closer, and the man to her right raised his rifle, centering it on her chest.

"You understand me? I'm taking the truck. Estoy tomando el camión."

The man tensed again. In stilted English, the gunman responded. "Who orders?"

Parker didn't know who these men were loyal to...

"Where are the DeSilvas?" Parker asked.

The rifleman closest to him responded. "They are here, safe for now."

"They are supposed to be released when we take the truck," Parker said.

"Who are you working for?" Parker felt the pressure as the large bore rifle barrel settled on him.

"Castaneda," Billie responded before Parker braced for the response.

"How do we know you aren't lying."

"Call him."

"We can't reach him."

"I can." Parker slowly withdrew a phone from his pocket. "Call him yourself."

The man shouldered his rifle while his partner covered him. He grabbed the phone from Parker.

"The number in there is his."

The gunman pressed the button for the number and waited.

"Jefe?"

The man listened, glanced to Billie, and hung up. He tossed the phone back to Parker and gestured for his partner to lower his weapon.

"The DeSilvas?" Billie asked.

One of the men tipped his head to the rear of the building.

In the back of the garage, past Billie's Ford and two farming tractors, a small office had been framed in to separate the business from the machine floor. Billie threw open the door. Two worried faces looked to them and immediately turned to relief when they spotted Billie.

Parker helped them up from the floor. "You're Armando's family?"

"Is he safe?" the man asked, rubbing a hand through his grey hair.

"He is, and he's waiting for you outside."

The old woman hugged Billie. "My heart is happy now. You and Armando are safe. I'm sorry you put yourself in danger for us—again."

Billie hugged the woman. "Let's get you to Armando. Quickly now."

The older couple shuffled out of the office. Parker and Billie escorted them to the garage door opening. Billie pointed at the truck on the street. And they shuffled toward a waiting Armando.

"They're too old to be Armando's parents, aren't they?" Parker said.

Billie stiffened. "They ain't. They took him in when his mother got in some trouble. They've been the only parents the boy ever had."

Billie waited until the brief hugs were exchanged, the old couple lumbered into the cab and the truck pulled away.

"My truck, then," Billie said.

The closest gunman gestured to the blue Ford.

Parker looked in the passenger window. "Keys are in it."

Billie strode to the truck's bed and threw back a tarp. Boxes of "medical supplies" were stacked and tied down on a wooden pallet. Billie climbed up into the bed and pulled open one of the boxes, tearing a flimsy metal foil seal. The box contained eight H&K MP-5 rifles, disassembled. A quick count of the twenty identical boxes in her truck meant one hundred sixty weapons were ready for transport.

Billie ran her hand down an odd-shaped box and found the seal was already open. She lifted the flap, revealing ten Mark II fragmentation grenades. Three boxes stacked beneath this one meant she'd be careful driving over ruts in the desert.

"Some serious firepower up here, Nathan."

Parker was watching over the tailgate. "All this on there when you made the run down here?"

She shook her head. "Looks like Castaneda added to it after I got here."

"Where you plan on taking this now? Castaneda wants to keep this out of Carmen's reach, for sure."

"Only one way to find out. Call him," she said.

Parker hit the speed dial button on the border phone and tapped the speaker button.

The line connected, and Castaneda remained silent.

"Where do I take this crap?" Billie asked.

"The address is on the phone you have in your hand."

"How far do I gotta go?"

"Maybe an hour—hour and a half."

"Who am I giving this stuff to?"

"You'll know when you get there."

Parker chimed in. "You sure? With Carmen pushing her way in?"

"My men will make sure she doesn't get in the way."

"Can you trust them? Because there's a pair of dead ones here."

CHAPTER THIRTY-SEVEN

"Echeverría's dogs. I took care of him. I can take care of them all."

"What do we do when we get there?"

"My men will unload, and you're free to drive away. Then I will order my men to release the DeSilva family."

Parker and Billie exchanged a glance. He didn't know.

"Are they safe?" Billie asked.

"For now—as long as you follow through."

"Why don't your men take the guns where they need to go?"

Castaneda laughed on the other end of the call. "I'm not going to risk my men. If you are found by the fools who follow Carmen or the authorities, as you say, it's on you. Quickly now. Your phone has limited battery life." The call disconnected.

Parker glanced at the burner's screen. Less than twenty-five percent battery remained.

"What do you make of that?" Parker asked.

"He doesn't know these guys released Armando's kin," Billie said.

"What else doesn't he know?"

Chapter Thirty-Eight

Billie adjusted the seat and started her truck. The gas gauge read half.

"Good thing we only gotta drive an hour or so," she said.

Parker spotted a ten-gallon gas can near one of the farm tractors in the garage. As Billie let the truck idle, Parker lifted the can and shook it, judging it half full.

He lugged it to the bed and hefted it over the side and wedged it in between the boxes. He tossed the tarp and retied the cover before hopping in the cab with Billie.

"Better than nothing," he said.

"Don't know how I feel about a gas can back there with them grenades."

She pulled the truck in drive and shot out of the abandoned Los Muertos garage.

"The gas can is probably the least of our worries. Wonder what made those two Los Muertos thugs take off like they did?"

Billie pulled to the road, glanced at the red dot on the GPS, and turned right, heading north.

"How come we're doin' this? It don't make no sense. Castaneda had them guns already."

"I've been thinking about it too. You brought the guns down here from Western Machine, right?"

"I did. On account of Armando and his family."

"Castaneda knew they were important to you."

"He knew Armando was important to me long before the night I run off—and—you know what happened after…"

"Echevarría snatched them up before you could deliver. No one knows who to trust inside Los Muertos—"

"Them two were fightin' for control of Los Muertos. Echevarría found out I was comin' down here and what I was bringin', and the only ones who knew I was on the road was them misfits at Western Machine."

"You didn't tell anyone else? Not Armando, or any of your people down here?"

"Not this time. I couldn't risk it. Once I saw the name in the paper, I hit the road."

"When did you pick up the guns, Billie?"

"The same morning I saw Armando's name in the paper, I get a call from a guy called Whisper at Western Machine Parts. They call him that on account of his voice gettin' messed up from him bein' stabbed in the throat. He told me Los Muertos had the DeSilvas and Castaneda would give them back when I delivered the shipment ."

Parker took in the last of El Encanto as the scattered buildings thinned out and the desert took over. "Castaneda had the weapons up north and needed a way to get them south to—what? Fight off any faction opposing him for Los Muertos?"

"I guess…"

"Billie, pull off at that market ahead."

She swung the Ford into the parking lot of an all-purpose market, the kind selling tools, food, and lotería.

"Wait here," Parker said.

He entered the small store. It was well-ordered, with shelves of non-perishable food on one side, clothing—mostly t-shirts and hats, in the center, and along the back wall, he spotted what he was looking for. Parker grabbed the last pre-paid cell phone in the store and brought it to the counter. An old man eyed him with suspicion and started to ring up the purchase. While he did, Parker gathered a handful of crackers, bags of jerky, and salty snacks. He didn't know the last time Billie ate.

The shopkeeper finished, Parker paid him and told him to keep the change.

"My friend and I are headed up the road a piece. What's around about an hour's drive from here?"

The old man wrinkled his brow. "You do not want to go there, Señor. There is nothing good."

"What do you mean?" Parker figured delivering a truckload of guns to Los Muertos wouldn't be a trip to an amusement park. But he wanted to know more about what waited ahead for them.

The old shopkeeper seemed reluctant to talk, so Parker continued.

"I'm a sheriff's deputy from up north. Will I find Los Muertos on the road ahead?"

The man nodded slowly. "There will be some. Mostly, this is Sinaloa Cartel land. Their villa is about an hour away."

"The Cartel?" Parker pondered. He'd been there once before but had been locked in the back of a truck, so he couldn't see the landmarks. The compound sat atop a hill with a winding road to the peak.

Parker thanked the man and gave him another twenty for his trouble, and, hopefully, it was enough to buy his silence here in cartel country.

With a couple of coffees, Parker brought all the items back to the truck and laid them on the seat next to Billie. He ripped open the package for the pre-paid phone and powered it up. Two bars of signal strength—more than Parker thought they might have.

He tapped in a number and waited. "Hello?" Linda said.

"Linda, it's me,"

"You on your way home?"

"Soon. I'm with Billie, and we have a predicament."

"Of course you do. What do you need me to do?"

"First off, are you and Miguel all right?"

"We're both fine. Miguel stayed with Leon and me last night. They're off at school today following up at the job fair from the other day."

"Good. Anything new on the threads you guys were looking into on the money laundering, or Los Muertos-connected businesses? We found out what Western Machine Parts was hiding in those cardboard boxes Leon saw. Guns—guns and explosives. Enough to keep a small army going."

"They were running guns over the border? Who's buying them?"

"I don't know yet. I'm hoping you and the guys can pull it together before Billie and I walk into more than we bargained for."

"We can start digging."

"Call Espinoza over at DEA. He might have some close-to-the-ground intel on what's happening. He called the Los Muertos internal struggle to a tee. Castaneda is losing his grip on control."

"Want to read in Lynne Finch?"

Parker paused. She was close to Castaneda's handler at Homeland. If Lynne went running to him...

"I'll take your silence as enough. I'll call you back on this number if we get anything. What happened to your phone?"

"It's a long story, Linda. Remind me to cancel the account on my phone. You take care of yourself—and Miguel. I love you."

"I love you too. You be careful and get home soon," Linda said before hanging up.

Billie was grinning at him.

"What?"

"You had to go buy a phone to tell her you loved her. Kinda sappy—but in a good way."

"Shut up."

Parker was putting the phone on the seat when a banner flashed on the screen. "Bluetooth device located. Press to connect to Air Tag."

"You have one of those little Air Tags, Billie? Those things you use to track your suitcase, car keys, or your lost pet?"

"I look like I want someone watchin' my every move?"

"Someone is."

Parker debated pressing connect on the Air Tag feature, but he wasn't sure if it would disconnect it from the watcher.

"Give me a hand for a sec, would ya?" Parker said, getting out of the truck.

He dropped the tailgate and hopped up inside, pulling the tarp back, exposing the boxes in the truck bed.

"What you thinking, Nathan?"

"Remember the crate? The open one?"

"Yeah, the one with them grenades inside."

"I'm gonna take a better look."

Parker found the crate and pulled the top off, revealing two rows of Mark II fragmentation grenades nestled in soft black foam cutouts. Each explosive had its own safe little cubbyhole. The edge of the right side was curled upward.

"This has been lifted up."

Parker removed the four grenades on the right side and gently placed them on the truck bed. They were safe with all the pins in place, but still, it was unsettling to have all this explosive material close at hand.

He pulled the foam padding up, and the Air Tag glistened in the sunlight atop bundles of one-hundred-dollar bills hidden in the bottom of the crate.

Chapter Thirty-Nine

With the bundles of cash laid out in the bed of the truck Parker estimated over a half a million dollars was hidden in the box of explosives. The neat stacks were tightly wedged in the crate except for two missing bundles. The two gunmen who disappeared from the garage probably took their cut and left before they were discovered.

"What's going on here, Billie?" Parker asked.

"What's in the rest of them crates is what I wanna know."

Parker placed the protective foam layer in the empty crate and lifted a grenade to place it safely back in the nest. His finger caught on an uneven surface on the bottom of the grenade. Turning it over, he saw a plug at the bottom was loose. Using his fingers, he backed the screwed plug out of the bottom, and it was empty—hollow.

"This is a dud. It's empty with no explosive inside."

"What would make Castaneda send a load of toys down here?"

Parker tore open another cardboard box, Rows of disassembled H&K MP-5 rifles. He took the pieces out and assembled a weapon.

"These look like the real deal." He turned it to the side and placed his finger in the ejection port. "I think I feel a firing pin in place. What gives? Real rifles with pretend grenades?"

Parker lifted his hand under the packing layer. No additional stash of currency was hidden beneath the lethal firearms.

"Only the crate with the cash had one of them Air Tag thingies in it."

Parker repacked the crates, removed the Air Tag, put it in his pocket, and covered the load with the tarp.

Leaning on the side of the truck, Parker mulled over the possibilities.

"The old man in the market. He said we were heading toward the Sinaloa Cartel villa, remember?"

"How can I forget?"

"How come you didn't mention it?"

"I don't know. Maybe 'cause they pretty much abandoned the place after El Halcón got taken out."

"They aren't using it?"

"Don't know for sure. They might have a few people there, but the new Cartel head been moving from place to place, so his enemies can't find him."

"Is the GPS dot leading us to the Cartel compound?"

Billie shrugged. "Don't know for sure, but it's in the general direction. I don't use them E-lectronic road maps much."

"We could be dropping this shipment off in a cartel compound?"

"I guess. What do it really matter? Cartel or Los Muertos, It's more of the same."

"Are they?" Parker rubbed the stubble on his chin.

"Pretty much."

"Castaneda sends guns and money down here? Why? And who is supposed to get them?"

"He told us it was his people. I'm thinkin' it was another lie. 'Sides he doesn't know Armando and his family are free."

"What if it's a payoff? What if Castaneda is trying to buy off the cartel so he stays in control of Los Muertos instead of Carmen?"

"Huh? Makes sense in a twisted kinda way. He's buying off the cartel and aligning with them before Carmen has a chance to set up camp."

"What if this stuff never gets delivered?" Parker said.

"Someone won't be happy."

"Castaneda won't get the bribe he promised to the Cartel. The Cartel will take it as a slap in the face, thinking he either couldn't deliver, or lied to them. The only one who wins is Carmen Delgado. She's then in a position to take Los Muertos and cozy up to the Cartel."

"The cartel doesn't need Los Muertos as much as Los Muertos needs the cartel," Billie said.

Parker closed the truck bed. "Let's take a drive up the road a piece. I have a thought."

Billie shrugged and climbed in behind the wheel.

Parker pointed at a wash curving around a small hill. Billie turned and pointed the Ford off road and after a half mile, Parker motioned for her to pull over.

"What you got in mind?"

Parker jumped out of the cab and jogged to the back of the truck. He grabbed the weapon he had assembled and opened three more boxes until he found one with fully loaded 9mm magazines for the H&K. He shoved one in the magazine well and pulled the charging handle, chambering a round in the weapon.

Parker sighted on a spindly downed log and pulled the trigger. Three rounds shot through the barrel, and then the weapon malfunctioned. Parker pulled the trigger, and nothing happened.

He grabbed another weapon, assembled it, inserted a full magazine and after three rounds, the weapon froze. Not even the charging handle would retract to eject a round.

Parker smiled. "I know what's going on."

"Wanna fill me in?"

"Castaneda knows he's on thin ice."

"I mean, sure. He has to know. He's up north slippin' info to the feds while Echevarría is taking over."

"With Echevarría off the board, Carmen is set to make a move to align with the Cartel, according to Espi. Castaneda knows he's the only thing standing in the way of her complete takeover. So, what does our boy do? He buys his way back into the cartel's good graces with a truckload of guns and money. And he's tight with the feds, feeding them good intel on Los Muertos and the cartel."

"'Cept the guns ain't workin.'"

"It explains why they were shipped from Western Machine Parts. Castaneda's guys there disassembled them and cut, or damaged the parts in the receivers so they would all fail. They're useless."

"I'm following. He's givin' the cartel weapons that can't be used against him. But the money? That ain't faked, too, is it?"

"I'm not an expert, but I think it's all real. It explains the Air Tag in the crate. Castaneda planned on getting this one back."

"He could be tellin' the feds where to find the guns. Sounds like the kind of double deal Castaneda would pull," Billie said.

"Either way, we shouldn't be sitting on these for long."

"We gonna take them up to the villa for Casteneda? If it's like we're thinkin' they'll there to take this stuff."

"What if the cartel doesn't get their payoff?"

"Someone will be mad as a hornet. What do we do with this stuff? Give it to?" Billie said, kicking the truck's rear tire.

"Like you said, the cartel will be royally pissed. Castaneda's gonna get cut off, and his intel value to the feds goes down the drain. They could get these weapons repaired with some effort. If Castaneda doesn't see his Air Tag moving soon, he'll know we're onto him."

A rumble from south of their position marked the approach of a heavy vehicle. Dust spewed from the wheels of a dump truck. The red and white paint job rippled in the heat mirage rising from the road. It was lumbering along and didn't show signs of slowing down as it approached Billie's blue Ford on the shoulder.

Parker waved to the driver who looked surprised to see anyone on the lonely stretch of road but kept on moving. Not that anyone would want to highjack his truckload of red dirt, but no one stopped for hitchhikers out here.

As the truck swept past, Parker snagged the Air Tag from his pocket and hefted it in the rear of the dump truck. As far as Castaneda knew, his shipment was on the move once more.

"Let's take care of this crap and get home, Billie."

Chapter Forty

"You sure we did the right thing?" Billie asked once they were on the road again.

"I hope so. It keeps those guns out of anyone's hands, and it puts a kink in Castaneda's scheme."

Parker's new pre-paid cell sounded, and he recognized the number.

"Miguel, everything okay?"

"Yeah, fine. Everything's fine. I got a lead on one of those missing college students."

"What'd you find?" Parker said, putting the call on speaker.

"Are you anywhere near Hermosillo?"

"We planned on giving the city a wide berth. Why?"

"A woman connected with me, saying her son was one of the missing. I didn't want to send her the photos without your say-so. Besides, I don't think it's the kind of thing you want to get in a text message from someone you don't know."

"You're right, good thinking. Her son is one of our victims?"

"The things she was saying—you know—about how he and his friends disappeared. She sent him off to live with family near Mexico City so he could attend a tech school."

"She happen to say when she last saw him, or her family last put eyes on the kid?"

"Three weeks ago."

"Puts it in our ballpark," Parker said. "Can you send me her contact information and address? And can you send me the photos? I don't know how much memory this pre-paid cell has, but give it a try."

"Will do. Is Billie okay?"

"I'm fine, thanks to Nathan. You takin' care of the office while I'm out? Don't want to come back and find it all nerded out."

"Yeah, yeah. You need to get into the modern age, Billie. Leon was working with me to upgrade our server here. He got a job so I'll finish it up on my own. You have your own Immigrant Coalition email address now, Billie. billiecarson.coalition@gmail.com."

"When have you known me to ever email anybody?"

"Now you can."

"Leon got a job. I'm sure he was happy. He was kinda bummed after we all told him to leave the Western Machine Parts job."

"Yeah, he was kinda pissed, but this time he gets to actually do work he's going to school for, like upgrading our server. I'll send you the woman's contact and see what I can do about the photos."

"Thanks, Miguel. Billie and I will stop and try to talk with the woman. Be home tonight—probably really late."

They disconnected the call and seconds later a tinny chime sounded on the pre-paid phone. A text from Miguel gave an address Northern Hermosillo 81 Ave Calpé and the woman's name is Theresa Mendonsa.

"I know where that is. Can you use your other-other phone and call Armando? He's not far. I think he should be there when we talk to the family."

"Probably not a bad idea."

Parker made the call from the phone he got during the jailbreak. The number was in the phone's memory because Billie had used it to call Armando for a ride from the city.

"He said he'd meet us there. What's the deal with the kid? I mean, the way you guys were talking, he does quite a bit for you down here for the Coalition."

"He does. Armando knows the dangers of moving north with the wrong people. He can try to give that message to those waiting in the camps to make the crossing. He gets the resources to the right people. We have a small warehouse, and he runs it for us."

"The Casa Segura."

She nodded. "We needed to come up with a name so people could find us. Turned out to be bigger than we expected."

"How so?"

"We've got a couple of teams who go out to the camps and provide medical care, nothing big, but some of them people are in a bad way when they get here considering they already put on a thousand miles from Central America and such."

"You've got doctors working for you down here?"

"Only a couple. We could use more. People are coming for the medical care who ain't even plannin' on crossin'."

Parker hiked a thumb to the back seat of the extended cab Ford. "You can afford a few more now." The crate of cash, now devoid of phony hand grenades, sat on the seat.

"Could solve some problems we been havin' about moving Coalition money out of the country. Bank regulations and such. We can use this money to support operations here until we get the banks and the SEC to understand we ain't runnin' no drug smuggling operation."

"Sounds like good use for the cash."

Billie pointed ahead to Ave Calpé. "That's our street."

The neighborhood was residential, with homes walled off from the dangers of the street with tall concrete block barriers. They were painted in shades of brown and grey, whatever tint managed to cover the graffiti spreading through the neighborhood like mold. No one was out on the street in midday.

Parker felt the cell phone on the seat next to him vibrate.

"It's Castaneda."

Parker connected and answered. "Yes."

"What are you doing?"

"Driving in the middle of nowhere, like you wanted."

"You passed the drop point."

"It all looks the same out here."

"Stop. Turn around now."

"We're following the GPS location your men gave us.

"I'm telling you to turn around."

"That's not what the GPS says. It's showing us going north for another thirty miles."

"No. That's wrong. Turn around."

"It's the coordinates your own people gave. Unless—they weren't your people…"

A slight pause from Castaneda marked the first shadow of doubt. "They made a mistake. Turn around. Now."

"I don't think so. Someone's expecting these weapons. I want to see how grateful they are to get them," Parker said.

"Don't fuck with me, Detective. I still have the DeSilva family."

"Do you?" Parker hit the end call button.

"Oh, that will get him to spinnin'. You know he's callin' his people now."

"Wonder if they'll even answer him?"

"Number 81, that's us."

As Billie eased the truck to the curb, Armando appeared and slid the gate open, allowing them off the street. Billie didn't relish leaving a half million dollars out on the graffiti-covered thoroughfare.

"I didn't get any photos from Miguel. I'll call and see what's up."

Billie and Parker hopped from the truck cab, and Armando met them in the courtyard.

"Miguel says he couldn't send the file."

"How can Señora Mendonsa identify her son?"

"I'm not sure. I think we should still go talk with her," Parker said.

"She's waiting for us inside," Armando said.

Parker and Billie followed Armando to the door, where he knocked and waited, taking a step back from the threshold.

The door opened and a woman in her forties beckoned then inside. She was a slight woman, barely five feet tall. Her black hair was streaked with gray and worry lines were etched into her forehead.

Armando made the introductions in Spanish.

"Señora Mendonsa, I'm Detective Nathan Parker. Do you speak English?"

"I do," she said in unaccented English.

"Thank you. My Spanish is not very good. I'm a detective from Maricopa County in Arizona. I've been looking into a case—migrants coming over the border, and something has happened to them."

"This has to do with the men found dead on the freeway outside of Phoenix?" She said.

Parker looked surprised.

"It's been on the news down here. My son? Was he one of the people you found?"

"I don't know. But from what Armando and Billie have told me, your son went to school and disappeared, is that right?"

She nodded slowly. "My Hector went back to university three weeks ago. He was to graduate this spring. We are so proud of him. The first in our family to graduate. I attended, as did his father, but we were not able to finish. We needed to come home and take care of family, you understand?"

"I do. What was your son studying?" Parker asked.

"Computer engineering."

Parker frowned, trying to make sense of it.

"Any idea if he and others would cross the border? It seems unusual to me."

"There was no reason for him to take such risks. He is smart. He had a job lined up here with a big company once he graduated."

"I bet he was excited."

"He was. He couldn't stop talking about working for Coyle Technology and how he was going to be able to make a good living and help us. We don't need him to help us, but he felt he should because—"

"Coyle Technology?"

"Yes. They offered him a position at their offices in Mexico City." She strolled over to a hall table and sorted through a stack of mail until she found the one she was looking for. "Ah, here it is." She handed the letter to Parker.

The correspondence was in Spanish, but it was on Coyle Technology letterhead. He handed it to Armando. "Could you translate this for me?"

Armando held the letter and read. "Congratulations, Hector. It is my great privilege to announce your acceptance into the advanced programming internship at Coyle Technology upon your graduation from the Institute of Technology in Mexico City.

"After successful completion of a sixty-day training program, you will be appointed as a Programmer I at one of our facilities. You are asked to report to the Coyle Technology Recruitment Office in Mexico City." Armando handed the letter back to Señora Mendonsa. "It said he was to report two weeks ago."

"He was so happy—I never heard from him after a quick phone call saying he was going to Coyle Technology in the morning."

"The police in Mexico City? Did they have any ideas? You aren't the only mother this has happened to..."

"They were too busy with real crime, they said. An adult like Hector can make his own decisions. Even if there were more than ten of us who reported the same thing."

"If you don't mind—I know it's an imposition, may I look at his room? Sometimes, we can see something in a missing person's room to tell us where they might have gone."

Mrs. Mendonsa shrugged. "This way." She led Parker to the rear of the house, crossing a large square courtyard in the middle of the residence. A fountain bubbled in the center of the tiled square. The evening sky cast an orange hue into the open-air patio, transforming this home on the fringe of the city into a peaceful oasis.

The woman opened a glass-paneled door and flicked on a light as she entered. A large room facing the courtyard was divided into two living areas. One to the right was Hector's bed, bureau, and bathroom. To the left, a living room and office with computers and two large monitors. The computer desk was crowded with boxes, wires, and notebooks.

"He really is into computers," Mrs. Mendonsa said.

"I'll say." Parker walked toward the desk, and three computer towers were on the floor near the desk, each in partial disarray. Parts were carefully laid out next to each one.

"Was he building computers?"

"His friends would pay him to make them fast gaming systems. They had a whole network of online players. All his off time—this is where I would find him. Working on these computers, playing online, and chatting with people all over. I wished he would have spent more time with his head out there—in the real world. Maybe this wouldn't have happened to him."

She reached for a photograph on the desk. A small silver frame held a black-and-white image of Hector and his mother. She handed it to Parker.

"This is the last picture I have of him. It was taken a few days before he returned to school."

Parker held the frame in both hands and the young man's face struck a nerve on the back of his brain because he'd seen him before—in the back of the cargo container.

Chapter Forty-One

The boy wasn't smiling when Parker spotted him tangled in among the corpses abandoned at Devil's Well. What made this face stand out from the other twenty-seven men was this one—the one in the photograph—was the only survivor. Hector was the unconscious man in the hospital.

"Señora, your son is alive."

"What? Are you certain?" She leaned on a computer desk to keep from collapsing."

"He's in a hospital in Phoenix. He had no identification on him."

"Hospital—Phoenix—is he hurt?"

"He was locked in a shipping container with over twenty other men. Many of the others didn't survive. He's stable and receiving medical care."

"But, he's alive. My baby is alive."

"He is."

She began weeping. The tears held back from the fear of losing her son. The not knowing. The emotions held in check while she prayed for her son's return. The dam broke, and she let it all go.

"Thank you. Can I bring him home?"

"I can connect you with the hospital and his doctors. I can help you go visit him."

"I can't get a travel visa in time to be of any use."

"I think we can help. Hey, Billie? Can you come in here for a sec?"

Billie popped her head in Hector's room.

"Billie, can the Immigrant Coalition help find a place for Señora Mendonsa to stay in Phoenix while she visits her son in the hospital?"

"Sure. Not a problem at all. Say, hospital, you mean Hector ain't—?"

Parker cut her off, not wanting too much information to overwhelm the shaken mother.

Billie understood and nodded. "I'll get it set up."

"That is very kind of you, but I don't have a travel visa."

"Can we sit and talk for a minute? Maybe we can figure out a way to deal with the visa issue."

They parked at a small table covered with computer parts, wiring diagrams, and tools."

"Señora, was Hector involved in any—political organizations? Any groups or associations with people who would oppose the cartels?"

"Hector was not at all political. If it didn't have to do with computers or his gaming, then he wasn't involved in it. I mean, he knows about the cartel. Everyone does who lives here in Hermosillo knows about them. We also know we don't draw their attention."

"Do you or your family know anyone in the FBI or Homeland Security?"

She shook her head. "We don't. Hector never mentioned it. He would have said if he had."

The honcho from Homeland Security presented Hector as a material witness, or an informant, and they were concerned for his safety. The same concern brought Esteban Castaneda to the hospital in an attempt to kidnap the comatose patient.

"Does the name Esteban Castaneda mean anything?"

"No. Is he one of the missing?"

Parker took the new pre-paid cell and dialed Miguel's number again. He picked up like he was sitting by the phone waiting.

"Are you in Hermosillo?" Miguel asked.

"We are, and we're meeting with Señora Mendonsa right now."

"Does she know? About the men in the shipping container?"

"Her son Hector is the survivor."

"The one in the hospital? That's good news."

"It is. Billie's going to arrange a place for her to stay so she can visit her son. I need to reach Lynne and see what we can do to expedite a visa for her. We can't wait the usual months. Can you get me Lynne's number? You're at home, right?

"I'm at Sarah's. Going to a late movie and some dinner."

"Oh, I was going to tell you to grab her number from my desk."

"I can get it—hang on for a minute."

Less than thirty seconds later, Miguel came back with Lynne's cell number. "You did want her personal cell, right? Because at this hour, no one would be at her office."

"Good thinking. How did you? How were you able to get her private phone number?"

"Please. Nothing is ever private. You got to know where to look. I have Lynnette Finch's phone number when you're ready."

Parker grabbed a scrap of paper from the desk and jotted down the number.

"Thanks, Miguel. Don't stay out too late. Billie and I will be home soon."

Parker tapped in Lynne's cell number.

"Hello?" Lynne said.

"Lynne, it's Nathan."

"I didn't recognize this number. Where are you calling from?"

"Mexico."

"Not Hermosillo, I hope. Billie's a person of interest down there for breaking out of jail. A police inspector was killed. She's implicated in his death."

"She didn't do it."

"I know you have this blind spot for her, but this is serious, Nathan."

"She didn't kill Inspector Lopez. It was one of Castaneda's men."

"How did you know it was Lopez?"

"Because I saw it happen. And his real name was Echeverría. He was fighting Castaneda for control of Los Muertos."

"Nathan—"

Parker cut off the lecture that was brewing. "Lynne, I'm calling about the survivor in the shipping container. I'm here with his mother. The

240

man's name is Hector Mendonsa from Hermosillo. This is where it gets complicated."

"Of course it does with you."

"Hector is not an undercover operative, or an informant. Homeland is lying to you. Be careful, Lynne. Your fed brothers aren't telling you everything. If Hector Mendonsa isn't an operative, why did they arrange to kidnap him from the hospital?"

Lynne was silent on the other end of the connection.

"Lynne?"

"I'm here, Nathan. Mom might not know all her son's activities. He could be working with Homeland and she's not aware of it. Moms are sometimes the last to know."

"This kid was a computer programmer down here and was abducted to end up in a box in the desert. Does that sound like someone working undercover? It's not who this kid is."

"What do you want me to do, Nathan? It's another federal agency. Homeland doesn't share their intel."

"Start with why they had Castaneda involved in his attempted abduction from the hospital."

"I don't like it either." Parker felt the ice begin to thaw. "I'll take a look, quietly, and see if there's anything there."

"Thanks. Can you help Mrs. Mendonsa get a visa to come and visit her son in the hospital?"

"You only call me when you need something, don't you?"

"Because you come through, Lynne."

"Is the mother there?"

"Yeah."

"Let me speak with her."

Parker handed the phone to Mrs. Mendonsa. "This is a friend with the FBI. She's very nice and she can help get an emergency visa for you."

She took the phone from Parker and spoke with Lynne. Parker stepped away, giving her some privacy.

He stood with Billie at the patio door.

"Lynne didn't break with Homeland. I think she's still buying the company line the kid is some sort of super spy."

"You've seen him. Skinny little boy. He's no informant, confidential or otherwise."

"She also mentioned the heat is still on here in Hermosillo. The locals are still after you for the Inspector's murder."

"I figured as much."

"How we gonna get you out of here? Did they snatch your passport when Echevarría busted you with the guns?"

"I got it in my truck. But if they're lookin' for me, it will light up at the border."

Mrs. Mendonsa handed the phone back. "Miss Finch says she needs to speak with you."

"Lynne? Can you help her visit the boy?"

"I think we can get a t-visa for both of them."

Parker knew the emergency t-visa was granted to trafficking victims, and from all indications, Hector clearly fit.

"Thanks, Lynne."

"I feel for the mom. And for what it's worth, I think you're right about her son. I'm not on board with Homeland. It smells."

"Be careful with Hansen, Lynne. He's only interested in his arrest rates and CompStat report numbers."

"I know the type. You heading home? Be careful."

Parker said goodbye and disconnected the call.

"Can this woman do what she said she could do?" Mrs. Mendonsa asked.

"Lynne is tenacious, and once she says she'll do something, there is no stopping her."

"She said she would have a courier from the American Embassy bring me the visa."

"Good. I know Hector will recover faster with you there."

"Thank you." She paused for a moment, then hugged Parker. "I don't know why you did this, but Hector and I both thank you and owe you a debt we can never hope to repay."

"You don't owe us anything, Señora. I'm sorry Hector got caught up in this mess. I know he didn't bring this on. He—and the others were trapped. I'm hopeful he'll recover quickly." Parker handed her one of his cards and told her to call her once she got to Phoenix.

Parker and Billie left the Mendonsa home and closed the front door behind them. Armando waited near Billie's truck.

"How much do you trust him?" Parker asked.

Billie took in the young man, who straightened when she and Parker looked in his direction.

"With my life. I did that very thing once. He's a good boy. I've known him since the day he was born. Helps with the family business—another electrician, it looks like. But he is my eyes and ears down here. Armando keeps the Coalition resources safe and makes certain they get to the people in the most need."

"How does the Coalition keep him supplied? I know you can't do it all by yourself."

"I get him what I can, as often as I can. He's managed to develop a few donors down here. I worry because I don't know when their true intentions will surface and the donors will use the relief effort for their own ends. It's dangerous for Armando to ask for money—you never know who's lurking out there."

"What if he didn't need to ask anymore?"

"He doesn't have a choice. There are too many who need the help and we don't have enough to go around. With Echevarría out, there might be a window where people can get across without the Cartel, or Los Muertos putting them in danger."

Parker nudged Billie, and they went to the truck.

"Armando, what could you do with a half million dollars?" Parker said as he opened the truck's passenger door.

Chapter Forty-Two

The six-hour drive from Hermosillo to Phoenix went smoothly, especially since Parker slept for part of the journey after the border crossing at Nogales.

Even in the late hours, the Nogales border station was open as it was one of the major international crossings. During the day, wait times could be over an hour, but at one in the morning, there was no traffic. The U.S. Customs officer asked for their passports, and a canine officer walked around the truck with the dog on a long lead and a mirror on a stick, looking under the lifted truck's frame.

The Belgian Shepherd barked once and sat. The dog alerted his handler.

Parker and Billy exchanged a glance. Neither of them had thought to look under the truck. If Los Muertos had hidden a kilo of heroin under the chassis, they were screwed.

The dog handler directed Billie to a parking area to the right, where a team of Customs officers waited to search the vehicle.

Billie pulled the Ford to the search area, where she and Parker were told to leave the vehicle. Another Customs officer took their passports and escorted them to an office. While the passports were checked again, the search team went through the truck.

Parker noticed the pedestrian walkway, the Morley Gate, wasn't scheduled to open for hours and at least a hundred people were lined up for their turn to enter the United States. Some of these people did this every day, working on the northern side of the split city of Nogales, Arizona.

The canine officer entered the office with his dog, and he let the dog try to catch a scent off of Billie and Parker. The dog didn't alert.

"You have any firearms or explosives to declare?" The officer asked.

Not anymore, Parker thought. "No, nothing," Parker said, hoping nothing was hidden under the truck.

The handler narrowed his eyes at the pair.

Parker pulled his badge from his wallet, identified himself, and the Customs man relaxed a bit.

"The dog hit on the truck bed. There's nothing there—now."

"Could have been last week's range day. We set up in the truck before we shot," Parker said.

The man nodded.

Parker felt the anxiety creep up over what was taking so long with the passports. Unless—

"Miss Carson," the Customs man called.

If the Mexican authorities had, in fact, tied Billie to the assassination of the police inspector, this was the end of the line—for both of them.

The man strode over, his six-foot-five frame towering over Billie.

"Here you go, Miss Carson, Mr. Parker. Welcome back to the United States."

Parker and Billie returned to the truck and were glad they buried the weapons in a desolate patch of desert.

Billie pulled out of the inspection area and followed the signs north toward Phoenix.

Once they were clear of the border station, Parker asked. "Why do you think the Mexican authorities didn't have an APB out for us?"

"The federales been known for their history of corruption, and no doubt once they realized what their inspector was, they'd be happy enough to let it go."

Parker's cell vibrated in his pocket. He pulled the burner out, and Castaneda's number blazed on the screen. "Oh, he can't be happy now. He has to know we didn't deliver his goods." Parker hit the end call button.

"Castaneda is runnin' out of time. If them guns were a peace offering to the cartel, then he's out in the cold," Billie said.

"And his value to the feds is running on empty."

"I only worry what he'll do next. He's like a wounded animal, and he's unpredictable."

Parker nodded and leaned against the passenger window. He drifted off into an uneasy sleep with images of Castaneda, McMillan, and all the innocents the Los Muertos thug killed and the lives ruined. Ellie McMillan's words echoed in his dreams—forgiveness. Not in this world or the next.

"Nathan. Nathan," Billie said, shaking Parker's shoulder.

He startled awake. "What is it? Where?"

"Nathan, you're home. Man, you were dreamin' something fierce. Talkin' in your sleep and everythin'. Somethin' 'bout revenge served cold."

Parker rubbed his eyes, and they felt like they were full of desert sand. He noticed they were parked in front of his home. He glanced at his watch—after four o'clock in the morning. Miguel's car was in the driveway. It was dark. The sun hadn't even considered making an appearance yet. Across the street, old Mrs. Estacio pulled her curtains open, keeping watch over the neighborhood.

"Billie, I was going to drive for a while to give you a break."

"You needed the rest. After my jailbreak and all."

Parker unbuckled his seat belt. "You want to come in, catch a few hours sleep?"

"Nah, I gotta go get my trailer, and then I'll crash for a while."

"Where is your trailer anyway? Your neighbor out at Rocky Wash saw you pull out."

"Storage yard behind the Immigrant Coalition offices."

"Oh, right. You sure you don't want to stay here?"

"Thanks for the offer. I don't get many, but I'll head to my own place."

Parker hopped down from the truck's passenger seat and walked around to the driver's window.

"Thanks for comin' to rescue my sorry ass, Nathan. I know the way I split and all had to look bad. I wouldn't have blamed you if you'd left me there."

Parker patted Billie's arm through the window. "You would have done the same for me. And you have. My world wouldn't be the same without a little Billie Carson in it."

Billie's eyes welled. He decided he'd keep the doubts that ran through his brain about what Billie had done and why she fled to himself.

Billie nodded and pulled her truck away. The street was quiet after she left, and Parker decided to sit on his patio for a moment and pause in the night air. The still warmth in the pre-dawn hours predicted a scorcher of a day ahead.

Parker had a few hours rest and his mind was already starting to work over the bits and pieces on the road from Hermosillo. Hector Mendonsa was lured to a job with Coyle Technology. A job which was supposed to be his entry into the high-tech world. Parker had no doubt the others in the shipping container were also IT job seekers.

In his years working in Arizona, he'd seen farmworkers by the thousands, laborers, skilled construction workers, and salesmen. The high-tech scene wasn't the usual draw for illegal immigration. Sure, there were guest worker visas for highly skilled tech jobs, and Parker knew Mexico and South America were more than capable of growing their own Silicon Valley companies and were becoming less dependent upon American expertise and other foreign influences. Why, then, were Hector and the others found here? Coyle Tech was the key.

The porch light flicked on, and Miguel cracked open the door. "I thought it was you out here."

"Hey, buddy. Sorry to wake you," Parker said.

"How long have you been sitting here?"

"Not long. Billie dropped me off." Parker glanced at his watch. He'd been sitting here ruminating for an hour.

"Is Billie all right? Are you?"

He nodded, his head getting heavy from the road trip. "I think she is. She had a rough go of it down there, but I think it's over for her."

"Oh, good. And you found Hector Mendonsa's family." After a pause, "I was worried that something would happen to you."

Parker felt the concern from Miguel—worry that he might lose another family if something happened to him.

"It's all good, thanks to you. His mother will be up to be with him in the hospital."

"Oh, wow. Good news. I found his online gaming profile. We like some of the same things. He's really good."

"Maybe once he gets rested, you can drop in on him."

"I'd like that. He has his mom, but it might be good for him to know other people care."

Parker patted Miguel's leg. "Armando DeSilva turned out to be a good person too."

"The name in the paper. The one that made Billie get all weird."

"Yeah, Billie's got him running most of the Coalition's business down in Hermosillo."

Miguel's face pruned up. "Really? I haven't heard the name before."

"You haven't run across Armando in your networking down there?"

"Not at all. First time I saw the name was when Billie found the newspaper."

Parker's neck tingled.

What was Billie withholding from him? She wasn't telling him the whole truth.

Chapter Forty-Three

After a scalding hot shower, Parker brewed a pot of coffee for Miguel and himself. The morning paper had dropped on the doorstep a hall an hour ago and Parker scanned it for any mention of the international entanglements he'd witnessed in the last twenty-four hours. Nothing on the front pages.

The business page was the usual blather of stock prices dropping in response to market influences. Blah, blah, blah. Parker started to turn the page until one line caught his eye. He straightened the page, and his attention went to an article about Coyle Technology. It seemed the company was the exception to the global tech stock devaluation. Their share price skyrocketed. The columnist attributed the increase to the visionary leadership of Randy Coyle. Although brutal staffing reductions were noted, Coyle managed to exceed all projections and increased the company's cloud server capacity. The article proclaimed Coyle and his organization were a model for the rest of the industry.

Parker didn't know how visionary the man was. He seemed distracted and scattered when he and Barry Johns paid him a visit.

Miguel padded out of his room and went directly for the coffee.

"Get any more sleep last night?" Parker asked.

He nodded and took another sip.

"What you got going today?"

"The usual. Classes this morning, and off to the Coalition offices in the afternoon. Was going to meet up with Leon, but he's ghosting me now that he's working."

"He's probably busy and distracted learning new stuff. Did you tell me where he was working?"

"Yeah, he wanted a real job. Coyle Technology." Miguel drew another sip of dark roast.

Parker stopped his coffee mug halfway to his mouth. Placing it back down on the table. "What did he say he was going to do at Coyle Technology?"

"I dunno. He mentioned programming and maintaining their servers. Kinda techie stuff. He hoped if he did a good job, they'd keep him on full time."

To Parker's ear, it sounded like the sales pitch Hector received in his letter from Coyle Tech.

He'd have to ask Linda what Leon said about his first days on the job.

Miguel put on some toast. While he stood there waiting, he said, "I still can't understand why Billie didn't tell me about Armando DeSilva if he was such an important part of the Coalition's operation in Hermosillo. She's been having me set up supplies, get relief packages mailed out, and arrange for people to pick up the shipments when she can't get down there. She's never mentioned him all this time. Does she not trust me, or something? Did I mess something up?"

"No, you didn't do anything. She's keeping this one close, and I don't know why. I met the kid and he seems like he's known Billie forever. His family was taken by Castaneda, and we got them back."

"No kidding? Lucky for them, you were able to get there in time."

"Yeah, lucky..."

Parker's stomach no longer agreed with the dark roast. "I'm gonna get moving. You call me—oh, wait, I need to get a new phone. Call me on the number we connected on last night." The prepaid cell.

Parker headed out to his Jeep. Linda had taken the department SUV before he left for Hermosillo.

The Major Crimes Bureau was quiet, with the exception of Barry Johns and Pete Tully, who were plugging away at their desks.

"You two got an early start," Parker said.

"I think we got a hit on the money laundering angle," Tully said.

Parker sat on the corner of a nearby desk.

"Twenty of the hundred-dollar bills were tagged as federal assets."

"Like a bank?" Parker asked.

"No. Like in funds allocated to a federal agency."

"Which one?"

"Barry's working on it..."

"And I got us an answer. The money came from an account in Homeland Security allocated for confidential informants."

"The only confidential source I know working with Homeland is Castaneda."

"They're paying the guy for spilling his guts."

"For now."

Parker filled the detectives in on Castaneda's ploy to double-cross the cartel with the defective weapons.

"He'd still remain in control of Los Muertos," Tully said.

"If his deal went through. We made sure there was a hiccup in his delivery."

"Means the Cartel will turn to Carmen and her Los Muertos faction," Johns said.

Linda walked over and hugged Parker and didn't care what Johns and Tully had to say about it.

"I was worried about you."

"Yeah, we were worried about you too," Tully said. "But I ain't the hugging kind."

"I'm kinda happy to hear that," Parker said.

"We were catching up on who's calling the shots for Los Muertos," Johns said.

"As soon as Carmen realizes Castaneda took his shot and tried to cut her out, she's going to do some cutting of her own. According to Espinoza at the DEA, it was her plan all along, but now she's got a bit more motivation."

"That would certainly do it," Linda said. "Should we alert Agent Finch?"

"She knows. I was able to reach her last night from Hermosillo. She's beginning to believe Homeland isn't telling her everything."

Parker caught a glance from Linda.

"The boys here were telling me the cash we processed from the trucker's place—some of it tied back to an account in Homeland used to pay off informants."

"How did the trucker get it?" he said.

"Homeland buying the trucker's services doesn't make sense. Homeland to Castaneda to the trucker fits a little bit more, but for what?"

"The link is there, but I don't get the 'Big Why.' What would Los Muertos get out of this arrangement?" Tully said.

"There's another piece we're missing here to make it all come together. Western Machine Parts was shipping guns down south. That's what these crates held. Billie and I disposed of them in the desert before they could get into the wrong hands." Parker decided to withhold the part about Billie being the one who smuggled the arms shipment over the border.

"Here's the kicker and where the machine shop comes into play. They tampered with the weapons so they would fail after a couple of rounds. The end-user was going to be holding a stockpile of useless weapons."

"Who was going to end up with them?"

"The cartel," Tully said.

"Castaneda made his play to push Carmen out," Johns said.

"Listen, we know Sinaloa has been vulnerable since El Halcón was overthrown. All the infighting weakened them to the point the Baja and Juarez Cartels started poaching on their territory. Los Muertos under Echevarría was one more competitive element," Parker said.

"Has a ring of truth to it," Tully said. "If the Sinaloa Cartel could bring Los Muertos back into the fold, they could hold off the other cartels. Casteneda made a promise to get in line."

"The other cartels have to be watching on the sidelines, ready to swoop in and pick up the pieces," Tully said.

"It explains why Castaneda has been secretly giving up small pieces of the cartel's operations to the feds. It would make them weak and desperate to shore up what they have. Pushing them to bring Los Muertos under their wing as muscle," Parker said.

"What does Castaneda hope to gain from a move like that? Wouldn't it make everyone vulnerable? Who wins?" Linda asked.

Parker paced across his office. Castaneda had moved in unexpected ways. Three or four moves ahead of his rivals. What was his end game here? He wasn't going to end his career as a federal snitch. He was using them for his own ends and they were too blind to see it.

Unless...

Chapter Forty-Four

P arker left the Sheriff's Offices with little more than a terse, "I need to take care of something," to his detectives. Linda offered to come with him, wherever he was going, but he asked her to stay and follow up on the money angle; if there were a few bills marked, there might be others.

Reluctantly, she agreed. He noticed the hurt in her green eyes. But where he was going, he wanted to make sure she was isolated from the fallout.

Parker pulled his Explorer into the underground parking lot at the law offices of Sutton, Witmer, and Hoster. He was relieved to see Sutton's Bentley parked in his reserved space.

The receptionist in Larry Sutton's office was on the phone when Parker arrived, and he strode past her toward the inner offices.

"Wait. Sir, you can't…"

By the time she finished her sentence, Parker was in Sutton's office, where the attorney sat across from a middle-aged, ruddy-faced man in an expensively cut suit.

"Mr. Sutton will finish with you later, pal," Parker said, pulling the rolling chair away from the table.

The client wasn't used to being treated in a rough manner and demanded to know why Parker was barging in on his meeting. "Who do you think you are?"

"I'm the guy who'll make your life miserable if you don't get out now." Parker's badge peeked from under his jacket, and the man's eyes popped at the brass star.

The client fled. Larry Sutton called after him. "We'll get you rescheduled."

The receptionist guided the man, who Parker pegged as a white-collar criminal, down the hallway to the outer office.

"Good morning to you, Detective. Care for a coffee, or something stronger based on your sudden appearance?"

"Sorry to interrupt, but I've got something that can't wait."

"I should thank you. From the expression on my new friend's face, I just added another zero to the price of my retainer. I should ask you to come and perform your theatrics more often."

"Your southern client has a problem, a big problem," Parker said.

"We've been down this road before, Detective. I cannot talk to you about any of my clients. Some of them—frown on law enforcement entanglements."

"Hypothetically speaking, then, what would you advise a client who you learned was being targeted for a hostile takeover?"

Sutton rested his elbows on his desk and tented his hands together. "Depends on how hostile?"

"Very."

"I would caution them to be vigilant in taking on new business ventures, especially where it might compete with others."

"What if it's more of an 'insider trading' problem?"

Sutton grew silent. Pushed back from his desk. "Let's take a walk, Mr. Parker."

Before Parker could respond, Sutton was up from his chair and at his office door, gesturing him to follow.

Parker joined him as Sutton told his receptionist he'd be out for a few minutes and to cancel his appointments for the rest of the day.

She looked surprised but tried to hide it behind her oversized glasses.

The attorney remained silent during the elevator ride to the street level.

Once outside the building, Sutton finally spoke. "What makes you believe my client is under threat?"

"It's not any threat, and it's coming from two angles."

"Go on..."

"You're aware Los Muertos and the Sinaloa Cartel have been at odds recently," Parker said.

"I'll take your word for that, Detective. I'm not involved in that kind of business."

The attorney mouthed the words, but Parker didn't believe him. Partially because he'd communicated with the Cartel before and represented their members when caught north of the border. And he was paid handsomely for his legal prowess and discretion.

"Let me fill you in then; stop me if you've heard this before. Los Muertos, under the control of Echevarría, were working against the cartel in many areas, trafficking routes and distribution of—"

"You said were?"

"Echevarría was murdered yesterday in Hermosillo. I know your 'contacts' down there can verify it. They should also know he was also an Inspector for the Federales."

Sutton nodded. "This explains a few things. But, if this is as you say, it's not a detriment to the Sinaloa Cartel."

Parker noted the attorney dropped the pretext of talking about his client in hypothetical terms.

"The new boss is the same as the old boss. Isn't it the old Russian saying? Esteban Casteneda and Carmen Delgado have been cozying up to the Cartel leadership, promising to bring Los Muertos under their umbrella."

"Again, this doesn't seem to be a bad thing for the Cartel. Wouldn't it make them more of a presence in the region?"

"What if it's a set-up for a run at the Cartel itself?"

Sutton pondered the theory for a moment. "You have proof?"

Parker nodded.

Sutton locked eyes with Parker.

"Come with me. I have someone you need to talk to," Sutton said.

The attorney turned on his heel and made a path to the parking level. When they reached the attorney's Bentley, Parker stiffened.

"Where we goin'?"

"Get in the back, please."

Sutton didn't bother to hold Parker's door because he got in the back seat on the other side.

Parker slid on the rear leather cushion while Sutton slid a panel down on the back-facing portion of the front seat. The attorney tapped in a number on a keypad and the screen bloomed to life until a Zoom video connection appeared on the screen.

An olive-skinned man with slicked back hair in a black long-sleeved shirt with pearl buttons sat glaring into the camera.

"What do I owe for this interruption, Mr. Sutton?" the man said.

"This is Detective Nathan Parker. Mr. Parker, may I present Joaquin Pimentel."

Parker didn't need the formal introduction. He recognized Pimentel from the Most Wanted List—the head of the Sinaloa Cartel.

"Detective, I've been following your career with great interest."

"I could say the same," Parker said.

"The detective was expressing some concern of over 'competing interests.'"

"Is that so? I assure you, I have no competition."

Sutton reached for the door handle. "I'll let you two speak privately."

Parker recognized the gesture for what it was. Sutton could claim deniability if his client divulged some nefarious activity.

"I'm certain you know about Echevarría?" Parker said.

"I do. One reason why there is little worry about competition."

"I have reason to believe things aren't as they might seem as far as Los Muertos is concerned."

"If you mean that lying dog, Castaneda. I know about his deal with the American government."

"Did he promise you something recently—something he failed to deliver?"

Pimentel started back at the camera for a moment. "He's always promising something to someone. Me? I know better than to expect anything from him."

"Curious, then. Why would Castaneda smuggle an arms shipment to Hermosillo?"

"When was this supposed to have occurred?"

"Yesterday," Parker said.

"Detective. I'm sorry, I can't help you."

"I take you at your word. If the arms weren't for you, who were they for?"

A shadow crossed Pimentel's eyes. Even through the video feed, Parker found it discomforting.

"Where are these weapons now?" the cartel boss asked.

"I've taken care of them. They are buried in the desert and are out of reach for whoever expected them."

Pimentel nodded.

"Echevarría and Castaneda are the same in many ways," Parker said. They're both opportunists, jealous of one another. They wanted Los Muertos to rival the cartel."

"We see how that ended up for them—one dead and the other turned into a government informant, soon to end up like the other."

"How well do you know Carmen Delgado?"

"What are you getting at?"

"I know from personal experience Carmen is capable of pretending she's something other than what she is."

Pimentel paused.

"If these things are connected—the weapons and Los Muertos... I don't like being played the fool."

"Nor do I," Parker said.

"I will look into the matter discretely."

Parker knew to the Sinaloa Cartel, discrete meant hanging rivals from freeway overpasses.

The cartel boss looked off-camera and motioned to someone off-screen.

"Detective, if this turns out as you say, I have to ask, why tell me about it?"

"Los Muertos has been preying upon the weak and vulnerable. Too many innocent people are caught up in their extortion and smuggling schemes. You're in a position to make it end. All I ask is one thing."

"And what is that?"

CHAPTER FORTY-FOUR

"Castaneda is mine."

Chapter Forty-Five

Parker left the law office parking lot feeling a little dirty. Did he make a deal with the head of the Sinaloa Cartel? The thought of it made him uneasy.

Pulling his Explorer out of the shadowy basement parking lot didn't make the queasiness fade. The sunlight showed it for what it was—he'd made a deal with the devil to cut off an attempted coup by Los Muertos and ensure Parker would have his revenge on Castaneda.

Ellie's admonishment echoed in his conscious mind. "Castaneda would like nothing more than to see you fall. You can't give him the satisfaction."

He promised—he swore to McMillan as he held him in his arms that night he'd find the man responsible and make him pay. He missed his chance once before. Parker wouldn't miss again.

His pre-paid cell vibrated, which reminded him he needed to pick up a new one today. The number on the display was a Mexican number.

"Hello," Parker said.

"Detective, it's Armando DeSilva."

"Armando, is everything all right?"

"I wanted to let you know the authorities down here have closed the case on the assassination of the police inspector. They are whitewashing his ties to Los Muertos and have caught the man who shot him. They had camera footage of the killing. It cleared you and Billie of any wrongdoing."

"Billie will be happy to hear it. Are they talking about her escape? I don't want to see her get in trouble on a relief trip and get snatched up by the authorities down there."

"They are releasing a dozen—at least—who were arrested by the Inspector. They know it's because of his Los Muertos involvement, but the government is saying lack of evidence. Billie is in the clear. I picked up a letter from the Federales clearing her of all charges."

"That is good news."

"I also wanted to thank you for entrusting me with—the contents of the crate. It has been safely deposited. I will message you with the account information so you and Billie will know where it is and what it is being spent for. Many people will have better lives for what you've done. Thank you."

"Thanks to you, Armando. I can't believe Billie never told me about your role in the Coalition down there."

"It was for the best. The fewer people who know, the safer—for all of us."

"How did you first meet? I know you saved her that night with Castaneda."

"We saved each other. We're family."

"She has a way of doing that."

"Take care of her, Detective."

"I'll do my best."

They disconnected the call and Parker spotted a cell phone store for the carrier he used. He pulled into the parking lot and entered the store to find it empty except for the young pimply-faced employee.

Parker picked out a plain, no-frills phone despite the kid trying to upsell him on the latest model with the extra camera on the backside. It was especially good for selfies, the kid had said.

"Do I look like I take selfies," Parker said, exasperated by the hour-long phone activation and setup.

When he turned on his phone, five text messages pinged, one after another: three were from Lynne at the FBI, one from the phone carrier asking if he wanted to upgrade his phone, and a third from an unknown number.

Thankfully the phone numbers were all downloaded onto his new device. He tapped Lynne's number and waited for the call to connect.

He winced when Delores answered, her acidic tone announcing, "ASAIC

Finch's Office."

"Detective Parker returning Lynne's call."

He waited for the offhand comment, but instead, Delores simply told him to hold and put the call through."

"Nathan?" Lynne said by way of a greeting.

"Hi, Lynne. Just saw your messages. What's up?"

"What's up is Castaneda has disappeared. Homeland is apoplectic. They don't know where he is."

"They didn't have anyone sitting on the guy? No electronic monitoring?"

"No. Nothing. They said the guy was a cooperating witness, so they had no reason to monitor the guy twenty-four-seven."

"He's going to run for the border and disappear again."

"That's the party line around here, too. We've alerted border patrol and ICE to stop him if he's spotted making a crossing."

Parker knew the man wouldn't use a public route. He was practiced in illegal crossings and knew where the borders were unprotected.

"They'll never find him that way. Besides, he'll want to finish what he started here."

"What's that?" Lynne asked.

"He'll clean up loose ends here, and then he'll make good on his promise."

"What promise? What are you talking about?"

"Lynne, thanks for the call. I appreciate the heads up."

"Nathan, wait,"

Parker hung up.

Castaneda would clean up his mess north of the border, eliminating any direct tie to him. He would head to the border and make good on his plan to overthrow Pimentel. But before that could happen, Castaneda had to clean up his mess.

Then the thug would take down Parker.

Chapter Forty-Six

Parker's next call went to Linda.

When she picked up, he started. "The boys still around?"

"Pete's here. Barry ran down to the nerd herd to chase down a technical point."

"Okay, put me on speaker so you and Pete can hear."

"Go ahead, we're both here."

"Castaneda's in the wind. Just got off the phone with Lynne, and they've lost track of the guy."

"You're kidding me?" Tully said.

"Nope. I think it has to do with the excursion Billie and I took yesterday. He's got to make amends to some folks down there, or his goose is cooked."

"Couldn't happen to a more deserving guy, if you ask me."

"We know this guy better than anyone. He's going after everything here, tying him to the crap he's been pulling. He doesn't like loose ends. The survivor at the hospital. Call them and make sure he's being guarded. Castaneda will make sure there are no witnesses."

"I'll make the call," Linda said.

"Where does this put Castaneda's immunity deal with the feds?" Tully asked.

"I don't know. If he can't give up the goods, then he's of no value to Homeland."

"Will he still get his immunity for what he did to McMillan?"

"Not sure. The feds bought his line that he was there but wasn't the one who killed him."

Parker wasn't certain if Castaneda disappearing would change their perception.

Linda came back on the line. "Nathan, I spoke with the hospital, and the feds pulled their coverage on the patient. They walked away, like thirty minutes ago."

"What's the deal with that?" Parker said.

"Hospital couldn't say. They said the two officers guarding him picked up and left after they got a phone call. Wonder who called?"

"I'm gonna head there," Parker said and hung up.

Parker started tapping out a quick text message to Miguel while parked at a stop light. What would he say? "Oh, hi. Hope your day's going well. BTW, the crazed killer who tried to get you once before is on the run. Be careful. Okay, bye."

He tossed the phone on the seat. This would have to be a conversation. The way Parker saw it, Castaneda tried to get rid of the survivor once before. He'd do it again.

Parker pulled into the Banner Memorial Hospital entrance and parked at the loading zone curb. Pushing into the lobby, he scanned the faces, and the collected grey hair, slumped backs, and shuffling steps didn't scream of a Los Muertos hit squad.

As he got off the elevator to the ICU, an icy prickle hit the back of his neck. The nurse's station where someone sat to monitor the screens and readouts from the patient rooms was unattended.

Parker rounded the corner into one of the ICU hallways and glanced back at the nurse's station. A pair of blue Crocs poked out from behind the counter. He stepped around the barrier, and a pair of wide blue eyes looked up at him. Tearstained and red-faced, the nurse was bound with zip ties, and surgical tape was across her mouth.

Parker gently pulled back the sticky tape, and the nurse drew in a quick breath. Through quivering lips, she said, "He said he was going to kill me."

"Is he still here?" Parker asked.

"I—I don't know."

Parker cut the zip ties using a pair of scissors the nurse had in her scrubs.

"How many other staff are on duty right now?"

"Seven."

Damn. "All right, get to the elevator and let security know. My people are coming. If you see them, let them know what's happening."

She nodded and crawled to the elevator. An electronic ding sounded and reverberated in the vacant hall. She leapt inside and stabbed the close door button repeatedly until they began to close.

Parker caught the shadow of someone approaching from the opposite direction. They'd heard the elevator. Tucked behind the nurse's station, Parker watched the shadow pad down the hall, and, when they found no one there, the man let out a grumble and turned in the other direction.

When the man faced away, Parker arose from his hiding spot and crept behind him. He spotted a handgun with a suppressor in the man's right hand. A black balaclava pulled down over his head obscured his identity. He was agitated, his free hand clinched into a fist.

"Where are you?" the man said behind his face covering.

Castaneda? Parker couldn't be certain. The man in front of him had the swagger, but he was concealed too much to be certain. The gunman turned slightly, and Parker thought he was going to whip around and face off with him. Instead, the man ducked into a patient room.

"Where is he?" Louder this time.

He wasn't finding the survivor he was looking for. It would be a matter of time until he did or hurt someone who happened to get in the way.

Parker glanced around and spotted a cart behind him. He grabbed the first thing he found and swung it at the man as he stepped from the room. The stainless-steel bedpan dented when it struck the gunman above his left eye.

The sudden attack caused the gun to slip from his grip while both hands went to his face. Parker swung the bedpan again and caught him under the jaw, toppling the man backwards. The metallic thunk echoed while Parker struggled to get the gunman cuffed.

Once on his back, Parker pulled the black balaclava off. It wasn't Castaneda. For a second, Parker was confused. He would have sworn the Los Muertos thug would be here taking out the last witness.

Then Parker recognized the face on the floor in front of him. The employment specialist from Coyle Technology, Lee Patterson.

Patterson tried to roll away, but Parker pinned him in place with a knee on his hip.

"Let me go," Patterson said.

"That's not happening."

The chime from the elevator sounded, and responding officers spilled out into the hall. Tully, Johns, and Linda followed behind.

After a pair of uniformed Phoenix police officers picked Patterson off the floor. Parker stood with a slight twinge in his knee.

"Find our survivor. This guy hadn't found him yet." Parker pointed at the weapon dropped on the floor. "Secure that, would you, Pete?"

Tully borrowed a cardboard evidence box, fetched by one of the Phoenix officers, put on a pair of nitrile gloves, removed the magazine, and rocked back the slide, ejecting a 9mm round. "Guy was serious. Jacketed hollow points and a suppressor." Tully placed all three in the evidence box and sealed it.

Linda huddled with the nurse Parker rescued. She'd returned after the officers had swarmed the ICU floor. She hooked the nurse by the arm and directed her to Parker.

"Nathan, this is Melissa."

"Thank you for—everything. We tried to stop him, but—"

"I'm glad you're all right. Where is the man he was looking for? The patient who was being guarded?"

"We moved him. When that man showed up, we knew what he was going to do. The other nurses on the unit moved him while I tried to slow him down."

"That was brave of you," Parker said.

"Brave or stupid," she said. "I didn't see the gun until after I confronted him."

"Where's the patient?"

"They rolled his gurney to the NICU next door."

CHAPTER FORTY-SIX

"The pediatric unit?"

She nodded. "Can I go and get back to my patients here in the unit?

"Yes. Absolutely. Tell your co-workers they can bring their patient back, too. Any change in his status? Is he awake yet?"

"No change, but his heart rate, blood pressure, and ECG are stable in a normal range. The doctors are feeling more positive about his prognosis."

Parker gave her his card. "Would you mind calling me the minute he's awake?"

She nodded and tucked the card away in her scrubs.

Nurse Melissa was shaking from her experience but was more concerned about the patients in the unit. She'd soon feel the weight from what happened to her and would need some post-trauma care.

A pair of Phoenix officers struggled with Patterson as they led him down the hall.

Barry Johns tapped Parker on the shoulder. "Isn't he the dude we followed from Coyle Technology?"

"The one and only."

"What the hell is his connection to all this?"

"We should ask him."

Chapter Forty-Seven

Lee Patterson sat in the interrogation room at the Maricopa County Jail. He hadn't been booked for the hospital assault yet, and Parker let the man stew for an hour in the small room.

As an interview technique, waiting let some suspects rehearse what they were going to say to the detectives. It was obvious when the answers were too pat, too planned. It gave Parker a chance to pry open those frayed edges the suspects often overlooked.

Then there was Lee Patterson, who suffered every minute that clicked by on the clock inside the interview room. Agitation, evidenced by a bouncing knee, constant eye movement, and a nervous tic in his left eye. Patterson wanted to talk.

Parker and Johns entered the interrogation room and took chairs opposite Patterson, whose eyes flicked from one detective to the other. Parker placed a digital recorder on the table, flicked the switch, and waited.

The silence was getting to Patterson. Parker sat quietly with a neutral expression and waited. Suspects hated the silence. They need to fill the void, often incriminating themselves.

"What?" Patterson said. The bouncing knee tapped the bottom of the table.

"You remember me reading you your rights? You don't have to talk to us—the right to an attorney—all that?"

"Yeah, yeah, I remember. You had me sign a little form before you locked me in here."

"Okay."

"Okay, what?"

"What do you wanna say?" Parker asked.

"You need to let me out."

"You broke into a hospital, held a nurse hostage, and the gun kinda leant a hostile air to the whole ordeal," Parker said.

"You don't understand."

"Apparently not. Why don't you enlighten me?"

"Let me go, and I will," Patterson said.

"Ain't happening."

Parker crossed his arms and waited.

"I have to finish what I started."

"And what's that, exactly?"

"I need to kill him—the one who survived," Patterson said. He looked surprised when the words finally came spilling from his own mouth.

"He has a name—Hector Mendonsa. That's what you went to the hospital to do? kill him?"

"Yes, I had to."

"You had to? Why?"

"You don't understand. If I don't kill him, my life is over."

"Some would argue the inconsistency of that statement. Why would your life be over?"

Parker began to wonder if there was some strange psychological delusion at play here, but the man's anxiety seemed more focused.

"He'll kill me and my family."

"The unconscious man?"

Patterson tensed and shook his head, sweat beads dipping on the table surface.

"No. The other man."

"This other man have a name?"

"I—I don't know it. He told me I had to kill the man in the hospital."

"Why?"

"Because of what he knew."

"Okay, we're going in circles here. Who wanted this man dead, and what

269

did it have to do with him being left for dead in a shipping container?"

"A guy—a guy who brought people in. Workers who weren't supposed to exist."

"Why is that worth killing over?"

Patterson squinted at Parker. "You know who I work for? Then you know why."

Barry Johns bumped his knee against Parker's leg, a signal to let him take a shot at breaking Patterson.

"Coyle Technology? What do they have to do with any of this?"

"Everything."

"Coyle Technology is in the human trafficking business?"

"It wasn't supposed to be like that."

"What was it supposed to be like? You said you were bringing people in to work."

"It sort of happened, you know?' Patterson's eyes searched for understanding. He couldn't sit still. "I've gotta go. You don't understand."

"Why don't you help me? How did this begin? Start with what you do at Coyle Technology…"

"I don't have time for this." Patterson started to stand, and Parker pointed a finger at the chair. Patterson slunk back down, scolded.

"I'm one of the recruiters at Coyle. My job is to hit up the tech market and steal the best and brightest away to come and work for us. It used to be that way until six-eight months ago. We all got called in for an executive meeting, and all but two of us were let go."

"Executive meeting? Who ran the session?" Johns asked.

"Randy Coyle himself. I'd never met the man before. Now he's telling us to cut costs to stay competitive and all that noise. We'd heard it before, but this felt desperate. Instead of finding experienced programmers, coders, and engineers from other companies, he wanted us to find the cheapest labor force we could find and bring on interns."

"Okay, why is that a big deal?" Parker asked.

Patterson squared his shoulders. "You can't expect a company to thrive and gain market share with interns. They don't have the experience and don't know the Coyle Technology proprietary software."

"Any new employee would need to learn the new system, right?"

"And they could, if they had experience. Interns don't."

"Interns like Hector Mendonsa?" Parker asked.

Patterson shook his head. "Am I supposed to know who he is?"

"Hector is the man you were trying to kill in the hospital. Seems only right you should know the guy's name if you're gonna go kill him."

"It didn't matter anymore."

"Was Hector one of your interns?"

"One of Coyle Technology's interns. He was one we pulled from a tech school in Mexico City."

"The men who died in the shipping container?"

Patterson nodded.

"How did you find these men, and why did they die on their way here?" Parker said.

Patterson's forehead creased. "They weren't on their way here. The crew was done working and on their way home."

"On their way back? They didn't get far, did they? Where were they coming from?"

"One of the server farms. That's not my part of the operation." Patterson tried to distance himself from the ugly parts of the business. Until a flash fell across his face when he remembered he was going to kill the lone survivor.

"Coyle Technology runs a few server farms, right? Johns asked.

"Ten of them, I think, if they are all up and running."

"What would these interns do at a server farm?"

"Keep it up and operational. It's mostly all automated. They need someone on hand in the event a server goes down, or when a DDOS attack slows the response rate."

"Denial of Service attacks? How often does that happen?" Johns asked.

"Every day. But we have pre-coded scripts to run when they are detected."

"These men were done working? Did they stay on site, or did you move them to a hotel every day?"

"Once they are at the farm, they stay there until the next crew relieves them in a month. They live, eat, and sleep on site."

"This crew was done working. That means a new crew replaced them?"

Patterson nodded.

"What happened to the men in the shipping container?"

"I don't know. They were supposed to be going back to Mexico City."

"Why were you trying to kill Hector, the last one left alive?"

"I had to."

"Not good enough. Why?" Parker raised his voice, and Patterson jerked back.

"Because he'll kill my family if I don't?"

"Who? Castaneda?"

Parker felt the puzzle pieces begin to slip into place. Castaneda was the mechanism to abduct the college students in Mexico and smuggle them over the border. There were no work visas to worry about and when they were done, off they went. Until this time…

"Castaneda? I don't know the name." Patterson said.

Parker pulled up a photo of the Los Muertos leader on his phone and slid it across the table to Patterson.

"Him. He connected me with some group to bring in workers from down south without the burdensome visa process. I've seen him spending a lot of time at Coyle Technology with the Homeland Security people.

"He threatened your family?" Parker asked. It was right out of Castaneda's playbook to use a man's family as leverage.

"No. Not him. Hansen from Homeland."

Chapter Forty-Eight

Parker and Johns left Patterson alone in the interview room, and they stepped into the hallway.

"Hansen threatened his family?" Johns said.

"I would have bet the farm on Castaneda being the muscle behind this. Why would a government hack threaten a man's family?"

"Right? That doesn't make sense. I mean, the guy's ego-driven as hell, but why would he abduct a bunch of college students and threaten a man's family?" Johns said.

"We need to make a run at Hansen. But I need to ask our boy here one more thing that's bugging me," Parker said.

Parker stepped back inside the room with Johns. Patterson glanced up, exhausted from the emotional drain.

"How many crews have there been before this one?" Parker asked.

"Three prior to this one. Two more are supposed to have come in this month. I don't know what's happening with them since all this."

"There's a crew at the server farm, one replacing the crew Hector was on?"

"Yeah."

"Another group of migrant college students?"

"No. I got this one local."

Parker strode out of the room and slammed the door behind him.

"What's up?" Johns asked.

Parker grabbed his cell phone and stabbed a number. "Linda's kid. He was supposed to start work at Coyle Technology."

"Linda, did Leon go to work today? At Coyle?"

"Yeah, why."

Parker clamped his eyes closed, trying to figure out a way to tell her.

"We're uncovering things about Coyle Tech and their use of interns. Linda, the men we found in the shipping container may have been Coyle interns. Can you call Leon and make sure he's okay? Maybe we can talk to him when he gets home tonight?"

"Are you sure? God, that's all he needs to get wrapped up in. He won't be home tonight. They told him to expect to be gone for two weeks. On-site training, they called it. Leon was excited for the opportunity."

"Did he say where he was going?"

"I know he had to arrive at the Coyle Tech offices today for an orientation."

"Linda, see if you can call him and give him a heads up. I know he's not going to want to hear this after the West Valley Machine Parts business. But it looks like it's connected."

"I'll call right now."

"Barry and I are heading to Coyle Technology now. You might want to meet us there."

She agreed and disconnected the phone call.

"You don't think they'd do anything to local college kids, do you?" Johns asked.

"I don't know what to think about this anymore. I know Castaneda's connected to this somehow, and it's more than the human trafficking angle of the deal."

As they left for the Coyle Technology offices, Parker's cell rang. He expected Linda's caller ID on the screen, but instead he saw Sam Turner's name displayed.

"Parker, here. What's happening in the CSI world?"

"Detective, I've got some interesting info, and as much as it pains me to say it, our new evidence tech, Willy, found it."

"What ya got?"

"The shipping container AC unit. You know how it malfunctioned?"

"Yeah," Parker said.

"There were gouges in the soft brass fittings, showing the connection was purposely disconnected. There were brass shavings in the threads—indicating something was attached and removed."

"Okay, I'm following ."

"This is where Willy comes into his own. The boy goes and searches the semi-truck you impounded. Behind the driver's seat is a hose with a brass fitting."

"A hose? What for?"

"What for is connecting the AC Vent system directly to the truck exhaust. There are matching tool marks on the truck's exhaust pipe behind the cab. Carbon Monoxide from the exhaust ran directly into the shipping container."

"Damn. That would do it. Now we need to figure out when and who connected the device to the exhaust."

"Which makes it even more painful for me to tell you what Willy found. He pulled prints from the exhaust pipe and was able to collect a DNA sample from the rough brass AC fitting. The DNA will take a few days to confirm, but the boy genius got a hit on the prints."

Parker felt his shoulders tense.

"The prints came back to Esteban Castaneda."

"You sure? Absolutely sure?" Parker asked. He couldn't risk a misstep allowing Castaneda to slip away again.

"We're certain. The way we figure it. Castaneda connected the device before the truck driver started his trip. The driver dropped the trailer and disconnected the hose, stashing it in his truck."

"Makes sense. We'll have to see if the driver's body—his hands—had any brass shavings."

"On the list of things Willy's gotta check."

"Good stuff, Sam. Let me know if anything changes."

Parker hung up. "We got him. Castaneda. We got him. Not even his immunity deal can save him from this one. Multiple murder." Parker slapped the steering wheel.

They pulled into the Coyle Technology parking lot and it was as vacant as the last time they were there. No one strolled around the campus and the entry lobby was unattended as it was on their first trip to the tech giant.

Parker gestured down the gold-toned carpet. "We've seen where the yellow brick road goes. You wanna explore this side?"

Johns shrugged, and together, they passed empty offices, blacked-out monitors, and vacant meeting rooms.

"What do you make of this?" Johns asked.

"Like they pulled up stakes and abandoned the place," Parker said.

At the end of the hall, a shuffling sound came from a classroom. A lone Coyle Tech employee, dressed in the button up shirt and dark pants uniform. The young woman accented the drab uniform with bright pink hair and long dangly earrings that sparkled when she turned her head.

"Meeting's over," she said without looking behind her. She was busy gathering papers from the tables.

"What was the meeting about?" Parker asked, and he glanced at the document at the closest table. The bold headline was *"Push to Unionize Coyle Technology."*

The woman turned and regarded the two detectives. "What, more union busters? You guys made your point. Don't need more of your capitalistic screed."

"That's not us." Parker showed the woman his badge. "Union meeting?"

"Not anymore. Coyle Technology made sure of it. Coyle's minions stormed in and shut the meeting down. Told us if we wanted to unionize, go somewhere else."

"What were you organizing for?" Johns said.

The woman stopped gathering the meeting notices and placed a hand on her hip. As she spoke, the earrings flashed with each word.

"Basic worker rights. Working conditions, health care, more accrued time off, profit sharing, and better pay. Management treats us as indentured servants."

"I heard Coyle Technology was voted one of the best tech companies to work for," Johns said.

"Used to be. Before my time. Maybe five years ago. Not now. They've laid off more than two-thirds of the workforce, extended the shifts from eight to twelve hours, and pay us squat while the company rakes in millions."

"Before your time? You knew what the landscape was like when you came here. What made you think it would change?"

"Because it's the right thing to do. We deserve a share in the profits we bring into the company and we have the right to set the company's future direction."

"Do you share in the risk too?" Parker asked. "What do you stand to lose if Coyle Technology goes into the red?"

"This company was built on our backs, and we deserve our share. Without us, Coyle Technology wouldn't exist."

"Tell me about these union busters you mentioned," Parker said.

"People like you. Who don't believe we should have a voice over the direction of the company. They made claims about the important work Coyle Technology does and how it cannot be interrupted by rabble like us. Rabble—he actually said that before he claimed the work here is a matter of national security."

Parker perked up at the last phrase. "You catch a name for this guy?"

"Yeah, he left his card." She shuffled through a pile of documents on the head table. She strode back and handed it to Parker.

The name and title on the card made everything a little more complicated. Why was Robert Hansen, Assistant Director of Homeland Security, acting as a union buster for Coyle Technology?

"Mind if I keep this?" Parker asked.

The pink-haired woman shrugged. "Whatever."

"Where is everyone?" Johns asked.

"They scurried back to work, afraid they would get laid off. This guy," she pointed to the business card, "actually said if there was any more talk of unionizing and strikes, we could find another job, and McDonald's was hiring."

"Where'd they go? We saw a lot of empty offices on the way here?" Johns asked.

"Most of us work in building 2."

"Is that one of the server farms?" Parker asked.

A dark shadow clouded her light brown eyes. "You know about those?"

"Sure, Coyle Technology made no secret of them?"

"Did they tell you they've shut down the server farms and outsourced them? I bet they didn't. All that Made in the USA garbage, and then they take our jobs and send them overseas."

"When did this happen?'

"Hey, listen, I gotta get back to building 2 before they lock me out. I need this job."

She swooped up all the loose union material and pushed past Parker and Johns.

Linda appeared in the hallway as the pink-haired woman hurried out.

"What did I miss?"

"You're in time to go meet the man behind it all."

"Randy Coyle?" she asked.

"The one and only. We can ask him what his employees are talking about when they claim his server farms are shut down and he shipped the jobs overseas."

Parker and the detectives backtracked to the lobby and took the gold carpet path to the executive offices. There were a few people working in cubicle farms off the main hallway. They seemed engrossed in whatever was on their monitors and paid them no attention as they passed.

Parker opened the heavy wooden doors of the executive suite, and the same young woman sat behind the reception desk. She looked like she hadn't slept or moved from the desk since Parker last saw her. Dark bags under her eyes and two paper coffee cups sat on her desktop.

She straightened and didn't seem surprised to see them. "Mr. Coyle is expecting you." She pointed to the office door.

Parker nodded, and he pulled open the office door.

Randy Coyle was scratching out notes on his whiteboard. The cubicle in the center of the office was overflowing with papers, books opened on broken spines, and colorful charts.

Coyle paid no attention to the arrivals, but the lone guest sitting on a sofa did.

Homeland Security Deputy Director Hansen recrossed his legs. "We had an understanding, Detective."

Chapter Forty-Nine

"What understanding was that?" Parker asked.

"You were ordered to stay away from Coyle Technology."

"Not how I remember it. My department agreed to let you 'handle' the shipping container and the survivor. Never said anything about Coyle Technology."

"I'm saying it now."

"Too late, don't you think? Especially with your star witness in the wind. You haven't heard from Castaneda, have you? Seems like he tried to kick off a war with the cartel while you had him as your lapdog.

The homeland executive's face reddened. "Nothing's changed as far as you're concerned. Castaneda and Coyle Technology are off your radar, you feel me?"

"What's the sudden interest in Coyle Tech, if you don't mind me asking?"

"I do mind, and you need to leave."

"Randy doesn't mind us here, do you, Randy?" The man absently waved a hand while he scribbled a mathematical formula on the whiteboard.

"See, he doesn't mind. But let me tell you why you've got your knickers in a twist."

"Oh, please do…"

"Coyle Technology has become too big to fail. There are too many Fortune 500 companies relying on the backbone Coyle has created. If Coyle Technology buckled, it would cause more than a ripple in the economic pond. Then I had to ask myself, why would this dick from Homeland Security care? Wouldn't it be more of an issue for the FTC or SEC?

"Unless the government was also a client. If the Department of Defense, or The Department of Energy, or maybe even Homeland Security had their systems running on the Coyle Technology platform and using the cloud."

"That's enough, Detective. I've listened to enough of your fantasy."

"Barry, isn't Coyle Technology known for hosting all of their services right here in the good ol' US of A?"

"Says so in their portfolio. That's what the latest quarterly report claimed." Johns picked up a copy of the official quarterly report from a side table.

"What would their clients and stockholders think when they find out the company has been outsourcing the server farms?"

Randy stopped moving his marker across the whiteboard surface.

Hansen stiffened.

"What would the media do with the story?"

"We'd bury it."

"Like you tried to bury the twenty-seven men who left their jobs here?"

Randy dropped his marker in the tray at the bottom of the whiteboard.

"What's he talking about, Robert? What twenty-seven men?"

"Never mind, Randy."

"I will mind. This is still my company. What have you done?"

Homeland fell silent and held his chin up. "We did what we had to do to repair the damage you've done."

"Tell him about the men in the shipping container. Go ahead," Parker said.

The pieces were all falling together—Parker was sure of it.

"What have you done?" Coyle said.

"You set up a server farm in China, for shit's sake. Our classified information was sent to one of the nation's biggest adversaries. The security nightmare you created because you were trying to save a dollar set our intelligence services back a decade. Do you realize the damage you've caused?"

"My server systems are bulletproof, and we could plug one inside the Kremlin, and Ivan the Terrible himself couldn't access it."

" China compromised the system during the first week."

"No, that can't be correct." He picked up a colorful chart and waved it at the Homeland Security executive. "All server farms are operational. We had Server 3 experience a temporary outage—wait—Server 3 is the farm we outsourced in Shanghai."

"Not anymore."

"What do you mean?" Randy held the chart in his hand and shook it at Hansen. "It's right here. See. All are running at full capacity, even Shanghai."

"We relocated all the server farms from offshore. They're all back here in Arizona. We cannot take the risk of foreign interference, or access to the systems."

Coyle stumbled to his cubicle desk and flipped through a thick sheaf of paper. "My personnel costs. They increased eight months ago, then dropped to less than a third of the baseline."

"Eight months ago, we shut down all offshore assets and moved them back."

"How could you do that? The government cannot interfere with my private enterprise. It's—"

"A matter of national security?" Parker said.

"You couldn't have reestablished the server farm operations in the U.S. The expenditures don't support your claim. Moving a major operation would cause a system-wide disruption. I couldn't afford to staff and maintain the server farms if they were moved back here. " Coyle said, searching his charts for the answer.

Parker strode to the whiteboard and noticed the columns of numbers corresponding with dates. "This date. Here. Six months ago. These numbers all dropped. What's this about?"

Coyle joined Parker at the whiteboard. "Yes. Good eye. It was a systemwide software update we had scheduled." Coyle turned to Hansen, "You used the software update to cover your server relocation. But I'm still paying for the offshore farms. That's why I'm bleeding my operational budget. You're running double the server farms."

"Technically, you're running them, but the U.S. Government is operating them. We pulled our systems off the overseas servers, then sold access to the Coyle Technology cloud platform to China, Pakistan, and North Korea. We exploited every one of their systems and have gathered more intel in the last six months than we have in the ten years before."

"I laid off half of my staff to make up for the operational losses I was suffering." Coyle shook. He was angry at being used and deceived.

Parker tapped the whiteboard and noticed a pattern within the columns. Every month for the past six months, server farm output would drop for a day, or two, then increase. Next to that, the dollars spent to maintain the server farm. The dollar amount never varied. The date of the last production downturn was the day the twenty-seven men were found dead in the shipping container.

"How many people do you need to run a server farm?" Parker asked.

"For twenty-four hours a day, we need about twenty-five to thirty to manage the traffic into and out of the servers."

"I know where they came from, Mr. Coyle. And I wonder if you know?"

Coyle reddened. "I don't know what you're talking about, Detective. I've been managing these server farms on a shoestring, and now I know it's because he was running a duplicate system operating off my server backbone. It's why I've had these latency issues, the production drops, and the cost overruns."

"Lee Patterson arranged for your labor force to run these servers. Ever stop to ask how he was able to get you all the people you needed at a fraction of the usual cost," Parker said.

"People want to work at Coyle Technology. Interns are nothing unusual in our field."

"Interns aren't usually smuggled across the border, Mr. Coyle."

Coyle glared at Hansen.

"We needed to keep the operation running, and the cheapest way to do it was with a workforce of interns who'd be willing to work for the experience and the idea of working for Coyle Technology."

"Interns like Hector Mendonsa?" Parker asked.

"I'm sorry, who?" Hansen asked.

"The one survivor from the shipping container left to die on the side of the road."

"That was us?" Coyle said.

"We had nothing to do with the deaths of those men," Hansen said.

"But you had everything to do with them being here in the first place. Smuggling in undocumented migrant labor? That's one way to keep your operations costs low," Parker said.

"Where'd you get the idea anyone working here is undocumented?"

"There's no record of them entering the country at a border checkpoint, they had no identification on them when they were found, and their families knew nothing about them crossing the border."

"I can assure you anyone recruited had a valid visa."

Parker knew by the time the dead were identified, a work visa would suddenly appear. They would cover their tracks.

What happens to these workers when you're done with them?"

Hansen shrugged. "Not my interest. Don't know, Don't care."

"Don't care if they end up dead in a shipping container?"

"Wasn't us."

"You hired untrained interns from another country and brought them into my company? We've set our standards for recruitment, retention, and have high expectations for the people we bring on board. What did you do to these workers?" Coyle said.

"All well and good, but you weren't getting the job done," Hansen said.

"And you made a deal with Esteban Castaneda to traffic them over the border for you," Parker said.

"He does know the most efficient routes over the border. And we needed to keep the operation quiet to prevent the Chinese from learning we'd moved the server farm. Who better?"

"You went into business with a murderer."

"That old saw again. Get over it, Detective."

"Get over it? He murdered my partner." Parker stormed across the room, and Johns stepped in between them.

"Not now, boss. We'll blow the lid off this, but not now," Johns held Parker from a career-ending move. Assaulting a federal officer was usually difficult to explain—although Parker thought he had a good reason.

"Mr. Coyle?" Johns said, trying to redirect the conversation. "Did you know about this morning's union meeting with your employees?"

"Union meeting?"

"Seems Assistant Director Hansen here took it upon himself to step in and do a little union busting. Are you really running Coyle Technology anymore, or is it another failing government operation like the Post Office?"

"You had no right. This is my company. I built it from the ground up, and I run it," Coyle said.

"You've done a piss-poor job of it and put our national interests in harm's way."

"Excuse me," Linda said. She'd been quiet while they were in the executive offices. Parker nearly forgot she was there with them.

She was pointing at a series of small monitors. "Where's this?"

The monitors were tucked in a small alcove next to the cubicle desk.

Coyle waved them off. "Those are the cameras watching the server farms. Had them installed three weeks ago. If I was getting downtime, I need to see why."

"This one. Where is it?" she asked. Linda pointed at the small screen on the far left.

"Server farm 3, the one in Shanghai."

"No, it's not." Linda's face drained.

"How would you know? It's farm 3."

"It's not in Shanghai. It's here, in Arizona. That's Leon," Linda said, pointing at the screen.

Chapter Fifty

"Where is this?" Linda said.

"I told you. That's my Chinese server farm."

"Not unless you've invented light-speed commercial air travel. This boy, right here, had breakfast with me this morning, less than three hours ago."

"I'm sure you're mistaken."

Parker closed in on the monitor. He studied the images for a moment. Linda pointed at Leon.

"Mr. Coyle? Your reasoning for opening offshore operations was to cut costs, right?"

"One major concern, yes."

"Part of it would involve hiring local Chinese employees to work in the facility—lower local wages and all, am I correct?"

Coyle nodded.

"Take a look at this monitor—all of them—do you see any Chinese workers?'

Coyle bent at the waist and peered at the screens. He glanced at Hansen, who remained stoic.

"Where are these facilities?" Parker asked.

Coyle couldn't answer. He kept studying the monitor images. He stiffened. "The signs, the employee warnings, and signs in the rooms are all in English. They have to be stateside."

"And no more than an hour away, if Leon was with me this morning," Linda said.

Hansen slow-clapped in the background. "Congratulations. You've discovered the Great Deception. Coyle Technology is a massive fraud."

"Tell me where these server farms are?" Parker said.

"I've had about enough of you locals trying to push your weight around. I have real work to do. Mr. Coyle, remember our conversation…" Hansen strode out of the room.

"What was he talking about? What conversation?"

"Hansen said interfering with the platform would make him invoke some kind of Imminent Domain action on the basis of national security interests."

"Can he even do that?" Parker said.

"I'm beginning to think there are no limits to what he's willing to do," Coyle said.

"Can you help us find where these facilities are?"

"I thought I knew where they were…"

Barry Johns tapped a section of the whiteboard. "Mr. Coyle? These figures. They're listed as staffing needs."

"Yes. We determine how many man-hours are needed to manage a server farm, and Lee Patterson fills the vacant positions to make sure we meet the demand."

"This one has today's date. Another tomorrow. You anticipate new workers being assigned to the facility? What happens when they don't show up?"

"That would be untenable. We need to keep the facilities operational."

"You might want to make arrangements, because Lee Patterson isn't going to be filling any positions for a long, long time."

Parker noticed a thick file near the monitors he'd been watching. He peeled back the cover and found energy bills from the Palo Verde Generation Authority.

He grabbed the file and held it behind him.

"Linda, Barry, time to move on. Mr. Coyle, I suggest you figure out who runs this company."

Outside the office, Linda put a hand on Parker's shoulder. "We can't leave without knowing where they've taken Leon."

"I think I know." Parker revealed a glimpse of the folder under his jacket.

The entrance gates of the Palo Verde Nuclear Power Plant were gated and manned by an armed security force.

Parker showed his badge to the gate officer.

"Your business here, Detective Parker?"

"Need to speak with someone about plant operations, maybe your head of security."

"What can I tell them this is about?"

"Radiation leaks," Parker said.

When the security man walked back to call, Parker said, "That should get their attention."

"Don't you think they'd know if they had a radiation leak here? There have to be more monitors and sensors here than an eavesdropping Russian Embassy," Johns said.

"You both still have your dosemeters?" Parker asked.

"Yeah, what are you thinking, Nathan?"

"Those first bodies, a couple of them were contaminated."

"But they said nothing was missing from the storage facility here," Linda said.

"Nothing missing. Doesn't mean it didn't happen here."

"You think Leon and the others are here?" Linda asked.

"It makes the most sense. The power bills from the Palo Verde Generation Authority back it up. Lots of electric service needed to run server farms. My bet is all three of them are here on site. If the weenie from Homeland is concerned about keeping the data on these servers secure, what could be more secure than the nation's largest nuke plant?"

The security man returned to the SUV. "Ms. Jamison will see you. She did ask me to tell you there is no danger of a leak here."

"Thanks."

"Follow my partner." The man pointed at a pickup truck pulling out of a parking spot with flashing yellow lights. It reminded Parker of one of those construction detour roadblocks.

"Stay in his path. Do not wander off on another side road. Ms. Jamison is doing this as a courtesy."

"I understand, and we appreciate it. Say, you guys ever have to deal with Homeland Security people here."

The security man's jaw tightened, and while he didn't verbally respond, the reaction confirmed a run-in or two with Hansen's people.

"Have a good day," the guard said and waved Parker forwards as the checkpoint arm raised and a metal barrier recessed into the roadway.

Parker followed the pickup truck as they made a slow and deliberate path to the main office building, a square block of a structure. The driver of the pickup pointed to a parking slot, and another security man waited for them at the front entrance of the office building.

"Detective Parker?"

Parker raised his hand.

"Come with me, please."

The offices were plain, unadorned with motivational art, and were all business. They were led to a conference room and asked to wait for Ms. Jamison.

The conference room doors closed, and Parker checked them to make sure they weren't locked.

A minute later, the conference room door opened, and a tall, red-haired woman entered with another woman in tow, presumably her assistant.

"I'm Lisa Jamison, head of security. What can I do for you?" The red-haired woman unbuttoned her suit jacket and sat at the head of the table. Her assistant handed her a folder.

"What can you tell us about recent Homeland Security activity here in the last six months or so? Specifically, their operation of computer servers here."

"Why aren't you asking Homeland?"

"Assistant Director Hansen is less than forthcoming."

"He would be. I can't tell you what they might be doing here. I'm not confirming they are, mind you. Several federal agencies use us as a temporary base of operations. I'm sure you can figure out why."

"I'm interested in what Coyle Technology is calling a server farm. Takes almost thirty people to run the thing. They need a place to sleep, eat, and whatever else computer nerds do for a month at a time."

Jamison opened the folder in front of her. "A few days ago, you asked about missing radioactive waste. This have anything to do with your server farms?"

"It does. We had victims who were exposed to radiation. We thought it might be medical waste. But we have reason to believe they were working here when the exposure occurred, or shortly thereafter."

Jamison shared a look with her assistant. "We tend to stay out of other agencies' operations. We have enough oversight from Department of Energy types; we don't need to bring in even more of them."

"We believe the people brought here were undocumented migrants, and twenty-seven of them died after leaving this facility."

"Are you referring to the incident at Devil's Well?"

Parker nodded.

"Jenny, ask Tom to join us." The assistant scurried from the room.

"Tom Heath is our environmental exposure lead."

"You suspect an exposure?"

Parker noticed Linda tense as he asked the question. Leon was in danger if he was here.

A beefy, barrel-chested man followed the assistant back into the room. He paused mid-step when he spotted the three detectives.

"Ms. Jamison?" Tom said.

"A few days ago, you briefed me on an exposure potential out on C-8."

"We got it cleaned up."

"What caused the exposure?" Jamison asked.

Parker felt the man's reluctance to speak with the detectives in the room. "We aren't here to dig up any problems for you, Mr. Heath. We're working a mass murder and they may have been exposed while they were here."

He nodded. "I know they were. The levels of exposure were minimal. We treated them as a precaution, then advised their team they should follow up with their medical provider after they left."

"Treated? Iodine?"

"And decon."

"How were they exposed, Tom? I don't remember from the briefing," Jamison said.

"They were in a restricted area near the storage pads. Remember the guys we needed to chase out of there?"

"Yes, now I do. They were playing soccer in the waste storage area."

"Scratching around in the dirt near where a medical waste container was spilled a few weeks back. It was enough to spread the radioactive particles. Nothing to cause permanent illness or injury unless they had some preexisting condition. That's why we needed them to follow up with their personal medical teams."

"They turned up dead anyway, but not from radiation sickness."

Tom's face tightened.

"We treated the area and cordoned it off. We haven't had anyone else wander around out there. The—contractor—erected fencing to make sure their people didn't enter the restricted area again."

"Can you show us where this is?"

Heath looked to Jamison. She nodded.

"All right then. We'll need to get you dosemeters to monitor levels as we go."

Parker, Linda, and Johns pulled their dosemeters and clipped them to their jackets.

"Oh, okay then," Heath said.

"Ms. Jamison, are you coming with us?"

"No. Don't need to. Make sure you give the detectives everything they need. I'm exhausted dealing with Homeland and if this gets their project off my campus, I'm all for it. Detectives."

Jamison left the conference room with her assistant.

"How far is it?" Linda asked. Parker could tell she was nervous from the tight jaw and anxious hands, wringing and fidgeting.

"Ten minutes. We'll take my rover. We'll all fit. It's out back."

They followed Heath through the warren of hallways to a loading dock door. Outside in the heat, six large electric ATVs were parked at charging stations.

Heath motioned to the first one. He unplugged the ATV, and Linda got in the front seat while Parker and Johns climbed into the back. Heath pulled the silent vehicle out of the loading area onto a smooth, blacktopped roadway.

The breeze cooled Parker a little, but he felt he needed to hold his breath as they rounded the large containment buildings where the real hot stuff happened.

In the distance, three metal buildings encircled with twelve-foot-tall wire fences came into view. Heath pointed them out to make sure they saw them.

Multiple air conditioning units perched on the tops of each building to cool the computer equipment house inside. There was no one in view outside as they approached.

The ATV pulled to a stop at the fence line. Heath pointed to a barricaded section of land to the south. "That's where we caught them playing soccer. Those concrete tubes behind them—store radioactive waste."

As they approached the fence line, a door opened from the closest trailer, and a uniformed Homeland Security Officer strode out to meet them.

"What's up, Tom?" the Homeland officer asked.

"Need to run a quick inspection inside."

"We didn't get notice."

"Just came up?"

"I'll need to call it in."

"Assistant Director Hansen won't like it if you delay us from getting our work done. You want me to call him for you?" Parker bluffed.

The Homeland Officer's eyes bugged. "No, no. I got you." He unlocked the gate for the party."

"Are all server farms up and running?" Parker asked."

"They are all operationally in the green. The second team of new arrivals are getting their orientation right now."

"Take us there," Linda said.

The Homeland Officer paused before he relocked the gate. "Um—I guess. We haven't had anyone come and check in before. You sure it's all right? We're getting this crew settled in."

"Show us," Linda said.

The officer led them to the building he'd come from. It was a large square metal structure with thick insulated walls to protect the valuable equipment from the desert heat. The space was divided, the largest was devoted to racks of computer servers, stacked atop one another. There were hundreds of them, row after row of flashing green and yellow lights. Neat bundles of cable ran from one row to the next, linking the servers together.

At the front of the server bay, two rows of monitors and workstations were arranged to oversee the operation. Parker didn't know what the lines of code scrolling across the screens represented, but the cascading indecipherable figures cast an ominous shadow on the video screens.

Parker counted ten workers, each wearing the Coyle Technology uniform shirts, at the workstations, or tending to the servers in the racks. A single Homeland Security officer stood to the side watching.

"You see Leon?" Parker whispered to Linda.

"Where are the others?" Linda said.

"Must be their off cycle. Twelve on and twelve off. They'd be in the barracks section."

They followed the officer to a thick door which operated with a keypad. The officer punched in a code and pulled the door open. Heat from the adjoining space hit them the moment the door cracked. The air-conditioning was in place for the equipment, not the people. The barracks was eighty-plus degrees and the smell of sweat permeated the space.

Barracks was a stretch. There was a communal dining room which consisted of two long tables with folding chairs. There were empty paper cups on the table and a trash can overflowing with government-issued MREs, the Meals Ready to Eat, prepackaged food usually provided to the military on deployment.

A long hallway beyond the dining room held a dozen rooms, each with an electric lock. Jail cells, really. When the workers weren't at their station, they were locked away.

Linda strode down the hall, looking in each window.

"When did we start locking them down during their off cycle?" Parker asked.

The Homeland officer tilted his head, and the creases in his forehead told Parker he should have known the answer.

"It's policy. We don't want another uprising. Server 2 damn near lost the racks when they refused to work and barricaded us out of the server room. Since then, we've been following the protocol to the letter. All non-workers are locked down. Makes them a bit more willing to go to their stations when they get released. Non-compliance is managed..."

Parker noticed the Taser on the Homeland officer's belt.

"Nathan, down here," Linda said.

Parker joined her and spotted Leon sprawled on a thin mattress on the concrete floor.

"Open this one. Number 11," Parker said, pointing at the number on the door.

The Homeland Officer shrugged and strode to a keypad on the wall at the head of the hallway. He tapped in a code, then the number of the room. The metal door slid back on tracks, opening the room.

Linda rushed to Leon's side. She shook him and he didn't rouse. "Leon, wake up."

The boy was groggy and barely registered her presence.

Parker put his fingers to Leon's neck. His pulse was slow, but steady. Parker lifted the boy's eyelids, and pinpoint pupils stared back.

"He's drugged," Parker said.

"What did you give him?" Linda asked. The Homeland officer leaned on the doorframe.

"The usual. It's policy. You should know that."

Linda propped Leon up and shook him.

"He'll be fine. Most of them never have a problem with the dose. We got NARCAN for when there's a problem."

"What you dose him with?" Parker asked.

"We only use what you guys give us in their food. Your people told us it was low-dose opioid—time released to make sure these bastards don't cause us any problems."

"We're taking this one."

"How come?"

"National security," Parker said. He'd heard the phrase so many times, and it had the effect on the officer, who shrugged and backed out of the way while Linda and Parker lifted Leon from the mattress, dragging him out of the room. His arms draped over their shoulders, he stumbled, and his body couldn't register what was happening.

"NARCAN?" Parker asked.

The officer took a bottle from a locker in the hallway and tossed it to Parker. A spray in each nostril, and within twenty seconds, Leon began to come up from his drug-induced sleep. His eyes flickered open, and he had difficulty focusing on the faces hovering above him.

"Mom?"

"Mom?" The Homeland officer stiffened. What—"

He didn't have a chance to finish before Johns shoved the officer in Leon's vacant cell and slid the door in place, locking it shut.

"We gotta get going," Parker said. "We need to help the rest of them."

Tom Heath hit a red button on the panel. "I think this will do it. I don't know what they were up to here, but this ain't right."

As Heath hit the button, red lights flickered on, and an alarm sounded. All the cell doors popped open. Johns slammed Leon's old cell door closed again. A few men roused in the hallway while others remained drugged and unresponsive.

"You get him out of here. I'll manage the rest of them."

"You sure you can handle this?" Parker said.

A Palo Verde security team burst through the front door.

"Yeah, we've got this."

Chapter Fifty-One

The server room was evacuated when they came through. Parker stopped for a moment.

"Barry, help Linda with Leon, would you?"

While Barry hefted Leon, Parker strode to the center of the server room, right in the view of the camera streaming the video feed to Coyle's monitors. With the alarm, Parker was certain Coyle was glued to the screen.

Parker stared at the camera lens and made a "cut it" gesture across his throat. Any question about whether Coyle was watching was answered in seconds when the entire building went black. The blinking lights on the servers went from green to red, then winked off as if someone pulled the plug. And they had. Coyle shut down the system.

The doors on the other two buildings flew open, and the workers streamed out. Into the holding area inside the fences.

They arrived at the locked gate, and Parker scanned the enclosure for one of the Homeland Security officers. He couldn't spot one in the crowd. Parker pressed buttons on the keypad and thankfully power to the lock was still operational, but he didn't have a clue about the correct combination.

"Seven-two-three-eight," Leon said. "What? You weren't watching when they let you in?" Parker punched the numbers, and the lock clicked open.

Johns started the ATV and once Leon and Linda were settled in the back, they headed to the main building. Parker picked up a radio mounted to the dash and clicked the microphone. "Get a bus to C-8 and pick up the workers." Parker recalled the designation from their meeting with Jamison.

Johns bypassed the office building and parked the ATV at their Ford

Explorer. Five minutes later, they were out of the facility's gates and on the highway.

"This was the worst job ever," Leon said from the backseat.

"How you feeling?" Linda asked.

"Tired, but okay. Did they really keep us in jail out there? Coyle Technology really needs to work on their employee retention program."

"What was so important they need to lock you all down?" Parker asked.

"Got me. I got a look at some of the screens as we got familiar with the workstations, and they were government web traffic; you could tell by the IP addresses and .gov websites."

"Doesn't explain what happened to our shipping container crew," Barry Johns said.

"I think it does. A couple of them were contaminated with the radioactive waste out there from playing soccer in the disposal site. They were told to get outside medical attention. If they did, all kinds of red flags would go up. Like where did this exposure happen? Other agencies would get involved. The news would spread pretty quickly."

"Like what happened after the Medical Examiner found the contamination. NEST flyovers, feds crawling all over."

"Exactly. But why they all had to die out there, I'm still not sure, other than Castaneda was responsible. His prints were on the hose pumping in exhaust fumes to the container. Why he would care, I don't know."

"If they couldn't be linked to Palo Verde, where they were contaminated, then-Homeland Security's project would go unnoticed."

"Sure, I suppose. But, why Castaneda was involved is troubling me."

"How you feeling, Leon?" Linda asked, huddled with an arm around the boy.

"Better. I'm—I'm kinda hungry."

"That's a good sign. Let's get you checked out and then a good meal.

The doctors in the emergency room at Banner Memorial gave Leon a clean bill of health. The quick-acting drugs they'd given him at Palo Verde had metabolized, which made sense if they expected him to work at the server station once he woke from his 'off-cycle'. The doctors took blood samples, but one was convinced it was a drug cocktail used by the military to allow special ops teams to rest, then perform at peak levels afterwards.

"While we're here, I want to go check on Hector Mendonsa upstairs. Take Leon home. You can crash at my place if you want. Might be good for him to be able to talk with Miguel. They have some shared experiences…"

"Why, Detective, are you inviting me for a sleepover?" Linda said.

Parker handed her the keys to his SUV. "Barry can drop me off when we're done here. And, yeah, I am inviting you to stay." His hand held hers momentarily. "I'd feel better with you and Leon with us for a while."

Linda squeezed his hand in return. "I'd like that too." She took the keys and said, "Don't worry, I won't redecorate—yet." Her green eyes sparkled when she smiled.

Linda waited for the results of a last scan for Leon, a precaution to rule out head trauma, and because he said he was a little dizzy.

Parker and Johns headed to the ICU, and it was a relief to see a nurse at the station this time rather than bound and gagged on the floor.

The nurse recognized Parker and waved him over to the station.

"Detective, the patient you're interested in—he's awake. In room 4. The doctor might be in with him now. And thank you for before…"

"I'm sorry for what you and the crew went through. I'm glad you'll all be okay. Is the hospital offering post-trauma counseling for you all?"

"They are. I don't know if I'll do it or not."

Parker remembered the same reluctance after his partner's death. "Trust me, it's worth the time."

They arrived at the patient room door as the doctor was leaving. A slight ebony-skinned woman in a starched white coat. She smiled when he saw Parker.

"Detective Parker."

"Dr. Oymingo. When did you leave the VA hospital?"

"I'm still on staff over there. Banner called and said they were short-staffed over here after an incident. I suppose that's why you're here."

"I may have had something to do with it. Your patient in there was the center of the action, though. Can you tell me how he's doing? I understand he's awake."

"He is. He's gone through quite an ordeal, but I think he's out of the woods. I'll let him tell you the details. How's Miguel, by the way?"

"He's doing okay. I'll let him know you asked."

"I've got to get going, good to see you, Detective." The doctor swept out to the next patient room.

Parker and Johns entered the room where a tired looking young man sat propped up on the bed, sipping from a juice box. He was connected to monitors and IV lines, snaking back to pumps and digital screens.

"Hello, Hector. I'm Detective Parker. This is Detective Johns. We'd like to talk with you for a minute."

Hector put the juice box on the tray. "Am I—am I in trouble?"

Parker put his hands up. "No, No, not at all. We've all been worried about you. Your mother, too."

"My mother knows where I am? The policeman who was here said I couldn't have any phone calls."

We can get you a phone. But your mom and I had a long talk, and the way you disappeared— let's say she was worried."

"You spoke with her?"

"I did. In Hermosillo."

"You went all the way to Hermosillo to talk with my mother? Why would you do that?"

"You had us all worried. We didn't know who you were, or what exactly happened to you. We've been able to put the pieces together, but you can help us get the big picture. We know you were on a job with Coyle Technology when you disappeared."

"Yes. Some job that turned out to be. We all met at the Coyle Tech office in Mexico City. There were about thirty of us. All programmers, coders like me, and systems engineers. Getting a job with Coyle was exciting for all of us. A chance to get inside of one of the big companies. We were all met in a large conference room. They had a big meal all ready for us. I don't remember what happened next—I don't remember seeing anyone until I woke up in a small room—locked in a small room."

"Sounds like what we found today out at Palo Verde at the server farm."

"Yes, the servers. They had us working the data."

"What does that mean?"

"The servers. I mean, you don't need anyone to support them. I mean, they store network data. It doesn't require thirty people—coders like me. What they wanted us to do was sift through the incoming system traffic and redirect some of it. They'd give us a list of keywords, like names, or phrases like defense spending, or democratic caucus, and we'd write some code to redirect or copy any message with those keywords."

"Why would they need someone to do that?" Parker asked.

"We wondered the same thing. I asked the guard watching us—which I thought was kind of strange—told me to mind my own business."

"Who were the keywords coming from?" John asked.

"I'd have them in an envelope on my workstation at the start of my shift. Never saw who gave them to us. It was clear what we were doing."

"What's that?"

"Spying. We were spying for Coyle Technology. We weren't there to support the servers; we were there to mine data from them."

"Any specific traffic you remember redirecting?" Parker said.

"Not at first. Each of us had a small piece we looked for. It wasn't a complete string. But if you got all the envelopes together, you could see it. We'd all huddle together after our shift and put the words together like a puzzle. We were searching for any system traffic related to Homeland Security and instances where other agencies mentioned them. Border security, and Nightshade were a top priority."

"What's Nightshade?"

"I have no idea. But it came up a lot and I must have redirected twenty data streams relating to it."

"Where would you redirect them?"

"It was strange. We were redirecting this in two places: back to another server in Homeland Security and to another one with an IP address I recognized in Hermosillo."

CHAPTER FIFTY-ONE

"In Mexico? Our government was sending information to Mexico?"

"Not everything—that's where the Nightshade messages were going. I know who they were going to—the Sinaloa Cartel."

Chapter Fifty-Two

"The Cartel? Why would Homeland Security divert messages to them? Are you certain?" Parker asked.

"I don't know what reason they had to send them the messages. One of the guys with us had hacked into the Cartel's network before to see if he could. We told him he was stupid to do it, but that's the kind of guy he was. He recognized the IP addresses and swore it was the Sinaloa Cartel."

"You're sure?"

"I am. We were all sure after he ran his mouth and said something about Nightshade, and the guards heard him. We were all fired."

"When was that?"

"I don't know for sure. How long have I been here? All I remember is they backed a shipping container up and loaded us in. They moved us out of there fast. I started to feel light-headed, and then I woke up here."

"Were some of you playing soccer outside?"

"Yeah, that was something else they got upset about. Four or five of the guys got bored and made a soccer pitch behind the building. They leveled out the field on one end. Some armed guards came and chased them off. We all got locked in the building after."

"Were you one of the soccer players?"

"Me? No. I've never been into sports, mostly into computers and gaming."

"Does the name Esteban Castaneda sound familiar?"

"No. Should it?"

"I'm certain he had something to do with your being here in Phoenix, and I know he's responsible for you being in the hospital."

"Phoenix. I knew I wasn't in Mexico. Where is everyone else? Did I get sick, and they went back home without me?"

Parker took a deep breath. There wasn't going to be an easy way to tell him the truth. "Your mother will be with you while you recover here. I'll let you call her and find out when she's coming. Hector, when we found you, you were in bad shape. There was carbon monoxide in the shipping container. You were the only one to make it out."

Hector's jaw trembled. Parker saw the pulse rate on the bedside monitor increase. "Todos?" He reverted to Spanish.

Parker nodded. "I'm afraid so. Parker slid his cell phone on the tray in front of Hector. You should call your mom."

Parker tipped his head to the hallway. Johns joined him outside of the room. Parker heard Hector speaking in a rapid clip. He'd connected with his mother.

"What do you make of what he saw out there," Johns asked.

"Homeland spying on other agencies. Seems clandestine enough for them—shady, but I get it. The part bothering me is the Nightshade thing. What's that about? Sharing intel with a criminal organization is a whole different ballgame."

"I can ask the guys in organized crime," Johns said.

"Might not be a bad idea. Tread softly. We don't know where this goes. I'd ask Lynne, but she might be too close to the source, and I don't know if Homeland is monitoring her. We have to be careful how we bring this out."

"I'll start with a couple of guys I trust in organized crime," Johns said.

"All right. I have an idea on how to approach Lynne."

"Detective?" Hector said from inside his room.

He was done with his call and held the cell phone out to Parker. "Thank you for letting me talk to her. She said things down there have gotten much worse with the Cartel. She's okay, and she's coming to see me. She said you had a friend who was able to get a visa approved for her. She's coming tonight.

"She said you and your friend risked your lives to find her and save me."

"I'm glad she'll be here soon. You rest up, Hector. If you need to get me, here's my card. I'll make sure the officer watching you lets you call anytime."

"Why is there an officer watching me? I won't go anywhere."

"They're going to be here to keep you safe. Until we unravel all this Nightshade business and the Cartel connections, I want to make sure you're safe."

Hector's eyes widened. "Oh, okay."

"What next, Boss?" Johns asked.

"Can you drop me back at the house? I want to check up on Linda, Miguel, and Leon."

Johns smiled. "Sure thing. Is this a soft domestic side I'm seeing, or what?"

"Shut it, Detective."

"Whatever it is, I know you both seem happy, that's all."

"Just drive."

Parker knew Johns was right. He was happy with Linda in his life. As much as he'd screwed up other relationships, this one felt different—in a good way.

While Johns drove, Parker made two phone calls explaining a problem he needed to run by them in person, not over the phone. He promised dinner and a show.

Chapter Fifty-Three

P arker asked Johns to make a quick stop at a grocery store. He came out with four bags overflowing with dinner ingredients for a houseful of people. Steaks, baked potatoes, vegetables, rice pilaf, and a coconut cream pie from the bakery case. Barry was invited, too, and Parker told him to call Tully and get him there.

When Johns pulled to the curb, Tully had already arrived. Johns pointed it out. "You tell Tully there's a free meal and this is what happens. Probably ran here code three."

They each carried two bags inside. Miguel and Leon were sitting on the sofa playing a video game. Billie was standing behind them, grimacing at the carnage on the screen.

Linda was in the kitchen and grabbed a bag from Parker when he came inside. She peeked in the first bag. "No pizza takeout tonight? You're pulling out all the stops, aren't you?"

"Leon, how's he doing?"

"I think he's okay. Spent a long time with Miguel talking. Did a lot of listening too. They've been hanging close tonight."

"We can get Leon in to see the counselor Miguel used. She's pretty good with this kind of thing—especially with kids with their background."

"Probably a good idea. If Miguel can convince him it's okay to do it and it's not a sign of weakness. You men..."

Parker started unpacking the bags. "I've invited a few people over tonight so we can put our heads together. There's more going on here than we thought. Parker ran down the details Hector provided: the redirected

305

server traffic, the Sinaloa Cartel connection, and Nightshade, whatever that was.

"How does Castaneda fit into all of this?" Linda asked.

"That's one of the pieces not lining up for me. Castaneda wouldn't risk everything to smuggle a container full of tech workers. High risk and low reward. And he's all about the reward. What's in it for him?"

"He got an immunity deal," Linda said.

"Still not enough for him. There's more and he's working the angles. His immunity for McMillan's murder was a piece of it. He needed the feds to help him take down his competition."

The men in the shipping container with Hector, they weren't Castaneda's competition. Why would he need to kill them?"

"I don't know. There must have been other workers shipped back home. They weren't killed—at least not that we know of."

Billie leaned on the counter separating the kitchen from the living room. "Castaneda don't do nothin' less there's a payoff. He don't care 'bout nothin' but what's in it for him."

"I don't see what killing a shipping container full of kids like Hector gains him," Parker said.

"He'd kill his own family if they got in his way," Billie said. There was an acidic edge to her voice.

"Does he even have family?" Linda asked.

"Not no more," Billie said and pushed off the counter, rejoining Miguel and Leon.

"What was that about?" Linda said. "Billie's in a mood."

Parker laid the rib steaks on a platter and seasoned them. "I've asked Espi and Lynne to come. We can ask them about the fed connections to this thing without Homeland listening in. Hansen is way off the reservation."

"You think they will give you anything but the party line? They seemed hemmed in by Homeland Security. Especially Lynne, and not because I'm jealous of your ex."

"It seems she wants to distance herself from Hansen. Espi will lay his cards on the table, because it's the kind of guy he is—good news or not, he'll tell you like it is. He gave me the intel on the struggle between Echevarría and Castaneda for control of Los Muertos."

Tully came in from the back patio.

"Wondered where you disappeared to," Parker said.

"Got the coals ready for you."

Billie answered a knock at the front door. Lynne and Espi arrived at the same time. Parker wondered if it meant they had rehearsed their party line.

He beckoned them into the kitchen.

"Thanks for coming, both of you."

"I haven't talked to you since you got back from your shitstorm tour in Mexico," Espi said.

"It wasn't my storm, but you were right on about the internal feud going on within Los Muertos."

"Apparently, the Cartel isn't happy with Casteneda. He'd promised them an arms shipment, and it disappeared. He's on thin ice with them and needs to prove his loyalty."

"How's he gonna do that?" Parker asked.

"That's the million-dollar question. No one seems to know. He needs a big score to get back into the fold. Then there's the matter of where does Carmen go? She can't merge Los Muertos with the Cartel if Castaneda's running and gunning."

Lynne took off her coat and laid it on one of the chairs in the dining room. "Castaneda's vanished. Assistant Director Hansen is beside himself. His big score, taking down a gang leader and turning him, blew up in his face. It happens. I get it. But that prick is furious."

"Could be because of what we uncovered at Palo Verde today," Parker said.

"The nuclear facility?" Lynne said.

"Yeah, and it has to do with Homeland Security running a computer server operation, redirecting government communications, and something called Nightshade."

Lynne and Espi shot a glance to one another.

"Where did you hear Nightshade, Nathan?" Lynne said.

"The victims on our shipping container were computer nerds, coders, programmers and were brought in to work at the server farms run by Homeland. They were instructed to search for specific web traffic. Some of it included Nightshade."

"And you believe it was at the direction of Homeland Security?" Lynne said.

"Absolutely. Hansen, specifically. He admitted setting up the server farms. Randy Coyle at Coyle Technology didn't even know about it."

Lynne turned to Espi. "What's the connection with Homeland and Operation Nightshade?"

"None. It's a JTTF operation, with DEA in the lead. Homeland is in the info loop, but they have no operational role in it."

"What's Nightshade?" Parker asked.

"It's classified," Lynne said.

"Not anymore," Parker said.

"There's too much at stake here."

"What would the Sinaloa Cartel do with the information on Nightshade?"

Espi stiffened. "If they got wind of Nightshade, it would put our people at risk."

"Homeland was redirecting these messages to servers in Hermosillo. Servers suspected of ties to the Sinaloa Cartel."

"It can't be true," Lynne said.

"It is." The voice came from behind them. Leon had paused the game and was listening to the conversation. "Our instructions were to search for any web traffic coming through the servers with certain keywords. Nightshade was one of them."

"What were you supposed to do when you found a message like that?" Lynne asked.

"Redirect it to another server."

"It was probably another government server to protect the information," Lynne said.

"It wasn't government. At least not yours. The IP address was in Mexico. I don't know where for sure. The IP address was within a block of numbers in Mexico. 200.50—I don't remember the rest."

"Also confirms what Hector Mendonsa told us," Barry Johns said.

"If the Sinaloa Cartel knows about Nightshade..." Espi said.

"Dammit. Are you gonna tell me?" Parker asked.

Espinosa sighed. "Nightshade is a covert operation to take down the Sinaloa and Juarez Cartels."

"Isn't that something we're always doing?" Tully asked.

"Nightshade authorizes the use of American military resources in Mexico. U.S. Troops on foreign soil without the Mexican government's knowledge."

"We're invading Mexico?" Linda said.

Espi shook his head. "No. It's a surgical strike against the two Cartels. Quick and clean. Eliminate the leadership of the two organizations and the threat they pose to our country.

"If the cartels knew about the operation?"

"They'd move the key players and make our strike ineffective at best or lure us into an ambush. Dammit, if the cartels know about Nightshade, we have to call off the strike package. Why would Homeland redirect the messages and alert the Cartels? I don't get the rationale. They have as much at stake as anyone."

"What if Homeland Security didn't know the messages were being redirected?" Parker said.

Espi shook his head. "I thought you said they did. The redirected the web traffic to Mexican IP addresses?"

"They were, but I don't think it was Homeland Security. It was Esteban Castaneda and Los Muertos."

Chapter Fifty-Four

Lynne picked at a napkin on the countertop. Her jaw was tight, and she looked away, keeping her eye contact away from Parker. He knew her tells, and this one meant she had plenty to say, but she was holding it in. He'd seen this more times than he cared to admit during the last days of their relationship.

"Lynne, what?" Parker asked.

She sighed. "Nathan, I get it. Castaneda's an asshole. But every bad thing that happens in the desert isn't because of him. You're obsessed. You want to bring him down for something—anything."

"Why would a career politician like Hansen give classified information to the Cartel? I mean, the guy's a power-hungry zealot, but this? I don't see it."

"Then why Castaneda? He was getting his immunity deal. Why would he risk it?"

"On account of who he is," Billie said. "That man don't care about immunity. He's only interested in power—keepin' and gettin' more of it. You're missin' the whole point here. What Nathan found out about them web messages—goin' off to some server in Hermosillo."

"No, I heard that," Lynne said. "I don't see what it has to do with Castaneda."

"It has everything to do with him. You said Nightshade was a strike on the Sinaloa and Juarez Cartels, right?"

Espinosa nodded.

"Then why was them messages only going to one cartel—the Sinaloa Cartel?"

"Maybe that's what Hansen wanted to monitor, and Castaneda took it a step further," Parker said.

"Think bigger," Billie said. If only one Cartel knew the attack was coming, the other would get wiped out."

"Getting rid of the competition," Lynne said. "You could be right, Billie."

"How do you figure Castaneda into this," she asked.

"He's been under the thumb of the cartel. He hated it. The arms deal and the cash supposta go to Sinaloa smells like a buy-off. What if Castaneda planned to take over the Juarez Cartel once the U.S. Government does his dirty work for him?"

Quiet around the kitchen.

"She may be onto something," Espi said, breaking the silence.

Parker rubbed the stubble on his chin. If Homeland Security didn't order the Nightshade messages redirected, then who did? Castaneda wasn't at the server farm according to Hector. No way he could get through all the security clearances at the Palo Verde facility.

"Leon, how did you hear about the keywords and the message redirects?"

"They were typed out in envelopes left at our workstations."

"That's what Hector said, too. Everyone had a piece of the puzzle, not one worker knew the whole picture, until Hector's crew got together and pieced it together. Did you ever see who put the messages at the stations?"

"Not directly. But I saw Lee Patterson from Coyle Technology hand a stack of envelopes to the Homeland Security Officers on site."

"Patterson again," Johns said.

"Coyle Technology, again," Parker said.

"But not a direct connection to Hansen, or Castaneda," Lynne said.

"I'm not so sure, Lynne. Patterson claimed he was forced to try to kill Hector. I thought it was Castaneda because we caught them together on the hospital surveillance video. But Patterson claimed he and his family were threatened by Hansen."

"Who told him his family was in danger?" Billie said. "Who told him that?"

"He said Hansen," Parker said.

"No, what you said was he blamed Hansen, but who told him his family was in danger? There is one person who you know was with Patterson. And he's the kind who'll threaten a man's family."

"Castaneda," Parker said.

"I know this man. Hurtin' someone's family to bend them to do what he wants. It's him. I can feel it in my bones."

"I respect that, Billie, but you can't know what Castaneda may or may not have done," Lynne said.

"Bullshit I can't. No one in the room knows him like I do. I know him better than he knows himself. He's ruthless and will stop at nothing to get what he wants."

"How would he even know Nightshade existed?" Espi asked.

"The way I have it figured—it's the whole reason he cozied up to Hansen and got his immunity deal. The intel he was givin' up to Homeland was to feel out for what the Assistant Director really wanted. He probably heard him mention Nightshade while he was giving up bottom-rung Los Muertos thugs."

"That makes a lot of sense, Billie," Espi said.

"It makes sense why Castaneda would give himself up to the feds. He was never interested in the immunity deal. It was always to carve out a Cartel for his own," Parker said.

"He played Hansen and Homeland Security," Lynne said.

"I gotta warn off the Nightshade strike teams," Espi said as he pushed back from the table.

"Wait on that, Espi. I have an idea."

Chapter Fifty-Five

"You actually think this will work?" Espinoza said over the radio. "Were you able to let the Nightshade strike team know what they'd be walking into?"

"The tactical commander wasn't happy about the change-up. He did finally come around to saying he was thankful for the heads up."

Parker keyed the microphone, "They move showtime up?"

"It's going down in one hour. I hope you're right about this."

Parker did, too. It was a risk he had to take. He put the radio on the table as Lynne opened the conference room door. On her heels, Assistant Director Hansen stopped at the threshold when he spotted Parker.

"What's he doing here?" Hansen said.

Even for a hastily called session, Hansen was dressed in a fresh suit, starched white shirt, and blue tie.

"Still no leads on your little pet?" Parker said.

"Castaneda will come back to the fold. You probably spooked him."

"Yeah, I'm a threat to a gang assassin."

Two other men entered the room, one in black BDUs with short-clipped grey hair. The second man was a tired-looking older man who carried himself with a comfortable swagger. A politician, Parker figured.

Lynne closed the conference room door and took a seat at the head of the table. "Gentlemen, we have a change in plans. Commander Willis will fill you all in."

Willis, the man in the black BDUs stood with an erect military bearing and addressed the room. "We have intel that Operation Nightshade has been compromised."

Hansen pushed back from the table and appeared surprised by the news. Parker wasn't sure how deeply the man's involvement ran in the deal to tip off the Sinaloa Cartel.

"How? Why am I only hearing about this now?" Hansen said.

"Agent Finch, if I may?" Willis opened a laptop computer and streamed the feed to a large video screen on the wall. The picture flickered and filled the monitor with a green and grey-hued image.

It took Parker a few seconds to register the night vision feed.

"This is from a Globalhawk drone, call sign Nightshade 1. It's running a racetrack pattern around the designated Sinaloa target."

Parker recognized the hilltop villa as the expansive Sinaloa Cartel base under the late El Halcón. The green image made the place appear even more sinister than his memories of the compound.

"When are we going to hit the target?" Hansen said.

Willis thumbed a switch on the remote, and the image changed to a darker hue.

"I/R shows the facility is empty. It's abandoned."

"That's not possible. We have intel the Cartel leadership is there. Have our team enter or take the place down with a Hellfire missile."

"There's no one to target. This one is a dry hole," Willis said.

As if to emphasize the point, an orange outline of a coyote, clearly visible on the screen, trotted into view. It raised its snout sniffing the air near the compound and ambled past.

"I'm telling you the Cartel leadership is meeting now," Hansen said.

"I can assure you the Cartel has not acquired some Klingon cloaking device, and this target is off-line. There's no one there."

Parker swiveled his chair. "Where'd you get the intel, Hansen?"

Hansen's face pruned, and before he could spout off about confidential sources, or national security interests, Parker stared back at the Homeland Security executive. "We all know where it came from, your new friend Castaneda. Wonder why this was bad intel? Oh, wait, too bad you can't ask him because he disappeared on you."

Hansen's face reddened.

Willis drew their attention back to the screen. "This is the secondary target location, the Juarez Cartel compound outside of Nuevas Casas."

The night vision image was slightly clearer, and when Willis switched to I/R, the screen lit up with scores of orange spots in and around the compound. Willis zoomed in on a pair of images. Two men with automatic rifles patrolled the edge of the compound. Parker's quick count was at least thirty men guarded the compound.

The interior of the villa was dotted with heat signatures of people moving throughout the estate.

"See. The intel pans out. A Juarez Cartel is meeting. Strike now," Hansen said.

"The intel we used to plan this operation said there would be less than half of the security guarding the compound."

"Doesn't matter."

"It does, actually." Lynne passed a folder to Hansen.

He snatched it from her and tossed it open. A series of photographs inside, obviously taken from the same drone, showed car after car arriving at the compound and depositing their passengers. Men, women, and scores of children."

"What am I looking at?"

"The gathering is for the Quinceñera for the daughter of the Governor of Sonora."

"What's he doing at a cartel compound?"

The older man, who'd been silent until now, cleared his throat. "That's where I come in. I'm Sidney Compton, State Department. The Sonoran governor is using his daughter's birthday festivities to broker a truce with the Juarez Cartel. There are negotiations going on as we sit here watching."

"Truce, what truce?" Hansen said. "I've not been informed about any truce."

"We couldn't risk the negotiations being compromised. If the Governor is successful, the Juarez Cartel will agree to cease fentanyl shipments over our border."

"And you'd believe them?"

"They've offered a good-faith gesture."

"Take the compound out, and there won't be any risk of the cartel smuggling poison over our border—ever. The Governor is using the Cartel to line his own pockets. He'd be collateral damage."

"And the families? The children there?" Parker asked.

"The message would be loud and clear," Hansen said. "We have authorization for a strike. We need to act now."

"Your authorization has been rescinded. There will be no military strike on Mexican civilians."

Hansen stood from his chair. "What? You can't be serious."

"Your intel was compromised. The strike packages were based on faulty, if not purposely misleading information. The Sinaloa Cartel was observed in a different compound a hundred miles to the south. They knew it was coming. And the Juarez Cartel—a strike on them would set back the Mexican government's efforts to reduce cartel violence. Assassinating foreign leaders, like the Governor, is not U.S. Policy."

"Castaneda played you. He used his association with you to warn the Sinaloa Cartel about Operation Nightshade. And we believe he intended to use the strike against the Juarez Cartel to move in and use Los Muertos to take over the territory."

"Not possible. Castaneda couldn't—he doesn't—"

"He used your own server farms to redirect web traffic to servers in Hermosillo. Servers we've tracked back to IP addresses the DEA has flagged as Cartel sources."

Hansen fell heavily in his chair. It was sinking in—the reality of being manipulated by the gang leader.

Willis gestured to the screen once more. "We do have our gesture of good faith." The track of the GlobalHawk drone shifted east. In the middle of a stark wasteland, a single structure came into view. There were no heat signatures of people in the area. A single strobe popped on and off on the building.

"We have a team on the ground painting the target," Willis said.

CHAPTER FIFTY-FIVE

"What is it?" Parker asked.

"Juarez Cartel's fentanyl manufacturing and distribution center."

"How do we know it's not an empty shell?" Lynne asked.

"My people entered about an hour ago and verified the target. It's packed full."

Willis tapped a series of buttons on his laptop, and the image on the screen shook for a moment. A small white flare dove toward the building. Moments later, the structure exploded into a massive fireball, engulfing the building completely.

The drone circled the facility, and Parker pointed out a huge crater in the center of the burning building. "Damn. There's nothing left."

"That was the idea," Willis said.

The drone turned to the north and caught the night vision image of a Blackhawk helicopter lifting from the desert floor. "That's Charcoal 1, our team on the ground," Willis said.

"Charcoal?" Parker asked.

"Charcoal is the antidote to Nightshade poisoning," Willis glanced at Hansen, but showed absolutely no emotion.

"I thought you said there would be no military strike. What was that?" Hansen jabbed a finger toward the screen.

Sidney Compton stood from the table, shot the cuffs on his jacket. "The Mexican authorities will report a fire erupted in an illegal drug manufacturing lab in a remote corner of Sonora. We...were never there."

The radio crackled near Parker. Espinosa's voice sounded over the speaker.

"It worked. Castaneda is on the move."

Chapter Fifty-Six

"Where did he surface?" Parker asked.

"The gentleman's club. Linda and I have eyes on him. Got into a blue panel van. Looks like he has a driver."

"Tully, Johns, you ready?"

"We're parked on Grand near the 10. We'll pick him up as he gets on the freeway going south."

"Good work, everyone. I'm coming to meet you now."

Linda shook Commander Willis's hand and thanked him. The tactical man didn't waste any time and left the conference room without fanfare.

Linda turned to Parker. "How did you know where to find Castaneda?"

"It was going to be one of a couple of places. He'd been spotted in the strip club before. We got word he'd been hanging around the place. If he expected an assault on the Juarez compound, he'd have people nearby. When they got word of the explosion at the drug lab, they'd assume the attack had begun. Castaneda got the news and scurried out from the rock he'd been hiding under. Granted, this was a glitter-covered and cheap perfume-scented rock."

"If you knew where he was, you had a duty to tell us. We could have taken him down," Hansen said.

"Not without risking innocent people inside the club. That might be your style. It ain't mine."

"Castaneda is my informant."

"Is he really? Or are you his?"

The Assistant Director pushed up from the table again. Parker took it for trying to reclaim some authority from his debacle.

"You withheld information from me and obstructed my investigation. You'll be charged—"

"Slow your roll, Mr. Hansen," The State Department man said. "No one's being charged with anything, unless you can charge him with cleaning up your mess. You nearly put us in a position where we went to war with a neighboring country."

"The Cartels would have been eliminated. The threat to our national security would be taken off the board."

"You don't get it, do you? The Cartels will always be there. It's a way of life. Killing off one only means another sprouts up in its place. You nearly put an entire year's negotiation with the Mexican government and the Juarez Cartel in the toilet. You're not bringing charges against anyone—you don't have the authority—anymore."

Compton removed two folded documents from his jacket and slid them across the table to Hansen. "Your services are no longer needed. There will be a congressional inquiry as to how a known criminal gang member was able to access our secured government servers. There's also a subpoena there to compel your attendance at the hearing."

"You can't—you—" Hansen said.

"Look who's the national security threat now?" Parker said.

Hansen grabbed the papers, clinched them in his hand, and strode from the conference room.

"What an ass," Linda said.

"Thank you, Agent Finch, for organizing this little get-together. It was an eye-opener. Nice to meet you, Detective."

Parker shook Compton's hand. "Can you tell me about the deals Hansen might have made?"

Compton's eyes softened. "The immunity clause for Esteban Castaneda? As far as the United States Government is concerned, it never happened. Which seems to be the theme of the night."

The State Department man strolled out of the conference room.

"What makes me think there's more to Compton than some State

Department functionary?" Parker said.

Lynne was about to respond when Parker's radio crackled to life. "Castaneda made a U-turn and is now heading North on Grand."

"Did he make your tail?"

"No, I don't think he did," Espi said. "He might have gotten an update from his boys down south and status on the Cartel. Wait, he's making a stop. A mom & pop store."

Parker heard Linda's voice in the background. He couldn't make it out.

Espi said, "Linda says it's one of the businesses Los Muertos tagged—the graffiti. Want us to intercept?"

Parker paused, lowered the radio for a second, then keyed the microphone. "Negative. Watch him for the moment. I think he's making a pickup. If I'm right, he'll hit the other businesses in the valley before he makes his final run. He's grabbing all the cash he can before he slips away."

"Where do you want us?" Johns sounded over the frequency?

"Espi, can you confirm the vehicle again?"

"Light blue Dodge Panel van, California plates."

"Running heavy?" Parker asked, meaning loaded, with the box riding low on the suspension.

"Negative."

"Barry, you and Pete head to Western Machine Parts."

"Affirmative."

Lynne crossed her arms and tilted her head. "What are you thinking?"

"The weapons. He lost his last shipment-the one that was supposed to buy some goodwill with the Sinaloa Cartel. He's going back for more."

"Didn't he buy all the goodwill he'll ever need by tipping off the Cartel to a military strike?"

"Some, but he did it more for himself to take over the Juarez operation. The cartel expected an arms shipment, and they still want one. Castaneda is trying to broker a truce to allow him to set up his new operation in Juarez territory."

"Why not let him go down there and wait for the surprise awaiting him with the fully intact Juarez Cartel?" Lynne said.

"Because he might disappear again. I can't let it happen. He will hurt someone again. He's threatened to kill anyone close to me: Miguel, Linda, you. I won't let that happen."

"What do you need from me?"

"A tactical team on standby? We might need a show of force."

"I'll make some calls."

"Thank you, Lynne."

Parker didn't expect the hug. It was an echo of times past.

"Nathan, don't do anything reckless. You have nothing to prove. McMillan doesn't need revenge."

"It's about making sure Castaneda doesn't make another McMillan. He's brought this terror and violence down on everyone, and it's time for it to end. Revenge is best served cold.

Chapter Fifty-Seven

"Here he comes," Parker said, watching the light blue panel van pull into the Western Machine Parts parking lot.

Espi and Linda had followed the van across the valley, where Castaneda made six stops shaking down businesses for cash.

The machine shop's lights were on after business hours, which meant they expected the arrival. One of the long-haired mechanics inside flung open the front door as the van jockeyed in the lot, backing up to the door.

From Parker's position in the shadows of the end of the strip mall, he could spot the outline of wooden crates being loaded in the rear of the truck. From the choppy steps and strained muscles, these were heavy loads, with a man gripping a rope handle on each end of the crate.

One handle broke under the load, and the end of the box crashed against the pavement. The thin wooden top popped off, and the box tilted, spilling the cargo. Parker raised a pair of binoculars and spotted the gleam of black rifle barrels—dozens of them crammed into the crate. Not the delicately packed and foam-secured shipment he'd found with Billie in Hermosillo. This one was rushed. Castaneda was clearing out the arms cache to make good on his deal with the Sinaloa cartel. Tribute to allow him to assume leadership of the neighboring Cartel.

There he was. Castaneda. He'd popped out from inside the machine parts store and grabbed the man who dropped the cart by the collar.

Parker lowered the binoculars and raised a camera with a telephoto lens. He zoomed in and snapped a series of shots with Castaneda and the weapons. The expression on the gang leader's face was smug and arrogant.

He was already acting as the Cartel boss.

Putting the camera away, Parker keyed his microphone two clicks. It was the agreed-upon signal that Castaneda was spotted, and the arms shipment was in play.

Two matte black armored vehicles sped into the parking lot, one blocking the light blue van and the other sealing off the lot. The only access was the rear, where Johns and Tully were posted, or out through the front door into the field of fire the FBI tactical team established.

A flash-bang grenade exploded at the front door of the machine parts store. Parker wasn't sure where it had come from the FBI team or from the Los Muertos thugs inside.

The FBI team was taken by surprise by the flash bang and momentarily paused their movement. It was enough to allow three Los Muertos gang members to flee before the FBI team recovered.

Two ran to the side of the shop building and sprinted to the rear.

"Pete, two coming in your direction, hot."

The third dipped at the van, grabbed a weapon from the open crate, and peeled away from the store. Castaneda.

"I'm on Castaneda. On foot, south on Grand."

Parker chased after Castaneda. He couldn't let him disappear again.

The thug ducked around a corner into a dense residential neighborhood. He twisted around and spotted Parker behind him. While running, Castaneda chambered a round into the rifle. Parker heard the metallic clacking sound from fifteen feet back.

Castaneda spun quickly and fired off a burst from the weapon before sprinting forward. Parker heard the shots scream past him and pepper the stucco of a home behind him. Parker ducked behind a short cinderblock planter and found a cholla cactus with his right hand.

He heard Castaneda's footfalls going away. Parker glanced up over the wall and spotted his black leather jacket pulling right, followed by a faint scream.

Parker caught a woman in the window, wide-eyed at the sight of a man crouched in her front yard. "Call 911," Parker called to her before he followed Castaneda's trail.

A toppled trash can and another muffled scream marked the home where Castaneda went to ground.

Parker radioed in his location, and seconds later, sirens sounded in the distance. The door was ajar, and Parker heard a pleaful moan from the woman inside.

He couldn't let Castaneda take another victim. Not another McMillan. He failed to save his partner, and the others who followed, he had to do everything he could to make sure this ended tonight. Now. Without another soul lost to this monster.

Parker ran up to the front of the older adobe-styled home. A short front step to a concrete patio and the crashing sounds came from the back of the home.

He ducked his head in the open doorway and pulled back quickly. No sign of Castaneda, but he heard him grumble at his captive.

Parker held his Glock in a low, ready position, elbows in, close to his body, and muzzle ahead, as he stepped inside.

The living room was orderly, and everything had its place. Photos on the wall told a story of a life in eight-by-ten slices. A yellowed wedding portrait, baby pictures, a photo of a man in an Army uniform, and a more recent photograph of a wedding anniversary with two smiling gray-haired people smiling at one another after a lifetime together. A single photo of an older man sat by itself with a candle burning beneath it. A memorial. Parker was determined the widow's life story would not end tonight.

"Castaneda. It's over," Parker called out.

"Detective Parker. I should have known you were responsible for this." The calm demeanor was gone, replaced with the anxious and desperate voice of a man who knew a trap had been sprung.

"Let her go and come out and face this like a man."

"I don't think so. I have more leverage here because you know what I'm capable of."

"I know you're always hiding behind women and children."

"Then you know I will put a bullet in this old woman if you don't back away."

"You have no place to go. Your reputation is taking a bit of a hit, don't you think? The second arms shipment you were going to offer to the Sinaloa Cartel goes up in smoke. I'm thinking they won't take you at your word anymore."

"I don't need them."

"If you mean your plans to take over the Juarez Cartel, you might want to put a pin in that for the time being."

Silence from Castaneda. Parker used the moment to creep closer to the back of the home. He perched near a wall separating the living room from the kitchen. A reflection in the window showed Castaneda holding an older woman in front of him as a human shield. He clamped an arm around her and held the rifle at the ready with his other arm.

"Go ahead. Make a call to the Juarez people, or whoever you had watching the place."

Parker watched as Castaneda shuffled around and adjusted so he could hold a cell phone and pin the woman against him.

"Get ahold of them yet? Wonder if they'll answer you?"

"Shut up." The agitation spilled from the kitchen.

"If they'd pick up your call, they'd tell you there was no attack on the Juarez Cartel. The Mexican government and the Cartel came to an agreement. And you don't figure in the deal. Where does that leave you?"

"Shut up, shut up, shut up!"

"Los Muertos isn't even returning your calls. You're ex-girlfriend Carmen is holding the reigns now. There you are again, hiding behind a woman."

Castaneda threw the phone down, shattering it on the tile floor. He tightened his grip on the woman. She shuddered in response. "Please, let me go," she said.

"You're done, Castaneda. Come out and face it like a man."

A tap on Parker's shoulder let him know backup had arrived. A black-clad tactical operator with an automatic rifle stacked behind him. Parker caught Tully's profile at the front door, and he waved him forward.

Tully knelt next to Parker, who signaled for him to hand over the shotgun he was toting. Tully squinted and gave Parker an "Are you sure" look before handing the weapon over. Parker checked the loading port, confirming a 12-gauge shell was ready to go. He chambered the round with a rack of the slide.

"Last chance, Castaneda. I'm coming for you."

"Bring it pendejo. I'm done with you."

Parker saw a change in the window's reflection. Castaneda held the rifle in his right hand, tucked close to the woman's body. He looped his left arm around her torso, gripping her tight.

His hostage must have felt the change in his demeanor. She began to sob and collapsed in Castaneda's arms. Dead weight, and he struggled to keep his human shield in place.

Parker saw his opening and sprung around the corner, raising the shotgun barrel.

Castaneda was watching the window reflection, too. He readied the M-4 rifle, and the moment the detective's head cleared, he jerked the trigger.

Click.

Castaneda glanced down at the malfunctioning weapon. The old woman fell to the tile. He didn't notice Parker press forward, centering the large bore barrel. Castaneda glanced up as a flash erupted from the shotgun barrel, and a deafening noise echoed in the small kitchen.

Chapter Fifty-Eight

Castaneda lay in a heap against a kitchen cabinet. The bean bag round struck him in the sternum, knocking the breath out of him, and his head smacked off the sturdy wooden cabinet dazing the gangbanger.

The tactical team flowed into the room, handcuffing Castaneda and gently lifting the old woman off the floor. She pivoted around quickly, removed her sandal, and started smacking Castaneda, cursing him in Spanish.

Parker handed the shotgun to Tully. Even though it was a less than lethal round fired, there would be administrative reviews, interviews, and inquiries from the Professional Standards Unit. There would be a mandatory time off while paperwork was sorted, stamped, and approved.

"It's over, Tully said."

Parker nodded. "For now."

The FBI tactical team drug the semi-conscious Castaneda from the kitchen, through the living room, and into an SUV. They spirited him away before the first news media van pulled to the scene.

Linda waited for Parker on the front porch. She threw her arms around him. "What were you thinking, going in after him?" The words came out in between ragged breaths.

"I couldn't let him disappear this time. For everything he's done, for McMillan, Miguel, Leon, all of it. I couldn't risk him slipping away to do it again."

The FBI team leader joined Parker and Linda on the porch. She shook Parker's hand. "Interesting choice of weapons."

"He needs to answer for what he's done, and a quick exit from this life would have been what he wanted."

"Still, you chose a beanbag round against an automatic rifle. You got lucky when his jammed, I guess."

"It didn't jam. When his weapon is examined, they'll find the trigger mechanism and firing pin were tampered with. The weapon failed."

The FBI man tilted his head. "How could you know?"

"He's predictable. The weapons being shipped from the Western Machine Parts store were going to the Sinaloa Cartel. They modified another shipment, and the weapons failed after a few rounds. These would do the same."

"A hell of a chance to take."

Parker shrugged. "He couldn't risk arming who he thought could be his rivals. By the time they got around to using the weapons, Castaneda thought he'd be tucked away in his Mexican villa and would probably blame what's left of Echeverría's Los Muertos contingent for the sabotage."

The FBI leader shook Parker's hand again and pulled the remnants of her team out.

Parker felt the adrenaline coursing through his system, and he noticed a tremor in his hands. The self-doubt began to creep in. Had he done the right thing? Would Castaneda find a way to manipulate the system again? Should he have killed the man?"

His attention went to the open ambulance bay where an EMT attended to the woman taken hostage in her own home. An oxygen mask was over her thin face, and her eyes were clamped shut, probably trying to make sense of the last few minutes.

Parker excused himself from Linda and made his way to the ambulance. "How's she doing?"

"Pulse is a little rapid," The EMT said.

"So's mine," Parker said.

"She looks okay. I'd like to get her checked out to make sure. She's been through quite a bit tonight."

"Excuse me, Ma'am. I'm sorry we made a mess of your home," Parker said.

Her eyes opened slightly. "As long as I never see that man in my home again."

"You won't. What's your name?"

"Rosa. Rosa Gonzales."

"Thank you, Mrs. Gonzales. If you need anything, you reach out and call me. I want you to let these people take you to a hospital to make sure you're all right." He slipped a card into her hand.

"Parker, a word." Captain Morris had arrived on scene.

"Hey, Captain."

"I got a call from a young Assistant U.S. Attorney, and he's telling me a story about one of my detectives going on an unauthorized trip down south, getting wrapped up in some wild Mexican prison break, then exposing a high-ranking Homeland Security official involved in an intelligence leak. You know anything about it?"

"Which part?"

Morris smiled. "Anything gonna blow back on the department?"

"No, sir."

"Okay then. I am hearing rumblings Castaneda's immunity deal is off the table. There is a silver lining to all this."

"If I could believe it. Defense attorneys will have a field day and might convince a jury the feds can't retract the immunity deal. My faith has been tested…"

"The U.S. Attorney did mention they are moving Castaneda directly to ADX in Colorado as we speak. They aren't going to take any chances losing one of the FBI's Most Wanted."

"They put him back on the list?"

"Funny how that happened, isn't it?"

"If he's in Supermax, I think people are finally understanding the threat he poses," Parker said.

Morris put an arm on Parker's shoulder. "Go home, get some rest. I've put off the Professional Standards interviews until tomorrow at oh-nine-hundred."

"Thanks for that, Captain."

"Go on now. Get your team and go. You've earned some downtime."

Linda joined him after Morris departed. "Everything good?"

He put an arm around Linda. "Yeah, I think it is. Let's go home."

Chapter Fifty-Nine

Out of habit, Parker woke up before sunrise. He slipped out of bed, careful not to wake Linda. Her face was peaceful, and for a moment, he wondered what he'd done to deserve this—deserve her in his life.

He snuck out of the bedroom, closed the door softly behind him, and went to the kitchen. This morning was going to require an extra scoop of grounds in the coffee maker. He'd been through a few Professional Standards interviews before and some of the rubber gun squad made him feel no better than a low-life criminal, this time, he didn't have the nervous apprehension in his gut. It wasn't because he was confident in his use of force, or rigid adherence to department policy.

There was a sense of peace, or calm, and it came from keeping his word. He'd kept the promise he'd made to McMillan. The man who was responsible for killing his partner now sat in a Supermax prison cell.

The coffee machine gurgled, and Miguel strolled out of his room.

"You're up early," Parker said, pouring a second cup.

"Yeah, got to get some last-minute cramming in for finals. They start today."

"Which ones?"

"Econ and International Relations."

"You've had a crash course in both," Parker said with a sip of coffee.

"My perspective isn't quite the same as the professor. She learned everything she knows by reading books. It's not quite the same."

"Is your friend, Sarah, helping you study?"

A grin spread on Miguel's face. "Maybe."

Parker topped off his cup. "You hear from Billie?"

"Said she had to take care of some stuff after we split up yesterday. I'm thinking it was Coalition business."

Parker felt the cell phone vibrate in his pocket and he took a deep breath before he looked at it. The brief peace and calm was over.

"Parker."

"Nathan, it's Lynne."

He tensed. "Castaneda. He's escaped?"

Miguel sat back in his chair.

"No, no. He's still locked up in ADX. But this call is about him. The U.S. Attorney wants to prosecute him for the twenty-seven men killed in the shipping container. And the attempted murder on Hector Mendonsa. He's throwing on arms dealing, providing material support to known terrorist organizations. The whole deal. Castaneda won't ever see the light of day again."

"Good, I'm glad they're taking him down, finally."

"Which brings me specifically why I'm calling you so early. There is an arraignment today, and you're needed."

"They need me in Colorado today? Geez, Lynne."

"No, no. The arraignment will be video only. No one's getting into see this guy. He's acting as his own attorney. He put you on the witness list."

"Why me? Witnesses at an arraignment?"

"I was hoping you could tell me," she said.

"I have no idea. Maybe he wants to swap recipes or something."

"Is there anything we don't know about this guy, maybe something you know that you haven't passed on to us?"

"What are you saying, Lynne?"

"Listen, I know this case is personal to you. This—this—man put you through so much and I get you want him to pay for it. But, if there's anything we need to know, anything you did, that might make it hard to get a conviction…"

"Yeah, Lynne, it's personal. It's personal you have to even ask if I beat the guy down, or entrapped him, or whatever you're trying to say. It's personal because I get to go tell McMillan's widow we finally got the guy. It's personal because Miguel can finally get a night's sleep without wondering if tomorrow would be the day Castaneda comes calling."

"Nathan, I didn't mean to—"

"Yeah, you did, Lynne. Maybe you should look in your own backyard. Hansen putting together an immunity deal for a cop-killer. And you went along with it. How do you think that's going to play with a jury, or the headlines when the media gets wind of it? Not to mention how the government was outwitted by a street thug and nearly started a war with another country."

"Nathan, I didn't mean it to sound—"

"I'm sorry, Lynne. I'm tired. It's been a long couple of days. I didn't mean to take it out on you. I want this behind us. I'm tired of Castaneda blaming others for his bullshit. Everyone seems eager to pile on..."

"I had to ask because Castaneda listed you as a defense witness."

Parker's coffee turned sour in his stomach.

"I don't know what he's thinking calling me as a defense witness. It's only an arraignment. He doesn't need witnesses. He's playing an angle." Parker pushed his coffee aside. "Where am I supposed to be, and what time?"

"Lynne gave him the details of the video arraignment, the only video part which would be Castaneda's appearance streamed in from deep within the Colorado Supermax prison.

Parker disconnected the call and tossed the phone on the counter.

"He's not getting out, is he?" Miguel said, clutching his coffee cup.

Parker placed his hand around Miguel's. "No. That's not going to happen. Where he's at in Colorado, they have to pipe in sunshine. You're safe. I meant what I said to Lynne: Castaneda doesn't need to consume all our waking thoughts and dreams. He's behind us now."

Miguel nodded and stared into his cup.

"The call was about a hearing today—an arraignment on the charge the feds have him on. The state will file charges this week, too. He will never see the light of day again."

"Why are you a witness for him?"

Parker shrugged. "I have no idea. He probably wants to muddy the waters, hoping the judge will toss a couple of the charges. I certainly won't be able to testify as a character witness."

"Can I come?"

"I thought you needed to cram for a final exam?"

"I am, I do—but they are this afternoon, late. I think this is something I need to see. To know he won't be able to get to us again."

Parker nodded and understood where Miguel was coming from. He didn't want to burst the kid's bubble that gang members in prison have a history of carrying out gang business from behind the walls. Supermax makes that kind of interaction with the outside more difficult, but not impossible. Evil always has a way...

Chapter Sixty

The Sandra Day O'Connor Federal Courthouse on West Washington in downtown Phoenix is a monochromatic, six-story structure wrapped in blue-green glass. Miguel had been in the building once before when he testified against members of the Sinaloa Cartel. He'd witnessed unthinkable human atrocities while they smuggled migrants over the border to further their drug empire.

Parker glanced at the young man, wearing his suit and tie over a light blue shirt, and couldn't help but feel proud of him. An orphan refugee from El Salvador and he'd gone through so much in his life. Struggling to find his way and his purpose. He was here today to face down a larger-than-life figure who represented all of the violence and trauma Miguel, and people like him have weathered.

After checking in, going through the metal detectors, and screening, Parker found directions to the courtroom.

On the fourth floor, the elevator doors parted and there were clusters of people hanging in the hallway waiting for their proceedings to be called into session.

He spotted Lynne's blonde hair and worried face in deep conversation with Espinoza.

Espi glanced up and waved Parker over.

"What's going on?" Parker asked.

"We have intel Castaneda has something planned," Espi said.

"Los Muertos elements aligned with Castaneda?" Parker said.

"We don't know. But it explains this witness list," Lynne said. She handed the list to Parker.

The document contained the witnesses called by both the federal prosecutor and the defense. Parker's eye went to several familiar names: his, Espinoza, Lynne, Billie Carson, Lee Parker, Randy Coyle, and at least twenty more he didn't recognize. Miguel peeked over and pointed at the last few names on the list. These were all migrants who came to the Immigrant Coalition for help after they lost a family member to Los Muertos.

"Everyone who could testify in the case against them will all be here. Tempting target," Espinosa said.

"The courthouse has doubled up security," Lynne said.

"I don't see Billie here in the hall," Miguel said.

"She's in the courtroom with most of the people on the list."

"Why don't you go in and wait with them, Miguel," Parker said.

He nodded and opened the tall, dark wood door to the courtroom, disappearing inside.

"We have five bailiffs inside," Lynne said.

Parker scanned the faces in the hallway, looking for someone who didn't belong. But, in a federal criminal courthouse, everyone looked suspicious.

A woman brushed past Parker in the hallway. "Excuse me. Sorry," she said.

Parker felt a folded note slip into his jacket pocket. He turned, and the woman blended into the crowd. He unfolded the note. "Men's room, this floor, ASAP." The note was unsigned.

"Where's the restroom?" Parker asked.

Espi pointed ahead down the hallway in the direction the woman had come from. "Better hurry. We're supposed to start soon."

Parker found the restroom sign and pushed inside. Larry Sutton stood in the center of the room.

"I can't take the risk of communicating in public. My southern client appreciates what you did to prevent a move against them. They found the buried arms shipment and quickly discovered they had all been sabotaged. They have been destroyed. And Los Muertos has been sent blowing in the wind."

"I didn't do it for them. There would have been innocent people caught in-between."

"Quite right. And there are innocents caught in the middle again."

He reached into a jacket pocket and removed an envelope. "This is from Carmen Delgado."

"Hardly an innocent," Parker said.

"It seems without Echevarría and Los Muertos, she finds herself alone on an island. She needed to make a choice."

"Never made me wish for global warming and rising sea levels more."

Sutton held the envelope to Parker.

He took it, unsealed it, and removed the single sheet of paper. The short, handwritten note inside read: *Esteban called you here today to take care of unfinished business. He ordered the few weak-minded followers to plant an explosive device in the courtroom. It is to be triggered during the hearing so he can watch. The remaining Los Muertos followers have been handled. Now you do your end. —C.*

"The authorities should be finding the device about now."

Parker looked in the envelope and found McMillan's compact body cam tucked inside.

The restroom door burst open. Espinosa rushed in. "Bomb threat. We need to vacate."

Sutton had turned to the sink and washed his hands—the symbolism wasn't lost on Parker.

The courthouse was evacuated, and the device was located under the witness stand. A large pipe bomb assembled from two sections of a metal mop handle. The bomb-sniffing dogs cleared the courtroom, and the rest of the building and the witnesses for Castaneda's hearing were escorted back to the courtroom minutes before the hearing was set to begin.

Parker and Miguel found Billie. She was dressed in a plain black business suit. It was a few years old but serviceable. What Parker noted was a smoke odor wafting from her. Billie noticed and said. "Had a fire at my place."

"Fire? What kind of fire?" Parker asked.

"Like an everythin' I own is gone kinda fire."

"Your place?"

She nodded solemnly. "Was able to grab some stuff before the damn thing went up like dried brush."

"I'm sorry to hear it. How did it happen?"

"I'm not sure. We been gettin' threats from some of the locals 'about how we don't belong. Can't be for sure 'bout any of it."

"You can stay with Miguel and me until you figure stuff out."

"Thanks. Maybe a day or two would be good. Nathan, I gotta tell you somethin—,"

"All rise. The Federal District Court for the District of Arizona is now in session, the Honorable Colleen M. Booth, presiding."

A slim Black woman in a robe took her spot on the bench. "Be seated, the bailiff called out.

She donned a pair of reading glasses and glanced at a video screen in front of her. "Matter of U.S. versus Esteban Castaneda. Do we have the video link up with the defendant?"

A large screen in the front of the courtroom came to life, Esteban Castaneda in a white prison uniform sat at a metal table in what looked like a glass fishbowl with green and white walls.

"Very well, is the U.S. Attorney ready?"

"We are your honor, Jefferson Parkes, Assistant United States Attorney, for the people.

"And Mr. Castaneda, have you reconsidered representing yourself in this matter?"

"I have not, and I will represent myself."

"Due to the unusual nature of these proceedings, the complications of video arrangement, and the serious nature of the charges brought against you, I'm denying your request and appointing counsel, at least for today's hearing in this court."

"That's not necessary, Judge," Castaneda leaned into the video screen, assessing who was in the courtroom. "I see most of my witnesses are there."

"Madam Clerk, who is up next on the conflict counsel roster?"

The clerk opened a binder and handed it to Judge Booth.

"Very well, the court orders Larry Sutton as conflict counsel. Is Mr. Sutton in the courtroom today?"

Sutton rose from the back row. "I am, your honor."

The judge motioned him forward. Sutton stood behind the defense table and shot a look at Castaneda on the video screen. An expression took over Castaneda's cocksure appearance—recognition. He knew who Sutton really represented in these proceedings and it wasn't him.

"I don't accept this, judge. This is a travesty, and you'll all pay for it." He looked at a clock on the wall in his video arraignment room. The smile on his face evaporated as the second hand swept around without the courtroom erupting into flames.

His eyes locked on Parker. "You. You did this to me."

Parker sat quietly without any acknowledgment Castaneda was speaking to him.

The judge tried to cut him off and Castaneda was working himself into a lather.

"You think you've won. I'm not done with you, Parker. Any of you. Parker, you think you're so smart? Ask that Carson woman what she's been keeping secret from you."

"That's enough, cut the video feed," the judge ordered.

The screen went black.

"I apologize to the court and Detective Parker for my client's outburst. The court may want to order a mental health evaluation before the next hearing."

"Anything else, Counsel?"

"I'd like the staff at ADX Florence, Colorado, informed by order of this court that my client is to be held in protective custody as a result of his cooperation with the government, your Honor," Sutton said.

"So ordered. The arraignment is continued for two weeks. That's all people." She rapped the gavel on her desk.

Everyone filed out of the courtroom unsure what it was they witnessed. Except for Billie. She sought out Parker and had trouble making eye contact.

Miguel grabbed one of her hands. It seems like she was having trouble

SERVED COLD

walking.

"Billie, I don't care what Castaneda said. He's trying to get under our skin, and we can't let him win."

Outside the courtroom, Billie found one of the uncomfortable wooden benches arranged for witnesses about to testify. They didn't encourage long-term lounging.

She held her head between her knees.

"Billie, you should go get checked out. You don't look so good." Parker ran his hand across her forehead, and it was clammy with a thin sheen of sweat.

Whatever secret Castaneda triggered with his rant cut deep. Billie didn't look this scared in a Mexican prison where gang members lurked all around her.

"I'm sorry, Nathan."

"Billie, stop. I don't care what he said."

Linda had exited the courtroom and sat next to Billie, rubbing her leg.

"If you knew, you'd never look at me the same way again."

Billie hung her head again and concentrated on drawing a deep breath.

"Let's get you home, and we'll worry about everything else in its time," Parker said.

Chapter Sixty-One

Linda convinced Billie to go take a long, hot shower and let the water beat the knots out of her muscles.

Parker and Linda sat at the dining room table. "What did you make of the attorney today?" she asked.

"Sutton? You've met him. You know he's not all above board."

"Yeah, he is an attorney, after all. But he happened to be in the courtroom? That was a little happenstance, wouldn't you say?"

"See, you are a detective, after all."

"The protective custody request was a little strange, too. Isn't that usually handled at the jail classification level?"

Parker smiled and took a sip of an herbal tea, which Linda had been substituting for his afternoon coffee.

"Sutton wanted to make sure as many people as possible knew Castaneda was a snitch working for the government. That kind of label gets around pretty fast. Castaneda won't be a popular guy around the cell block."

"It's the kind of information that could get a prisoner in trouble."

"If by trouble, you mean a shank in the kidney, then yeah."

Parker changed up the conversation. "Billie give you any idea what's got her stirred up? I mean, I know she lost her house and everything in it—maybe it's catching up to her."

Linda pursed her lips. "Billie is—I don't know. You know her a lot better than I do, but she doesn't seem hung up on things. She is not a material girl."

"True, but something's eating at her…"

Miguel came from his room, backpack slung over a shoulder. He seemed lighter after seeing the man who was responsible for his torment locked away behind bars.

"Hey, mind if I go over to Sarah's for a while? We've got a couple of hours and are gonna study before the final this afternoon."

"All right. Got your phone?"

Miguel patted his pants pocket and nodded. He swept out the door and Parker wondered how much actual studying was going to happen.

Parker poured more hot water into his mug. He held the kettle out to Linda, and she shook her head.

Linda's phone buzzed. A text message notification hit her screen.

"Leon at school?" Parker asked.

"He is. I told him no one would blame him for taking a break for a while." She clicked on the message link.

"He says turn on the Channel 7 news."

"What's this about?" Parker said while he strode to the television and powered it up.

"You could use a new television, this one must be ten years old. Look how long it takes to come on."

"You sound like Miguel."

When the picture blossomed on the screen a petite reporter with long dark hair cascading over one shoulder centered in the shot. Behind her the Coyle Technology offices. The banner on the bottom of the screen read, "Coyle Technology Scandal Unveiled."

"Employees of the largest tech firm in the nation walked out today in protest over what appears to be the company's use of undocumented migrant tech workers. Our sources tell us Coyle Technology knowingly brought tech workers from Mexico and other countries to staff some of their critical systems. The workers were subject to harsh working conditions and held in prison-like settings while they performed their duties at a fraction of the cost. We've learned over two dozen workers died in a shipping container abandoned along I-10 just days ago.

"When asked about the use of foreign migrant labor, Coyle Technology

CEO and namesake, Randy Coyle, said, 'A subcontractor made the choice to use undocumented labor. No customer data was compromised to his knowledge.' We've learned there were system-wide data breaches, and despite the company's highly touted policy claiming all data systems were maintained in America, sources tell us Coyle Technology operated foreign-based facilities that maintained highly classified government data.

"Upon learning of the scandal, stock prices plummeted in a rush to sell off shares of the beleaguered tech firm."

The news went on to report about an upcoming Salsa Festival planning in Tempe. Lives lost and forgotten—the news cycle was searching for the next big story.

"Who do you think the source was?" Linda said. Her buzzing cell phone answered her question. Leon. "Leon says he didn't tell them about any overseas operations; they got that from someone else, but he did reveal the part about undocumented workers and pointed them to the connection to the dead men in the shipping container."

Billie came down the hallway and didn't make eye contact with Parker.

"Thanks for the clothes, Linda. I'll get them back to you as soon as I can."

"Don't worry about it. They fit nicely."

"Been a while since I had something this nice to wear."

"You look nice. Tea?" Linda asked.

She shook her damp head. "Nathan, what I gotta tell you—you ain't gonna understand. I don't even understand how I let it happen. It was years ago. I was a different person then. If you never want to see me again, I'll understand…"

"Billie, nothing could change the way I feel about you. You're part of my life."

"I know you mean it. I mean, why else would you have come to Mexico and bust me out of prison? But I do have a secret, and I can't keep it from you no more. Better you hear it from me."

Parker nodded but kept silent.

"I—I have a son."

"What?" Linda said. She covered her mouth with a hand after she blurted out her surprise.

Parker looked at Billie. She'd raised her head and stiffened her jaw when she revealed her secret.

"Huh. Armando DeSilva."

Her eyes widened. "How did you..."

"I saw the way you two interacted when we were down there. He's the reason you go to Hermosillo so often. Now I see it: he does have your eyes. And your kind heart."

"It's been safer to keep him away from me. I couldn't risk him gettin' caught up in the mess that is me."

"It's more than that, isn't it? Armando was with you when Castaneda killed McMillan. You said he knew Castaneda planned to get rid of you, and he warned you. There's only one reason you'd bring a young child with you on a smuggling run..."

She steeled herself a stiffness in her shoulders. "Castaneda is his father."

Parker tried to imagine what Billie had gone through.

"You kept your son hidden down in Hermosillo to keep him safe. You knew if Castaneda got his grip on him, he'd be drawn into his world—his control."

"I don't expect no one to understand. Back then, I was a different person. Young and stupid, mostly. But I didn't always look like this—be like this. I fell for this handsome bad boy before he was involved in Los Muertos."

"I know what that's like," Linda said.

"Once he got involved in Los Muertos, he changed—everything dark came to the surface. He'd take his problems out on me and, when he could, on Armando. I knew it was a matter of time until he'd kill us or draw Armando into his life. The night Esteban killed your partner, he also said Armando was his legacy. That night scared both of us, and we had to escape."

Billie stood there, shoulders slumped, and her head fallen once more. She felt shame for the mistakes of a much younger and naive woman.

Parker got up from the table and stood in front of her. He tipped her chin up with a finger so he could see her tear-stained eyes.

CHAPTER SIXTY-ONE

There was nothing left to say.

Parker hugged her, and he felt her weep in his arms. The years of hiding the truth, of sneaking around to keep Armando's identity safe, all came out in shuddering sobs.

She tried to speak in between ragged breaths. "I'm sorry for—"

He held her tighter. "It's okay now, Billie. Armando's safe, and so are you."

She pushed back and wiped her eyes with the back of her hands.

"I'm sorry for everything."

"You have nothing to be sorry for, Billie. You did what you needed to do to keep him safe."

"You're not mad at me?"

"Of course not. Now, with Castaneda locked up, what are you and Armando going to do?"

"I want to be with him without worrying about who's following me, or wondering who knows about him. The DeSilvas have been wonderful to keep an eye on him all this time, but it's my turn.

"Hermosillo, or up here?"

"Prolly a little a both. I got a whole new life with him now."

"Wherever it is, we're all here for you."

Chapter Sixty-Two

In the six months since Billie revealed her secret, she'd spent weeks in Hermosillo with Armando and the DeSilva family. With the help of Lynne and some arm-twisting by her immigration contacts, Armando would be legally coming over and living with Billie.

Parker got a call from Billie telling him to meet her at the place she last parked her trailer, out near Rocky Wash. She was a little scant on details, but said it was important and she needed him there first thing in the morning.

Parker rinsed out his coffee cup, and Miguel came plodding down from his room. He grabbed a mug before he muttered a single word.

"Up early today," Parker said.

"Got a busy day at the Coalition office," he said after his first sip. "Billie's sent me a bunch of emails of things she needs me to jump on. I should have never taught her how to use email."

"What kind of things she have you working on?"

"A whole laundry list. Transportation, large food orders, coordinating with shelters, and clothing donations. It almost sounds like she's—"

"Bringing migrants over."

"Right? But she hasn't mentioned anything."

"Before you get too wrapped up in the day, you have some mail from last night."

"Last night?"

"Messenger service brought it by." Parker pointed to a spot under the telephone. A large white envelope leaned against the counter, addressed to Miguel. The return address is what caught his attention first.

346

"It's from the Arizona State University."

"I see that."

Miguel hefted the envelope and tried to suss out the content based on the weight of it. "If they didn't accept me, it would be a letter, wouldn't it? Maybe I'm waitlisted."

"Why don't you open the damned thing and find out."

Miguel carefully opened the envelope like it was a delicate gift-wrapped present.

He pulled a cover letter out and silently read the first few words, then aloud, "We are pleased to accept you into the fall class. And they gave me a scholarship. Not a big one, but look." He thrust this letter at Parker.

"I'm so proud of you, son."

Miguel hugged Parker before pulling away. "I gotta call Sarah."

"All right. Congrats and I'll talk with you later. Maybe I'll drop by the office."

"K...Hey, Sarah, I got in..."

On the way to Billie's old camp, Parker stopped at the memorial out on Rocky Wash. The wooden cross for McMillan had been freshly painted. Parker wondered about it for a second and knew he hadn't done it, neither had Ellie, his widow. Which meant Billie had applied the fresh paint. Her way of making peace with the past, perhaps.

"We did it, Mac. We got him. Sorry it took so long." Parker patted the top of the cross and got back in his Explorer for the ride out to Billie's last hideaway.

He turned on the dirt road and found a gravel covered track instead of the dirt ruts the last time he came out here looking for her.

The spot Billie's trailer last stood was a blackened section of earth. The debris had been hauled away, but what took Parker's attention was a two-story home nearly complete next to the site.

Billie stood on the front patio and was pointing at a roof rafter with a construction worker. She spotted Parker and waved.

"Whatcha think?" she called out.

"I don't know what to think."

Armando strolled out the front door and raised his hand at Parker. He had a paintbrush in hand, and based on the color splotches on his shirt, it was an off-white tint.

Parker climbed up the porch, taking the big step to the landing.

"I gotta get them steps in."

"Hey, Armando. Good to see you."

"You too, Detective. I gotta go paint, or the boss will get all pissy."

Billie smiled. "Yes, she will."

"What's going on here?"

"This here's my new place. 'Bout time I put down some roots. Me and the boy need it."

"You deserve it. But won't the neighbors complain? I mean, they burnt you out last time."

"Don't got no neighbors no more. I bought them out. Hundred and fifty acres, and it's mine. I been sitting on all that money and thought it was about time to put it to some use."

"I don't know what to say."

"There's also a house out back for temporary housing for Coalition people who need a little help on the way."

"Must be what Miguel was going to work on today: food, clothing, and everything."

"Right."

"I'm happy for you, Billie, you deserve it. Everything you've sacrificed these past years. It's your turn."

"Maybe. I'm still grateful you understood my—didn't hold my secret against me."

"I get it, Billie. It's what we do for family."

Parker's cell phone chirped in his pocket. "Excuse me for a sec, Billie."

"Parker, here. What's up, Lynne?"

"Thought you'd want to know, Castaneda got stabbed last night. Don't look good for him."

"How did someone get to him in protective custody in the most secure prison in the world?"

"Seems another protective custody inmate was what they call a 'sleeper,' an inmate waiting for an order to take someone out."

"It was bound to happen."

"Castaneda gave up his role in the death of the Coyle Technology workers in the shipping container."

"Of course, Hansen claims no knowledge of the plans, I'm sure."

"You got it. He's not scot-free. They have him on mishandling classified data, fraud, and some international espionage stuff, which will see him in federal prison for a while. Coyle and Patterson, the grand jury indicted them."

"That's something, I suppose."

He disconnected the call and shoved the phone back in his pocket.

"Everything all right, Nathan?"

"Yeah, everything's fine.

She stared at him.

"It happened, didn't it? Esteban's gone."

She didn't look relieved, and her reaction surprised Parker.

"Not gone, but according to Lynne, it doesn't look good."

Parker figured Billie must have some difficulty processing the impending death of a man she shared a son with.

"It's happening then."

"What?"

Billie ducked into the house and returned seconds later with a letter.

It was handwritten in the same script as the note handed to him in the courthouse.

"*Esteban was a cruel man, and he will pay for his transgressions. I will do this for you. We are even now.* —*C.*"

Carmen.

"She's in tight with the Sinaloa Cartel. They ordered the hit on Esteban. With him out of the way, Armando will be safe. I didn't ask them for this; they wanted him gone for what he tried to do.

"What does she mean, even?"

349

Billie shrugged. Another secret took root.
Everyone's entitled to a secret or two.

Acknowlegements

During a scorching heatwave in 2022, a semi-truck and trailer were found along a Texas freeway. People were observed jumping from the rear of the moving truck and when authorities responded, the found more than fifty undocumented migrants dead in the trailer. Sixteen others were hospitalized for heat-related illness and dehydration. The driver and three others were arrested and acknowledged they knew the air-conditioning unit in the cargo container was broken. The tragedy underscores the callous disregard for human life—all in pursuit of profit.

That event stuck with me as I wrote Served Cold. I wanted to know the origin stores of the people in that container. My fictionalized account changes the narrative and asks, "what if" these migrants weren't destined for the fields and who stood to gain from their work?

I'm forever grateful to my friend and editor, Shawn Reilly Simmons, at Level Best Books. Shawn is superhuman and I love working with her. She's guided this series and enabled us to share Nathan parker's story with you. Most of all, I'm happy to call her a friend.

The book community is incredible, and I appreciate the support of independent bookstores like Face in a Book (Tina Ferguson and Janis Herbert), Book Passage (Kathy Petrocelli and Luisa Smith), Mostly Books in Tucson (Tricia Clapp). They make a bookstore feel like home.

Sometimes it's words of encouragement that came when they were most needed. J.T. Ellison, Wendall Thomas, Karen Dionne, Hank Phillippi Ryan, Baron Birtcher, Claire Booth, and Bruce Robert Coffin. I thank you for your support. Thanks to my ThrillerFest and International Thriller Writers crew for the kick when needed. A special shout out to my fellow Mystery Writers of America, and Capitol Crimes Chapter of Sisters-in-Crime members for the love and support.

Thanks to my kids, Jessica, and to Michael—I love you guys.

I wasn't always alone at the keyboard, and I owe Emma and Bryn the Corgis extra treats for all the plot points they helped me work through on countless walks. The book would have been done a month earlier if not for their constant demands.

A special thank you to Ann-Marie L'Etoile for tolerating my nonsense over the years. You let me disappear behind my keyboard and still love me when I come up for air. Love you.

And finally, thanks to you, dear reader. It's only possible because of you.

About the Author

James L'Etoile uses his twenty-nine years behind bars as an influence in his award-winning novels, short stories, and screenplays. He is a former associate warden in a maximum-security prison, a hostage negotiator, and director of California's state parole system. His novels have been shortlisted or awarded the Lefty, Anthony, Silver Falchion, and the Public Safety Writers Award. Served Cold is his most recent novel. Look for River of Lies, coming in 2025. You can find out more at www.jamesletoile.com

SOCIAL MEDIA HANDLES:
  Facebook: @AuthorJamesLetoile
  Instagram: @authorjamesletoile
  X (twitter) @jamesletoile
  Threads: @authorjamesletoile

AUTHOR WEBSITE:
  Jamesletoile.com

Also by James L'Etoile